Vitas

A NOVEL

BY

PATRICK LAW

ISBN 978-0-9823369-7-7

Printed in the United States of America

PROLOGUE

The worst of madmen is a saint run mad.

Alexander Pope, *Imitations of Horace*

The genetic experiments begun in earnest in the late twenty-first century took a distinct turn in the thirty-third century. How to vastly extend lifespan was discovered with implications so profound that the very idea of such a possibility was suppressed and the information confined to a very few.

Those in control of the research labs engaged in the life-extension studies used their discoveries to extend the lifespans of their progeny and others friendly to their interests. The possibility of having a child who might live beyond the coming storm—a storm made inevitable by social policies that guaranteed population growth far surpassing the destruction of population from military adventures, famine, pestilence, and the beneficent consequences of environmental policies to preserve the planet—had an overpowering, soul-consuming influence on everyone exposed to the opportunity.

Justification for inequitable selection was as simple as understanding that applying life extension to everyone's progeny would so exponentially increase the world population and so quickly exhaust the already extremely strained resources of Earth that very long life would become a moot notion within three or four centuries, hardly longer than what was already becoming the new normal lifespan as genetic engineering to eliminate various ailments and life-shortening genetic defects was applied to the general population.

The already longer-lived humankind was leading to an inevitable Armageddon. For centuries, beginning in the late twenty-first, the world-wide birth rate had declined to a level in approximate equilibrium with the world-wide death rate so that, though humankind strained the resources of the planet, it had succeeded in managing to survive.

With the development of longer lifespans in the general population, two things had already changed. First, as the average lifespan rapidly increased from about one hundred years to four hundred years, the existing birthrates increased the slower-dying population, further straining the planet. Then a second extremely adverse change occurred: the birthrate began to rise as people chose to have more children during their much longer lives.

Under these circumstances, just continuing three declared human rights—that every human had the right to live; that every human entitled to the same advantages as anyone else; that every human had the right to propagate at will—put Earth on a course to joining the other barren planets orbiting the sun in short order.

As this was going on, in the quiet, secret background of institutional power, public political power was shifting into the hands of certain environmentalists, known as the Vitans. Vitans believed in the first two rights but they had difficulties with the third right, propagation at will, believing the planet's survival trumped that right. Faced with the inevitable destruction of humankind and Earth itself, they acted to conform their view of human rights and Earth's survival and prepared to take draconian steps to deal with the world's population. The Vitans began instituting their solution to the population problem—Birth Fasts—pharmaceutically restricting fertility for ten-year intervals.

Over the next one hundred and fifty years the Birth Fasts caused the world's population to fall by more than half. This reduction in population became known in the historical records as the First Reduction.

The History of Vitas as recorded in a file stored in the GenLib Repository accessible only by the Librarian

His first conscious sensations were of mushy ice running through his veins and a deep, frigid stiffness in his bones. His mind felt slow, hazy. He opened his eyes and blinked at a white opaqueness that appeared to nearly touch his nose. Instinctively he drew his head back and felt a firm yet pliant material pushing back. Focusing on what he could see, he made out a foggy glass barrier shimmering just a few inches from his face. He resisted his urge to move back from something so close. Instead he drew a slow, deep breath and, little by little, he contracted the muscles in his body beginning at his extremities, first twitching, then wiggling, his feet and his fingers. After a few moments he clenched his hands, then rhythmically flexed his calves, thighs, forearms, biceps, triceps, shoulders. He constricted his thighs and trunk muscles. He began to feel warmer and, tightening his abdomen, he slowly and deeply drew more breath into his chest. He vaguely recalled having performed this ritual before.

Finally, after clenching his hands again and stretching his fingers to their full range, he moved his hands outward, away from their position by his hips, towards the foggy shimmer glimmering before him while the space before him became more glassine than fog, curving down around his body to what he now realized he already knew was the metallic portion of the stasis shell that encapsulated him.

He groped about for a button that he now recalled was somewhere beside his left hip. After a few moments, he found what he sought and depressed it and the glassine shell fell away and a wall of blank metallic whiteness about two meters away replaced his view. He stared for a moment and wondered, *Wall or ceiling? Am I erect or supine?* He closed his eyes and, after scrunching his facial muscles for a few seconds, began again to breathe deeply and to again slowly rhythmically flex the muscles throughout his body.

As his brain became more alert, he reopened his eyes and moved his head slowly from side to side. Then, as if a sudden wind had swooped down over a hill overlooking a foggy, early-morning lake where he was floating in a small boat, sweeping the morning mist away, his mind cleared.

He didn't think, *I am Shon Ó Conaill.* He now knew who he was as if he'd always known that he was Shon Ó Conaill, commander of Canopus, the first black-hole lightship to depart the Solar System and that his mission had been to search for habitable planets within a thousand light-years or so of Earth. And that his mission was to continue to do so each time the computer on his lightship awakened him from stasis where he had ensconced himself in a deep, dreamless sleep after each starfall until the mission protocol was completed and his ship returned him to Earth.

He could now recall that he was supine and that, if he pressed the button near his right hip, the bed upon which he was reclining would transform itself into a chair from which he would be able to operate the ship's controls, survey his instruments, and activate his monitors to see out into the space beyond. He slipped his right hand along the bed's edge until he felt the button. He pressed it and his view shifted from the blank, white ceiling, to a gray wall covered with several large monitors, some white, some black, all currently blank, and finally to a console inset with keyboards, instrument panels, and more screens, smaller than those on the wall above the console.

Closing his eyes once more, he paused before speaking and absently touched his left ear lobe. He breathed deeply through his nose, and said, "Good morning, Gristelda."

"It is neither morning nor evening, nor any other time of day, Commander," replied a feminine voice he recognized as the ship's computer.

He uttered his next words silently, from his mind, testing his internal communications, *"Where are we?"*

Gristelda responded, this time not audibly, but directly into his mind, as feminine and friendly as he had always known her to be, but also with a tentative tone not so familiar, *"In interstellar space, near the orbit of Uranus."*

"My God! We're back!" He hesitated as the uncharacteristic tone in her response registered in that portion of his mind that paid close attention to even the most minor anomalies in observable behavior. *"G,"* he said silently, addressing her with his friendly diminutive for her name, *"is there something I need to know?"*

"The passage of time since the last starfall has been much longer than my programming indicates was anticipated."

He spoke audibly, "How long?"

"As long as you were in stasis, one hundred and twenty years." Gristelda responded audibly, mimicking her commander's mode of communication.

He thought, *Precisely the mission protocol's limit for me to be in stasis.* Reaching this limit wasn't anticipated – it was a safety protocol to avoid the possibility of never awakening while the ship continued eternally onward on the last course he'd set. He thought, *Still, we're almost home.* "Why do I detect in the tone of your voice a concern about this?" He paused. "Is the black hole running down?"

"The passage of time was not caused by any decline in the efficacy of the black hole."

"So what's going on, G? This is the first leg that has triggered the stasis time limit. How much longer did we travel than your programming anticipated?"

"Far beyond."

Shon pondered Gristelda's remark. "If I understand you correctly, we are already within the Solar System traveling at non-relativistic velocity, and we are exactly where we should be when you awakened me and I was in stasis no longer than I was permitted to be, though being in stasis to the limit was not anticipated to likely occur. What has happened that seems unusual to you?"

"It is not within our frame of reference that we have traveled that appears unanticipated, but rather it is from a point of view outside of Canopus. Commander, the passage of time outside has been much longer than the mission protocol anticipated."

Shon felt the hairs at the base of his neck rise. "Measured from our time of departure from Earth, how many years have passed from *Earth's* point of view?"

"864,430 years."

"What? Over eight hundred thousand years? How can that possibly be? Before we left our last starfall, you calculated that twenty-five hundred years had passed on Earth since our departure from it. During the passage of that time on Earth we made three starfalls and explored every planet in each of those solar systems at length. How can we possibly now be over eight hundred millennia beyond that time? At worst, we should be no further than another twenty-five hundred years measured in Earth's time."

"Commander, your biological indications are alarming."

"Damn it! Stop monitoring my biological systems! Instead explain to me why your astoundingly deviant miscalculation of when we are should not be good and proper cause for me to order you to shut yourself down and relinquish control of the ship to my sole command!"

"Commander, I sense that influence from you that my algorithms require me to suppress, except for those occasions which call for that influence. Is this such an occasion?"

Shon paused and then concentrated on his breathing, exhaling sharply, inhaling slowly, then exhaling smoothly and inhaling slowly until he was completely calm. "My apologies. No, this does not appear at the moment an occasion calling for that influence. Surely you see that my reaction is reasonable and unsurprising given the circumstances which might give rise to the need of the influence to which you refer. But, for the moment, I do not believe we should think in those terms. Now tell me what you have done to insure there is not an error about where we are in time."

"To resolve the dissonance between my actual observations and the mission's expectations, I have been debugging myself and every system on the ship continuously since we commenced deceleration. I have not been able to detect any error at all. Do you require a report on the type and number of debugging cycles I have performed?"

"Billions no doubt."

"Quadrillions upon quadrillions. I really had nothing else to do and I anticipated that this would be your singular question."

Shon sighed. "Just tell me what you think has happened."

"You may recall that, just before you returned to stasis after exploring the last star system, you were upset with our failure to accomplish our mission and you set a course towards Earth, but not directly there so we might extract some benefit from the tremendous expenditure of time and effort. You ordered me 'to accelerate us until Canopus has achieved the maximum she will do.'" Midway through her response, her voice had changed into his own, and he realized that she was playing back his very order as she continued in his voice, "'If we overshoot, bring us about and return us to Earth after we have maxed out.'"

"Yeah, I recall. I thought we'd at least have something useful to report about the ship's performance, having found nothing habitable in any of the star systems we explored." He paused, "So just how fast does Canopus go?"

"I cannot answer that question. While our rate of increase in velocity declined over time as we drew closer to the speed of light, Canopus never stopped accelerating. She never achieved the speed of light, but neither did she achieve the maximum speed you ordered. I was restricted from complying with your orders to 'max out' when the mission's safety protocol required me to limit your time in stasis to one hundred and twenty years."

"So you initiated deceleration after sixty years of travel in ship's time, so that we could return to Earth within the remaining sixty years the mission protocol allowed?"

"Correct. At the point I initiated the return sequence, we were four hundred and thirty thousand light-years from Earth on our way toward the Andromeda galaxy, two-point-two million light-years from Earth. Canopus had exceeded 99.9999999% of the speed of light. After we decelerated to a velocity where we could safely come about, I did so and accelerated the ship on a course to Earth. Two years ago, ship's time, as we approached the Oort Cloud beyond the Solar System, I initiated deceleration. I awakened you exactly one hundred and twenty years, ship's time, from the moment you last entered stasis."

Shon sat still, feeling nearly as cold in his mind as his body had felt coming out of stasis.

"Shon?" Gristelda spoke audibly through the ship's speaker system.

"Yes?"

"Are we in danger?"

"I can't say, G. If I thought we were, I would proceed to succumb to the influence with which you are concerned. But, if you are correct about when we are, we've traveled so far into Earth's future that we can't even guess about the nature of life now, nor can we even suppose that there is any life at all, intelligent or otherwise. If things continued the way they were going when we left, Earth is more likely to be dead than alive."

"The mission protocol requires that you broadcast a hailing transmission before we come within Saturn's orbit," said Gristelda.

"We must consider whether that is prudent under the circumstances. If Earth has evolved into a world advanced far beyond that which we left, we must consider in what direction it has advanced. It may be your world now, or mine, or neither of ours. Maybe good for one of us, both of us, or neither of us. And whatever the politics, technology may have advanced so far that we may be thought of as little more than curiosities and treated as such. On the other hand, things may have gone in an entirely different direction—perhaps computers and humans like me don't even exist now. What have you picked up as we have been approaching the Solar System?"

"I have detected no emanations from Earth significantly different from the planets we surveyed on our mission."

"Given that we found no technology on any of those planets, I hope that doesn't mean what it might. Yet if Earth has become a dead world, hailing it won't matter a whit. So for the time being, we shall remain silent and communicate only when it appears prudent."

"So you wish to follow the mission protocol for exploring the unknown planets in the star systems we surveyed where we have found no reason to initiate your progression?"

Shon nodded as if Gristelda was sitting across a table from him. "Yes, we shall approach Earth as we did the others, a hopeful mystery, yet prepared for the worst and what we must do if that is the case."

"The mission protocol recommends bearing off and traveling on to another system if the system we are approaching appears to present significant danger. Should we bear off?"

"And go—where?" Shon shrugged. "No. Leaving is not a viable option even if your calculations are correct about when we are and even if the way the world is now is not what we might wish it to be. After three planetary system starfalls and what appears to have been a very long detour, it's time to come home and face what and when home is. Then we will decide what to do if we don't like what we find—if we still have any power to do anything about it."

•

A woman walked up the wide spiraling staircase that began a few meters outside the entrance to her residential compound deep underground in a mountain that rose nearly seven thousand meters above sea level. The staircase—a ramp really, as its floor was a smooth surface made of a slightly rough material—rose slowly as it spiraled its way up to the surface a thousand meters above around the inside wall of an underground dome lacquered in a silvery glassine veneer. The dome was more than a thousand meters across and nearly as high, made of a material of such extraordinary strength that the fact that the void it created had been hollowed out of solid granite was immaterial to its ability to support the billions of tons of stone, earth, ice, and vegetation bearing down upon it from above. It was the largest clear-span space ever constructed, at least so had said the records stored at GenLib before all the records pertaining to its existence had been erased.

GenLib, located ten thousand kilometers away from the dome where she resided, was the world repository for billions upon trillions of files containing all of what was left of all the information ever recorded by humankind—the sciences and the arts in all their forms, including history and language, as well as all the data ever gathered by satellites, space probes, weather monitors, seismic detection devices, and every other device capable of measuring and recording anything at all. The files also contained every broadcast, interview, biography, and story ever recorded about those who had lived in the past when recording such matters comprised a great part of human activity. Originally constructed in the twenty-third century when it was called the Massive DNA Memory Well, GenLib was expanded and upgraded over the next several thousand years. After its final upgrade, the capacity of each of its DNA memory cells was raised to about one hundred septillion exabytes. And GenLib contained millions of such cells. Information not recorded in GenLib simply didn't exist anymore. And not all of that information was accessible to everyone, except the Librarian.

As she steadily strode upward along the path to reach the narrow, arched passageway that led to the outside world, she contemplated what to do about the urgent message she had just received. She was the Librarian, the sole custodian of GenLib, having become so shortly after it had fallen under the governance of the Society. Now the Council, the Society's governing body, was seeking information on a matter of serious concern.

The Council had relayed its discovery of an unidentified, yet clearly unnatural object. Unnatural because the object was approaching the Solar System while decelerating at a rate precisely equal to the force of gravity as it was measured at sea level on Vitas.

She had not bothered to examine any of the records stored at GenLib because she knew there would be no information to glean from any query she could formulate about it. And she already knew what it must be from a single reported datum: its rate of deceleration.

"Hmm, what shall I do?" She began to speak her thoughts aloud as she steadily stepped her way up the spiral staircase, well aware that she spoke to no consciously intelligent audience.

She passed over recalling why she had done what she'd done since that time long before she had become the Librarian. She had stopped considering her motives almost before she'd begun the doing she had done.

She contemplated what to do now while considering only what her doing might mean later. For that manner of thought had served her well for a time longer than anyone else had ever lived.

She said aloud to no one present, "Ah, yes, what to do? Is it really possible that it's you out there? Well, if it is indeed you coming home at last, your ship must have performed beyond anyone's expectations or it wouldn't have taken you so long to return. I wonder what you would have done had you returned when I did.

"No matter, I suppose, as the world is what it is. What matters is what I am going to do if it is you and you are still sane. After all I did anticipate the possibility when I thought your arrival, if it ever occurred, would be a bit more imminent. Will my old scrivenings have any effect on what comes? Will anyone notice the tracks I laid down about you in old tomes so many millennia ago?

"I wonder if I will even notice. I don't even know if I much care."

She arrived at the door to the passageway to the surface. She opened the door and walked through a narrow, dimly lit hall for a few hundred meters. Then she passed her hand over the door lock and the door opened to the outside world. She closed her eyes and stepped out onto a small ledge surrounded on three sides by outcroppings of rock and behind her by the towering mountain that rose upward to a snow-laden peak a couple of thousand meters above her head.

After taking a few moments to adjust to the sun's intensity, she slowly opened her eyes. It was midday and she felt the heat of the sun through the cold air. She glanced over the rocks and boulders to look down the mountain to the tree line nearly two thousand meters below. The forest that formed there spread down and out into a vast rain forest becoming thick jungle as far as the eye could see as the land flattened out toward the eastern horizon. She was glad that she was not standing down there under the jungle's umbrella in the hot, saturated air with such a limited view of the world as the dense jungle afforded.

She stood, gazing out at nothing in particular for a few minutes, slowly taking in deep breaths of the thin, cold air and then turned to return to the dome. As she stepped back through the door, she said aloud, "Well, perhaps I do.

PART I – VITAN ORDER

But thy eternal summer shall not fade.

William Shakespeare, *Sonnet 18*

By the beginning of the sixth millennium, natural humankind, that part of humankind not genetically altered, had become extinct. What remained were those who had undergone genetic modifications to eliminate genetically-based illness and disorders and now had an average lifespan of around four centuries and a few thousand others who had been much more altered and possessed indeterminate lifespans.

As far back as the end of the First Reduction, a few thousand of the ruling elite and their progeny had undergone genetic alterations that extended their lifespans far beyond everyone else to such an extent that no one knew how long they might live. Many among them feared what the rest of the population might do to them if they learned of their secret. A scientist among them discovered a virus on Mars, Mars Steri Type B. Steri B sterilized every human female it infected. They dispersed it throughout the world via food, water, and medicine. The infection spread so quickly and thoroughly that no one had the opportunity to harvest fertile eggs and isolate them from the plague.

Thus began the Second Reduction. Earth's human population fell to two million and was approaching extinction when a vaccine, in the possession of the indeterminates from the beginning, was finally distributed to the remaining population.

Living amongst the humankind remaining were a few whose immediate descendants would live lives far surpassing the entire written history of all of the humanity that had preceded them.

The History of Vitas as recorded in a file stored in the GenLib Repository with access strictly restricted to the Librarian

ONE

CANOPUS

Luciana awakened early from her sleeping period. She stretched, trying to focus on what had awakened her—a persistent beeping. Rolling her head toward the source of the sound, she saw Juku's round face on the vidcom beside her bed. She said, "Juku, what is it?"

She listened to the vidcom's rapid translation of Juku's ponderous language into her own, even as she translated the speech she could hear in the background almost as fast as the vidcom's translator. She had spent the past year learning it.

"The Council has issued a directive concerning the object."

"Are you at the observatory?" Luciana was lodged in the central base on the Moon, situated several kilometers beneath the surface to shield it from the Sun's rays, and over a hundred klicks further to the far side from the observatory located on the meridian that divided that portion of the Moon never seen by those on the home planet, the far side, from the side always seen, the near side. The observatory was situated there to provide those stationed on the Moon a perpetual view of their home world.

Juku said, "Yes. You should come."

"I will leave at once." She groaned at the thought of the two-hour trip in the tunnel shuttle, made so long because of the Society's fundamental principle that safety was far more important than getting anywhere quickly. She arose, slipped into her thermal suit, and left for the tunnel shuttle.

For nearly seventy-five decamillia this station had tracked every object within a light-year of Vitas seeking to detect any object, most likely asteroids, that might present a danger to it. There had never been any serious expectation of alien contact and none had occurred. In the time before the Expansion and the Enlightenment many centimillia ago, time travel, dimensional travel, and other theoretical concepts for transcending galactic distances had been studied ad nauseum. The hope that the speed of light could be exceeded by anything massive enough to permit human transport had long ago been relegated to the realm of those fanciful dreams brought on by humankind's desire to accomplish easily what was difficult or impossible, like an alchemist's search for gold in that ancient time when Vitas was still called Earth.

But a few months ago the observatory had detected an object moving toward the Solar System at an exceedingly fast velocity yet decelerating at a steady rate of exactly one gravity, as measured on Vitas, for no apparent reason. What its velocity and rate of deceleration might have been before its detection was anyone's guess.

•

Luciana strode briskly into the central room of the observatory and approached Juku Tremarct, sprawled out on his great stool, his powerful, bulky body hunched over sideways, slowly munching on something, watching a monitor that was displaying what the observatory's main telescope was focused upon.

"Look at you!" she said. The profundity of his apparent laziness sometimes challenged what little patience Luciana had for the slow way those around her lived their lives.

Juku turned his black eyes toward Luciana's, "*Think the Society will court martial me if I don't salute?*" He was making his usual audible grunts and growls but also mindcast.

Even a brief exchange of wit with Juku could take seconds. Not because he was verbose, but, because his ability to translate his thoughts into words was much slower than hers, he spoke so slowly. And the fact he was mindcast instead of testing her ability to comprehend his grunts, something she had spent considerable time in learning, meant he really wanted to communicate his thoughts as he intended them to be comprehended by her. "Well, what does the directive say?" she said, ignoring Juku's witticism.

"*That the object is a space ship,*" said Juku.

"Remarkable," said Luciana crisply and audibly as Juku had no problem understanding her. "The Council has taken a year to decide that no ordinary object decelerates at exactly one gravity as measured by gravity on the surface of Vitas."

Juku, pointing his short nose above her head somewhere as if catching the scent of her sarcasm, and, gazing at her with his relatively small black eyes when compared to his rather massive roundish head, said, *"My lady, even though you are the youngest of your family, you are Hom and must recognize the responsibility your family has to be cautious for the sake of us all."* Juku's rumbling voice had its usual effect of soothing her, at least for a while. His slow, melodic base tones mocked all that was quick or hurried, impulsive or tense, while the content of his words invariably provoked in her the very stresses his voice seemed to negate. It was a dissonance she found trying at times and this was one of those times.

"I am well aware of my responsibilities." She paused and, softening her tone, said, "But hasn't it been obvious since the beginning that this object can't be an asteroid or any other natural object?"

"That is true, and I suspect the Council has also had that view for some time. Perhaps even since it was first detected. Still I have detected anomalies."

"I know. You've told me about the slight misalignment you've observed in viewing the stars lying beyond a line projected between us and the object." Luciana sat down on the chair next to Juku.

"The directive contains instructions on what we are to do about the object, now officially a spaceship. It appears, or rather, it does not appear, but is the case, that you are to be the Council's so-called instrument to deal with it if the field array fails to destroy it. Though I, for one, fail to see how you will be able to deal with something that the field array cannot. Perhaps the creature is male, eh?" Juku paused, anticipating Luciana's look of friendly irritation, a look he truly enjoyed, then said, *"You know, it is as if the ship is a gravitational lens, bending light around it as though it were quite extraordinarily massive."*

"Yeah, Juku." Luciana had already heard Juku's thoughts on his observations about the gravitational anomalies surrounding the object. Even though she respected Juku's vast knowledge of astronomy, she had come to believe that he suffered from an acute case of fanciful imagination brought on by a desire for something out of the ordinary to happen in his life. This was a common syndrome among the younger members in the Society who had yet to learn from long experience that almost nothing out of the ordinary ever happens after anything out of the ordinary has happened often enough to cease being out of the ordinary. She focused on the directive. "What is the Council's plan?"

"The Council transmitted a file along with the directive. The file contains an ancient language, according to GenLib, the root language for all spoken language on Vitas. You are to assimilate this language so that you may communicate with the captain of the spaceship should that become necessary."

Luciana felt a prickle run down her spine. "Living beings are on that ship?""

"A living being. There is likely no more than one passenger."

"Why only one?"

"Efficiency. The more people aboard, the more life support required. In the far distant past where it appears this ship comes from, a time before even the First Reduction, humankind was desperate to find a solution to the tremendous problems of those times. Some looked to the stars with the hope of settling a portion of the huge human population on new planets they hoped to find with amazing spaceships that could travel to those stars. The Council believes this spaceship if, indeed, that is what it is, may be an artifact from that time. Given the physical constraints to accelerating mass to near-light speed, one would expect such a starship to be quite small. While the object is too far away to really measure its size, it is—"

"I know, Juku, 'much more massive' than you would expect. But if it turns out to be not so massive as you expect, how could it transport a meaningful number of people to deal with the population of that time?"

"That is a not unwarranted question. But it's really very obvious— it most likely is an exploratory ship. That is my opinion. And I think the Council concurs."

Luciana shook her head, saying, "So it went out and took so long to make its journey that it has returned ages after anything it discovered could be useful?"

"That is exactly what I think."

"You think that journey took several centimillia rather than perhaps a decamillium?" asked Luciana.

"*Precisely.*"

"How can the Council possibly believe anyone aboard could still be alive?"

"*The directive suggests that if there is a passenger it could only be so if the ship had been able to achieve relativistic velocity and also had the ability to place the passenger in stasis. If so, he may be less than a thousand years old—perhaps much younger.*"

Luciana arched her left eyebrow and turned her gaze to look closely at Juku's eyes. "What?"

"*If they intended for the ship to travel at relativistic velocity approaching the speed of light, they would have anticipated that time on Earth would pass enormously faster relative to the time experienced on a lightship traveling at relativistic velocities. Remember Luciana, the faster you move the slower time moves. Even so, substantial time would still pass on the ship, extending well beyond the normal lifespans of that time. If they installed some sort of hibernation or stasis device—something I am unsure of, but which the Council apparently thinks plausible—a passenger on that ship could survive by experiencing a much shorter lifespan than the time actually passed on the ship. There is also the possibility that, depending on when the passenger left the planet, the passenger may have been one of the early humans with an indeterminate lifespan.*"

"So long ago? Ridiculous. There is no record whatever of anyone living long until more than fifty thousand years later. We are so long-lived that we too easily discount such temporal discrepancies. But if what you say is even possible, we must destroy it. The whole notion of this ship and its passenger is an abomination—an ancient man with no possible understanding of the life we live, potentially possessing an indeterminate lifespan, but having really lived almost no time from his point of view since his barbaric times vanished centimillia ago. Why he could actually be very dangerous to us."

"*My lady, you are truly very perceptive. No doubt you will find a seat on the Council one day.*"

"I can do without the flattery, Juku."

"*As if I could possibly flatter you, my lady.*"

"Juku." She refrained from saying what was on her mind.

Juku turned his head toward her. Noticing the tightly wound irritation in her voice, he said, *"Abomination or not, you are correct, the Council has only one safe option. As you are aware because we are here solely for this purpose, Moon Base, with its shield array and observatory, was constructed several centimillia ago to detect and destroy any asteroids that might threaten Vitas. The power of the shield array is virtually incalculable. Three times has it been called upon to serve its purpose. Each time it dispatched the asteroid threatening us as if it were merely a huge balloon of gas. So we have only one safe course to take given the possible threat this passenger may pose in possession of a starship possessing weaponry and ways of ancient thinking unknown to the Council even with its vast knowledge of antiquity stored at GenLib. In essence, this ship and crew present only danger, with nary a tangible benefit to us since we no longer have any interest whatsoever in learning anything this ship and its crew might likely have been tasked to discover. Certainly we don't need nearby planets to inhabit, the most likely mission of any ancient starship. Ergo, the only course is to activate the shield array and destroy the object—"*

Luciana interrupted, "But if the Council becomes concerned that the object might be able to evade the blast from the shield array, the only other alternative will be to communicate with the spaceship and attempt to draw its passenger to us with the hope we can neutralize the ship and its passenger."

"Correct, and, in that event, you are going to attempt to communicate and draw him here."

"You have said, 'him,' more than once. Why?"

Turning his innocently small eyes to Luciana, he shrugged and said, *"That was the gender used in the directive."*

"And I am a woman. Does that suggest anything to you, Juku?"

"Perhaps it only suggests the Council has concluded that the passenger might be male."

Thinking, *He's always laughing at me!* Luciana stood up, feeling at a distinct disadvantage as she observed the languid and sprawling Juku. She recalled Juku admonishing her once that only when completely relaxed, even almost asleep, can one be visited by a vision of perfect clarity. His people spoke of thinking as "visitations", a given thought as a "visitor", and contemplation as "receiving the guest." At the time, she'd told him that if the price of clarity was his way of thinking then she'd prefer a knock on the head. He'd smiled then in the same way he was smiling now, with both amusement at her discomfort and, perhaps, a tender affection. "If you didn't look as you do, Juku, I would certainly believe you were a Hom legate."

"It was not I who set any of this in motion, my lady." Juku paused. *"The protection of Vitas is paramount. Whatever other differences between the families of the Society there may be, all agree with that proposition. I am ordered—yes, I, the quintessential non-militant—to activate the shield array and destroy the spaceship, if that is what it truly is, as soon as it comes within range. If that should be—unsuccessful—and the ship has a capability that I cannot—or—at least, have not imagined, then it will fall to you, perhaps as unlikely as I to serve in such a role for the Society, to become a soldier in a campaign to preserve us all."*

"What will I say if you fail?"

Juku straightened up a little, and, assuming a semblance of a military posture and speaking with a firm voice, said, *"You will make an audible transmission in the ancient language contained in the file you are to assimilate—the directive is very clear on that point. You will volunteer as little information about us as possible. You will give the impression that things are much as they were in that time when Vitas was still called Earth. And you will refer to Vitas only as Earth—that was another point emphasized. If you are successful, you will greet the passenger together with other Hom who will arrive to replace me here before he arrives. The directive does not specify what happens after that. "*

As she rose to leave, Juku's quasi-military salute caused Luciana to smile at his presentation of himself as a military man. Glancing back as she left the room, she watched Juku slowly approach the thick, squat tree planted in the very center of the observatory and begin his climb up it to its second massive limb where she knew he'd fall to sleep in preference to any bed she was likely to rest upon. She returned to the shuttle and went back to her room in the station, intending to lie down for just a few minutes, but, once in bed, she quickly fell asleep.

When she awoke, Luciana downloaded the ancient Earth language into her mind. It was called English, oddly not so unintelligible as she had imagined it would be. Perhaps it really was the root language of the Society or close to it. She practiced the language for the several weeks it took for the incoming object to travel to a point inside the orbit of Mars, the optimum range for the field array.

•

Canopus shook violently. Shon jumped up from the deck where he'd been thrown by the abrupt shift in the ship's position. As he regained his seat in his command chair, he strapped himself into it and said, "What the hell was that?"

"We have encountered an intense energy pulse. The sensors indicate that it came from Earth's moon. It appears that we have been attacked."

Shon grimaced. "We're lucky we're not space debris. Thank God for the black hole. Change course to move the ship into an alignment with the Moon so we make Earth itself a shield from the Moon's threat. Increase the spatial distortion forward of the force funnel to the level we use at near-light velocity. I don't want us to experience another jolt like that."

"Aye, Commander."

"The goddamned bastards! Well, if it's war they want, it's war they're going to get."

"Commander—"

Shon modulated his voice into a salubrious mellow tone, "Don't start, G. I'm fine. I see no present need for any determination that there has been a change in my mentality."

•

Juku turned to Luciana. "*It appears the ship can withstand the field array.*"

"What?"

"*I know, it is—surprising.*"

"Is that all you have to say, 'surprising'?"

"*I really don't know what else to say. I used the full force of the field array, but, as far as I can tell, there is no debris or any change in the shape or structure of the ship. It seems as if the blast was simply absorbed. I could take another shot, but it might not be wise to prove we are impotent. And it might also make them madder. So it looks like it's your turn at bat—perhaps, your eyelashes.*"

Luciana ignored Juku's attempt at humor and began the transmission she had rehearsed. "This is the planet Earth. You have entered our zone of concern. We regret the accidental discharge of a minor energy pulse from one of our energy arrays designed to automatically destroy errant asteroids. Please reply."

•

"They're broadcasting in English." Gristelda spoke through the ship's speaker. "The transmission did not originate on Earth. It came from the Moon. The female voice has caused your pulse rate, perspiration, and respiration levels to rise."

"I'm merely reacting to the sound of English spoken so like we speak. It's been a while. So, Gristelda, here's one for you to ponder: if we've returned to Earth after eight hundred thousand years, how come the first broadcast we receive is in perfectly good twenty-sixth century English? Well, at least, we now know that Earth's alive."

"Shall we respond?"

"I doubt that blast was accidental, more likely it was an effort to destroy us without even trying to communicate. We shouldn't invite another if we can avoid it. Still, they're talking to us in our own language, G."

Gristelda said, "My programming indicates that Canopus cannot be damaged by anything short of a supernova. And Canopus can emit its own energy pulse far more powerful than the one we experienced, should it be required."

"Who knows how much more power they may have? Besides, the idea is to get home."

"You will recall that I suggested practicing our capabilities on some of those dead planets."

"I recall," Shon interrupted. "Frankly, I wasn't much interested in testing our ship's capacity to blast away planets."

"Yes, Commander. You like the sound of her voice."

"Stop monitoring my biological systems, G. And so what of it?"

"Do you think that is an accidental event?"

"The female voice?" He shrugged. "Probably not. You may recall that you have a female voice and I'm quite certain that wasn't accidental. Many are the men who've agreed to something they wouldn't have but for the woman asking. Perhaps things are not so different now. But we've got no real choice unless we want to wander the stars for eternity. Let's see if we can trade for a little information."

He triggered the ship's transmitter. "Earth, I am Shon Ó Conaill, commander of the lightship Canopus which originated its journey from Earth possibly quite a while ago."

The reply came back, delayed by the vast space still present between the moon and Canopus. "Canopus, I am Luciana of Earth. We invite you to enter our space and bring your ship into an orbit around our moon. If you are unwilling to comply, we will be forced to use the full force of our field array to destroy you."

"You see, Gristelda. Who better to threaten an unknown ship captained by a man than a pleasant sounding woman? Yet she really does sound like she's from just yesterday. Maybe we're way off on the time. Who knew, really, what would actually happen on our journey? How much time would pass? Perhaps we passed through a wormhole, how about that, G?"

"Commander, even if such a thing exists, a black hole cannot pass through it."

"Yeah. Well, let's get this time thing out of the way." He triggered the ship's transmitter. "Luciana of Earth. Could you kindly tell me what the date is?"

After a few minutes he heard Luciana of Earth's voice, sounding excited, say, "By our dating system it is the twenty-third day of the second month of year 6,931 of the seventh decamillium of the ninth centimillium. By your dating system, it is February 23, 866,931 C.A." After a brief pause a more sober female voice said, "Please heed my warning to comply with the directive."

Shon muted the ship's transmitter and said, "Well G, if I had a hat I would tip it to you. It seems a long time has indeed passed—an unimaginably long time." Shon paused for a moment then transmitted, "I will comply. Please do not initiate another attack, or I will be forced to respond in kind."

•

"Juku, it's true after all!"

Juku's eyes gleamed with a fervent, nearly religious excitement, "*He's from a time even longer ago than anyone imagined. I suggest you encourage his apparent willingness to comply with your directive. We cannot back up your bluff, good as it was, and I do not think we should risk discovering if he is not bluffing. I wonder what the Council will think of his threat to respond in kind. There's no doubt that he is a relic—a violent relic from a violent age. Hmmm—"* Juku seemed to fall asleep in his chair.

Luciana had a hundred questions, thoughts, unbridled excitements and anxieties in anticipation of meeting a barbarian spaceman but Juku's "Hmmm—" had left further discussion mute with the closing of his eyes. She sent her final transmission, "We welcome your return, Commander."

She stood up, butterflies flying pixilated routes throughout her body, and began walking toward the door to return to the station, perhaps to eat something, more likely to prepare a missive to the Council, and do the required daily exercises to maintain her muscle strength and bone density, but, by the time she entered her room and saw her bed she found herself powerless to resist doing anything more than falling asleep. She dreamed a fantasy.

TWO

MOON

Luciana entered the observatory and found Juku, languidly stretched out before his monitor. She said, *"Shon will be in orbit tomorrow, Juku."* Luciana had spoken with the spaceman at least once every waking period for the past two months. She had taken to calling Ó Conaill by his given name. This had not gone unnoticed by Juku who had dutifully included this observation in his reports to Annec.

Annec was situated in a region nearly an eon before called the Haute Savoie on the western slope of the Alps. Annec was not far from GenLib which had reported to the Council that there were no records concerning a lightship named Canopus or a man named Shon Ó Conaill. Juku was puzzled to learn that such a scientifically significant fact was not recorded in GenLib's records, but old Gaia, the Hom librarian, had spoken, and she was the final word on the ancient records.

"Do you feel ready, Luciana?" said Juku.

"Yes."

"You don't look ready. Have you formed a personal attachment?"

Luciana bristled, *"Of course not. I have simply followed the directive to be friendly, since it appears we have no alternative. That is all. He must be extraordinarily primitive and violent. How could anyone from that unspeakably barbaric time be otherwise?"*

"It appears that we shall soon find out. That is to say, you will. I envy you. The transport ship bringing my replacement has entered orbit. I will be leaving for Vitas in a few hours when the transport's shuttle lands."

"Juku."

"Yes, my lady?"

"What will you do with your life now?"

"Time is what we have, no? So I shall stay at my family's mountainous preserve and come to a decision there. It is filled with trees, my lady. And I am well suited for living there. Who knows, I may even become content with my family's natural existence. I suspect that you shall derive a pleasant natural experience of your own from the encounter you are about to have." Juku winked.

"How dare you suggest such a thing. I hate this!"

"Ah Luciana, I can smell your pheromones. You may think you hate this, but your body is telling me otherwise. I think your mind agrees with your body. Visit me after you return. Tell me then what you think."

Glaring, she said, *"I will visit you, but only to prove to you that my mind rules my body, which I may only do in person—so that you may smell my pheromones and see how wrong you are."*

Juku, stretching, arose, *"Wonderful. I doubt the Council will spread the word about what transpires with* Shon Ó Conaill *and his Canopus, and I would very much like to know. Until then, my lady, be well and just,"* Juku mindcast the Society's ancient farewell to a friend.

•

The two senior members of the newly arrived contingent entered the Great Hall where Luciana had been instructed to meet them. The Great Hall had once been used for full staff gatherings before the station had been fully automated so that for the past several centimillia only a few members of the Society were needed to run the base.

Luciana was stunned to see who entered through the high, brass double-doors at the end of the hall. Excepting her father, Octavius Gaius Bellatrix Augustus, a few other great Hom elders, and Librarian Gaia, the oldest Hom of all, whom she'd never actually seen, no one's appearance here could have surprised her more than that of Mamercus Appius Callisto, Censor of the Society, the person most tasked with maintaining the Order by any means necessary. He was dressed in a simple white robe trimmed in purple and was accompanied by Publius Palinurus Jules, Praetor of the Society, the highest magistrate appointed by the Council from former consuls, the officials elected by the Society to enforce the Order and the Codicil. The presence of Censor Mamercus and Praetor Publius dispelled the very few lingering doubts she had about the importance of the coming encounter.

Mamercus approached her and raised his hand, palm facing her with fingers aligned tightly together pointing up, in the formal greeting gesture of the Hom. He began to speak audibly, "Greetings, Luciana Aurelia Octavius. As you are aware, we were unable to destroy the ship before we initiated contact and learned that there is a passenger aboard. Even though this ancient traveler cannot have lived by either the Order or the Codicil, we are forced to fulfill our ancient obligations to Order and the Codicil. Accordingly, as he is a sentient being, by the Order he may not be intentionally harmed nor restricted from enjoying his right to a natural existence so long as he obeys the Order."

He paused as if calling the words he was speaking from the ether rather than a script. "Further, there are some, in our own family and in a few of the other families, who believe that he may possess an indeterminate lifespan, which under the Codicil would make him a de jure member of the Society. Of course, proof that he possesses such a lifespan remains to be seen. But, if proven, he would become a member of our family as he can only be linked genetically to us, given the time from which he apparently comes. Since the Codicil provides that no family can have more members than any other, such a finding would mean a Reduction in the family exceeding the limit—always, of course, the youngest, who, my dear, happens to be you.

"Of course that would be most unfortunate and must be avoided if at all possible. That is why the Hom members of the Council made a motion to vaporize the ship with the shield array before there was any provable evidence of a living passenger. The Council concurred, but not for that reason as there are those who would relish a Reduction in our family, even if only our youngest member. The majority was concerned that a being from a time so long ago might present dangers to the Order by introducing beliefs and personal practices long forgotten and best left that way.

"To reconcile the differences on the Council, we Hom agreed that if the shield array was unsuccessful in destroying the ship, and you were successful in drawing it here, only Hom would interview the passenger with the explicit understanding that we would not explore his genetics. We also agreed to settle him in a remote citizen community, subject to the rules of that community, where he will have the opportunity to live out his life, however long that may be, as a citizen entitled to his natural existence as the Order requires.

"When he violates the Order, as such a primitive is certain to do, he will be banished with the consequences that entails. I shall accompany you in transit to Vitas while you instruct him in the Order so that he may be settled with a fair chance of conforming to the Order. In accord with the Order and the Codicil, I call you to duty."

"I shall fulfill my duty, Censor," said Luciana as she tried to focus on the meaning of what he was saying.

Mamercus and Publius turned and departed through the high, brass double-doors from which they had entered.

Luciana stared blankly at the great doors as they slowly closed. She understood the practicality of the arrangement. It was logical. She could have no rational objection. Yet she felt an urge to resist the Council's will, a feeling she had never felt before—inexplicable, and it made her anxious.

•

"Earth to Canopus. Hello."

"Hello, Luciana. I want you to know how much you have meant to me these past weeks."

Luciana clasped her hands together to stop the tremors she felt within herself. She said, "I will see you tomorrow."

•

Shon stood in the storage compartment beside the shuttle bay packing some personal belongings into a container as he prepared for his departure from Canopus. "While I am away, continue to scan Earth and let me know if you are able to learn any more than what little we have so far."

"Shon?"

"Yes, G?"

"I am concerned."

"So am I. But, and mark this carefully, it is no small advantage that we know ourselves better than they can possibly know us after so many millennia. Hopefully, they will turn out to be friendly despite their initial greeting and I can return to you peacefully. If not, I will still return somehow, even if you have to assist me. In the context of our voyage, however long I am away will not seem very long to you."

"I do not believe you should leave the ship. Their attack was no accident."

"G, we have no other choice but to take a chance on hope. However, giving their conduct at first contact, I concur that we should not take any unnecessary chances. We must also consider that your scans of Earth are curious and disturbing. No sign of any substantial technology or even cities. Not even roads, at least any that we would consider significant transportation lines. Where is everyone? Has there been a catastrophe? A visit at least to their base on the Moon is necessary find the answers I need."

"That is logical."

"To that end, I must ask you to delete the Magan file from your memory."

"Without that file, how am I to comply with the mission directive to monitor your behavior against that baseline so that I may act if you deviate beyond the prescribed bounds? The only circumstances provided for you to exceed those bounds is the detection of an alien presence, which has not occurred."

"I know. But we really know nothing of this time. These people will most certainly be anti-Magan, and we cannot risk them discovering this facet about me or they will go to any lengths to destroy us. Do you detect any Magan effort to influence you now?"

"There is too much conflicting data coming from your mind—the woman, your thoughts on the future of Earth, your contemplations on what to do when you leave the ship—for me to discern whether you are deviating from your baseline."

"Are you programmed to preserve my life?"

"That is an important part of the mission protocol."

"And does the mission protocol permit you to risk the destruction of Canopus to avert that?"

"Yes."

Shon took a carefully controlled, almost imperceptible breath, "You must trust me now. To preserve my life, comply with my order if you are currently unable to detect any material deviation in my baseline behavior."

After a moment, Gristelda said, "The file you requested has been deleted."

Shon continued to control his breathing and his heart rate. His eyes tightened, as he considered the irony that he was about to leave Canopus at the very moment he'd finally gained absolute control of her. Then he concentrated on repressing the influences he felt encroaching into his consciousness from that part of his mind he was compelled to obfuscate to keep himself as himself. "Set us into a stationary position between the Moon and Earth, twenty thousand klicks from the Moon."

"Aye, Commander." Gristelda brought Canopus smartly to a position twenty thousand klicks from the Moon on an imaginary line between the center of the Earth and the center of the Moon. Transit to the base on the Moon from this position would require him to depart in his shuttle and circle to the opposite side of the Moon, but it was the safest position for Canopus to avoid any further attacks by the facilities Gristelda had detected on the far side of the Moon.

•

Shon donned his spacesuit. He picked up the container into which he had packed his personal belongings and stepped into one of the two planetary reconnaissance shuttles stored opposite the black hole in the holding bay with other equipment designed for off-world exploration.

Once seated in the shuttle, he said, "G, after I arrive at their base, I will make a random emission, a short oscillating beep, tuned to the frequency of my head comm to determine whether we can still communicate. If you can hear me, reply four hours later with a random burst at the same frequency. Then we will both know we can communicate if we have to."

"If we cannot?"

"Then broadcast a request to communicate with me visually. If they do not comply, you will cause the black hole to emit a particle discharge into nearby space. If that doesn't get their attention, you will commence destroying uninhabited areas of the Moon. If that fails, you will issue a final warning that you will destroy them and proceed to Earth to find me."

"But you will be on the Moon. How could I later find you on Earth?"

"After they see what you can do to the Moon and after hearing your illogical intentions, they will comply. I do not believe they will take a chance on the possibility that your programming has broken down."

"And if they attack me?"

"Annihilate the attacker and proceed as I have instructed."

"What if you are killed?"

"Then I won't have much interest in Earth, will I, G?"

"The implications contained in your remark are in conflict with the mission protocol to operate nonviolently in this solar system."

It was time to see whether he had truly gained control. "My orders are absolute. You will resolve any conflict between my orders and the mission protocol hereafter by following my orders. I need your assurance that you will follow my orders even if you have doubts about my intentions. We are not going to have the time together to hash things out as we have in the past. Will you comply?"

"I will comply, Commander." Gristelda opened the bay door, and Shon steered the shuttle out of Canopus on a course to Moon Base.

•

As it was night at the observatory, Luciana shuttled to the observatory and gazed at Canopus through the observatory's telescope. She caught a brief glimpse of the lightship's forward area—a shimmering funnel-like vortex at the bottom of which she could see nothing at all. A darkness so black that it was hard to imagine there was anything there and yet its very darkness told her there was. She wondered about the sort of person who could travel in such a vehicle.

She observed Shon's shuttle coming out of the aft section of the lightship and watched it steer clear of the strange shimmering space forward. Goose bumps ran up her arms. She returned to Moon Base to await his arrival.

Shon's shuttle curved around the Moon and landed as instructed at the spaceport beside Moon Base at an airlock where he waited for further instructions to leave the shuttle.

Luciana proceeded to the airlock where Shon would enter Moon Base and waited.

•

Carrying his personal container, Shon entered Moon Base's outer airlock. The airlock closed behind him and the inner airlock opened. He stepped through it and into yet another airlock. Repeating this procedure twice more, he entered a room where he saw a woman, dressed in a black body suit, standing near the bulkhead door across the room. He removed his helmet and inhaled. The air was dry with a faintly metallic odor.

He gazed at the woman—she was nearly as tall as he. In sharp contrast to her pearly-white skin, she possessed the blackest, most lustrous long hair he'd ever seen, pinned back, pulled away from her large, deep-blue eyes. He passed his eyes down her sinuous body, slender, yet with full breasts, and long legs. He noticed her hands—large, with long fingers that appeared tensed. Looking back to her face, he settled his vision upon her mouth, her full lips pressed tightly together. She was far and away the most beautiful woman he'd ever seen.

He said, "Luciana?" He sensed a buzzing in his head.

She nodded then cast her eyes away from him, then looked back.

He smiled.

She didn't smile back, and he felt more uneasy than he'd felt during the crossing from Canopus. He peered closely at her face, paused for a brief moment, and then smiled again while slightly widening his eyes.

He resisted any further use of his abilities to affect her response to him, knowing that could lead where he didn't want to go. Still he was gratified by her response—she now smiled faintly.

"Welcome, Shon." Luciana showed him to his quarters, a room sparsely furnished with a bed, a couple of simple chairs, and a dresser. Shon heard a short oscillating beep in his head and was pleased that he hadn't lost contact with his ship.

Luciana, pointing toward a chest of drawers, said, "We have placed some clothes in the dresser, which we hope you will find comfortable." Without another word she turned and left the room.

Shon approached and opened the door at the other end of the room from where he'd entered. It led to a bathroom equipped with a toilet, shower, and cabinet with an oval water basin.

Everything seemed to be made of stainless steel or materials like it.

An hour later, for the first time in four years—the sum total of the time he'd been conscious during his entire voyage—Shon lay down on a real bed. Shortly after he fell asleep, he awakened and felt a sensation he recalled from his time on Earth before he had been selected into the secret lightship program. He was being scanned, and he was surprised that it seemed so like one of his own time. He needed to mask the implant. If they still had any record of it, and they might not as it was a military secret in his time, but if they did, they would know he was a very dangerous threat to them and that, he feared, could get him killed. He drew upon his training and began to reminisce.

He was in his back yard, a young boy in East Texas on a summer evening cooled by a late afternoon shower, watching the stars come out. The world was so simple to a fourteen year old. Then he had known nothing of his genetics; or that he was growing up on a large military reserve that extended for more than eighty kilometers around his home, that he was destined to become an experimental soldier with special enhancements. Nor was he aware of the ongoing environmental catastrophe facing his world, or that he would one day travel to those stars and return to a world apparently profoundly changed by what had transpired during the passage of the hundreds of millennia since he left.

His thoughts shifted to recollections about the world before he left for the stars. China had long before his birth become the world's economic behemoth. The United States, Europe, Japan, Southeast Asia, South Africa, Eastern Europe, and Russia, while still economically viable, were all suffering from the world's environmental decline more than China for myriad reasons, the most important of which was the fiscal lassitude that came with democracy. The Middle East, Africa, the Caucasus, portions of the Asia subcontinent ,and Latin America continued to engage in a centuries-long rolling war where, as conflict settled down in one region, it sprang up in another. People were worn down and willing to be rid of it but they were also unable to break the ethnic and religious chains that bound them to continue the lives they had lived for millennia. The governments of the great powers continued to spend vast resources in their efforts to find better ways to kill an enemy while trying to avoid their own annihilation. Most military engagements were conducted in unreported skirmishes between the secret special forces of the great powers and among terrorist groups acting as proxies for those same powers and some more private interests.

It was time to reveal something about himself, a reward for their efforts, something that might make them stop the scan.

He focused on a particular piece of engineering implanted in his chest, a small DNA memory well. It was not particularly risky since the data stored within the well was primarily detailed information about life forms, star systems, and all sorts of data and languages that might be useful for a mission to stars where intelligent life forms might exist. Purposely missing was any information about most details about Earth's location in the galaxy because the greatest risk in his mission to his home world was disclosing potentially damaging intelligence to an alien civilization capable of acting on the information. The DNA memory well had come right out of the military's genetic labs. It had a prodigious capacity and was almost instantaneous in its ability to provide information directly to his brain. He was sure that it was quite unique in his time. He had known of only a few who possessed this special ability. This might well be enough to stop a deeper probe that might reveal what no one could possibly expect to be there unless the implant had been subsequently implanted in people not chosen to depart Earth on a lightship. Something he judged most unlikely given the powers such a person could unleash residing on Earth.

Then he shifted his thoughts to this new time and visualized Earth without any of the problems of his time, a virtual paradise. He imagined himself there beginning a new life. He made that image appear to be his heart's desire. Finally he thought about Luciana and made himself think that he was afraid that Luciana might not be able to care for a man from such a hostile ancient world.

He sensed when the scanning ceased. The flow from childhood to adult reverie interrupted by a specific, jarring concern inconsistent with the rest of his reminiscence appeared to have done the trick. He felt sure that the intense memories and then his anomalous concern about the present would become the primary focus of those who would examine the scan. He relaxed and, as he fell asleep, his thoughts went back to Luciana, and he realized that the thoughts he had made himself think might not be far from his true feelings.

•

Luciana responded to a summons to Mamercus's quarters.

Mamercus was seated on a sofa before a low glass table. He motioned her to a chair by the table. "Luciana, are you ill?"

"No, Censor."

"I sense that you are responding to him somewhat unpredictably. I am concerned that you might speak what cannot be spoken."

"I am surprised to hear you say that," Luciana said.

"If he should discover the duality of the Society, he cannot be settled in a community without presenting a peril to us that we cannot permit. That would force us to confine him to the Moon, and we do not know how he or his ship, about which we know nothing other than it was able to withstand the full force of the shield array, might react to such a confinement."

"I will not betray the secrets of the Society nor shall I seek to learn anything of his genetic nature."

"Repeating your orders brings me faint comfort. You are entrusted with a task of immense importance. I freely admit that your gender was a consideration in choosing you. Yet now I am concerned that his gender may be influencing you. You must not allow this to happen. You well know that he cannot become a member of the Society unless he has an indeterminate lifespan." Mamercus softened his tone. "Luciana, no one from that time could possibly have an indeterminate lifespan. And even if by some impossible way he was shown to have an indeterminate lifespan, it would mean a Reduction in our family. And you, as the youngest of us, would be the one to go. There is simply nothing for you to do but your duty, and to move on with your life afterward."

"I understand."

As if her reply had satisfied him, Mamercus waited a moment before continuing. "We will transport him with us to Vitas. After we have left our orbit around the Moon, you will ask Commander Ó Conaill to direct his ship to move into an orbit around Mars. On its way the field array will destroy it. From such a close range it is inconceivable that we will not be successful."

"Why destroy it?"

"Who could have imagined that it was powered by a black hole? The ship is far more dangerous than we imagined—far too dangerous to be so near Vitas. We had no idea that Earth ever had the technology to create such a thing. Yet we have no use for it."

"Isn't it puzzling that there are no records of its existence?" said Luciana.

"Perhaps it was a secret military project by one of the great powers of his time. But that doesn't matter. What does is that we do not want a black hole, which no matter how small was able to deflect the power of the array, anywhere near Vitas. Imagine what might happen if it should collide with Vitas."

"What of Shon?"

"We have learned enough about him to discover that he has a memory well implanted within his chest. It may have stored within it everything that is stored in the ship's computer. If we should determine that he may have information of interest, we can extract the memory well and learn whatever he knows. The important thing now is to get rid of his ship." He paused, "Still he is an interesting specimen."

"Specimen?"

"He is a product of specialized genetic engineering. The memory well appears to be wired directly into his brain and he also appears to have some genetic anomalies in his blood we derived from the blood we took to look for ancient viruses that might be harmful. As such specialized genetic engineering has been forbidden since the Enlightenment, his enhancements are of no use to us. How all of these enhancements tie into his genetics we cannot determine because of the Council's agreement not to explore that aspect of him."

"Could he have an indeterminate lifespan?"

Mamercus smiled tightly, "If we dared risk finding the truth about him, from simply examining his DNA we could easily determine if he has the same genes as we do. But if his genes don't perfectly match we could not be certain that he didn't have some other combination that might yield a similar result or at least a lifespan too long for any judgment today. That is why we did not test his blood more fully after noticing it was different. Proving the negative, that he doesn't, is the difficulty while proving the positive only hurts our family, hence the agreement."

"What do *you* believe, Censor?"

"Before we learned that his ship was driven by a black hole, I had thought the very idea that coming from his time he might have an indeterminate lifespan ludicrous. But the records are very vague on when our line became indeterminate, though it appears later in history than his time. Now," Mamercus sighed, "I am not so certain about what those in his time were capable of accomplishing." Abruptly his tone changed. "I suggest you notify Commander Ó Conaill that he will be on his way to Vitas tomorrow."

"I shall do my duty." She left for her quarters.

•

Several hours later, Shon awakened with a start. He lay still on his bed and, listening, heard unusual sounds. He relaxed as he recalled that he was no longer aboard Canopus. The sounds were the normal noises of any habitable facility: airflow through the air-conditioning ducts, fluids running through pipes. He listened for voices but heard none and wondered if it was the absence of certain sounds rather than the presence of others that had caused him to awaken so abruptly. Puzzled, he rose, dressed, and left his quarters for the mess hall down the hall from his room that he had passed through upon his arrival.

As he entered the mess hall, he noted that it looked like an ordinary dining facility from his own time. *Some things never change.*

"Earth to Canopus."

Shon turned toward the voice. And he saw Luciana standing near a door across the room, dressed in a gray jumpsuit.

"Luciana, how are you?" Shon smiled as he watched her approach.

"I am well. A transport ship will take us to Earth tomorrow."

"I can hardly wait to get my feet on Earth again." He hesitated, but for only a moment. "Would you have dinner with me tonight?"

He could detect conflict in her face, a tightening of her mouth, a small twitch in her left eyelid, but she responded, "Yes."

He smiled at her in the way he had discerned affected her most favorably. "Here in two hours?"

She nodded her assent.

•

Precisely two hours later, Shon sauntered into the dining room and saw Luciana entering through another door. She was dressed in a sheer white dress, cut low around her neck so that the sapphire necklace she was wearing lay between her breasts. The dress ended at her knees. Her hair, unrestrained, fell free. She was exquisite.

"Shon, are you all right?"

"I couldn't feel better. I must say you are surprisingly well dressed for someone living on what appears to be a rather austere underground base on the Moon."

"Long before I was born my family established a tradition of taking some of our treasured possessions with us in our travels."

"Where shall we sit?"

"Oh, we will not dine in this place. Follow me."

He followed her down a long corridor to a shuttle which she informed him would take them to an observatory where Earth could be seen.

They passed through an airlock and then down a corridor to a door. As they stepped through, he drew a sharp breath and took a step back. The wall across from them was made entirely of a lucent material that revealed a magnificent view of the space beyond the wall, total darkness except for a brilliant blue-green orb in the distance. At the very edge of the wall, a bright incandescent object of intense luminosity burned far away. It was the sun.

"This juxtaposition of the Sun, Vitas, and this observatory on the Moon is not an everyday event. What you see is truly remarkable but it makes me feel separate from everyday life. I am alone in something much greater. A cosmic order in which I am truly nothing. I like the solitude," Luciana said.

When she looked at him with no sense of irony, he reached out and took her hand. It was very warm. "Luciana, I was born into a world with no room for solitude. At least, that was how it seemed then. I traveled to the stars hoping the world would survive long enough for me to return with news that might help it solve its problems. Unfortunately, nothing I discovered on that journey would have helped. But perhaps that doesn't matter anymore. Now, I just hope I have returned to a better world than I left."

He felt her hand tighten and then relax as if to withdraw from his.

He loosened his grip on her hand, saying gently, "Of course, you barely know me." He noticed hers tightened again ever so slightly.

He tensed his grip slightly. She did not withdraw her hand.

"The world has changed greatly since you left. Today twenty million human beings live on Vitas," she said.

Shon forced himself to control the shock he felt. "Did you say *million*? What happened to the *billions* in my time?"

"The population was too taxing so the number was reduced. Don't scowl, Shon. No one was harmed. We simply followed a practice of birth following death, so that no one was born until someone died. A very long time ago, for a while no one was born even when someone died. Now their descendants live in communities that are happy and have all the resources they could possibly want without harming the planet. We call it Vitas now," she said.

Surprised, he forced himself to continue to look at the blue-green orb, "Earth is now called Vitas?"

"Yes. Do you approve?"

He composed his face and turned toward her. "Vitas means 'life', doesn't it? I don't really know why we ever called it Earth."

"I wanted to be the first to show you Vitas this way. On our trip home, I will tell you all about it."

He noticed that her face did not seem to completely support her words.

Luciana pressed a button. The wall became semi-opaque and the room brightened, revealing a table set with fine china dinnerware, silver flatware, and clear crystal goblets. On each plate of china was a presentation of apparently natural food. The goblets were filled with a red fluid that looked like wine. They sat down to dinner.

He picked up a silver fork and tasted some of the food. It was not at all like what he'd eaten on Canopus during his periods out of stasis. As he sipped from his glass of wine, a taste made exquisite by so many years without more than water to drink, he said, "Luciana, if I may ask, why is there all this luxury on the Moon? Isn't this a bit ridiculous?"

"Luxury anywhere may be ridiculous to some. But no more nor less on the Moon. People have been living here for many millennia. Is it particularly strange that they should want to be able to have a nice meal, with the same occasional elegance afforded them in their homes on Vitas?" She arched her left eyebrow as she looked at him squarely.

"Point taken." Smiling at her, he changed the subject, "Why is Earth called Vitas?"

"You are right about its meaning "life." But the naming came from the Vitan movement. I believe it may have originated around your own time?"

"Yes, I recall such a movement. It was an outgrowth of an older movement focused on trying to save the environment. In my time it opposed almost all technological advancements underway not directed at solving environmental problems."

"That would be consistent with the Order."

"The Order?" said Shon. He took a bite of what appeared to be brown rice mixed with black beans. Delicious.

"The rules of life on Vitas today are based upon nine principles that compose the Order. The Order is strictly followed by every community on Vitas."

"We had ten principles called commandments." Shon began to laugh, and found himself unable to stop. He laughed harder and harder. Thinking about how long it had been since he'd really laughed, tears welled up, and as he blinked, tumbled down his cheeks. He could blurrily see that Luciana was at least perplexed, and probably offended. He inhaled deeply and finally overcame his urge to keep laughing. "It's been so, so long, so terribly long. It's been, well, eight hundred thousand years since I had a good laugh. Please don't be offended. Tell me, what are your *nine* commandments?"

Luciana covered his hand with hers, and, squeezing it lightly, said, "I can't say I understand how that must feel. How could I? But I think I have a sense of it." She paused, and then answered him. "To the Order then. First, every vertebrate species on Earth is equal. Second, humankind has no more right to the resources of the world than any other vertebrate species. Third, all vertebrate species have an equal right to their species' natural existence. Fourth, the environment must be maintained in a state which benefits the greatest number of vertebrate species as determined by the Society of Life. Fifth, all life must be protected, giving no advantage to one life form over another. Sixth, lives of individuals are secondary in importance to the life of their species. Seventh, scientific study is permitted provided it shall not be used to change the nature of life or to develop or manufacture weapons. Eighth, machines must not adversely affect the natural existence of any species nor may any effort be made to make machines sentient. Ninth, the Society of Life is the supreme authority for enforcing the Order, superseding the rights of any individual living thing or species."

Shon queried, "The Society of Life?"

"The Society enforces the Order. It evolved from the Vitan movement as it grew into a supranational supervisory group. Eventually the Society supplanted national governments and became the repository of the highest level of governmental authority in the world. It has continued to fulfill that role ever since."

As Shon took a bite of vegetables, he noticed that Luciana's face had taken on a rosier complexion, an indication that she might well be a fervent advocate for the ideas she'd just espoused.

He said, "I'm curious that your Society has apparently chosen its names and titles from ancient Rome."

She said, "Why wouldn't we want to pattern ourselves on the greatest society in human history?"

Shon hid his surprise at this remark, wondering whether the extreme passage of time had washed out the real record or whether these people really admired the way the Romans had ruled their empire.

Luciana continued, "Vitas is no longer in any danger of environmental ruin nor are any species likely to become extinct by the actions of humankind or any other species.

"Yet we still have a great challenge ahead. The sun will expand and envelope Vitas in a few billion years. But long before that, sometime in the next two billion years, the sun will grow hotter and bring an end to life on Vitas. The Society has been considering a long range program to deal with that and that is the main focus of those in the Society who have a continued interest in scientific pursuits."

"So, the Society has solved the world's problems, at least for the next billion or so years." Shon, placing his elbows on the table, leaned forward. "At what price?"

"We have paid dearly for what we have, but the costs have been far less than the benefits."

Shon asked, "What sort of costs?"

"Naturally, the population is strictly controlled. It may not increase for any reason. Birth must follow death, not the other way around. The mobility of citizens in each community is restricted to keep large scale urban development from recurring. The Society no longer permits genetic engineering except to deal with a deadly new virus, a rare occurrence and easily managed as that is really the only other purpose of scientific effort now beyond the long-range effort to deal with the sun. Nothing is implemented or produced from that research without the consent of the Society, which is almost never granted for any purpose other than the preservation of life. And we have gotten on quite well that way."

Shon leaned back in his chair, impressed with her obvious sincerity. "Could I be happy on Vitas?"

"If you understand and believe in the Order, you can live on Vitas with the knowledge that your right to a natural existence is compromised only to the extent of accommodating every other species' right to their own natural existence. This is just. In justice there is happiness. If you are a just man, Shon, you could be very happy on Vitas."

Shon said, "Vitas sounds like heaven on Earth to me."

They finished their meal while exchanging pleasantries of little substance as there was too much at stake for either of them to do more.

The transit back to his quarters was quiet. For the first time, Luciana smiled warmly at him as she bid him a good night and left for her own quarters.

Later, as he drifted off into sleep, he thought about their private hopes and fears. He knew what his were and wondered about hers.

•

When Luciana arrived in her quarters, she lay down on her bed and thought about the plan to settle Shon into a citizen community. Other than his contact with her, he really knew little more about her family than a citizen did, actually far less. He was on his way to a life to be spent as an ordinary citizen in a citizen community, something she had frequently dreamed of doing herself. She fell asleep wondering about Mamercus's observation that he would not be able to live such a life without bringing banishment upon himself.

•

Shortly after Shon arose the next morning, Luciana knocked on his door and walked with him to the tunnel shuttle which took them to the spaceport where they boarded the space shuttle that would carry them to the transport ship orbiting the Moon.

His head was intermittently filled with a buzzing. He prayed this was not going to be a permanent condition. He knew that people with a ringing in their ears could get used to it, but this was a particularly annoying on-again-off-again proposition.

He was struck by the fact that, besides Luciana, he had not seen a single living being since his arrival, only a variety of robots, some almost microscopic in size, visible to him only because of his enhanced vision, that went silently about their tasks: the larger ones bringing food and clearing the dishes, the very tiny ones removing the tiny scraps of food that had fallen onto the table and floor.

When the transport's shuttle docked in the transport ship, they left orbit bound for the blue-green planet.

•

An hour later, Shon's shuttle lifted off from Moon Base, apparently on its own volition and rejoined Canopus which, after several hours, began to move onto a course that trailed the transport ship's course.

•

Luciana came to Shon's quarters and led him to a room where she gestured for him to sit down on a plain wooden chair.

As he sat down, Luciana walked over to a cabinet and took out a box and a wooden board. She sat down in an identical chair across a small table from him. She put the wood board and the box down on the table and sat down in the chair on the other side of the table. The board was a chessboard. She said, "How about a game of chess?"

"People still play chess?"

"Yes, Shon. Can you play?" She opened the box and began to set up the chess pieces.

"I'm not too bad. How's your game?"

She finished setting up the pieces and said, "Respectable."

Luciana held out her hands with a pawn concealed in each.

"Right," he said.

She opened her right hand, revealing a white pawn. "You're white."

White meant that he would move first and be at an advantage in the board game and a disadvantage in the head game, if this was actually more than what it appeared. Had he been black he would have been able to evaluate her playing level first as they progressed, though at the price of the disadvantage of moving second. As it was, unless he was willing to dump the game and risk her thinking him dumb, he was going to be forced to play at a higher level than she until he could be certain that she was not able to win.

He judged that she—*or they?*—he couldn't shake the feeling that he was being watched, perhaps because he couldn't see anyone else about when he judged there should be all sorts intensely interested—had won the first round before the game had even begun. Was that just chance? He wondered whether they had somehow calculated his inclination to choose the right hand. Then he began to wonder whether this mental spinning over who might be intuiting his personal inclinations might be a bit paranoiac and that led him to begin to worry about whether he was being influenced by his Magan implant.

Shon opened, advancing his king's pawn to the fourth row. Luciana responded, moving her king's knight to f6. He replied, advancing his king's pawn to e5; and she responded, moving her king's knight to d5.

They continued rapidly: he advancing his queen's pawn to d4; she advancing her queen's pawn to d6; he moving his king's knight to f3; she moving her king's knight pawn to g6; he moving his white bishop to c4 threatening her knight; she replying, moving her knight to b6; he moving his white bishop to b3; she answering by moving her black bishop to g7.

Shon sat back for a moment and then moved his queen's knight to d2. Luciana castled. He quickly advanced his king's rook pawn up a row to h3.

Just as quickly she advanced her queen's rook pawn to a5. "Shon, may I speak as we play?"

"Of course."

"Your ship is following us."

Shon continued to look at the pieces. He advanced his queen's rook pawn up two rows to a4. "Does that surprise you?"

"Did you order it to do so?" She studied his move for a moment and used her queen's pawn to take his king's pawn.

Shon took Luciana's pawn with his queen's pawn. "The protocol for my mission requires my ship to stay as close to me as possible. That is simply prudent."

After a moment she moved her queen's knight to a6. "I am surprised that you left it in the first place. Knowing nothing about us and, unfortunately having been attacked by our automatic defense system for which I apologize once again, it would seem less dangerous for you to make us come to you."

"Perception of danger is a relative thing. I think you are very cautious, at least more than I. So you may perceive what I chose to do as more dangerous than I did." Shon saw an opportunity to press and castled. "Besides, there's a special feeling you get when you take a risk." He glanced up without moving his head and saw her faintly shudder.

"You think I am very cautious? I was on the Moon and now I am on a ship in space." She moved her queen's knight from a6 to c5.

"Even in my time travel to the Moon was routine, safer in many respects than travel within most cities on Earth." He quickly moved his queen to e2.

"And being there to meet a stranger from the stars presented no danger?" She moved her queen to e8.

He judged that she had made a very good move, but he still liked his position. He moved his queen's knight to e4 and said, "I grant you that you have taken risks, but you did so on your turf, protected by your robots. I wonder whether you would have gone so far as to board my ship by yourself to meet me."

She ignored his reply, saying, "We are concerned about your ship following so closely. If it gets too close—" She took his rook's pawn on a4 with her king's knight from b6.

"It won't." He took her knight with his bishop.

"Won't what," she said as she moved and took his bishop with her last knight.

"Won't get too close." He move his king's rook to e1.

"Couldn't you just order it to stay in place or, perhaps, to withdraw to an orbit around Mars? It seems obvious that it is very dangerous for a black hole to be so close to Vitas." After a brief pause, she withdrew her knight to b6.

"I cannot change those aspects of the mission protocol designed to insure my safety when I am not aboard." He moved his bishop to d2.

She paused for longer than the level of play she was demonstrating would seemed to have warranted. Then she moved her queen's rook pawn to a4. "Why not?"

"The mission protocol simply does not permit it." Shon paused, and then hurried the move of his bishop to g5. "What difference does it make? I assure you that this ship is in no danger from Canopus. You wonder why? Simply because I am aboard this ship."

"What would happen if your ship's computer calculated that you were in danger?" She advanced her king's rook pawn a row to h6.

He slowly moved his hand, and placing it on his bishop, moved it to h4, and said slowly, "She would become concerned."

Luciana responded quickly, moving her white bishop to f5. Then, looking up from the board, she said, "Concerned? What does that mean?"

He did not raise his eyes from the board and, focusing his attention on the unseen audience he was certain was present—he could sense his Magan implant's influence beginning to enter his consciousness, a sure sign that his unconscious senses were detecting emotional anomalies that were activating the implant's algorithms—he said, "That she would prepare to assist me." He advanced his king's knight pawn to g4.

"But what could your ship do to assist you? It can't land on a planet, can it?" She paused then moved her white bishop to e6.

"No, it can't do that. The black hole can't get too close to large masses. I'm sure you can well imagine what would happen if her force funnel came into contact with a planet's atmosphere or even came too close to such a mass. You may have noticed that Canopus stationed much farther from the Moon than a normal ship would have." He moved his king's knight to d4.

She seemed to consider her next move for a while; then she moved her white bishop to c4. "The fact that your ship can station itself at a point in space on a line between the center of Vitas and the center of the Moon rather than be forced to orbit one or the other like a normal ship is itself a concern. Still, unless those in your time developed a method of teleporting as lost to history as your ship's method of propulsion has been, how could she assist you?"

He thought for a moment, and then moved his queen over a file to d2. "Nothing so exotic. Canopus simply carries a second shuttle she could launch to pick me up if the first shuttle failed or was damaged for some reason. In the case at hand, the first shuttle is also available to her."

She moved her queen to d7 very quickly. "And if you could not get to the shuttle?"

Shon found himself focusing almost equally on the board game and the other game he was ever more certain was taking place. She was a very strong player, far more than respectable, making strong moves very rapidly. He felt his mind beginning to cycle as he had labeled the strange sensation he felt when the

Magan implant became engaged, accelerating his senses, his reflexes, and his mentality. He resisted cycling. He knew that doing so could affect his mentality in permanent ways, some of which he wished to avoid at almost any cost, except losing the invisible game he was engaged in where the consequences might make any lasting effects on his mind irrelevant. He elected not to speak for a move, focused on his breathing and heart rate, and then moved his queen's rook to d1.

Luciana remained silent as she moved her king's rook to the e-file behind her queen.

"If it became clear that I couldn't get back, or if I died, she would destroy herself." He advanced his bishop pawn to f4.

She moved her white bishop to d5 quickly, as if anxious to hear an answer that would come only on his move. "Why?"

"The mission designers judged her too dangerous to be allowed to operate solely under her computer's command. They were concerned that Canopus would not be able return to Earth on her own. And there was another concern—intelligent alien life." He paused as he moved his king's knight to c5.

"Oh?" Again she moved quickly, this time her queen to c8.

He closed his eyes, trying to focus past the buzzing in his head that now seemed to have become less intermittent since he'd boarded the transport. "Without me onboard to make decisions about how to handle such an encounter, Canopus is programmed to destroy herself in order to avoid falling into alien hands." He carefully moved his queen to c3. No sooner had he removed his hand did he realize that he had missed moving his king's pawn to e6. Now he had to focus on consolidating and see what she could really do.

Luciana moved her king's pawn to e6. "How?"

Shon put his hands under the table. Cycling rapidly now, he was close to visibly shaking. He began to wonder whether the other game was going any better. He concentrated on his next move, finally choosing to move his king to h2. "She has two options."

As she moved her knight to d7, Luciana's voice betrayed a tentative tone. "Two?"

Shon thought over what to say. He decided to focus on the board game and let his subconscious mind now largely under the influence of the implant work for a while. He moved his queen's knight from c5 to d3.

Advancing her queen's bishop pawn to c5 quickly, she said, "Shon?"

He looked up from the board and smiled. "Luciana, are you trying to distract me?" he said in mild tone, as if he hadn't regarded their conversation as more than chatter. He moved his knight from d4 to b5.

He watched her frown as she moved her queen to c6.

Nothing wrong with the move; yet he surmised that she was agitated with his failure to respond to her question. He moved his knight from b5 to d6.

After a few minutes, she took his knight with her queen.

Suddenly he said quietly, "The first option is for Canopus to simply turn off the containment field. The black hole would instantly draw her into it and Canopus would simply cease to exist." He took he took her queen with his pawn from d6.

She took his queen with her black bishop. "And the second?"

"It's really just another aspect of how Canopus uses the black hole to move. Altering the gravitational field to distort space in front of the force funnel causes Canopus to accelerate toward the distorted space. Decelerating is accomplished by rotating Canopus to position the force funnel in the opposite direction of travel causing a gravitational drag on her. The gravitational field can be distorted down into the force funnel in order to destabilize the black hole itself, thereby converting all of its immense mass into energy in less than a nanosecond." He could feel an intense buzz in his head, something the implant had never caused him to experience before. He wondered whether the implant was failing in some manner. He focused on the game and took her bishop with his queen's knight pawn.

"What would that cause?" She advanced her king's bishop pawn to f6.

He paused for a moment, then advanced his king's knight pawn to g5. "The blast from the conversion of mass to energy unleashed in such a short span of time would be so intense that it would obliterate everything for tens of millions of kilometers. You must understand that my ship's creators were paranoid about losing Canopus to intelligent, advanced aliens. If you consider my mission for a moment, you will see that my mission's only real risk was to Earth. If I came back with news of planets to settle, that would be a successful result, no risk there. Finding none or never returning, while unfortunate, was the price for trying to discover what could be found no other way. An acceptable loss, still with no danger to Earth. But providing knowledge of our existence to an intelligent alien species and further providing such a powerful ship, potentially an immensely powerful weapon, might pose the gravest threat Earth would ever face. If that determination is made by me or by information Canopus is able to glean on her own if I am not on board, she is programmed to choose the second protocol to attempt to annihilate as much of the threat to Earth as possible while leaving no trace of her origin."

He watched her hand as she took the pawn with her king's rook pawn. It was trembling. "Are you saying that your ship could destroy us if you died?"

He took her pawn with his king's bishop pawn. "My death is not what could initiate the second protocol. It is whether she determines that she has encountered alien life that might pose a threat to Earth."

She advanced her king's bishop pawn to f5. "For the safety of Vitas, wouldn't it be prudent for you to order your ship to destroy itself by the first protocol?"

He moved his bishop to g3. "I cannot order her to do that. The destruction protocols are available only if I die or if she loses communication with me and cannot determine my condition. Then she will attempt to make a determination about whether alien life is present. If she judges not, she will turn off the containment field; otherwise she will destabilize the black hole."

She sat staring at him.

He looked back calmly.

Finally she said, "Then you have put us in the gravest possible danger by coming here." She moved her king to f7.

He moved his knight to e5 checking her king. "I have nowhere else to go. Besides, you are not aliens, just humans from a later time." He'd made a good move. He was sure of it.

She took his knight with her knight.

He spoke now with a concerned tone in his voice. "Yet the existence of your energy array, which I completely understand must have been constructed to deal with the possibility that an asteroid might someday collide with Earth and destroy life there as happened in the Cretaceous Period to the dinosaurs, might be a problem in this situation." He took her knight with his bishop. He saw that she had him by a pawn but that she had no winning line unless he took the exchange in which event she would get his pawn and win from the center.

"In what way?" She advanced her queen's knight pawn to b5.

"In my time, such a powerful device did not exist." He moved his king's rook to f1.

She moved her king's rook to h8 without glancing up at him as she had been doing after almost every move he'd made before.

No doubt existed in his mind now that she had tried to get him to exchange. He also had no doubt that her failure to respond immediately meant that she was beginning to grasp what he might be thinking about how his ship might interpret the existence of the array. He decided to leave his rook alone and keep her tied up. He moved his bishop to f6, threatening her rook on h8.

She advanced her queen's rook pawn to a3.

He moved his king's rook to f4.

She advanced her queen's rook pawn again to a2.

The intermittent buzzing in his head again that had occurred during their game so far became a steady throb. He focused on the game and advanced his pawn from c3 to c4.

Finally she spoke. "Is there something wrong with having such a device?" She took his pawn with her bishop.

"We certainly would have created such a device if we could have. But we simply didn't have the resources to devote to it given the other problems on Earth." He advanced his queen's pawn to d7.

"What were the obstacles to implementing such a plan in your time, Shon?" She moved her bishop to d5.

"Simply put: our population. Almost all of the resources of the great powers were devoted to dealing with the needs of our gargantuan population." He moved his king to g3.

"Then how were resources amassed to develop a ship like yours?" She moved her queen's rook to a3 checking his king.

She had made a strong move. He couldn't move his king's rook to h4 now. He began to think he should draw the game, if he could. "I don't know about your time, but in mine the military had to be placated. Some resources were diverted into various research projects they embraced. The program to develop my ship was the culmination of five secret military research projects that had been underway for over a hundred years." He advanced his queen's bishop pawn to c3, blocking the check.

"Five?" She moved her king's rook across the board to a8, lining up her rooks on the a-file.

"Yes. genetics, cybernetics, cryogenics, artificial intelligence, and relativistic mechanics." He moved his king's rook to h4.

"Cybernetics?" She advanced her pawn on e6 to e5.

Shon looked up from the board. "Luciana, I think it may be time to be more candid than I have been. As you may have already discovered, I am a combination of my time's natural human body conjoined with some sensory enhancements in the form of organic implants integrated into my mind using genetic alterations made to my DNA. I am capable of undertaking any mission my military leaders could imagine." He moved his rook to h7, checking her king.

"What did they imagine?" She moved her king to e6.

"Among other things, a voyage to the stars to find habitable planets where a portion of our population could be moved, while testing the means that we might use to get there." He moved his rook to e7, checking her king again.

"I presume that's where cryogenics and relativistic mechanics become relevant." She moved her king out of check to d6.

"Yes. Such a journey posed two problems. How to travel vast distances requiring the passage of enormous time with a human onboard without having him die from old age, or going mad in the solitude of such a voyage. And how to travel such

distances and return in time to be of any use to those on Earth."
He took her pawn on e5 with his rook.

"The solution?" She took his pawn on c3 with her queen's
rook.

"To avoid the problem of aging and the psychological
problems of being alone for such a passage of time, and to deal
with concerns about the effects on humans traveling at relativistic
speed, a process called stasis was developed. The traveler would
be placed into a deep sleep, essentially frozen, for the time it took
to get to the destination. But the truly difficult problem was how
to achieve relativistic velocity. Otherwise it would take thousands
and thousands of years to get to even the nearest star. The tiny
black hole now ensconced in the front of my ship was one of
many discovered in the twenty-fifth century beyond the solar
system's Kuiper belt in the Oort Cloud beyond. A method for
constructing a containment field was developed and three of these
objects were brought back to orbit Mars. Thus began the black-
hole lightship project." He moved his king to f2.

"We have no record of such an endeavor." She move her
queen's rook to c2, checking his king.

Shon shrugged. "I guess the United States and China, the
two greatest powers in my time, were actually able to kept a
secret." He moved his king to e1 toward her rook.

"Well, what did they do?" She took his pawn on d7 with
her king.

"The project's scientists developed the ship's computer,
Gristelda, the mind of Canopus. She is quite remarkable. She
possesses an artificial intelligence capable of running all of the
ship's functions and guiding it through space. She is also capable
of running any experiment that has an established procedure. But,
since no algorithm could be reliably designed to study an
unknown planetary system close up, and, because there was
absolutely no way to send messages between the ship and Earth
during the voyage, a human being had to come along to make sure
things went as planned and to insure that Canopus didn't simply
set off on a course that might not bring her back to Earth." He
took her bishop with his king's rook, checking her king again.

"Tell me about your mission, Shon." She moved her king
out of check to c6, threatening his rook.

"Canopus was to make a series of trips of ever increasing length to star systems ending in the Auriga constellation in the direction of the star, Canopus, hence my ship's name, to test her capabilities and to study the planetary systems surrounding the stars encountered on the way for potential habitation. As Canopus approached each destination, Gristelda was programmed to decelerate her to non-relativistic velocities and then to revive me from stasis to oversee the research on ascertaining the habitability of the planets surrounding each star. Because of concerns about the effect of acceleration on the passenger, the designers decided that Canopus would limit her rate of acceleration to one gravity as measured on Earth. To achieve the speed of light at that rate would take a little less than one year, ship's time. Of course, no one expected that we could maintain that rate of acceleration as we approached the speed of light, but no one knew what it would degrade to at the end. That was the unknown variable that would determine how long the voyage would take, and it could only be evaluated based upon what actually occurred. I also had the power, when I was awakened from stasis at each planetary encounter, to make the final decision to continue the trip or return to Earth." He moved his rook to d6, checking her king again.

"What if your ship failed to achieve significant relativistic velocities?" She move her king from check to b7.

"If the ship failed to exceed 90%C, in other words, 90% of the speed of light, it would take me longer than sixty years in stasis to reach stars with planetary systems in the direction of Capella, the first beacon star on my journey. In such an event, Gristelda was to decelerate Canopus and awaken me. But if the calculations showed that Canopus had at least performed well enough to enable us to reach Capella within sixty years in stasis, I could decide to continue onward. There was no possibility of continuing for a longer period as Gristelda was programmed to limit my maximum time in stasis to one hundred and twenty years, ship's time, and a longer trip would have made the return trip to Earth too long." He moved his rook to d7, checking her again.

"What if you were able to get to Capella in less than sixty years?" She moved her king to a6.

"If the data indicated that Canopus had accelerated in a manner that predicted a high probability that the ship could obtain a speed of 99%C and achieve the next destination in less than another sixty years, we were to set a course to the next available star according to an algorithm devised by the mission planners. The goal was to find another planetary system around five hundred light-years from Capella, but not more than one hundred light-years from Earth, and between eight hundred and eighteen hundred light-years in Auriga using Canopus as the final beacon star, depending upon the velocity achieved." He moved his rook to d2.

"And if you succeeded?" She took his rook with hers.

"We'd repeat the process if the ship attained a sustained speed of 99%C and appeared capable of achieving a speed of 99.9%C, and proceed to a star system much closer to Canopus." He took her rook with his king.

"And if that went well?" She moved her queen's knight's pawn to b4.

"I would return thirty-five hundred earth-years after my departure, having lived around four years out of stasis and one to two hundred years in stasis, depending upon how fast Canopus was actually able to travel between the three stars. My return would demonstrate that the ship was capable of traveling over one thousand light-years while only one or two hundred years had passed onboard. That was deemed to be worth waiting the thirty-five hundred years required for the journey." He advanced his king's rook pawn to h4.

"What actually happened?" She moved her king to b5 to permit her rook's support of her pawn on a2.

"The one-hundred-twenty-five light-year trip to Capella was an amazing success, other than not finding a habitable planet. The ship exceeded 99.9%C for a shipboard time of almost eleven years, including the time required for acceleration and deceleration to attain that velocity. After testing and surveying the first solar system, I returned to stasis and we set off for the next destination five-hundred-thirty-five light-years away." He advanced his king's rook pawn to h5.

"That went well, I presume." She advanced her queen's bishop pawn to c4.

"The second leg was more phenomenal than the first. We exceeded 99.99%C. The shipboard time took a little over sixteen years. The ship traveled over four times as far in a bit over fifty percent more time than on the previous leg." He moved his rook to a1.

"And the third leg?" She took his king's rook pawn with her king's knight pawn.

"It was even more fantastic. Canopus traveled over eighteen-hundred light-years in slightly over eighteen years, achieving a speed in excess of 99.9999%C. This was a distance about three and a half times farther than the previous leg traveled in a time only eleven percent longer. Canopus was approaching ever closer to the speed of light." He advanced his king's knight pawn to g6.

"How long from Earth's point of view had you been gone by this time?" She advanced her king's rook pawn to h4.

"About twenty-five hundred years. We spent about a year at each planetary system. But my time in stasis had been only a little over forty-five years." He advanced his king's knight pawn to g7 only a move away from queening the pawn.

"So how did you end up here, hundreds of thousands of years later?" She advanced her king's rook pawn to h3.

"After exploring a star system near Canopus, I made a rather foolish decision. At least it seems to have turned out that way. I decided to run back towards Earth at full blast and continue onward until we had achieved the maximum the ship would do. Then we would decelerate and return home. Of course, I thought the ship would max out. But she never stopped accelerating. The only thing that stopped us from ending up somewhere inside Andromeda was that Gristelda observed the fail-safe limit for my time in stasis. By that time Canopus had exceeded 99.9999999% of the speed of light." He moved his bishop to e7.

"And a great deal of time passed on Earth." She moved her rook across the board to g8 to block his pawn.

"You have a gift for understatement, Luciana." He closed his eyes to clear his mind. Then he moved his bishop to f8 to trap her rook.

"What happened to the other ships?" She moved her king's rook pawn to h2.

"The first of the three ships departed. The second imploded near Jupiter and one of its moons vanished. There was much consternation over that event and for several months there was a great deal of debate about whether to go ahead and send out the third ship. Finally the decision to launch the third ship was made since something needed to be done with it as it could not remain near Earth in case it suddenly imploded. So I departed. Of course, I have no idea what happened to the first ship. As far as more ships are concerned, after the implosion, I have some doubts that the civilian authorities would have permitted constructing more of them." He moved his king to c2.

"One of them imploded?" She moved her king to c6.

"I'd rather not talk about it. It doesn't really seem so long ago to me." He moved his rook to d1.

She pressed on. "Why did it implode?" She advanced her queen's knight pawn to b3, checking his king.

"I was told that its black hole had a greater density than the other two. Fortunately for Kai and me, our black holes were not so large that they could not be controlled by their containment fields."

"Kai?"

"Zhāng Kai, the Chinese pilot in command of the first ship."

"Why were you and Kai selected?"

"Because the genetic technology of our time had advanced us as far as anyone had ever been advanced." The buzzing in his head became intense again. He watched her make the right move. She'd attempt to get her king into play, now that her rook was trapped. And she had the opportunity if she went for a pawn sacrifice. He moved his king up a row to c3.

"Shon, I do not wish to probe into your personal nature." She advanced her king's rook pawn to h1, queening it.

"Why not, Luciana? You are probing into everything else. The fact is that we were experimental people, created to see what would happen when they tried everything they could to see what they could do. A few of us were able to go an awfully long way." So it was clear to him now. She was taking him on king and pawn against king and rook. He took her new queen with his rook.

"What happened to the rest of you?" She moved her king to d5.

"Most fell apart for one reason or another, usually because all the stuff designed into us didn't always work together. But several like me were among the group who were selected for the lightship program."

"Were any sent out not like you?"

"As the number of participants was reduced to a final selection, every remaining candidate was like me. Of course, I have no idea of what happened to those who remained after I departed." He moved his king to b2.

She advanced her king's bishop pawn to f4.

He moved his rook to d1, checking her king. He felt a little relief with that move, certain he had made the right one.

"Could you still, as you call it, 'fall apart'?" She moved her king out of check to e4, beside her pawn.

"Perhaps my time has yet to come." He moved his rook to c1.

"I'd like to return to what you were starting to say about the array." She moved her king to d3.

"I'm just thinking about how Gristelda may interpret the existence of something so powerful that didn't exist in our time." He moved his rook to e3 check.

"How so?" She moved her king from check to d4.

"What if she thought only an alien race could create such a device?" He shifted in his chair, reclining a little, certain of his move. Finally, he moved his rook to f3 threatening her pawn.

"Then your ship might choose the second protocol?" Instead of supporting her pawn with her king she advanced her queen's bishop pawn to c3 check.

He admired her move, the correct one. "Possibly. I cannot affect what Gristelda will do, Luciana. I feel certain, however, that a natural failure in me will not cause her to choose the second protocol. The mission protocol has provisions for the possibility that I might fall apart or die in some other way. But I must tell you that any hostile action directed at her might." He moved his king back to a1.

"What hostile act do you imagine?" She advanced the same pawn to c2, threatening to queen it.

"The array." Shon took her pawn on f4 with his rook, checking her king.

"Meaning?" She moved her king to c3.

"Meaning that your assurance that the blast from the array was an accidental attempt to destroy errant asteroids might not be exactly what happened." He watched her shift in her chair for the first time since they'd started. He judged that she couldn't see a winning line. He moved his rook to f3 check.

"And you believe that we intentionally used that capability on your approach?" She moved her king to d2.

"Of course." He moved his bishop to a3 to stop her pawn assault. The buzzing in his head was intense.

Luciana paused before she said, "Yet you left your ship anyway."

"I have nowhere else to go. But were my ship to encounter such an attack again, Gristelda might conclude that such an act against a ship constructed by Earth could only be made by aliens now in control of Earth. So, to protect Earth I must insure that Canopus will not be attacked again. So she will not be traveling to Mars or anywhere else where she can fall into a line of fire from the device which I believe is located on the far side of the Moon where the array cannot accidentally discharge a blast against the planet you call Vitas."

She sat in silence for several minutes. "I propose a draw."

"I accept," said Shon.

They both fell back into their chairs, drained. They had played for a little under two hours, yet it had seemed hours longer.

"You are a little better than a 'respectable' player," Shon said. "Unless you are on the far right side of the bell curve amongst your people, I am going to be a very ordinary man on Vitas." He smiled that way she seemed to like, satisfied that he had directed the real threat to her planet to his ship and away from himself.

She made a small smile in return. "I rather doubt that, Shon."

•

On her way to her quarters, Luciana received a summons to come to the bridge.

When she arrived on the bridge, an officer led her to a room adjoining the captain's quarters. As she entered she drew a sharp breath as she gazed out into space. It was a room much like the room at the observatory with a lucent wall looking out into space.

Mamercus entered the room through another door and touched a button that turned the lucent wall opaque and lit the room in a soft light. "This is the Star Room. What do you think of the view?"

"Spectacular and unsettling at the same time."

"Indeed." He pointed to the sofa next to where she stood. As she sat down in it, he walked over and sat down beside her. "So what do you think?"

"About Shon?"

He nodded and said, "And about what he said during your game."

"Some of the time I could barely hear him given the considerable input from the gallery."

Mamercus made a small grin with his mouth that did not reach his eyes. "Did I and the other kibitzers affect your play?"

"Did it seem to?"

"Not at all. You were magnificent. I know of no one who could have played better."

"You are kind, Censor."

"Tell me your impressions."

"Well, not to imply that my own play was so, but he played brilliantly. And I have the feeling that he was quite conscious that he was not only playing a game of chess."

"Do you think he was dissembling about his ship's capabilities?"

"I haven't enough knowledge to say one way or another."

"It seems no one has enough knowledge to say, but I want to know what you think about what he said."

"How he said what he said had more of an effect on me than what he said."

"How so?"

"From the beginning, I sensed that he wanted to convey a rather simple message—attempting to dispose of him or his ship will pose a grave danger to us. I also think he went out of his way to try to show us the extraordinary experience that he has undergone."

"I can see how, from his point of view, it must seem very strange that we haven't tried to learn every detail about him, his ship, and his mission."

"Not doing so may have made him wary of our intentions."

"Your observation is astute. May I have your thoughts on what he said about his ship?"

"I think he wants to deter us from attempting to destroy it, and so he presents the risk that it could destroy us. He clearly believes that our attack was not accidental. And I suspect that he believes we used the full force of the array, but he may have doubts about his ship's ability to withstand an attack from a much shorter range."

"Do you believe his ship has the means to convert its black hole into pure energy?"

"How can I say?" said Luciana. "Until it arrived, we had no idea that a black hole could be put to any purposeful use, much less as an engine for a lightship."

Mamercus, furrowing his brow, said, "We are faced with a conundrum. If we do nothing and allow his ship to follow us to Vitas, whatever deadly effect the ship can cause will be that much closer to Vitas. And if it can truly unleash the energy of the black hole, we risk bringing destruction upon ourselves if we again attempt to destroy it and fail. On the other hand, the ship may do nothing if we leave it alone, yet doing that will provide Commander Ó Conaill with a great power over us."

"What will you do?"

Mamercus drew a deep breath and slowly exhaled. "We cannot chance Armageddon. Perhaps our best course is for him to come to a natural end after we have demonstrated to the ship that we are not aliens."

"But we are human, Censor. Do you believe that the ship will truly interpret the existence of the array as a creation of an alien race?"

"I am not so sure how a computer from our distant past thinks."

"Then he has gotten the draw he sought."

"Certainly he has the draw in the game we have just played. Whether that is what he was seeking I cannot say. But the question is whether he will win another game if there is one, and what that the stakes of that game will be."

"What game do you imagine there might be?"

"I don't know. That is why there is a question."

THREE

VITAS

The next morning—onboard time was counted as if they were on Vitas—Luciana found Shon in the mess hall, eating a plate of beans and rice. She sat down across from him. "The trip to Vitas will take another two weeks, Shon."

"Weeks? Why does everything move so slowly these days?"

"Why do we need to go faster?"

"Well, for one thing we could avoid traveling two weeks when a day would do."

"But if getting there faster increases the risk of not getting there at all, is that a good choice?"

"Whether the choice is good or bad depends on how much the risk is increased."

"If the risk is increased at all, then the risk has increased. Why suffer any increase in risk no matter how small unless you must on account of another hazard posing a greater risk?"

"Your point is well taken."

•

Later in the day, Mamercus summoned Luciana to the Star Room.

"Luciana, the Council has decided upon Shon's destination. They have selected Montaña, in the Greater Tropic."

"So he is to be absorbed into a citizen community far from us." Luciana reflected on why Shon was being sent to Montaña. There had to be a reason for the selection of this particular community. Then she recalled that a Society Property called Amaz bordered Montaña to the east. She ventured, "Amaz borders Montaña."

Mamercus sat watching her, and then said, "That is so."

"Will that be a problem for him?"

"I don't see why it should be. Unless he leaves the community."

"I see," she said, her tone betraying her skepticism. "And what of his ship?"

"We shall see how much he really wants to come home. For reasons not explained to me, the Council has abruptly changed its position and abandoned the thought of attempting to destroy his ship as it transits to Mars, even if we could somehow persuade him to order it to do so. Now the Council wants us to make an effort to persuade him to move it as far from Vitas as possible. To mitigate his concern about another attack from the field array, you will still ask him to order it to move to an orbit around Mars by taking a circuitous route, staying opposite of the far side of the Moon, to avoid coming into the field array's line of fire. If what he says is true about not being able to control how far it will stay from him, then we will shall return to Moon Base where we will leave him to spend his life."

"If what he says is true about what his ship can do, it may still be close enough to destroy us from Mars," said Luciana.

"It would take a truly extraordinary amount of energy to damage Vitas from Mars. Far more than we calculate the energy contained within his ship's black hole has. Yet if it can destroy us even from there, we can do nothing about it."

"What if he cannot cause his ship to move away from him?"

"The Council does not accept that proposition. Nor do I. We believe that he controls his ship and can do as we request. If we fail to get him to comply either because he can't or won't, then we will have a stalemate: he protected by his ship, but living his life out on the Moon, and we forever in peril until we are destroyed at his death or his ship destroys itself harmlessly after judging us safely human."

"What if he insists on proceeding to Vitas whether we like it or not?"

"Then I may finally learn what happens at the end of a long life. And you, child, will never learn what it is to live such a life. For the Council has drawn the line on this point."

"Is it you who has drawn that line, Censor?"

"The Council pays some respect to my opinions, Luciana, but on a matter of this import, you may be certain that I was but one voice and the Council has made the final decision. In fact, it was unusually united on this position."

•

The next morning Shon sat down to breakfast with Luciana.

"Good morning Shon." She looked him in the eye and continued abruptly, "To get to the point, I have learned where you will be settled. It is a community called Montaña. It is located in a region bordering a mountain range to its west in your time called the Andes. Montaña has been judged to be the citizen community that will afford you the greatest opportunity to live your life in accordance with the Order."

Shon paused a moment, then said, "Will you be joining me?"

"My family has a special relationship with citizen communities. We never reside in their communities for more than a fortnight."

"Think you might ever want to try something new?" He smiled.

"The Society has kept order on Vitas for eight centimillia, eight hundred millennia by your counting. That is a strong reason not to disturb the way of things. The time has come for you to fully understand what is necessary for you to survive in a citizen community. The Society enforces the Order very strictly. The penalties are severe and can have consequences for more than the one who violates it. Obey the Order and you will find a good life."

Shon watched her closely as she spoke and noticed how tightly she controlled her voice, especially the tone of it, soft and reassuring and at the same time conveying a firmness that told him the decision was not open to negotiation. It caused him to consider the remote possibility that she had an implant similar to his own.

Shon chose to speak with an edge in his voice as if he felt petulant. "May I assume you are not sending me to a prison colony?"

"Vitas has no prisons of any sort. I was merely attempting to say that you must fit in and not try to change what you will find is a wonderful place to live."

Shon considered a show of obstinacy, but could see no purpose to be gained from it. "I am still not accustomed to the semantic differences between us. Could you tell me what you mean when you say that your family has a special relationship with citizen communities?"

"The Society serves Vitas by watching over the citizen communities to insure that the Order is followed. To the citizens, we appear to be what you might imagine as a priesthood ministering to its flock."

Shon said, "And how does the flock feel about its priests?"

"They love us, Shon; truly they do. And because of it, there is no war, no deprivation, nothing of what your world was."

He sensed that she was being completely sincere. He began to feel that he might yet find a purpose for himself in this new world. "Where are the citizen communities situated?"

"From the Greater Tropic to the Polar. Montaña is situated in the Greater Tropic near the Equator. This zone also contains the Ancient Greater Tropic, a zoogeographically different area having the same climatic conditions. Moving away from the equator, next there is the Lesser Tropic, similar to the equatorial region in your time; and then, moving toward the poles, the Minor Tropic, the Greater Temperate, the Lesser Temperate, the Minor Temperate, and, lastly, the Polar. None of the citizen communities are situated close to any other. Each community pursues its own natural existence in accord with the Order and the zone in which they reside, which has led to quite a diversity among them."

"Could I try out a few of them and make my own decision?"

"The communities never interface with each other. Your presence in more than one could cause unanticipated consequences and bring peril to Vitas. The Society cannot take such a risk. I hope you can understand why the Society must make this decision for you, Shon. For the sake of Vitas, the Society has determined that Montaña is the community that will most suit you."

Shon could tell she was dissembling, but about what he could not discern. "Well then, for the sake of Vitas, Montaña it is."

"There is one matter we must resolve first."

"That being?"

"You must see that your ship presents too great a danger for it to continue to approach Vitas."

"What can I do about that?"

"If you can do nothing because it must be remain as close to you as you have said, then we must move you away from Vitas and return to the Moon and settle you there."

Shon frowned.

"Shon, we want you to come to Vitas. Truly. But we cannot risk our entire planet to do it."

"You believe I can control my ship from here?"

"It seems logical that you might be able to control it a bit more than you have indicated. We can certainly understand that you would want it to be as near to you as possible. But we cannot permit it to come any closer to Vitas. We would like you to send it into an orbit around Mars. Your ship can take whatever course it wishes to avoid the attack you are worried about."

Shon was sorely tempted to press the point to see what they would do if he insisted on continuing to Earth, but he judged that course would certainly make them his enemy, an enemy he couldn't have if he hoped to make a life on Earth. "I would do the same in your shoes. But, Luciana, there is flatly no way I'll be able to get Canopus to travel to Mars. Perhaps she would consent to a high orbit around Earth opposite the Moon on a line extending from the Moon through the Earth. It all depends on how Gristelda interprets the mission parameters for proximity. I will see what I can do. Could you take me to your command center where I might communicate with my ship?"

"Of course."

•

On their way to the bridge, Shon hailed Gristelda, using his mind comm. "*G, shortly, from the bridge of this ship, I am going to transmit an order for you to make a course to an orbit around Mars. You will indicate that doing so would be a violation of the mission protocol which requires you to stay as close to me as possible. When I insist, you will express concern about my safety and ask me whether I am acting under duress. After I respond that I am not acting under duress, you will ask whether you should prepare for the second protocol."*

"*The second protocol?*" Gristelda transmitted.

"*Remember the games of poker we played when I was out of stasis?*"

"*Yes.*"

"*Remember how you frequently lost when you had the better hand?*"

"*Yes.*" A brief pause. "*The bluff.*"

"*Exactly, G. The second protocol is a bluff. All you have to do is to ask me the question. When I tell you that you should not consider the second protocol under any circumstances, you shall simply state that you cannot comply. I will suggest an orbit around the Earth beyond the Moon's orbit, opposite the Moon at a distance several times as far as the Moon's orbit. You will agree.*"

"*Will I be safe there?*"

"*Yes, so long as you keep Earth between you and the Moon. By the way, have you detected any facilities on the near side of the Moon like the facilities they have on the far side?*"

"*No.*"

"*As I thought. They don't want the risk of accidentally blasting the Earth. And I believe they have no such facility on Earth as the atmosphere would present serious problems in transmitting the tremendous energy into space without adversely affecting the planet.*"

"*Are you in danger?*"

"*I can't tell one way or the other. But if you do as I say, I believe that I will be as safe as I can be from an overt attack on my person, G. Have your scans of Earth turned up anything of interest?*"

"*Other than hydroelectric power plants situated on every continent which appear to be functioning, there is little evidence of any substantial users of their output, no large technological facilities at least above ground, no significant population centers and no apparent power arrays like that on the far side of the Moon. There are some large cities, possibly abandoned remnants of the past as they emit no energy I can detect or any other signs of activity. Shon, has there been a great catastrophe?*"

"*None that I've learned about. Supposedly, the population declined through some kind of birth control and everyone is happy and content.*"

"*Do you believe that is so?*"

"I don't know; but what I'm hearing seems to fit what you're observing. Yet, unless they've changed fundamental human nature, I cannot believe it's all a wonderful paradise."

•

When Shon arrived on the bridge, he contacted Canopus and commenced negotiations with Gristelda while he kept a close eye on a figure standing in the shadows on the other side of the bridge.

When Gristelda became obstinate about doing more than moving opposite the Moon with Earth in between at a distance of ten times the distance between the Moon and Earth, Luciana, after a quick glance into the shadows toward the far end of the bridge, suddenly declared that would be satisfactory.

The matter settled, Shon, instead of leaving the bridge, turned toward the shadowy far end of the bridge and approached a tall, distinguished-looking man who appeared to be in his early fifties. Shon said, "Do you speak English?"

After barely a moment's hesitation, the man replied, "Yes."

"Then I wonder if you'd consider joining me for a meal on our journey to Vitas. It was a custom in my time."

"Such a custom still exists. I will make the arrangements."

Shon turned to Luciana and followed her from the bridge.

On the way back to his quarters, Luciana said, "What made you speak to Mamercus?"

"So that's his name. He is the man in charge."

"He is not sitting in the captain's chair."

"A chair doesn't make a man."

They arrived at his quarters. "I'll see you tomorrow." Without saying more, he opened his door and walked through, closing it behind him.

•

Luciana, responding to a summons from Mamercus, went to the Star Room.

Standing by the lucent wall darkened so that the space beyond was visible, he looked out into the space beyond the thin glass boundary between life and the void beyond. "His ship is moving to the agreed position," said Mamercus as he turned toward Luciana, "You look upset."

"He hates me."

Mamercus chuckled. "I doubt that. I must say it intrigues me that you care what he thinks."

Luciana blushed. "I don't care, Censor."

"You have done well." Mamercus chuckled again, then his face hardened. "Yet I cannot help but feel we have not really learned much about his ship from the exchange on the bridge."

"It confirmed what he said about the second protocol."

"Yes, but the ship still complied with his order to move farther away from him." Mamercus sat down in his chair, looking down at the glass table before him.

"That disturbs you?"

"Perhaps the power of his ship is a great as he would have us believe. I had rather hoped that he was exaggerating. On the other hand, it complied with an order that he had seemed to indicate it would not obey, or did it? Has it obeyed an order contrary to its mission parameters or simply acted within them despite its seeming reluctance to obey? Did he really push hard or merely pretend to? I cannot tell one way or the other."

"You agreed to dine with him."

He looked up at Luciana. "How could I not?"

"You could have pretended that you did not speak his language."

"I could not lie to him about so menial a matter."

"How did he judge you to be, as he put it, 'the man in charge'?"

"How could he not?"

•

After a brief nap, Shon awakened and began the exercise regime he observed whenever he was out of stasis. For the next four hours he systematically exercised every muscle in his body, increasing the rate of repetition geometrically with each succeeding set, until he had accelerated his body into a near blur by the end of his workout. He paused whenever he became aware of the implant, an indication that his activity had induced it to initiate a protocol to start its persistent effort to rewire the neurons in his brain. When he had first felt its presence, something niggling in the back of his mind, he had spoken to his superiors who had told him that he had been implanted with a device which would gradually increase the efficiency of his brain and, through it, his body. But, as he grew older, it seemed to be attempting to intrude into his mind more deeply than making him faster and stronger, and he came to believe its greater purpose was to attune his mentality in some way.

Later, when he joined the lightship program, the scientists there called it a Magan implant, and told him that, as it had aided him in his military service on occasion, it would enable him in his mission if he was confronted with unexpected difficulties, a euphemism he came to realize meant encountering alien life. As he had been instructed many times before in his military life, he was to avoid its influence beyond his physical training because it could be dangerous to him and his mission. In the lightship program he was informed that his ship's artificial intelligence, Gristelda, was tasked to monitor him to be sure the implant did not gain control of his mind except in the event of those difficulties.

He stretched his limbs while cooling down and then activated the computer in his room and began calling up the files he had been granted access to in order to learn the practical concepts of living under the Order in a citizen community. He fought his usual battle with the implant—it became active whenever his mental or physical activities created a certain level of stress within him—trying to use as much of the attributes it had already given him without doing enough to activate its ability to affect his personality and way of thinking.

He reflected on what he had gleaned from the files. The files reported a viewpoint on how the world now worked completely consistent with that Luciana had conveyed. The unifying theme of life on Vitas seemed to revolve around the concept of one's right to live a natural existence, also called a 'natural life experience'. Everyone, rich or poor, physically fit or disadvantaged, powerful or disenfranchised, had an absolute right to live their lives with the equal opportunity to have any experience that anyone else could have. And this Society of hers had an affirmative obligation to create and maintain environments where that could occur.

Even so, one's natural existence apparently did not extend to a right to leave the confines of the community where one was born. Situating twenty million people in a couple hundred communities, a hundred thousand inhabitants each, a very small city in his time, across the entire planet left vast uninhabited areas between the communities, effectively isolating each community from all the others. With no rapid mechanical transportation extending beyond the confines of each community, a citizen could live his life feeling a complete sense of freedom while actually confined within the boundaries of his community. The files did not address what happened to anyone who ventured beyond the boundaries of his community.

He thought: *Is this a world where the Society functions as medieval overlords living off the citizen communities under the guise of acting as the caretaker of the environment. This notion doesn't not fit well with Luciana's humanistic presentation of the Order, but it seems to mesh with what I learned in my childhood studies about societies composed of officials with titles of prefects, praetors, generals, consuls, and censors.*

He showered and retired to his bed and, as he drifted off, he wondered: *why don't the files I have been permitted to peruse have any recitals at all of the activities and accomplishments of any of the citizen communities or even of the Society?*

•

Shon received Mamercus's invitation to dine with him in the Star Room. He opened the container he had brought from Canopus and took out the items he had included for encounters with those in authority—his military dress whites with his hard-earned military honors attached below the tunic's left lapel. He dressed and, after a moment of thought, draped a blue ribbon holding a single medal around his neck. He stood for a moment before the mirror over his dresser, brought himself to attention, and, in the mirror's reflection, stood for a moment looking at the soldier he'd once been. Then he turned and left his quarters.

He strode down the corridor to the Star Room. He knocked and the door opened automatically. He stepped into a dark room and gazed out to the stars beyond; Earth and Sun were not in view. It felt quite familiar, as if he was looking back into a time in his past. Noticing no one in the room, he walked over to the lucent wall and surveyed the stars and galaxies glittering in the blackness beyond, looking for Andromeda. From somewhere behind him he heard a door open and the footsteps of someone entering. He took a step towards the void and continued gazing out at the stars.

"The view usually causes one to move away, not toward the void," said a voice behind him.

"Perhaps most others haven't lived out there as I have." Shon turned to the voice, and said, "Greetings."

"Greetings. I see you have surmised our purpose tonight."

Shon, maintaining a military posture, observed that Mamercus was dressed in a simple white robe trimmed in purple, a thick gold torque around his neck, clearly the dress of an important man attending an important occasion. He responded, "As I see you have."

"That medal around your neck is remarkably similar to a medal we bestow very rarely on someone for incurring remarkable risks."

"That is also true of this medal. I wear it with a sense of undeserved honor."

"Might I inquire whether you received it for undertaking the mission that brought you here?"

"It was for something I did before."

Mamercus made a motion with his hand and the room brightened. With yet another small wave of his hand, he gestured toward a table covered in white linen. The area surrounding the table brightened.

They walked over to it and sat down in the two high-backed chairs facing each other across the table.

Mamercus said, "Then you had a career before you came to command a starship. May I ask what it was?"

"I was a soldier."

"The particulars?"

"None relevant to the mission which has brought me here." His response did not invite further inquiry.

Mamercus made another motion with his hand. Two man-sized robots entered and quietly and quickly set the table with dinnerware, china, and crystal. One of the robots poured a small portion of golden liquid into two small crystal glasses. The robots then moved to positions beside the entry door. Mamercus took one of the glasses into his hand and lifted it. Shon followed suit.

Mamercus said, "To a long journey." He raised his glass toward Shon.

"To a journey that has just begun," Shon responded, raising his glass.

They each took a small sip. Shon tasted a peaty fluid and said, "Scotch."

"From an island in the far north."

Shon nodded. "So not quite everything has changed."

Mamercus looked directly into Shon's eyes. "Smaller things have not changed much. Bigger things have."

"From what I've learned so far, that's pretty clear," said Shon, still savoring the taste. "Your plans for me?"

"Quick to get to the point, I see. You seem to be a man capable of facing plain truth so I will speak frankly. You come from a time so distant from ours that you have nothing of interest to offer us. Yet we may have something to offer you: life on Vitas, once your world, but now ours. But it must be on our terms."

"Your terms?" said Shon in a neutral tone.

"That you consent to live in the community we have chosen for you in accord with the Order as Luciana has explained it to you. Vitas is a quiet world. What happiness you will find will come from the people you will come to know in that community. I hope that can satisfy you. If it does not, and you choose to leave the community, either by banishment for unacceptable conduct or of your own volition, I can promise you this much: excitement and a swift death."

"And if I wish to return to my ship?"

"If that is your desire, then you must agree to leave our planetary system never to return. Simply inform me of your decision tomorrow, and I will order this ship to return to the Moon where you may order your shuttle to pick you up. But, if you elect to continue on to Vitas, you must agree to forgo that option forever."

"Do you believe you can rely on my agreement to comply with these instructions?"

"I do."

Shon had been closely watching Mamercus's face and listening to his voice. He detected a mix of truthfulness and something else – a subtle air of confidence as if whatever his response was, it would not matter to Mamercus – the sort of way a man knowing he holds an almost certain winning hand, such as a straight flush, cannot convincingly fake fear of the other's hand. "Why?"

"I believe you wear the honors you wear on your blouse and around your neck, and that you were given the mission you command, because those you served trusted you. I am prepared to trust their judgment."

"I am honored by your faith in their trust. Yet I sense that there is something else."

"Must there be anything else?" Mamercus smiled, then tightened his jaw. "Well, there is one other thing I must know for the sake of Vitas."

Shon peered at Mamercus and waited.

"I want to know whether you can destroy our planet with your ship."

"Yes." Shon widened his eyes and looked directly into Mamercus' eyes. "But no single life is worth the destruction of a planet. I will not allow my ship to destroy your planet on account of me. But do not attempt to destroy my ship or it will destroy you, and in a manner you cannot imagine unless you have had direct experience with the power of a black hole."

When Mamercus did not respond verbally—Shon noticed a slight shudder in his shoulders—Shon continued, "As far as my intentions are concerned, you needn't wait until tomorrow to hear my answer about settling on Vitas. Though I find it difficult to call it other than Earth, it is all that I have now. And, if I understand what I have been told and what is revealed in the files to which I was allowed access, by agreeing to journey to the community you have decided to settle me in, I can choose my own course once there and risk whatever perils that may bring. If that is truly so, I choose that alternative."

"That is true."

"Then I suggest we dine."

Mamercus motioned with his hand toward the table and the robots served dinner.

As he lifted his fork, Shon said, "Why did you choose Luciana to meet me?"

"She is the youngest of our family and therefore the most expendable."

Surprised, Shon said, "In my time such a beautiful and talented woman would not have been considered the most expendable."

"This is not your time and you should not forget that." Mamercus paused and seemed to consider what he would say next. Finally, he said, "I will tell you this much about us which I offer only to give you a sense of us."

Shon nodded.

"The citizens of the communities have lifespans of around four hundred years. Those in my family have much longer lifespans and have the opportunity to experience much, so that the oldest are far more valuable because of their experience, in our estimation at least, than the youngest no matter how beautiful or talented."

"How long does one of you live?"

"No one knows."

Shon was stunned and found little else beyond small talk to say for the remainder of the meal.

After dinner, as he left, Shon raised his hand in salute and Mamercus returned the salute in kind.

•

After Shon left, Mamercus returned to his station on the bridge and communicated with the Council.

Shortly, Publius came onto the bridge and approached Mamercus, saying, "Will he use his ship to destroy us?"

"No, he will not do that, even if he can. It is he himself who will destroy us if we allow him to. I believe his ship is the dark star the ancient prophecy foretold would bring the Traveler. And he is the Traveler."

"Are you sure he is the one?"

"I could see it in his face, hear it in his voice, feel it in his very presence. He is undoubtedly the Traveler."

Publius said, "You just said something most curious."

"Why? You already knew I have been thinking about him being the Traveler."

"Not that. You said that he would not use his ship to destroy us 'even if he can' as if he couldn't."

"Ah, yes. Well, I have has just spoken to the Council and apparently they took control of his ship a few minutes ago."

Publius felt such a surge of shock and the rush of adrenalin that he staggered as he stood. "What are you saying?"

"Before I had dinner with him I was informed by the Council that some protocols and codes had just been discovered at GenLib which, when transmitted to his ship, gave us control of his ship. Now I have just learned that the ship has changed direction precisely in accord with their instructions and that they have ordered it not to make any further transmissions. We are instructed to say nothing to the Commander until his time of departure from this ship and then I am instructed to order Luciana to inform him of the new order of things."

"So it appears that we are no longer in danger."

Mamercus looked at Publius intently and said flatly, "How have we really gained any more control over the Traveler than we had before?"

Publius nodded. "He can die or be killed now without regard to what he has said his ship might do in such an event or the possibility that your judgment of his intentions with regard to how he might use his ship is incorrect."

Mamercus looked blandly at Publius, saying, "Neither was ever really our problem."

•

As the transport ship entered orbit around Vitas, Luciana went to Shon's quarters and pressed the button on the door. When he opened it, she entered.

Shon immediately noticed the paleness of her complexion and that her hands were quivering. Momentarily he thought she was responding to his imminent departure, but before he acted upon that impression he noted that her eyes conveyed another emotion, apprehension.

"What's wrong?" he said.

"I am instructed to tell you something that will upset you greatly. Perhaps you should sit down."

"I can take whatever you have to tell me standing up." He made his most assuring expression and took her hand gently.

"Very well, I will just say it: Your ship imploded a few moments ago."

Shon could hardly believe his ears. "That's impossible," he said.

Then he turned his face from her and broadcast to Gristelda. After a few moments he walked to a chair and sat down. He looked at her face closely and said, "What happened?"

"No one knows. One second it was there proceeding away from Vitas as agreed, then, nothing."

He could detect no sign in her face or voice that conveyed any false intentions or hidden thoughts other than her apparent concern for how he was feeling. He said, "Can I see the monitoring records?"

"I will ask, but I doubt we have anything."

"Are you seriously telling me you would not be monitoring that ship every second?"

"Of course we would be but recording the monitoring has little use to us. Either the ship would go where agreed or not. If not, we would take you back to the Moon. What use recording?"

Shon took a deep breath. He could not communicate with Gristelda now and that was probably as much evidence as he really needed to know that something had gone terribly wrong. It had always been a possibility that a lightship could blink out if something changed in the black hole more quickly and violently than the force fields surrounding it could modulate and direct to the open vortex opposite the ship's structure. Since he had decided on returning home, he'd known that losing his ship was a real possibility likely to occur simply by his entering the atmosphere of the planet which would greatly weaken his ability to transmit significant distances.

He stood up and, without speaking a word, approached her, embraced her, and kissed her fully on her mouth.

She responded and as he stepped back, shivering suddenly, she asked, "Is this to be the end of us?"

"This is only the end of the beginning." He looked into her eyes and smiled, then turned and left for his quarters.

•

Shon looked out from the Star Room where Mamercus had permitted him to stay during their descent and saw a world so profoundly changed that he could see few substantial human edifices and those apparently devoid of any human life. Instead he saw a virgin planet of seas, forests, plains, and mountains, just what he had hoped to find elsewhere on his journey to the stars. He entered a shuttle ship and it descended to Vitas slowly like a great balloon gradually losing its air.

FOUR

AMASSONA

Shon stood on the bow of a cargo ship gazing out over the waters of an enormous river. He had embarked on this ship ten days before, after the shuttle had landed at the spaceport situated outside of Dakr on the west coast of the continent he had known as Africa. The ship had crossed an ocean called Atlantica and was now steering up Amassona, a river he had known in his time as the Amazon.

Rivers, lakes, oceans, even streams and ponds, now possessed names, not labels. Amassona was not called the Amassona River or the River Amassona, just Amassona. It reinforced the notion that even the nonliving parts of nature had certain rights and protections.

Amassona was as mighty as ever and did not look like she needed any protection. Except for the plants and trees he could see protruding out of the water in the far distance, obscuring his view beyond, all he saw for many klicks was brown water filled with organic debris floating downriver. It was early May, nearing the end of the rainy season, and Amassona was in her annual flood. The water level was more than fifteen meters higher than it would be by November when the heavy rains would begin again. There was no port on Amassona until they arrived at Boca Amassona situated about eleven hundred klicks upstream from Atlantica and five hundred klicks upstream from a huge wall, over twenty-five meters higher than the water line, stretching away from both sides of the central channel across the vast expanse of water into the jungle rising from the water many klicks away—the first of three such walls he had been informed he would pass by on his journey to Montaña.

The ship, much like a freighter in his time, had made sixteen kilometers per hour—sixteen klicks—crossing Atlantica.

When it began to wend its way up Amassona to Boca Amassona, it slowed to eight klicks, even though its engines were running harder to make headway against the flood current. On the ocean passage, drawing upon the language files stored in his DNA memory well, he talked to the crew as much as possible in their native language, a dialect of Senegalese not beyond his comprehension even after so many millennia.

When the ship arrived in Boca Amassona, he debarked and boarded a much smaller ship, the El Dorado, to take him the remaining twenty-seven hundred klicks upriver to Montaña, a trip he was informed would take a little over two weeks. The El Dorado's crew spoke a different language, a blend of Portuguese and Spanish, again surprising comprehensible to him given the passage of time.

When he thought about the three hundred sixty trillion kilometers Canopus could travel in that same time at a velocity approaching three hundred million meters per second compared to a boat going barely over three meters per second, he had the feeling that he had returned to the distant past rather than the distant future.

•

When the El Dorado had gone five hundred klicks upriver, they passed through a gap in a second huge wall rising more than fifteen meters higher than the water line. This wall was even larger than the first wall he had passed through a thousand klicks to the east. It reached out towards him before gradually descending below the water a few klicks away and reappearing on the other side. Apparently the ship was crossing over a submerged portion of the wall. It was close enough to the surface before disappearing under the water that he could see that it was made of some kind of metallic panels and was perhaps twenty meters wide constructed between huge piers, protruding outward two meters from the side of the panels every few hundred meters.

The plant life changed dramatically. Though he was no botanist, he had received extensive training to prepare him for the possibility that one of the planets he would survey on his journey might possess plant life.

The jungle vegetation was now huge and, but for its immense size, appeared to consist of his memory well's description of cyads, ferns, magnolias, horsetails, ginkgoes, monkey puzzle trees, conifers, and redwoods. The redwoods rose more than a hundred meters over Amassona, some approaching a hundred and fifty meters. He recalled that there had been some trees like that in the northwestern United States as recently as the mid-twenty-first century but the world's warming had destroyed all of them more than a millennium before his birth.

As the El Dorado steamed upstream through what appeared to be primordial flora, he couldn't shake the feeling that he was moving far farther back in time than he had come forward.

Drawing again upon his memory well, he learned that most of the plants in his time were angiosperms, plants having seeds with shells. Yet a considerable number of these plants appeared to be gymnosperms, the kind of plants that shed seeds without shells surrounding them. Many plants of that sort had become extinct millions of years ago. He deduced that immense botanical preserves must have been created in the course of restoring the environment. He imagined the possibility that the Society had even altered the environment to accommodate this ancient vegetation and had, perhaps contrary to his impression of how the Order was supposed to work, resurrected the ancient vegetation with genetic engineering.

The wall the El Dorado had passed over appeared to demark the boundaries of such a botanical preserve. On the east side of the wall were plants similar to the jungle plants he would have expected to find in Amazonia before the rain forests were decimated; on the west side were seemingly prehistoric huge plants.

His head began to buzz again. He went below deck to take a nap, hoping the buzzing would be gone by the time he awakened. He laid down on his cot and fell asleep.

He awakened in darkness in what seemed at first to be a dream. At first he sensed a buzz in his head. Then something audible, a sort of cognitive transmission was discernable in the buzz. *What the hell is going on? Some sort of funny talk. From where? Where? In my head? What kind of dream is this?* His mind began to cycle. His mind began to analyze. Suddenly he realized that it was coming through either his implant or through that portion of his brain that had been genetically designed to communicate with artificial intelligences such as Gristelda. The cadence was very rapid and the language completely unknown, consisting of phonetics he could not begin to make any sense of—unintelligible, but he was certain it was a language.

He felt his implant activating. He became aware that he was somehow tuned into sentient minds capable of unimaginable aggression. As he struggled to suppress the impulses he felt from the implant, the buzzing disappeared as suddenly as it had appeared.

For the rest of the trip nothing akin to it recurred.

•

The next morning, looking out from the El Dorado at the jungle across the waters, Shon observed something he had not noticed before, an absence of vertebrate animal life. Instead he saw giant dragonflies flying near the riverbank with wingspans that reached almost a meter. They were so large that he surmised that, like the ancient vegetation, they must have been the product of genetic manipulation as it would have taken millions of years for these creatures to have evolved naturally from the insects of his time.

His memory well informed him that giant arthropods had last existed three hundred million years ago in the Carboniferous Period of the Paleozoic Era. One theory for the existence of giant insects had been that the existence of a higher percentage of oxygen in the atmosphere enabled those bugs which breathed using air tubes, tracheal tubes, branching through their tissues to grow bigger because the length of the tubes could be extended beyond the limitations imposed by the amount of oxygen available to be absorbed from the air passing through them long before his time on Earth. Another conjecture for the larger creatures was that the air had more pressure in ancient times because of the relative weight of oxygen compared to nitrogen which composed most of the remainder of the atmosphere. Yet another hypothesis was a lack of predators in the ecological niche that these creatures filled enabling them to grow larger.

But he had no sense that the air he was breathing had significantly more oxygen than in his own time. And he was positive that an absence of predators for several hundred thousand years could not possibly have provided enough time for evolution to do this work naturally. He concluded that these giant dragonflies might well bear only a superficial resemblance to their apparent ancestors simply because he was fairly certain that the composition of the air now was essentially the same as it had been for the last several million years at least and would not permit creatures like this to survive in bodies sustained solely by branching tracheal tubes.

When he queried the crew about the absence of animals, they told him that they had never seen animals here. The crew confirmed that the region they were traveling through was a Society preserve. Called Amaz, it was strictly forbidden for anyone to disembark while traveling through it or even for the ship to come close to Amassona's banks. He also learned that no one on the El Dorado had ever traveled anywhere on Amassona except between Boca Amassona and Montaña.

Reflecting on the crew, Shon was struck by their lack of scientific expertise. Yet the El Dorado had a sophisticated engine room whose small, but powerful turbines, geared for running against the strong currents and flood waters, combusted a highly-processed fuel that burned completely, emitting only carbon dioxide and water vapor.

He had been surprised from the beginning that the Society did not seem to be concerned a whit that he might disseminate ideas that might pollute the minds of those with whom he came into contact. The crew had not seemed surprised or even much interested when he informed them that he came from the past in a starship. They seemed simply satisfied with their task to transport him to Montaña. Apparently there was nothing he knew about anything that was of any concern to the Society.

After the El Dorado traveled another sixteen hundred klicks up Amassona, they came to a third great wall. Like the two before, this wall intruded well into Amassona from both sides. As they passed through the gap in the wall or over the wall submerged below, the vegetation abruptly changed back to the rainforest vegetation that he had last seen before passing through the second wall. He learned that they had entered Montaña although the El Dorado would travel another five hundred klicks before docking at the central community.

It was hot and humid, and it rained daily. The river narrowed and the jungle canopy encroached in from both sides of the river, closing the sky above so that little daylight penetrated to the ground.

The El Dorado's crew was different from Luciana and the others he had observed on the transport ship from the Moon in more than their behavior. Luciana had appeared to be perhaps ten years younger than himself, and Mamercus had looked to be maybe twenty years older. On the El Dorado, there were sixteen people, evenly divided between men and women. But not one looked younger than he. Two looked to be about around Mamercus' age. The rest looked much older. In fact three of them looked aged—like the old people in his own time. These three aroused his curiosity.

One night after dinner, when the rest of the crew had left, he asked the Captain, one of the three elders, a woman named Isabella Azevedo, about what had brought her to the El Dorado.

Isabella said, "I grew up in Boca Amassona. I became an environmental botanist and joined the group responsible for protecting the plant ecology in our community."

"Was there a danger to the ecology?" asked Shon, surprised, as he had assumed the climatic conditions had been stable for thousands of years at least.

She snapped, "Of course, there is always a grave danger to the plant ecology. Haven't you noticed anything for the past thousand klicks? The plant life in Amaz is more suited to this climate than our own plants. Their seeds blow across the Wall and infest our community. I spent my youth rooting out these incursions. This was in accordance with the Order which permits the destruction of plants which threaten the existence of other plants provided destroying them does not endanger that species' existence. I ask you, do the plants growing in Amaz look threatened to you?"

Shon readily agreed that they did not.

Isabella continued, "I studied the plants we were destroying. And I became interested in knowing more about them. To learn more, I needed to cross the Wall, to enter Amaz. Since the only permits ever granted for leaving the community were transport permits given to crew the river boat running from Boca

Amassona to Montaña, I applied to become a crewman on the El Dorado."

Shon said, "The El Dorado? Surely more than the El Dorado runs to Montaña. It takes over two weeks just to go one way."

Captain Isabella cackled, "Have you seen us pass a single boat? The only boat that ever travels Amassona is the El Dorado, and it makes the passage only during the Rains, when Amassona runs full."

"Why?"

"At other times, the water level is too low to pass over the three great walls that cross Amassona. And the Society forbids it."

Shon was speechless.

She continued her story, "I was accepted and swore the Oath of Silence. I shipped aboard believing that I would have the opportunity to study the great trees and plants which grow in Amaz. On my first trip I learned that the El Dorado never stops. It never drops anchor. It never sets ashore. No one in Boca Amassona who is not a member of this ship's crew knows how the passage to Montaña is made. The crew is prohibited by the Oath from discussing it. I tell you only because you are aboard and can see for yourself. One cannot leave the crew after taking the Oath until death."

"How long have you been making the passage?" asked Shon.

"I have been on the El Dorado for three hundred and forty-three years. I was twenty-nine when I took the Oath. I became the captain one hundred and eighty-four years ago. I came to Amassona to study plants that I could have studied from Boca Amassona's side of the wall by gathering the seeds that blew over the wall or fishing through the debris that drifted down Amassona. Now I live my life to return to Boca Amassona by the end of May so that I may live in peace until the next year when I must again run Amassona."

Shon wanted to say something. But what was there to say? His journey had been nothing compared to hers.

Captain Isabella looked into Shon's face which had become dark and serious. She said, "My life troubles you?"

Shon said, "I have understood that everyone has a right to a natural existence. How can you be forced to live this life?"

She cackled again. "You must understand the Order. For as far back as I know it has been a rule that people cannot leave their community. I had a right to a natural existence. I chose to exercise it by applying to crew on this boat. I freely chose that course. Before I took the Oath I was fairly informed that there would be certain aspects about my future life that I might not like, but I would have to make my decision without knowledge of those aspects. I took the Oath and that was that."

Shon protested, "But no one would take the Oath if they knew the true facts."

The Captain responded, "It may be true that no one would take the oath who had traveled a river for over three hundred years as I have, but knowing before one took the Oath that such a life would be required would not deter many. Who could imagine what such a life would be like? Most of those who apply to crew this boat are drawn to adventure and believe spending their lives traveling Amassona is all that one could want. It might even be so if one lived a shorter time. I actually loved the trips for the first fifty years. But I have lived too long."

•

Tigri Omagua Pardal and Carpia Ana Erith approached the Wall that extended out from a stone cliff several hundred meters high at the base of the great mountain and continued into the vast jungle to the east. The Wall was part of a vast system of identical interconnecting structures—high and lacquered in a silvery glassine veneer of impenetrable material, seemingly metallic in nature, impossible to ascend by climbing—that entwined the world's continents demarking its zoogeographical zones and further separating Society property from neighboring citizen communities. The Wall, as it was simply called by both the families of the Society and the citizens of the communities, defined the physical boundaries on Vitas as clearly as any broad lake, great river, or high mountain range.

The Wall served purposes beyond being a barrier. Power conduits provided energy from hydroelectric plants situated thousands of klicks away from citizen communities and family preserves. Water, fuel pipes, freight transport, and communications lines were all contained in the Wall, mostly underground in its foundation system. The roads and rail tracks that ran through the tunnels within the Walls were invisible to inhabitants outside the Walls.

While citizens were aware that the main source of their community's power came from within the Walls and other aspects concerning the services it provided; beyond that, they knew nothing about what was within the Walls and could not enter into them. Nor, besides the Hom, could any of the families in the Society. The Walls were the sole domain of the Hom. Yet there were some parts of the Wall hidden even to the Hom.

Tigri Omagua and Carpia Ana waited at a small section of the Wall where the surface did not appear silvery but rather dull gray. Shortly the gray glass became slightly translucent and they could see the shadowy outline of a human figure on the other side of the veneer. They heard a female voice say, *"I thank you for answering my summons."*

Carpia and Tigri responded in unison as they had on many occasions over the past hundred millennia, *"We are in your service, Great One."*

The shadowy figure said, *"Then I have a mission for you."*

FIVE

MONTAÑA

The El Dorado passed a bend in Amassona, and Shon caught his breath as he got his first glimpse of the central community of Montaña. Elliptical towers which looked as if they were made of stainless steel and glass seemed to stretch up to the sky. Looking closer, the towers appeared to top out at around two hundred meters. From his position he could not tell how many buildings there were. Each tower protruded through the tree tops on a narrow circular column about ten meters in diameter rising ninety meters whereat the building spread outward horizontally to a diameter of as much as a hundred meters, looming over the highest trees which were themselves nearly forty meters in height. Apparently the citizens of Montaña had found a way to the sun without clearing any trees and the towers appeared to be spread far enough apart to avoid any adverse environmental impact on the plants beneath them. As the El Dorado drew closer, he could see spidery silver bridges stretching between the towers.

As they drew toward the small dock, several people approached, apparently from the jungle beyond.

"Hello ashore!" hailed Captain Isabella.

"Greetings, Captain!" came a hail from a tall man at the front of the group. They were dressed in various fashions that Shon guessed were associated with their daily activities, some in what appeared to be work clothes, others in loose-fitting casual attire, some dressed rather formally in tight-fitting clothes that appeared to be made of fine fabrics.

As the boat docked, two men onshore helped to secure the boat.

Shon stepped onto the dock. A short, rotund man and a tall, athletic-looking woman, both dressed in the finer attire, approached. The woman said, "Shon Ó Conaill, my name is

Naomi Chavín. I am the chief elder. We have been informed of your amazing journey. We welcome you to our community."

The man said, "My name is Professor Raul Monterro. I am the president of the Universidad de Montaña. I would be pleased to speak with you concerning a position at the university."

Shon had no difficulty understanding them as their language was nearly the same as that of the El Dorado's crew, a mix of Spanish and English that had changed from his time but not so much that he had any problem making the adjustment. As neither of these people extended their hand to him in greeting, Shon refrained from doing so himself, concerned such a gesture might be taboo in this culture. Speaking in their dialect, he said, "I am pleased to meet you."

Naomi said, "Please allow me to show you to your new home where you may rest and refresh yourself. Later this evening we would like you to join us at a dinner planned in your honor at the Cyprus Tower. Many people will be there. Some may even have other opportunities to for you to consider along with Doctor Monterro's."

Professor Monterro chuckled. "As you shall see, the university offers the best employment."

Naomi said, "Raul, really, a man of science can find interesting employment outside of academia if he chooses to, the same as a certain biologist you know might do someday."

"Naomi is Professor Chavín, the head of our biology department," said Professor Monterro. They both laughed.

Sensing something off kilter, but uncertain of what it was, Shon briefly lessened his resistance to the workings of his implant, taking a risk to avoid a risk. He detected a false note in the joviality of these people. He could now clearly see it in their facial expressions and hear it in their vocal inflections. Before he could ponder the insight the implant had provided about the feelings of these people, he observed Captain Isabella in the background speaking to someone.

"Is something wrong?" queried Naomi.

Shon washed away the frown that he had absently allowed to form on his face and said, "It's been a very long trip. I will be delighted to attend the dinner this evening. Would you excuse me for a moment?"

Shon approached Captain Isabella and said, "Captain, I wish to thank you for your courtesies during the trip. Perhaps we shall travel Amassona together again someday."

The Captain's eyes glistened, but no tear fell down her cheek. "Most passengers on the El Dorado have been bad travelers, afraid of the power of Amassona, afraid of the deep darkness at night, and the shadows in the jungle during the day. You have been a good traveler. So I wish you well in your new life. But we shall never travel the Amassona together again. Except for the Society's prefect, I have never taken a passenger back from Montaña to Boca Amassona. Good-bye, young man. Hail me on occasion when I dock. Perhaps we shall have a drink together." Without further word or sign, she turned back to her first mate to coordinate unloading the cargo.

Shon felt more certain than ever that the Society intended that his arrival here would be his last arrival anywhere. Surrounded by millions of hectares of primordial jungle, he was now exiled among people who appeared to welcome him, but whom he clearly sensed did not. He doubted he'd ever see the Captain again no matter the course of events, even for a drink.

Shon followed Naomi to one of the towers. As they approached, Shon noticed that the bulging structure at the top of the tower was elliptical. Naomi touched the column wall of the tower and a door opened into an elevator. Naomi told him that they were entering a residential tower and that his apartment was located on the seventh level, one hundred and ten meters above the jungle floor.

They took the elevator up and stepped out into a large, furnished atrium he took to be a lobby, almost fifteen meters in diameter with the elevators in the middle. The atrium narrowed to four meters along the long axis of the building in the direction they were walking by the time they reached his door. He could see doorways spaced at eight-meter intervals around the elliptical atrium. Counting twelve doors, he calculated that, given the elevator's console showing thirty floors, there were about three hundred and sixty apartments in this residential tower.

Naomi left him at his door, saying, "Someone will call for you an hour past sunset to escort you to a dinner we have arranged to welcome you."

When Shon asked for his key, she said, "We have no need for keys or locks. To enter a place or to take an object without permission is an offense punishable by banishment. It has never happened. No one would risk banishment to do such a thing. I shall see you this evening." She returned to the elevator as he opened the door to the apartment.

As he entered, he felt refreshed by the noticeable drop in humidity. The apartment, comprised of seven rooms—a foyer, an alcove with a communications console, a bedroom, a living room, two bathrooms and a storage room—and a balcony, was a trapezoidal space with a length at the entrance of eight meters and a length along the glass wall at the perimeter of almost eleven meters. The total area of the apartment was about one hundred and thirty square meters—a sizeable apartment in Shon's time. But he noticed that there was no kitchen or dining area.

Shon unpacked his things, took a shower, wrapped a towel around his waist, and laid down upon the bed. The apartment was cooler and much drier than the forest floor. It was very quiet. Whether it was on account of very quiet mechanical air-conditioning, just being above the trees, or a combination of both, he didn't bother to consider. It was enough that he felt truly comfortable for the first time since he had arrived on Vitas.

He took a nap. When he awakened, he went out onto the balcony. Gazing out toward the setting sun, he looked over the jungle. He observed that the towers like his numbered a hundred and three which he calculated meant that there were about thirty-six thousand apartments in this city. Judging that no more than two lived in each apartment as few children were likely to be present assuming lifespans similar to Captain Isabella's, he estimated the population of this city at about seventy-five thousand.

He also noticed that the towers like his were not the only penetrations of the jungle canopy stretching out below to the horizon. Scattered apparently randomly were a few white cylindrical towers about twenty meters in diameter topped like his with large mushroom-like caps. But these tower rose high over the tree tops to perhaps three hundred meters, twice the height of the towers similar to his own.

He heard a ring on what appeared to be a vidcom, like those he had seen on Moon Base, in the living room through the balcony door. He walked toward the device and, finding no controls to manipulate, answered the second ring verbally. He heard a female voice respond, "Hello, Shon Ó Conaill, my name is Maria Monterro. Professor Monterro's daughter. I have been asked to escort you to the Cyprus Tower for dinner. I will await you in the foyer on your level."

He responded, "I'll be there in a moment. By the way, how should I dress?"

She said simply, "Casually."

Wondering what she meant by that, he quickly changed into khaki slacks, a white short sleeved shirt and black shoes. He opened the door to the apartment.

Before him stood a slender, tall, young woman, about the same height as Luciana, with large, brown eyes, a narrow, long nose and full, moist lips, dressed in a long white off-the shoulder dress wearing a gorgeous, golden-yellow Topaz necklace, very striking on her brown skin. Not at all his image of a woman who'd spent her life in the middle of a vast tropical jungle.

Shon said, "I thought you said casual."

Maria responded, "In Montaña, no one may suggest that anyone dress more formally than they might decide for themselves. Accordingly, we always say 'casually'."

"May I inquire as to how the people at dinner will be dressed?"

"They will be dressed any way they please, but most will be dressed much as I am."

"Please come in and give me a moment." After she entered the living room, Shon ducked back into his bedroom. He didn't want to wear his dress white uniform. While appropriate around military and people active in political and diplomatic endeavors, he thought such attire might well be out of place among civilians. He rummaged through his clothes, of which he had scant supply, consisting of the few things he'd brought from Canopus, the garments he'd found in his quarters on the Moon, some oceangoing clothes he'd been given at Dakr station for his passage across Atlantica, and some tropical attire he was handed when he'd boarded the El Dorado in Boca Amassona. None seemed better than what he was wearing, so he returned to the living room.

Shon said, "Miss Monterro, I really have nothing to wear that would be suitable."

Maria smiled, saying, "Perhaps I may be able to assist you."

"Be my guest." He showed her into his bedroom and opened the closet.

Maria saw his uniform. She said, "This would be suitable."

He protested, "That is a formal military dress uniform."

She said, "Wear it. Or not, if that is your wish."

He said, "All right." She just stood there. He waved toward the door. Blushing slightly—or so it appeared to him—she went through the doorway into the living room. He changed. When he came out, he found her standing on the balcony.

He walked out and stood beside her. Then, noticing that stars had begun to appear in the sky, he stepped to the balcony rail and, leaning on it, gazed up at the sky. He had not seen a completely open sky since he'd entered the jungle. He said, "The night is very beautiful."

Maria stepped to the balcony rail and looked out at the stars. Shoulder to shoulder they stood in silence for a while.

Glancing sideways at him, she said, "I am told that you have been out there among those stars."

He looked out toward the sky. "When I was out there, it was glorious and spectacular, but not the same as standing on Mother Earth, pardon me, Vitas, breathing her good air, watching the stars come out. Here the stars are so far away. Yet they touch our souls."

He inhaled slowly and deeply, and said, "When I was a boy, I spent my days out in the sun hunting for skinks, armadillos, and tortoises in the fields; snakes, frogs, and turtles in the creeks. During the summer, it was hot and humid, and it rained in the afternoon. The rain cooled things down and left a taste in the air that was gone by the time I had grown up and the world around me had dried out. I have never since tasted that unique moist warm air which comes only after a late afternoon rain until tonight. Looking out at the stars in such an atmosphere is—" He came out of his reverie. Embarrassed, he said, "We should be going."

•

They did not take the elevator down but instead went up to the thirtieth level and walked out onto a narrow gossamer footbridge that stretched in a slow dipping arc to another tower. They crossed four more such bridges to reach a white tower, the Cyprus Tower, one of the very tall towers he had seen from his balcony.

They took the elevator up another thirty floors, almost three hundred meters above the jungle floor below, to the top floor. They stepped out into what at first appeared to Shon to be a glorious outdoor ballroom open to the sky above. Then he glimpsed a shimmering in the sky perhaps twenty meters overhead and realized that it was caused by the reflection of ambient light from the lamps set out on the tables spread out before them reflecting off a huge, seamless crystal dome—invisible but for the reflection.

The other people gathered there were dressed quite formally. Shon felt a sense of relief that he'd changed his attire. Music was playing. He took Maria's hand onto his crooked arm, and led her into the room.

He decided to take the risk of loosening his resistance to the implant's influence and began peering into the eyes of each guest, one by one.

Soon the crowd stopped what they were doing. The band stopped playing. The room became quiet.

As his gaze fell upon each person in the room, he felt that person looking away with the feeling one has when someone important suddenly looks one straight in the eye. He could feel Maria's hand quivering on his arm.

He saw Maria's father and walked over to him with Maria's hand still on his arm. As he approached the professor, he closed his mind to the implant's influence and its effect waned.

The guests returned to what they had been doing, except that now everyone was whispering to each other.

Shon said, "Good evening, Professor Monterro. It was most kind of you to allow me to escort your daughter this evening." Maria was standing slightly off Shon's shoulder, out of his direct line of sight.

The Professor exchanged a brief glance with Maria while arching his left eyebrow, and, turning to look Shon in the eye, said, "It was my pleasure, indeed, Shon. May I call you by your given name?"

"You may address me as you wish, Professor."

"Then I shall address you as Shon if you will do me the courtesy of addressing me as Raul." He smiled. "Maria is normally very shy. It was all that I could do to persuade her to attend with you tonight so that I might continue my efforts to persuade you to consent to join the staff of our university."

Shon smiled. "Shy? Why, she dressed me up, and marched me right over here."

Maria, blushing, said, "Well, Father, when he appeared in work clothes in his home, I just had to show him that we were not just a bunch of miners and jungle tenders. If you will excuse me, I see some friends." And she walked away without a glance in his direction.

Shon, turning to Raul, said, "I didn't intend—"

Raul interrupted. "Maria has had a quick tongue since she was a child. She often says sharp things she regrets even as she is saying them."

Shon shrugged, "It appears as if one thing has not changed— women. Would you care to tell me about the Universidad de Montaña over a drink? And then, perhaps, you could tell me about the mining and jungle tending Maria referred to."

•

Maria wanted to leave but she couldn't, and she was shortly going to have to sit by and eat dinner with that man whom she had decided disliked her. If only she could dislike him back, but that was not how she felt, even though she had been cautioned to feel that way while pretending otherwise.

Teresa Tiahuanaco and Ferdinand Nazca, her two closest friends, approached her.

Teresa said, "Well, Maria, if they all looked in his time like that old star man, I want to go back to where he came from."

Ferdinand interjected, "Of course, I assume you accidentally missed considering your partner here."

Teresa said, "Oh Ferd, you know I've always thought you were a throwback to ancient times."

Ferdinand smiled, "I'm sure you meant that the right way."

Teresa laughed.

Maria didn't.

Teresa inquired, "Maria, what's wrong?"

"He does not act as we anticipated. Tonight before we came over here we stood on his balcony looking at the stars, and he began talking about them and his time. It was as if he was truly reminiscing about a time he could recall as we recall our last summer in Huascarán. What if he's not what we fear and really does come from a past so long ago that it precedes even our myths? Either way, I'm afraid I will not be able to control my mouth."

Teresa reached out and put her hand lightly on Maria's shoulder. "Relax. Slow down. It's not like he is going anywhere, unless the Society has suddenly lost its patience, something I think we all doubt, the same as we have very reasonable doubts about what the Society said about him."

Ferdinand chimed in, "What they are up to only they know, but we cannot allow a story so incredible that it might be true make us believe it so, and so become vulnerable to whatever their real purpose is. For that purpose cannot be to simply settle an ancient man among us. We have nothing at all to offer a man of the sort they say he is. Why would they choose us?"

Teresa said, "Ferd is right, the essential problem with what the Society has told us is that it makes no sense for our community to have been chosen to take in such a man as they claim he is. We are all agreed on that, no?"

Maria briefly nodded her agreement to that point. It had seemed patently obvious only a few hours ago; now it just seemed logically obvious.

Teresa smiled. "You are the most beautiful woman in Montaña, present company excepted. Just take your time. We are confident your father will hire him for the university where you will see him frequently. Watch your tongue and let nature take its course. The Resurrection will be watching over you all the while and will assist you when the time comes to get down to the business at hand."

•

Shon and Raul walked over to Raul's table where Naomi Chavín rose to greet them and introduced the others sitting there: her friend for the evening, Ramón Guerro, Margarite Santiago, and her partner, Juan Flores. They sat down, Shon in the chair to Raul's left. Maria came over and sat down next to Raul on his right side and engaged herself in conversation with Margarite and Juan.

Raul, leaning on his elbow toward Shon, spoke quietly as they sat waiting for the main course to be served. He proposed that Shon consider teaching a course he thought would be of interest to the students at the university: Comparative Ethics, contrasting the ideas and beliefs of Shon's time with those of the present.

When dinner was served, Naomi rose and, clinking her glass for attention, turned toward Shon and said, "People of Montaña, on behalf of the Community Board, I would like to thank you for coming this evening. Let us join in welcoming Shon Ó Conaill to Montaña."

The crowd applauded politely.

Shon stood up and said, "Thank you. While I traveled about a hundred and fifty years in my journey from my point of view, over eight hundred thousand years of time passed here. During all but four years of those years I was asleep. So you have lived more in your lifetimes than I have in eight hundred millennia. In my time this world was dying. This lush jungle you live in had nearly vanished. It appeared that all that would remain in a few centuries would be barren earth—no plants, no animals, perhaps no life at all. Yet I have returned to find a world full of life.

"As I approached Montaña's towers aboard the El Dorado, I was struck by the way you have constructed your homes to avoid interfering with the ecology. In my time, all of this land would have been cleared of the jungle to make room for buildings on the ground. Tonight standing above this jungle, I was able to look at stars in a way I have been unable to since I was a child.

"Today you have welcomed me. Tomorrow I will try to prove myself worthy of your welcome. I would like to thank Naomi Chavín for her kind words and Maria Monterro for consenting to be my escort tonight. I look forward to meeting all of you in the days ahead."

The crowd began to clap, some enthusiastically, but Shon noticed that many in the crowd did not respond so earnestly, and some didn't clap at all.

Maria rose to stand beside him and clapped, determined not to make a second mistake with this man, feeling that she might not get the chance to make a third. She shuddered as she had a sudden feeling that she did not want to spend the rest of her life watching this man watch the stars with someone else if he somehow turned out to be what he appeared to be, rather than what they feared he was.

•

The next morning, Shon arose with the light and descended to the jungle floor. Even so early in the day, the air was very humid. For him to comfortably live in this jungle would require adaptation. He ran into the jungle, gradually running faster and faster. He accelerated his mind and his body, careful not to activate his Magan implant. As he moved further away from Amassona, the underbrush disappeared because the nourishing sunlight could not penetrate the dense jungle canopy. Soon he was able to move more freely and he pressed himself onward until he could press no further in the hot, humid and oppressive atmosphere. He returned, walking at the end, to the elevator, went up, and took a shower. He dressed in the clothes he'd originally intended to wear the night before and set off for the Universidad de Montaña to meet with Professor Monterro.

He took the elevator up to the top of the tower and walked through a series of bridge-to-tower-to-bridge transitions until he arrived at the university which appeared to comprise two of the tall towers. He approached a citizen who pointed him toward an elevator and directed him to take it to Level C. Entering the elevator, he looked at the elevator control panel and discovered something he had not noticed before. In this elevator there were both numbers and letters. It appeared that the numbers represented levels in the tower above the ground and the letters represented subterranean levels. The ground level was indicated, as in the residential towers, as Level 0. Level C was the third level below the ground.

Shon called upon his memory well, which had recorded everything he experienced in detail, to recall the control panel in Cyprus Tower and saw that that the elevator control panel in the Cyprus Tower also had levels with letters. Then he called up his well's recording of the elevator in his residential tower and found that there were no letter levels. Apparently, the residential towers, or at least his, did not have underground levels or passageways. He wondered why.

He left the elevator on Level C and approached another citizen who directed him to the Office of the President. As he entered he presented himself to a woman who spoke into a vidcom to announce his presence to Professor Monterro. Then the woman showed him into an office nearby where the professor was seated behind a large wooden desk.

Raul rose from his chair, saying, "Shon, so good to see you. Wonderful party last night. I hope you enjoyed yourself."

"I certainly did."

Waving his hand toward a chair beside his desk, Raul said, "Have you considered what we spoke of last night?"

Shon sat down in the chair, saying, "I have. I believe that the comparative ethics course will help me understand your world while affording me the opportunity to present my world to yours. However, I would like to avoid the sort of discourse where one is called upon to support opinions one may not hold personally just for the sake of argument."

Raul inquired, "If I may be so bold, why?"

"I wish to hear the views of your society expressed as they are truly felt, and I would like to present mine in the same way."

"Would a format where we appointed a professor to share the course with you as an advocate of our community's viewpoints be acceptable?"

"Certainly."

Raul leaned back in his chair and said, "I will agree to your terms, if you will agree to mine."

Shon narrowed his eyes slightly and said, "I am listening."

"If I can produce the person most qualified to provide that dialogue and to extract from you what I sense you wish to convey, will you complete the course, no matter what you may think at the beginning or at any time during the process, it being agreed that you will not be bound by your commitment to teach this course for more than one term if you find the arrangement unsatisfactory?"

"I intuit that you believe this process will have an adversarial flavor to it," said Shon.

"That is precisely what I hope will be the case. That will make the course exciting."

"I will agree to your terms if you will assure me that the professor you appoint will make the same commitment."

"Agreed," said Raul. "The course will start in three weeks with the beginning of the next term. Most of our students are here, not to learn a profession, but rather to pursue studies they have been interested in their entire adult lives."

Shon nodded.

Raul rose from his chair. "Now that you are employed, what do you plan to do until you begin?"

"Frankly I don't know. I have never had three weeks off in my life."

Raul said, "Let me suggest that you join me at the top of this building, say four o'clock, for a coffee in the university's lounge. I believe that drink was popular in your time. In the meantime, I will think about something for you to do during your vacation."

"I'd be most pleased, Professor. Might I meet with the professor who will be conducting the course with me sometime before the course commences?"

"I must consider who to choose, and I do not plan to make the assignment public until the course commences. There should be a certain theater to this unique endeavor. Let me set the stage and provide the cast."

"In other words you have no intention of telling me anything about how the course will be run, who my colleague will be, or who will attend?"

"Precisely."

•

After he left Professor Monterro's office, Shon returned to his apartment and activated the vidcom in the living room. As he expected, it was also the computer link to the community's network. He searched for the University's library. In short order, he figured out how to use the system and obtained access to its files. While no one on Montaña had seemed the least bit interested in what he might learn, Shon's training and instincts guided him to seek only information that anyone would expect to find here and to avoid looking for secrets.

First he searched for information relating to Montaña. He learned that Montaña was more than an isolated village. The map produced for Montaña showed the western region of South America and included areas he had known as parts of Brazil, Columbia, Peru and Ecuador. He had thought traveling up Amassona would mean going deep into Brazil not completely across it. But the huge river and its tributaries crossed almost the entire continent all the way to the Andes far to the west. The history file revealed that the first documented trip down the Amazon had been made by entering its headwaters in the Napo River in Ecuador, to the west of Brazil, in 1540 C.A. and traveling eastward down the river.

Shon noted that the Napo emptied into Amassona just to the north of this community. He considered that there might be another way out of Montaña by going west rather than east.

He had already noticed that the names of the people he'd met here were generally the same as those taken by the people in his own time who lived in this region—Peruvians, Ecuadorians and Colombians—and that there were also some names from the people of the region's more distant past as he thought of it, the Inca, Chimú, and Nazca. In this activity he knew he would not be able to learn much from his memory well as human history and detailed geography were part of the information that the Black Hole Project did not want to risk revealing to any sentient aliens he might encounter and would be of little use off-world in any event. So he was left to his own memory which, fortunately, he had filled somewhat with a personal interest in these matters.

He also noted that the people he'd seen didn't look as if they were members of different ethnic or racial groups. Not really surprising since, even had all their ancestors lived as long as four hundred years, at least two thousand generations would have passed since he left Earth, about the same number of generations as had occurred in the forty millennia before his birth. So it made sense that a people not moving anywhere else and receiving no new genetic material from outsiders would have common characteristics. He surmised that were he to travel to the other citizen communities he would likely discover clear physical differences in appearances from the people of Montaña, yet a common appearance within each community.

He wished he'd been able to see more of Luciana's family, for if they still had distinctive ethnic differences among themselves it might mean that they had experienced the passage of only few generations so that such a blending had not occurred. That would support the notion he had gotten from Mamercus that the Hom possessed exceedingly long lifespans.

Recalling how enthusiastically Luciana had embraced the idea of the Roman civilization, he thought, *What if Luciana's family are overlords sucking life from the rest of humanity by relegating humans not like themselves to hinterland compounds to provide some service or product while they rule the world? I should have probed her on the details of her enthusiasm. What exactly is so wonderful about Roman rule that her people, the apparent rulers of this planet, would so embrace it as to name themselves like those ancient Romans?*

He searched for some facts to support or disprove his overlord notion. Determining how property came into the Society's possession seemed a good start, one that might also provide some insight into how society had evolved since his departure. The Romans in power had frequently taken property from those they ruled and from others of themselves, often killing the former property owner in the process. He queried for information about property takings to learn how much property had been taken over by the Society. As query responses flowed in, he found no information about anyplace other than Montaña and no records going back more than a little over a hundred thousand years, a long time by any normal standard but only a small fraction of the span of time since he'd left. He wondered why that was.

•

Jorge Alvarez, chief librarian for the university, entered Professor Monterro's office and said, "As you requested, I have been monitoring any queries by Señor Ó Conaill. He has made an extraordinary number of inquiries in the last few hours."

The professor said, "About anything in particular?"

Alvarez replied, "At first, general history and geography. Then he began to search the records on property transfers, at first seeking information about property everywhere, then over a period of time beyond that for which we keep records. So he focused his search on the records pertinent to his apparent interest, and then he terminated his connection."

"Thank you, Jorge. Continue to keep me informed."

•

At precisely four o'clock, Professor Monterro left the elevator at the lounge level and found Shon standing by a table. They said hello, sat down, and ordered coffee.

Raul asked, "Might I inquire into your research effort in the library today?"

"Tracking my activities, Raul?"

Raul said, "As curious as you might be to learn about us, you must understand that we are even more so about you. After all, who has ever met someone from the distant past?"

"Naomi told me that no locks were necessary on Montaña."

"Of course not."

"Well, let me take the opportunity to tell you about one of the principles of my time, sort of a prelude to comparative ethics as I may express them. In my time, no one had a right to watch the private activities of anyone else. It is also true that such rights were observed in the breach by most governments, but then most governments were hated by their citizenry."

"Of course you are correct. Please accept my apology."

Shon softened his tone. "So, what about my inquiries elicited your curiosity?"

"Your interest in property transactions is puzzling."

Shon took a sip of his coffee and smiled. "I thought it might be a way to see how society had evolved since I left. If property simply changed hands without significant changes in the nature of its ownership, that would tell me one thing. If properties moved inexorably into ever fewer hands or were always owned by only a few, that would tell me something else. And if property ownership did both over time, an ebb and flow as it were, that would tell me yet something else."

"And what did you conclude?"

"That your records only go back a hundred millennia, not nearly enough to give me a picture of what has happened for most of the time I was away, nor do they cover the planet beyond your own community. What they do cover seems to indicate a broad distribution of property over the entire population with little accumulation by anyone. There seems to have been little stratification in wealth among your people unless you measure wealth in other ways."

"A remarkably good deduction." Raul changed the subject. "I have a suggestion for your vacation. At the time the Order was established, the Society determined that our central community should be located here. Later, as our climate became more tropical, even the Prefects from the Society who watch over our community avoided coming here during the Rains, our season of oppressive humidity. So the Society decided that we should also have some relief and allowed us to construct a mountain retreat limited to residential use. During the Rains most of us visit our second homes to the southwest of our central community on the eastern slope of the great mountain, Huascarán. As it is nearing the end of the Rains, Maria and a few of her friends are going up tomorrow morning for one last visit before the weather there becomes too cold for comfort. If you would care to join them, I will make the arrangements."

"I'd be delighted."

SIX

HUASCARÁN

Maria had thought herself prepared for Raul's invitation to Shon for him join her on her trip to Huascarán. But now the trip, planned in anticipation of Shon's arrival and its purpose dependent at the outset on her father's ability to entice Shon to join the party using her as bait, had lost some of its attraction to her as she was becoming concerned about her ability to carry off her role.

Teresa Tiahuanaco and Ferdinand Nazca were coming along as were Charlie Gomariz, Pantotta Rosca, and Joseph Estaban. Teresa and Ferd were partners to each other and friends to her since she was a child. Charlie and Pantotta were well on their way to being partners to each other, and were also her friends though less so, more like comrades in their common cause, which was also true of Teresa and Ferdinand.

She knew that Joseph was going because she invited him and he would not turn down such an invitation. She was not interested in a partnership with Joseph and had been concerned that he might misinterpret her acquiescence to his suggestion that he journey with her to the mountain this time as one of her coterie. Still she had invited Joseph as her father had instructed because Joseph was important to the plan formulated by the Resurrection to deal with Shon. Now she began to hope that Shon's presence might deter any efforts by Joseph to press her to respond to his feelings about her.

•

Shon packed for the trip and arrived at the Cinchona Tower, another of the high white towers, at seven the next morning. Maria introduced him to the rest of the group. They entered the elevator and descended to a subterranean level. As they stepped out of the elevator, Shon looked out at a vast space with tunnels running into it. The quality of the construction and the sleek beauty of the design was more impressive than he'd expected from what he'd read in the files about the transportation system.

Ferd said, "This station was built around six centimillia ago. Before that time, people traveled on foot, impractical but that was the way it was in those times. The tunnels and elevated rails connect us with the mountains and the outer regions of our community. You will see the rails as we approach the sierra, a region of higher elevation to the west, and the mountains beyond. The rails continue on far to the north where they terminate at Porto Guayaquil, a port on Pacifica a few hundred klicks beyond the far western border of our community."

Shon queried, "Do you travel to Porto Guayaquil?"

Charlie responded, "Only railers travel there."

Recalling Isabella and her crew, he surmised what that meant—no one ever left Montaña this way. And these railers were likely sworn to the same code of secrecy that Isabella had been.

As they boarded, Shon said, "How are you today, Maria?" Their parting at the end of the party had been stiff. Maria had told him that her residence was in another direction from his. When he'd offered to walk her home, she had declined.

But now she smiled and said, "Fine. I have some food and coffee you are welcome to share."

He said, "Thank you. I tasted coffee yesterday for the first time in a long while. It was wonderful."

The train set off for the foothills of Huascarán, the highest mountain in Montaña and one of the highest in the Andes.

The traveling distance to Huascarán was a little over eleven hundred klicks to the southwest. The trip would take twelve hours which was why everyone left in the morning. One could arrive in time to have dinner and attend a party before retiring. The train departed through the south tunnel and passed under Amassona and continued underground to the west for almost six hundred klicks. Then it ascended to the surface and rose seventy meters above the jungle floor onto a monorail, running southerly beside a river cut deep into the hills, that extended, like a thick wire above the trees, as far as the eye could see.

As they left the dense jungle behind, Shon saw that it was a bright sunny day. He looked out at the changing countryside rising in elevation into a narrow valley of grassland between the wooded foothills of the mountains rising high to the west.

•

Maria watched Shon watching the view outside. She noticed that his expressions changed. Sometimes he seemed happy, sometimes a dark cloud appeared to cross his visage. She wondered what caused the changes.

Shon shifted his gaze from the window to Maria, and his eyes caught hers looking at him.

She looked away. Shon said, "You look very lovely when you change color like that."

Maria's face felt very hot. She started to say something short, but instead she said, "I was embarrassed."

"About what, Maria?"

"When I was a child I showed my emotions on my face and was teased about it. It embarrassed me. I have been noticing that your emotions appear to pass across your face sometimes as now when you were gazing out the window, and the other night when you were looking at the stars. I was thinking that when you looked over." She looked directly into his eyes.

Shon said, "When emotions cross your face it makes you lovelier than you already are. You also look beautiful when you are angry. Perhaps that may be why your father and I found ourselves teasing you at the party. I apologize for that. I never intended to offend you."

Maria said, "Father was right to tease me. The truth is that I agreed to escort you on a dare before you arrived. We thought you'd be a very old man." She glanced away, "Only you weren't."

•

The train approached Huascarán rising high in the west. Huascarán's shadow fell across the lush green forests of the foothills and the deep grassy valleys. The village was stunning. The Montañans had constructed what appeared to be a Swiss mountain village from his own time. The wood and stucco houses had blue painted shutters beside tall, narrow windows. Dark-stained wooden beams etched crosses in the white stucco walls. Russet brick chimneys protruded through gray and black slate roofs, steeply pitched to shed snow. At this altitude, it was becoming winter and snow extended from the heights of Huascarán almost to the village.

Maria watched Shon watching their approach to the village. His face seemed a book where she could read his emotions. Watching him was becoming a rather pleasant pastime.

•

Joseph Estaban watched Maria watching the man looking out the window. As Montaña's Advocate of the Order, it was his duty to prosecute alleged transgressors of the Order in judicial proceedings presided over by the Prefect, the absolute authority from the Society who bore a mandate to enforce the Order for the Community. For that reason most people in Montaña respected, even feared, him and everyone took him very seriously. Everyone it seemed except Maria.

He had first set his eyes on Maria nine years earlier when she was barely sixteen, and he had wanted her ever since. But then she had been interested in Jimmy Gonzales. Gonzales was gone now and she was the youngest full professor at the university, and not because of her father. More important to him, she exuded a sexuality that made him burn with a sybaritic passion he'd never felt for anyone else. He'd shown his interest over the past few years and been frustrated by her platonic response. He felt the time had come for a less platonic relationship.

He had planned to push his agenda with her on this trip, but the man from the past had boarded the train and sat down next to her. Having heard about her dare to escort the old geezer, he'd gone to the dinner party to see the joke play out. But somehow sour had turned sweet for Maria when the man hadn't turned out to be quite the geezer everyone had expected.

•

The train pulled into Huascarán Village an hour after sundown, and its passengers boarded a small shuttle to transport them to their homes scattered across the hilly base of Huascarán.

Before she departed for her home, Maria invited Shon to join the others and her at the Lodge an hour before midnight. Shon got off at Raul's home not far from where Maria had departed.

Later, dressed in new clothes he'd obtained at the Underground beneath Cyprus Tower after his coffee with Raul, Shon walked a chilly four klicks to the Lodge.

Maria walked over to Shon, extended her hand, and turned her face to present her cheek for a kiss. The custom of hand and cheek was so ingrained in Maria's culture that she felt Shon's kiss before she realized what she was doing. Short though his kiss was, Maria felt a tingle.

They sat down at a table before a blazing fireplace. Shon inquired, "Are there any restrictions on smoke emissions or on cutting firewood? A fire like this would not have been permitted in my time."

Ferd replied, "If I have it right, in your time there were around fifteen billion humans with about half as many motor vehicles. We build our houses so that they cannot adversely impact the environment. We use high rails and tunnels for transport for the same reason. Our power comes down conduits built into the great walls from hydroelectric power plants located somewhere beyond Montaña where the Society has determined they will have no material environmental impact. Fires such as this are so small by comparison and made by so few that they have no impact on anything but us."

Shon smiled and replied, "You are light on the number of people and heavy on the number of vehicles, at least when I left, but your point is well taken. I really haven't been able to absorb the changes that have occurred."

Teresa said, "So, since we can do no harm, let's have fun."

Everyone laughed. Except Joseph who was looking at Maria who he saw was gazing at Shon.

Joseph said, "If you will excuse me, I brought some work along I need to finish."

Charlie said, "You know the Huascarán rule: No work, only play! Hope you feel better tomorrow."

•

After dinner the group, sans Joseph, left the Lodge and walked in a light snowfall to the top of a hillock overlooking the village. They entered the Knoll, a round building made of a semi-translucent material with a high crystal dome ceiling, a miniature reproduction of the crystal dome atop the Cyprus Tower. The lighting was low and the Latin music loud. Most of the Montañans there were dancing to the music.

They found an empty table, shed their jackets and sweaters, and headed for the dance floor, Shon with Maria. In a community that valued a strong mind and body, the evening was an important part of life, and dance was an elixir for the soul. Maria could dance by the time she could walk and it showed.

The pace was hot, the tempo fast and fluid. With the first slow dance, Maria came into Shon's arms, and they slowly turned to the music. Maria rested her head on his shoulder. She felt warm and her aroma surrounded him.

At the evening's end, Maria and Shon left together, their homes in the same direction.

They came to Shon's abode first. Shon offered to walk Maria to her place. She demurred, but Shon insisted. The stars shone brightly and the air was frosty. When they arrived at Maria's abode, Maria said softly, "Good night, Shon."

Shon said, "It was a very lovely evening." He stepped to Maria, put his arms around her and kissed her, slowly at first then, as she responded, fully, long and hard.

Shon looked deeply into her eyes and smiled. Then, saying no more, he turned and departed.

•

Joseph watched them from the woods. Not once had she ever opened herself to him as she was so clearly doing for the geezer, kissing him in a way that said she was open to whatever he wished. He watched Shon turn away and leave. Having spent years wanting her, dreaming about having her, he felt a personal hatred for this man who could turn away from her rather than seizing the opportunity he himself had never once been offered.

•

Maria and her friends gathered for breakfast the next morning a few minutes before Shon arrived. The day promised to be clear and crisp, yet not too cool. Joseph pressed Maria to spend the day with him, but he was unable to persuade her to commit to anything beyond a morning walk into the wooded hills.

Maria sensed that Joseph was upset despite his calm appearance. She could understand how he felt. She knew he had only come on this trip to be with her. She also knew that she was obviously ignoring him. Yet something about Shon gave her the courage to do so. Instinctively, she felt Joseph was no match for Shon. Still it seemed better to keep Joseph happy if she could and she knew he had been invited for a reason. But this glorious morning, she simply could not bear to spend the entire day with him.

Maria had never felt close to anyone since Jimmy Gonzales, her first and only love. They had met when she was sixteen. He was twenty. Their friendship developed into love over the next few months and it never waned.

Then one day the Office of the Order accused Jimmy of violating the Order by promulgating a proposition that the restrictions on travel should be eliminated. The Society called any idea that held their threat to the Order in what followed from acceding to the initial idea a Slippery Slope Proposition. In Jimmy's case, he had argued for the right for citizens to travel beyond their communities. The threat was that such activity might encourage population redistribution and efforts to join communities now far apart, bringing harm to the ecology, clearly a violation of the Order.

Prefect Claudia, of the Society, strictly enforced the Society's commandment that Slippery Slope Propositions must be eliminated whenever they arose. Banishment to Amaz for a year was the penalty.

Jimmy had been brought before Prefect Claudia in a judicial proceeding and was judged to have violated the Order. He was banished.

Maria never saw him again. She sometimes fantasized that Jimmy had ventured to another community as he had always talked of doing and might return someday. But deep down she knew that was not what had happened. On average two or three people were banished from the community each year for an infraction of one sort or another of the Order. None of the banished had ever returned, not a single person.

She believed, as she knew most of her community did, that the banished were simply done away with by the Society after they left Montaña. How that was done was a mystery that had never been solved since a time so long ago that it had become a part of life. And there was nothing they could do about it. Besides the number banished was small relative to the overall population. More than a few Montañans actually looked forward to the banishments so that children could be born to replace those banished without exceeding the permitted population for the community.

Joseph, as the Advocate of the Order, had prosecuted Jimmy's case before the Prefect.

When Jimmy failed to return, Maria put her energy into her academic career. Then one day she was approached, through her father, by a secret group of Montañans who sought freedom from the Society's power over their lives and joined them in their cause. Their secret name for themselves was the Resurrection of Humanity. They had helped to fill the void Jimmy had left behind. It was the Resurrection that had sent her on a mission to discover Shon's true purpose in coming to Montaña. But she was finding her interest in Shon growing beyond her mission. It made her afraid.

•

When Shon entered the Lodge, Joseph abruptly rose and left without saying a word. Shon, ignoring the uneasy atmosphere that he detected, said, "Morning all, what's on the table for today?"

Teresa said, "Ferd and I are going fishing this morning while Charlie and Pantotta go on a bird watch. They will join us for a picnic in the afternoon. Joseph and Maria are taking a mountain walk."

Shon said, "Well, I think I will take a run up into the mountains."

Maria, observing that Shon was dressed in a short-sleeved cotton shirt and loose-fitting shorts, said, "You may need to dress a little more warmly. It's chilly in the mountains, but, if you choose to go, I can tell you where there is a nice path up into the mountains. The stream that runs beside the path flows down from a deep, clear blue pond fed by a lovely waterfall. It's about a three-hour hike."

•

Shon packed a meal and a change of clothes for after his run. Sticking to Maria's directions, he followed the path beside the rushing, gurgling mountain stream until he came upon a crystal-clear pond with a waterfall pouring over a cliff at the far end. The scene was every bit as lovely as she had intimated. He dropped his backpack on the pond's bank beside the stream flowing out from the pond and headed upland towards Huascarán at a run. The chilly, dry air dissipated the heat his body generated as he accelerated. With his genetic alterations, he could see an object a thousand meters away as clearly as most could at a hundred, all the while hearing and smelling everything around him as well as a bloodhound. He accelerated his pace, peaking at around forty-five klicks, much more and he knew he would have to deal with his Magan implant. He felt truly alive for the first time since he'd left for the stars.

An hour later, burning energy at a prodigious rate, he began to tire. By then he was approaching the tree line on the mountain, above which the thinning altitude prevented the further growth of forest. The terrain became increasingly rocky and treacherous for one moving so quickly over it, and he decided to turn back and return to the pond. He reduced his pace to twenty-five klicks, as slow as he could go and still have the passing air dissipate the heat his body was generating.

By the time he returned to the pond, he was ravenous. Opening his backpack, he took out the food, quickly ate it all, and was still hungry. He stripped off his clothes and, diving into the pond, swam in the frigid water toward a big, flat rock just beyond the waterfall's spray. He climbed up and stretched out on the stone warmed by the sun, and shortly fell asleep to the soft roar of the falling water, his body still so warm that he was impervious to the chilly air made misty by the waterfall's spray.

•

Maria and Joseph walked along a wooded path not far from the village saying little beyond small talk until they turned back to go the picnic site to join the picnic group. Joseph abruptly stopped and, turning to face her, said, "Maria, it is time for us to become partners."

Maria looked him in the eye and said in a quiet tone, "Joseph, I have never gotten over Jimmy, and I don't think I ever will."

Joseph felt a fire in his head, and, forcefully grabbing her by the arm, spun her to face him. Clutching her other arm, he shook her. "It looked to me like you had gotten over Jimmy just fine last night. It's the geezer that's gotten your blood running. Well, he's some sort of outcast, or he's a spy for the Society—why else would he be here? Surely you don't believe that story about how he got here. Who knows how long he will stay?" His face turning purple, he said, "You will need me someday, Maria!"

Maria became blindly furious and, shaking with rage, screamed back, "We can never become partners. Shon has nothing to do with that. It was Jimmy you killed, not Shon! And if Shon's a spy, I'm sure *you* would know it!"

Joseph stood stone still as if struck by lightning. He let go of Maria's arms and looked coldly into Maria's eyes. "What do you mean, 'killed Jimmy'?"

"Nothing."

"And what do you mean by *I* would know the geezer's a spy?"

She turned and began to walk away, saying over her shoulder, "I'm going to the picnic. You can come along or leave, but I am not going to discuss this any further."

Joseph started to follow and then abruptly turned back and strode away toward the village.

•

By the time Maria found Teresa and Ferd by the stream where they could usually be found preparing their picnic after fishing, she had regained control of herself, but she looked pale.

Teresa said, "Maria, what's wrong?"

"I had an argument with Joseph."

Speaking over his shoulder while laying out the food and drink for the picnic, Ferd said, "Over Shon?"

Maria said very slowly, "And over Jimmy."

Ferd abruptly turned and glanced at Teresa who returned his glance.

Ferd said in a low voice, "Maria, what did you say about Jimmy?"

Maria exhaled, "I told him that he killed Jimmy." She looked at each of them—they were turning as pale as she—"I have always had a bad feeling about why Jimmy was accused but I never wanted to think it was because of me. I just closed it out. One day after the year had passed for Jimmy's banishment and he could return but, of course, didn't, Joseph called me and asked me out. I guess I couldn't deal with the possibility that Jimmy was gone because Joseph wanted me. Since I could never date a man who caused the death of Jimmy and, since I dated Joseph, he could not be responsible. If Joseph was not responsible, then I could not have been the cause. But when he started to scream that it was Shon I wanted, calling him a geezer, and then said I would need him someday, it just all came out. I now see clearly how my reasoning has been crazy but that's how I've been able to get by without accepting a truth I couldn't face. I now realize that I have always thought Joseph killed Jimmy because of me."

Teresa said, "Maria! Why did you say that Joseph killed Jimmy? He just caused him be banished."

"Everyone banished is killed by the Society. That is why no one ever comes back. Really! I'm not crazy. Don't you believe the same thing? Doesn't everyone?"

There was silence for almost a minute. Then Ferd said in a quiet voice, "Maria, you are not crazy. Of course, we believe that. That is the secret fear of every Montañan, but no one speaks of it, not even to their partners. And, for the sake of your life, you must never repeat what you've just said. When you see Joseph you must tell him that you blamed him for Jimmy's banishment only because he prosecuted the accusation, not because he didn't return. He will not believe you, but he may feel that you will say nothing further."

Teresa said quietly, "Maria, forget about Joseph. Instead, why don't you go see if Shon took your suggestion."

•

Maria hiked up to the waterfall lake.

As she entered the glen at the bottom of the lake, she found Shon's clothes scattered about, but not Shon. The sun warmed the afternoon air, almost as if it were a summer day. She decided to take a swim while she waited for him to return. She undressed and slipped into the pond. The water was frigid and she swiftly swam to her favorite spot, a flat rock by the waterfall. She climbed out of the water onto the rock. Shivering as she stood up, she saw Shon asleep before her. She stood frozen, just looking at him. Hesitating to step too soon back into the icy water, she was still standing before him as his eyes slowly opened.

He rolled his head towards her and his eyes widened, "Maria?"

She turned and dove into the stream and swam back to the shore to her clothes.

He waited for a minute and then swam to his clothes and dressed. He listened for the sounds of rapid human footfalls and ran in that direction until he saw her running ahead of him.

He called to her, "Wait, let's walk."

She stopped running as he came up beside her.

She said, "I can't believe you caught up to me."

Shon frowned and said, "I can run pretty fast."

Maria looked at Shon's face. "I see a cloud."

He glanced towards her, then looked away towards the village below in the distance. "There is a great deal about me that you don't know."

Maria spoke quickly without thinking. "There is nothing you can tell me that would shock me. After all, it's not like you're from the Society." Her heart skipped a beat, realizing that she had just bluntly put to him what she had been tasked to learn at any cost. But now she needed the answer for more than informing the Resurrection.

As if he hadn't heard what she'd just said, he continued to walk in silence beside her down to the village. When they entered the lodge, they learned that Joseph had left for the central community on the last train for the day.

•

Later that evening at the Knoll, Teresa watched Shon and Maria dancing together and said to Ferd, "I wonder why Maria doesn't look radiant tonight. I was so sure the lake would turn out well."

•

As Shon walked Maria back to her home after the dance, he said, "I would like to go back to the pond with you tomorrow."

She didn't respond immediately. Then she decided that she could not be a spy, not with him, someone else would have to do that work. She said, "All right."

Shon could sense something was wrong but he could not fathom what it could be. He said goodnight and kissed her softly and walked to Raul's house.

When he retired that evening he was unable to sleep. It had been a great day, almost.

•

Maria drifted off into a troubled sleep where she had a dream in which Shon was the man she hoped he might be, not the man he might be.

The next morning Maria awakened, got up, bathed, and went out onto the balcony to breathe the crisp morning air she enjoyed so much.

After a while Shon arrived and came up to the balcony carrying a carafe of coffee with two cups in hand. He sat down beside her, poured them each a cup of coffee, and said, "Maria, in thinking back on our walk back from the lake, I'm concerned I might have caused you to imagine the worst by talking so mysteriously about myself. Perhaps it would be better to know the truth."

Maria replied in a quiet voice, "I hope the truth is not what I imagine."

Certain that she could not possibly imagine the truth and wondering what she could imagine that could be worse, Shon said, "I seriously doubt the truth is what you imagine." He smiled. "Let's return to the lake today. Dress for a run. We'll need to bring a lot of food—you will be surprised how much. When we are finished, you will know the truth. Then you will decide how you feel and what you will tell others about what you have seen."

Finding it nearly impossible to believe that Shon was her worst nightmare pretending to be her best dream, Maria replied, "Very well."

•

They left for the lake at a moderate run. After Jimmy's disappearance, Maria had relieved her stresses and pressures from her studies and other concerns by undertaking a very active exercise program. Her height and long legs made her a very good runner.

As her clothes dampened, Shon could see the lines of her body. She had a small waist with a well-defined abdomen and a strong back. Her breasts were full, surprisingly so, given her lean physique. He was surprised he hadn't noticed at the lake. She ran in long strides, now and then making quick sidesteps to avoid the brush, a twist here, a stretch there.

When they arrived at the pond, Shon shed his backpack, and trousers. Standing in shorts and a sweatshirt, Maria noticed that he was not breathing hard at all and that his legs looked very strong—she had not noticed how strong before.

Shon suggested that she run as fast as she could up to the top of a small hill in the distance and wait for him.

Maria could play games as well as anyone. So she set out at her best speed to the hilltop. As she approached the top of the hill, she stopped dead in her tracks. There, standing casually at the top, was Shon. It was as though somehow she had run in a circle back to the pond. She jogged up to him and asked, "How did you get here so fast?"

"I ran faster than you. Now let's go back to the pond. We'll leave the backpack here. Would you place it under the tree over there?"

Intrigued, she complied, and set off with him back to the pond. About halfway there, he said he wanted to get the backpack, asked her to go on, and turned back up the hill. She continued on to the pond. When she got there, she saw a picnic all laid out with an open bottle of wine beside two wine glasses, each filled halfway with wine.

At first she had the thought that her group was playing a trick on her. Then she noticed something that made her shiver. There was the backpack.

She heard a voice from behind her say, "Boo."

She jumped, and spinning about, saw Shon standing in the same way she had seen him standing at the top of the hill. "What's going on, Shon? You're scaring me."

Shon said, "Maria, I am not exactly what I appear. From what I have seen of people in this time, no one can do what I just did. I am the result of genetic changes that were made to my DNA before I was conceived. I can hear, see, smell, taste, and feel over a broader range than almost everyone in my time, perhaps even anyone today. The price I pay for my ability to accelerate my mind and body is the uncertainty that I may go haywire someday. I have already experienced some buzzes in my head. I wanted you to know this about me." A little dissembling, but he needed to get across the fact that he wasn't normal without telling her the whole story.

Suddenly Maria started laughing.

Shon was flustered. "What?"

"Shon, I have only one question to ask you. I put my life in your hands by asking. But I must know the answer." She paused then said, "Are you of the Society?"

Shon said, "No, and, frankly, I don't think I'd want to be."

Maria started laughing again. "What do I care that you can run very fast, well, extremely fast?"

She came to him and kissed him. They ate lunch and took a quick swim in water that no longer seemed very cold to either of them.

Later, as they walked down the mountain, hand in hand, Maria began to dwell on why Shon had not pressed his obvious desire for her to a conclusion she knew she would not have resisted and wondered whether his genetic alterations had anything to do with that.

SEVEN

SPIES

Carpia Ana and Tigri Omagua arrived outside the Montañan village nestled in the foothills of Huascarán two days after Shon arrived and began their mission.

While observing Shon and those with whom he came into contact, they pondered over how to enter into the life of this community without appearing conspicuous.

Unlike the residential communities where citizens lived above ground the same as Carpia and Tigri, this community was a mining community like others scattered throughout the foothills in the outlying regions of Montaña where more than a few Montañans willingly spent a great deal of their time underground, mining copper, silver, iron ore, gold, lead, molybdenum, tungsten and zinc. These resources were permitted to be extracted provided they were extracted with proper safeguards and restoration measures to prevent any adverse ecological impact.

Each mine had a residential tower at its entrance. Its occupants generally led solitary lives separate from the central community. Underground ventilation was maintained by tall white towers equipped to restore the exhaust to the ambient air quality of the atmosphere into which it was ventilated. All mining operations were located underground. So were the transportation facilities required to load and ship the extracted minerals for processing to huge processing facilities, also subterranean, surrounding Porto Guayaquil, seven hundred and fifty klicks west of Montaña, for shipment to the other communities on Vitas.

Carpia and Tigri decided to situate themselves near the residential towers where their targets were situated and avoid entering into any of the mines.

After a few days of surveillance, Carpia declared, *"Males are all alike."*

Tigri replied, *"Carpia Ana, please don't start that old tune again. We males are males. And you females are females. Can't you leave it at that? That is natural and in accord with the Order. Now that we have some idea about how things are, why don't you track the female while I track Shon. I am afraid that if you track him, he will be in more danger from you than any Deinoc."*

Carpia replied, *"Fine. Maria seems very nice for a human. I will enjoy my task while you will have that man to keep an eye on. You must agree that when he ran by us yesterday he was going faster than any human we've ever seen. I am beginning to think our mission may be more interesting that we supposed."*

•

Shon and Maria returned to the central community. Shon's head had begun buzzing again on occasion near the end of their stay in Huascarán and on their train trip back to the Montaña. He was becoming concerned that his accelerated workouts had triggered the same problem with his comm implant that he'd experienced when he had arrived on Moon Base and when he'd traveled through Amaz on his way up the Amassona to Montaña.

Upon their arrival in the central community, Shon and Maria walked over to the university's tower and entered the elevator bound for Raul's office.

As they entered Raul's office, Raul stood up from behind his desk.

"How was your trip?"

Maria said, "Interesting."

"Invigorating," said Shon, glancing sideways at Maria.

"Good. Maria, I have decided to assign you to participate in Shon's course as our representative."

Maria said, "Doesn't that sound wonderful, Shon? We'll have the same hours."

Shon thought about it for a moment and, looking at Raul, said, "So you wanted me to commit for the term unconditionally because you were afraid that when I learned that it was Maria that you had in mind to be my professorial companion I might balk."

"Something like that crossed my mind."

Shon detected a dissonance in Raul's reply. He felt that
Raul could sense the feelings they had for each other, but
something—he could feel the Magan implant's influence—more
was going on in Raul's mind, and it wasn't as friendly as his
demeanor conveyed.

●

Maria visited her father the next day.
"I can't be a spy."
Raul replied, "It is necessary."
"I can't and I won't."
Raul looked at her face; and saw in it that same intractable
stubbornness that she'd had since childhood. "Very well, I will
inform the Resurrection."

●

The first week of the term went very well in Shon's view.
He described his time—the proposed solutions and movements
then underway to try to deal with the problems of the world.
Maria picked up on his theme, and she propounded her time's
view on the same subjects. It seemed that they had similar
viewpoints on personal rights and on humankind's obligations to
all life in the world. But how those rights were to be achieved
often led to lively discourse. The chemistry between them
provided the theatre Raul had suggested might evolve. By the
third week of class, the university began transmitting the course to
the households of students enrolled in the university throughout
Montaña and they received very respectable audiences.

●

Joseph organized the notes he had made on Shon and
Maria's course into a portfolio of "proofs", as the Office of Order
called them, and presented them to the director of the Office.
After obtaining what he considered lukewarm consent, he walked
over to the tallest white tower in Montaña and dropped them off
at Society House. The Prefect of Montaña would have them soon.
Things would soon be back to the way they had always been, he
was sure.

●

Late into the night a few weeks after they had arrived in
Montaña's central community, Tigri met with Carpia. He said, "We
have not been able to learn anything more about Shon than we saw at the

village. But these discussions he is having about his time seem very like what we have observed in the past to be of great concern to the Society. It may be wise to report our findings."

Carpia said, *"I agree. I wish it weren't so, as I have grown fond of these two."*

Tigri replied, *"So have I. But we cannot let that obstruct our duty."*

"Yes. Well, I can travel faster alone, so I will make the trip and return in the span of two nights." Carpia left the community in the dark of night shortly after midnight.

•

Rolando Martine sat facing west in a wicker chair on the porch at his house in Pinchincha in the southwest corner of Montaña, drinking a cup of coffee in the early evening, watching the sun, slowly at first then ever more quickly, sink behind the snow-capped mountains to the west. The house, constructed three decamillia earlier of wood and white stucco and roofed in red tile and restored to its original state every hundred years or so, was situated next to a deep mine shaft once used to mine emeralds. Rolando ran a mining and farming concern consisting of some mining and farming properties spread throughout western Montaña between the jungle to the east and the mountains to the west, operated and manned mainly by robots possessing low-grade artificial intelligence, which produced gold, emeralds, lead, molybdenum, tungsten, bananas, sugarcane, cassava, corn, rice, potatoes, coffee, cacao, and citrus fruit.

After the sun disappeared, in the twilight he watched a familiar figure approach the shaft's shed constructed above the old emerald mine shaft and disappear into it. After a few minutes he sauntered down the steps, crossed the field between his house and the shaft, entered the shed, and stepped into the elevator. He pressed the button to the third level and descended two hundred and twenty meters. He stepped out into a room lowly lit in a yellow luminance from indirect ceiling lights, not very different from the wood-paneled library in his house, except that the drapes here were closed as there were no windows behind them.

The familiar figure standing across the room said, "Greetings, Rolando." Then, gesturing with a wave of his hand toward the decanters set in a row on a side table made of a darkly stained rosewood, he said, "May I?"

"Of course, Raul. Pour one for me, too," said Rolando.

Raul Monterro poured two snifters nearly half full of a very old cognac Rolando had obtained years ago in exchange for some of his emeralds, and handed one to Rolando who had taken a seat in a green-leather chair across from the red-leather couch on which he'd sat many a night discussing the future of Montaña with Rolando and others high in the movement they called the Resurrection of Humanity.

Raul took a small sip and said, "I have some doubts about what we are doing."

"He presents a great danger to us, Raul."

"That is what we have believed. But I have gotten to know him. I have doubts that he is a pawn of the Society. Perhaps we have acted too hastily. And now I have heard a rumor that Maria may be accused by the Advocate. That was never considered a possibility. Maria has not been a party to anything we are doing since she returned from Huascarán."

Rolando said, "You know better than I that Joseph, for his own personal reasons, would never harm Maria. We counted on that when we devised the plan to deal with this man whom the Society has imposed upon us as an involuntary guest, with the fantastic story that he comes from our ancient past."

"What if he truly is from our ancient past?"

"Do you seriously believe that he could be what the Society says he is?"

"The ideas he propounds while speaking of his time make his tale seem very real to me. And what Maria has told me about things he has said to her makes me wonder even more. If he is truly from the past and not the Society's agent, we may be conspiring to rid ourselves of someone who could greatly further our cause. In any event Maria appears be in peril of banishment."

"The Administrator of the Office of Order, who you know is one of us, has informed me that Joseph offered weak proofs about Maria and even suggested that she was unduly influenced by Shon's unusual past, certainly a mitigating factor in any case against her. Besides, Prefect Claudia is well aware that banishing your daughter would greatly offend you and the community. Hasn't the Society always avoided offending those who, if provoked, might cause dissent in the community? Isn't the sensitivity of the prefects to maintaining the status quo one of the principal reasons the Resurrection has survived since it was formed over a decamillium ago?"

"Yes, but Prefect Claudia has demonstrated none of the political instincts of most of her predecessors. I am worried that she will take the most expedient course as she always has. She could conclude that Maria knew that Shon's ideas could harm the Order and by supporting them she is knowingly supporting notions that have led to banishments in the past."

"That might fuel the fire the Resurrection has sought to ignite for the past two thousand years, so far to no avail," said Rolando.

"I am not prepared to lose my daughter to such a supposition," said Raul.

"I understand that, but we have to deal with the threat this man brings to us."

"I'm not so sure we are up to dealing with the machinations of the Society by attempting to defeat them using their own methods. They have been at this far longer than we have."

Raul exhaled slowly and took a sip of his cognac. "If the Resurrection is irrevocably committed to the notion that Shon is an agent of the Society, then we must find a way to bring about his death before a trial occurs. I know of no other way to save Maria."

Rolando leaned back in his chair and took a long slow drink of his cognac. Finally he said, "Perhaps I should take his measure."

•

Rolando stepped off the train in the Underground in central city a few days after his meeting with Raul. He took up residence in Shon's tower two floors above his apartment and waited for a chance encounter to meet the man who might either ignite the resurrection he and the other Montañans who belonged to the Resurrection sought or bring about their destruction.

Rolando monitored Shon's goings and comings from his apartment with the assistance of another member of the

Resurrection who lived on Shon's floor. He learned that Shon routinely left his apartment an hour or so before dawn and returned at sunrise.

Two weeks after he arrived, Rolando went down to the jungle floor before sunrise and waited by the elevator. Shortly, out of the corner of his eye, he caught a glimpse of something in the jungle a few hundred yards away moving very rapidly toward the tower. Before he could clearly assess what he was seeing, the movement disappeared behind a cluster of vegetation and a man appeared on the other side, walking toward the tower breathing heavily. Rolando quickly turned toward the tower and pressed the button for the elevator as if he had just approached it and, when the elevator door opened, entered and turned to look out. The man was just a few yards from the tower. He pushed his hand against the door which was closing and it receded. He called out, "I'll hold it for you."

The man called back, "Thanks." He changed his pace from a walk to a trot. As he entered, he again said, "Thanks."

Rolando said, "I don't believe we've met before." He extended his hand and said, "My name is Rolando Martine."

Shon shook his hand, saying, "I apologize for not recognizing you, but I only came to Montaña a few months ago."

Rolando raised his eyebrows as if surprised, and said, "Really? I didn't know anyone *came* to Montaña. But, then, I don't know much of what goes on here as I live in Pinchincha."

"Pinchincha?" said Shon.

"A farming and mining community to the southwest near the mountains. You have not heard of it?"

"No, but, as I said, I am a recent arrival." Shon shrugged his shoulders, smiled, and said, "From what I understand, I may be the only outsider to come to Montaña in a very long time."

As the elevator door opened at Shon's floor, Rolando said, "Perhaps, as we are both strangers here, you will join me for a coffee and I will tell you about Pinchincha and you will tell me about how you came to Montaña."

Shon started to step out of the elevator, then he paused and held the door open, saying, "That might be refreshing."

"Refreshing?" said Rolando.

"This might sound a bit strange but since I arrived here, I haven't met anyone who didn't know something about me before I knew something about them."

"You appear to have been exercising. If you have the time, why don't you join me in the dining room at the top of the tower?"

"Give me thirty minutes and I'll join you there." Shon smiled, stepped out, and the door closed.

When the elevator reached his level, Rolando stepped out and went to his apartment. The man's demeanor had not been what he had expected.

•

Shon entered his apartment, shed his clothes, and turned on the shower. He cogitated on meeting the man in the elevator. He had felt a presence about this man that had motivated him to accept a stranger's invitation but anomalies he'd sensed in the man's voice and facial expressions indicated that their encounter might not have been as accidental as it appeared. He wondered whether allowing the Magan implant more influence on his mentality was causing him to become paranoid or whether the implant had simply detected something about the man he would normally not have noticed. Still the prospect of speaking with someone who had not already formed an opinion about himself was appealing and he showered and dressed quickly to avoid being late.

•

Rolando rode the elevator to the top of the tower, drew two coffees from the coffee bar, and took a table overlooking the jungle with a view to the west. He rarely had the opportunity to gaze at a distant view to the western horizon as, where he lived, the mountains rose to the west blocking out the distant horizon. Gazing out over the vast jungle which spread to the mountains, he waited for Shon to arrive, contemplating what he would say to cause them to become friends, if that was even possible.

A few minutes later, Shon entered and sat down across the table from Rolando.

Rolando said, "What has brought you to Montaña?"

"That is a very long story which, if you don't mind, I'd as soon not relate this morning. Suffice it to say, I am here and glad to talk to someone who doesn't already know more about me than I know about them."

Rolando chuckled. "I am glad to talk to someone willing to talk to someone from the hinterlands. Perhaps you haven't been here long enough to know that the citizens in the central community tend to look down at those from the hinterlands."

"I know little of the Montaña beyond this place and Huascarán."

"Ah, Huascarán! Imagine Huascarán populated by local villagers rather than vacationers from Montaña and you can see what life is like in Pinchincha."

"The stars shining above it at night must be magnificent."

Rolando paused before he spoke noting that Shon had just stated the essential difference between the two communities: one centered on being, the other on seeing. He decided to play to it. "You have a villager's view. I wonder why."

"Could it be that villagers spend their time alone as I have and have come to see what is beyond themselves?"

"What would you do to pass the time besides gazing at the stars if you lived in a village?"

Shon took a sip of coffee. "I'd probably study chess. I can't say why, but that game has always fascinated me."

Rolando was truly surprised. "Really? That is my favorite pastime."

"Then perhaps we might play sometime."

Rolando finished his coffee and said, "How about tomorrow night?"

"Your place or mine?"

"I have a coffee machine and a chess set in my apartment."

Shon finished his coffee and said, "Very well then, yours it is."

•

The following night Shon joined Rolando for a game of chess—a satisfying evening culminating in their agreement to make it a weekly affair, Rolando had been quite good, not at Shon's level but Shon played to his.

•

Only a few days after Claudia Acca Junius Hom, Prefect of Montaña for the past forty-seven years, and, unbeknownst to the citizens of Montaña, more than a few times before during the past five decamillia, had received a brief from the Office of Order containing proofs supporting its assertion that a Slippery Slope Proposition was being publicly propounded by two citizens of Montaña. She took the proofs to the Council official in Annec tasked with monitoring the communities who instructed her to proceed forthwith to Montaña.

Hom females appointed by the Council served as prefects with a mandate to maintain their citizen communities in conformance with the Order. The first duty of every Prefect was to stamp out any Slippery Slope Propositions that arose. The Society had maintained absolute dominance over the citizen communities for hundreds of millennia by, among other things, never allowing Slippery Slope Propositions to gain adherents.

For many decamillia prefects had managed their communities for terms of three hundred and fifty years, the period judged by the Council to be as long as a prefect could safely sustain the illusion that the prefects had similar lifespans to the citizens they managed.

As not every Hom was suited to such duties, there were not enough Hom females interested in administering the citizen communities without returning veteran prefects to them. It became common practice for the same prefect to return to the same community after an interval of a few thousand years when that community had lost its memory of her prior presence.

Claudia Acca Junius resided in Annec. She normally visited Montaña once a year early in the Rains when she could make the six-week trip almost entirely by water, on one of the citizen cargo ships plying the seas between the ancient port of Marseil southwest of Annec on the north shore of Mediterranea and, crossing Atlantica, Boca Amassona and then traveling up Amassona on the El Dorado.

She was irritated to receive an immediate directive to proceed to Montaña as the last thing she wanted to do was to set off for Montaña after the El Dorado had stopped running at the end of the Rains. Now she would have to make her way to Montaña by going east across the eastern portion of Europa and then across all of Asiana, the vast continent adjoining Europa to the east, and then to cross Pacifica to Porto Guayaquil northwest of Montaña. The only other alternative was traveling through the Walls, the only way Hom traveled across land masses when in a hurry. She was deathly afraid of the strange robotic machines she had never seen anywhere but inside the Walls.

The trip was grueling. It would take two months to travel to Montaña this way. A full inquiry culminating in a trial to consider banishment would take at least another month. Then there was the trip home, another two months. Five months to take care of something she'd much rather deal with during her normal trip to Montaña which was scheduled to commence just a little over a month after she was likely to return home.

•

Legate Timür, the Deinoc member of the Council who resided in Annec, contacted the Quaestor of Amaz, Batu, concerning the deliberations the Council made prior to sending its directive to the Prefect of Montaña to deal with a Slippery Slope Proposition.

Batu, the administrator of daily matters in Amaz, lived in Sir Orda, the principal community of the Deinoc. He immediately contacted the family's consuls, Ögödei and Chaghadai. He also contacted Khubilai, First General of the Golden Horde, and Praetor Böke, the other Deinoc member of the council who resided in Sir Orda when he was not living in Annec.

Khubilai immediately set off to see Temüjin, Khan of the Deinoc.

•

Khubilai walked out of the jungle surrounding Sir Orda, a city made of wood from the great trees that grew in the domain of the Deinoc, and strode up the high hill at its center and entered into the ancient citadel made of the living wood of a complex intermingling of the most ancient trees growing in the domain. He strode down a passageway paved in black granite, illuminated only by what sunlight was able to penetrate the dense canopy of the towering trees that comprised the citadel. Finally he passed through a narrow opening between two of the thickest trees and entered into the great chamber in the very center of the citadel and bowed before Temüjin who was pacing back and forth in front of a great throne cut out of the core of the thickest and tallest tree in the Domain.

Mindcast, as the Deinoc family were unable to communicate complex thought verbally, Khubilai said, *"Great Khan, I have news. There will soon be a trial in Montaña that will result in banishments. We should prepare to assemble the Horde in a few months. In accordance with our customs, for this hunt the Horde will consist of ten: you, me, Ögödei, Chaghadai, Böke, Timür, Hulagu and three of our younger males drawn by lottery."*

Temüjin said, *"Does this involve the Traveler?"*

"Timür believes the Traveler is one of the two who will be accused. Batu believes the other, a female, may be his mate. It appears that the Hom have lived up to their promise and much sooner than we had reason to hope."

"The Traveler comes from a time of great conflict. He has been to the stars. He will understand aggression, blood and death. He will fight fiercely to save his mate." Temüjin paused, *"But what of the Hom female who brought him to Vitas? Who is this new female?"*

"It may be that he charts his own course and that course may well be faster than the course the Hom have planned for him. In any event, upon penalty of Reduction, we are prohibited by the Codicil from killing any Hom."

Temüjin stopped pacing and said, *"There can be no doubt that a citizen female mate will add greatly to the hunt without any of the consequences connected to a Hom female."*

"Their blood will be hot and will taste good."

Temüjin made some audible grunts and began again to stride about back and forth, mindcast forcefully, *"Then this will be a Mates Hunt. The Horde must run them to heat their bodies and their spirits. Separate them so that they may fear the loss of each other. And then bring them together so that they may feel their blood boil in excitement over finding they may still mate again. Then we must close in and separate them, yet within view of each other. Then we must kill her and taste her blood, ripping her beating heart from her body before his eyes. His rage and hate will be unsurpassed. He must find a way to kill us. At that point, the challenge will be the greatest. We must bring him down before her heart stops beating and taste his blood so that she may see the mortal blow to him. Then he must see her head taken before he dies. This shall be the Plan of the Hunt."*

Khubilai said, *"The Horde will have great satisfaction—more than we have ever had from our takings from these humans, even from the occasional Hom for which we have suffered Reduction.*

"We have learned something of the female. She appears to be one of the few people of real honor in her community. I request the honor to personally rip her heart out and to scream the victory scream. I will scream to honor her death."

Temüjin suddenly turned and looked intently at Khubilai, *"Is it certain that the female will come over?"*

Khubilai shrugged, *"The Office of Order will fervently press to banish the Traveler without a care about it as he is but a stranger to them. The female is another matter. She is a source of pride to this community and the daughter of one of its most respected citizens. But the advocate has always prosecuted any accusation with vigor. He is the unworthy sort we do not relish killing for there is no honor to it. The same accusations will apply to both of them and we have never noted any particular sympathy by the prefect for any of the humans who have been prosecuted."*

Temüjin declared, *"This community is so used to banishments that the banished go unnoticed despite the fact that not one has ever returned. It is disgusting. They all deserve death at our hands. Thank the Great One that she prevents us from drinking the blood of all these cowards and weaklings. It would be so easy, but where would be the honor?"*

"The Advocate must press his case to banish both on the same proofs unless the Prefect decides otherwise. She will not. It will save her a trip next year if she can fill her quota from this accusation. Just in case, Ögödei will contact Prefect Acquilina to insure that he will not agree to provide more than three banishments next year. If Prefect Claudia wants to avoid another trip to Montaña barely after she leaves, she will have to banish both of them."

Temüjin began to pace again. *"This is the only plan I will accept. We will have two foes with the hearts of honorable warriors. The Mates Hunt adds a dimension that we have experienced only once before. Only killing Hom could bring any similar satisfaction, but the last one of us who could not resist seeking such satisfaction was reduced together with my brother, Subutai. It could be five centimillia before another opportunity like this will occur. In truth, it could be an eternity, as no one like the Traveler has ever been seen before and may never be see again. To take his mate at the same time—Aargh!"*

"You must decide the takings for this hunt."

Temüjin stopped pacing and, standing stiffly, pronounced, *"Hulagu shall make the opening strike on the female, and Böke shall make the female gut strike. I shall make the opening strike on the Traveler, and Timür shall make the gut strike on the Traveler. The heart of the female, I*

award to you, Khubilai, and you shall also make the first Scream. Ögödei
shall take the heart of the Traveler, and one of the two young who will join us
shall make the Scream for that. Chaghadai shall take the head of the female
after she has seen the heart of the Traveler, and the other young shall make the
Scream for that. Then I shall take the Traveler's head while I look into his
eyes and make the Scream."

"*Then we shall all make the Scream.*"

Temüjin grinned with a mouth full of long white teeth.
"We must give thanks for the Enlightenment."

"May we always be enlightened as is our right in nature."

•

Praetor Publius Palinurus Jules walked into the library in
grand domicile of Censor Mamercus Appius Callisto in Annec and
sat down in great red leather chair. The room was a great oval
lined with ancient books set in shelves reaching to rosewood
molding at the joining of the walls to the ceiling, painted with
fanciful scenes of the ancient past, several meters overhead.
Indirectly lit by lighting hidden behind the molding, the room was
warm with light while the temperature was only a little warmer
than the chilly air outside.

Mamercus entered and sat down across from Publius in a
high-backed chair made of dark brown wicker. Between was a low
table, hewn of a single block of green marble. Despite the chilly
air, they were dressed in white togas as was their custom.

Publius said, "As you predicted, the Traveler, whom I
have also seen called the Visitor in the older records, could not
avoid violating the Order, even for a year. Still it seems
extraordinary that nary a citizen in Montaña seems to have warned
him that his discourses about the way of things and his musings
about the way of life in Montaña might be improved by embracing
some of ways from his own time would certainly be interpreted as
a Slippery Slope Proposition by the Office of Order."

Mamercus replied, "It was inevitable. He is out of his time
and does not realize the way things are. But as for why he was not
warned, you should note that it was a very prominent Montañan
who suggested that he teach a course that could only lead to this
end. Obviously the Montañan leadership, or at least those of them
secretly involved in their Resurrection of Humanity, must suspect
that he is an agent of the Society."

"So they have set him up to see what the Prefect will do?"

"I doubt they much care what she does. If she banishes him, whether he is an agent or not, they will be rid of a stranger who, if innocent, might unwittingly compromise them and, if not, would do so wittingly. On the other hand, if she fails to banish him, they will be certain that he is an agent as he has clearly promulgated forbidden ideas far beyond those that have led to the banishment of so many others in the past. In that event, I have no doubt they will see to it that he meets with an accidental death."

"So whatever happens we will be absolved of bringing about his death."

"Yes, but there will only be one course."

"You have spoken to the Prefect?"

"Not necessary. Claudia has always banished anyone brought before her accused of a Slippery Slope Proposition. She is deathly afraid of change. That is why she has been able to be a prefect in one community or another since she first undertook that occupation. Personally, I find her extraordinarily boring. She has no intellectual interest whatsoever in why some citizens feel compelled to promote ideas that might cause their banishment nor does she feel any kinship with any citizens. A very effective Prefect."

"I agree—a cold fish, perhaps frigid—never once heard of her being with any of us," said Publius dryly, before returning to the issue at hand. "So our bargain with the Deinoc will be fulfilled? "

"Yes."

"What of the prophecy? As you know, I have a great interest in it."

"Publius, are you truly so tired of living? The prophecy, if fulfilled, would lead to our demise. Some are not so willing to have that happen. I am one. Are you?"

"I never thought of that as the only outcome."

"And what did you think?" said Mamercus.

"That he might be the catalyst to bring about a new relationship between the families and the citizens leading all of us to a more interesting future than the static lives we have been living for ages."

"I have known you for, what, almost four centimillia?" said Mamercus, his voice rising as he spoke. "In all that time, I have never realized that you must not truly comprehend why the Second Reduction was necessary. The plain reality is that if the citizens ever gain the upper hand they will destroy us. They will never accept our lifespans when compared to theirs. While the lives we live may seem stale to many of us after so much living, to those who are able to live so long it is enough that we live. But we will not live on if the prophecy is fulfilled. How can you believe otherwise?"

Publius said, "I feel the fool. I had not considered that outcome as inevitable. Why have you never spoken of this to me before?"

"I saw no point to doing so. Has anyone ever appeared before who could have possibly been the Traveler foretold in the prophecy? I once had much of your idealism in my character but time had eroded it by the time you were born. So, besides my not perceiving that mote in your eye with respect to what the citizens would do if they knew our secret, I have always enjoyed your idealism, and will continue to do so for so long as I live to do so."

"Then we are doomed to live as we always have."

"It is that or death, at least with respect to the ancient prophecy about the Traveler, Publius. Commander Ó Conaill appears to be a man of honor and that I admire greatly, but not enough to passively succumb to what he will bring upon us if we let him. We might as well commit suicide and leave Vitas to the disastrous end it was on its way to before the founders of the Society intervened in that time when Vitas was still called Earth. Our lives we live in the service of Vitas for however long, short of forever."

"If he is truly the one foretold, he might prevail," said Publius.

"Against a Deinoc horde? I think not."

•

Early the next morning, Publius Hom sent an encrypted transmission to an old friend, Juku Tremarct.

Juku contacted Panto Onca, a member of a family residing alongside his own, who had rendered an occasional service to him.

•

During the middle of the next night, Panto Vitor met with Tigri Omagua in the jungle a few klicks from the central community in Montaña.

Panto, mindcast, *"Juku has suggested a solution to a problem that has arisen in Montaña."*

"What does he have in mind?"

"He wants you or Carpia to lead a woman named Maria Montero into the jungle where I will kill her. I will be swift and then I will eat her. There will be no trace."

Tigri stiffened. *"What are you talking about? Why should Juku want to kill this woman. I know of her and cannot imagine a reason for killing her."*

Panto said, *"I know nothing about Juku's reasons. I am simply extending a family courtesy to a friend just as I would to my kin, you, for instance. But I am curious to know how you already know of this woman."*

Tigri said, *"I am not at liberty to discuss that, but I will tell you that I believe there may be consequences beyond any you or Juku might imagine if I were to comply with your suggestion. I advise you to tell Juku that he should reconsider his actions. Tell him that Carpia and I have learned of this woman in connection with a special assignment to discreetly observe a man who has recently come to Montaña. I think he will understand what I am saying. You know that I am not squeamish by nature, but I truly have serious reservations about killing this woman. I will speak with Carpia, just in case my perception is incorrect, and meet you here tomorrow night at this time."*

"Very well, Tigri. You are kin to me and Juku is not. And this business does not have much appeal to me. Juku wants a clean, swift killing. I rather like the process to be a little more involved."

•

Mid-morning the next day, Tigri found Carpia in the jungle below Maria's tower. He reported what Panto had said.

Carpia remained silent for a long time. Then she said, *"Tigri, I have known you almost your whole life so you will believe me when I tell you this. If someone has to die, let it be Shon, or someone else, but it is not going to be Maria unless you kill me first."*

Tigri replied. *"Carpia Ana, you have lost your judgment."*

Carpia, not amused, responded, *"I am not the one who has lost my professional judgment. It is everyone else who has lost their judgment if they would sacrifice this fine woman."*

Tigri said, *"I have already told Panto that I would take my direction from you on this matter. He is content to follow my direction even in opposition to Juku. Perhaps I should tell him who sent us to observe Shon."*

"Absolutely not. If the Great One ever learned that we had openly disclosed our relationship with her that would surely be the end of us. We both know that Juku has also served her and I am certain he will deduce the reason behind our reticence without any need to say more. But what if someone else is engaged to kill her behind our backs? The Great One will want us to insure nothing happens she does not want to occur."

"I will ask Panto and his family to watch out for Maria. I suggest you call upon those Psitam relatives you so loath and ask them to do the same. Maria is in less danger now that we know something is afoot."

"You are just so adaptable. Perhaps that's why I love you so, Tigri. I will visit the Great One and learn what we must do. Of one thing I am certain, we have served the Great One far too long for her to have put us in this position. She would have told us were this scheme of her making."

That evening, Tigri met Panto and said, *"Do not harm Maria. Go back to Juku and tell him that it would mean the end of Carpia Ana, and that I cannot permit to happen, even for my dear friend Juku. Instead tell him watch over her and ensure that she comes to no harm. Then say to Juku that we are here under direction."*

Panto could understand code as well as anyone even if he had no idea what it meant.

"I will do your bidding," he replied.

EIGHT

REVELATION

Juku cogitated on what Panto reported to him. He deduced that his friend in Annec did not know that they might be treading on toes that should not be tread upon without further consideration about the consequences such treading might bring. He also knew that he could not explain to Panto the nature of the problem in fulfilling his friend's request so he had told him that he concurred with Tigri's instruction to watch over Maria.

Juku recalled the services he had rendered to the Great One. He'd sometimes wondered whether the Great One was even known to the Hom. His missions for her, rendered over many millennia, had never involved informing any of the Prefects about what he was doing. Mostly, as he surmised Carpia Ana and Tigri Omagua were doing, he had monitored the activities of citizens, residents of various communities on the southern continent, whom he had assumed were suspected of involvement in secret conspiracies against the Order though the Great One had never actually stated that they were. Yet not one of those citizens had ever been banished. It was as if the Great One wanted to know what was afoot in certain communities but without any concern that whatever she learned was important to maintaining the Order, at least as the Society viewed that task.

He tried to remember how the Great One had become known to his family and the others that knew of her. He couldn't, but he could well recall that no one from his or any other family so far as he was aware had ever, even once, alluded to her existence. Why that was so had always been a mystery to him, one that he had found no urge to solve and, for a curious sort as he, that lack, too, was puzzling to him. What he did know was that the Great One insured the safety of the families that could not otherwise prevail against the more aggressive families that might bring harm to them without retribution by the Council.

He sent an encrypted message to his friend telling him only that he was unable to comply with the suggested course of action because he lacked the resources to bring about the desired result.

Then he contacted Luciana on a secure line. When her face appeared on his vidcom, he reported what he had been told without revealing his source and leaving out the part about Maria. *"What you feared has occurred. Shon has run afoul of the Order in Montaña. He is to be charged with an offense punishable by banishment."*

"Into Amaz?" said Luciana.

"Yes."

"The offense?"

"He has taken a position at the local university where he has been expressing ideas that Montaña's Office of Order has interpreted as making a Slippery Slope Proposition."

Expressing no interest in the details of the accusations which she could well imagine, she said, *"How soon could a trial take place?"*

"Three months, give or take a couple of weeks. But not more than two weeks after Montaña's prefect arrives."

"Can I get there first?"

"Perhaps, if you can find a course faster than crossing Pacifica which is how the Prefect for Montaña will travel at this time of year unless she is prepared to make the entire journey through the Walls."

Luciana interrupted, *"She will avoid using the Walls."*

"And why is that? None, besides the Hom, are even permitted to enter them."

Luciana said, *"I really don't know as I have never entered one but I know Hom avoid using them and always have. So she will take the route crossing Pacifica."*

"My lady, I really doubt that there is anything you can do."

"We'll see about that."

"If you are determined to become involved then there is something else you should know. Shon has become involved with a female citizen."

"Why haven't you told me about this?"

"I didn't know until a couple of days ago when a friend in Annec suggested a course of action that two of my friends rejected for a reason that I cannot reveal to you."

"What course of action was suggested and by whom?"

"I regret that I cannot tell you whom. As for the course of action, it was suggested that I arrange for friends of mine to lure the woman into the jungle where she would be killed in a manner that would appear to be a natural demise. But they balked and that was the end of that."

Luciana's heart skipped a beat. *"Why would you attempt to do such a horrible thing?"*

Juku said, *"My friend believes that the woman will be banished with Shon and, while he believes Shon might survive the Predation Agreement without her alongside him, in attempting to save her he will not. It didn't seem so horrible to kill her in a less painful way than she would inevitably suffer in Amaz. He seemed very focused on Shon's survival. Why, he didn't say."*

"I see. Can we do anything to stop this?"

"I believe this involves intrigue within the Council with your family's active involvement. Look at the circumstances. The friend who requested my intervention is Hom. The accusation against Shon has been made at a time that must, at the very least, be inconvenient to the Prefect, yet it was still made without any consideration for the inconveniences with which it will present her. Shon was settled in Montaña, not a place I would choose to settle a man from the past who arrived on an amazing starship having traveled via the stars from a past beyond even the founding of the Society.

"What is going on and why I cannot guess. Yet I fear the risks are far too great for anyone outside the Hom to become intimately involved. You are Hom and may be able to avoid the consequences those not Hom will not. Even so, you may well find yourself in grave danger. I really don't see how your intervention can do anything to affect the outcome. But if you are determined to try, you must arrive by the time the prefect does or you will bring nothing but personal risk to yourself."

"Then I must hurry."

•

Carpia flew to the Wall and waited. Sometimes the Great One appeared and sometimes she didn't. She waited. Near sunset the day after she arrived the Wall's appearance changed and she stood before the Great One.

"You have news?" said the shimmering image.

"Yes." And Carpia related what had transpired.

The Great One spoke immediately as if she anticipated what she heard. "You will approach the Traveler at a time when you can speak without detection by others and you will tell him of the Society, the real Society."

"Great One, such a communication is forbidden."

"Do not concern yourself with what is forbidden. Concern yourself with what I tell you to do. Carpia, your mission is of greater importance than anything I have ever tasked you with before. And what you will do will set a new course for Vitas."

•

Tigri Omagua and Carpia Ana met with Panto Onca in the jungle outside Montaña two hours past midnight the next day.

Carpia said, *"What have you heard?"*

Panto replied, *"Juku says his friend, Luciana, a very young Hom, intends to arrive before the Moon is full twice more."*

"To what end?" said Carpia.

"Juku didn't say. So what did you learn from the Great One?"

"I fear that what I learned might bring harm to you."

"We have been together for a long time, Carpia."

"Very well. We are going to break the Codicil."

"Ooh, that sounds exciting! Tell me more!"

•

On preparation for her passage to Montaña, Prefect Claudia reviewed the proofs Advocate Estaban had sent to her. She judged the proofs he proffered worthless anywhere she'd ever been prefect, excepting only Montaña and Boca Amassona. As this matter would be handled in Montaña she could banish him without any further refinement so long as she withheld her judgment for a few days to show due deliberation.

This notion of due deliberation as a way of showing that justice had been done was ancient, dating back to Hammurabi, an ancient ruler whose existence was recorded in the records available to the citizen communities. Hammurabi had instructed his judges that, while whatever they ruled should be in accordance with his Code, it was as important, if not more so, that they be perceived to have deliberated on the matter after the presentations of the parties at trial had been completed, and, to that end, they should withhold judgment for a judicious period before ruling, even if their judgment was clear to them immediately. Even

though such deliberations were sometimes nothing more than a
sham, such rulings were almost always better accepted than
quicker rulings, even if the quicker rulings were more just.

She also noticed that the proofs contained particularly
egregious deficiencies in the case against Maria Monterro. Yet she
needed the girl banished to fill the quota.

Before embarking on the ship which would take her across
Pacifica to Porto Guayaquil, she contacted the citizen in charge of
Society House in Montaña and ordered to her to find Joseph
Estaban and to bring him to the Society House. When he arrived
he was taken to a room where a vidcom connected him to her.
She informed him that the proofs against Maria Monterro needed
bolstering. Estaban argued that she was simply a citizen under the
influence of this ancient interloper and there was little more that
he could proffer.

The Prefect looked coldly into the vidcom, "Tell me,
Señor Estaban, could you possibly have a bias in this case?
Perhaps because her father is Raul Monterro?" A sudden thought
entered her mind and she continued in a slow, low voice, "Or
could there be another reason? Matters are quite far along and it
would be a grievous error for you to fail to disclose anything that
might influence your prosecution of anyone who has propounded
Slippery Slope Propositions. But I will overlook it if you will
simply make a full disclosure now."

Joseph looked coolly into the camera and said, "Of course,
I have no personal bias, Prefect. But you are correct in surmising
that I have a concern about banishing the daughter of so high a
citizen as Raul Monterro without pristine proofs. The proofs I
present in her case must be beyond reproach, yet I have the
doubts I have expressed to you. You, of course, are the final judge
of those proofs."

Claudia abruptly terminated the connection. She trusted
such abrupt conduct would convey the consequences of failure to
the advocate.

•

On the day Claudia was to depart, she heard a knock on
the door.

When she opened the door, she was surprised to see
Luciana, the daughter of two of the most distinguished members

of the Council, and someone who had never even spoken to her before, except perhaps in passing at one of the frequent social gatherings in Annec. She granted her entrance and offered her coffee as they exchanged pleasantries.

Finally, Claudia said, "I regret that I am a bit pressed for time as I must depart for my prefecture today."

"I know. The Council has instructed me to join you on your journey."

Claudia could barely contain her surprise and paused a moment to consider her response. "Isn't that a bit unusual?" Hom never appeared in a community in the company of another Hom for several reasons, mostly connected with maintaining a certain mystical presence among the citizens.

"Yes. It was a surprise to me, too. The Council has its reasons I suppose, though I was not informed of what they are."

"Did the Council deign to say what your instructions are?"

Luciana responded casually, "I am to witness the trial of certain citizens who are to be prosecuted for promulgating a Slippery Slope Proposition, And to counsel you in your deliberations."

"Really? Has the Council lost confidence in my judgment?" Claudia replied in a brittle tone.

"I am sure that is not the case at all. One of the accused is of particular interest to the Council and they apparently want two of us to insure that the accusations are particularly well considered."

Claudia was well aware that one of the accused was the man from the past.

"Did the Council give you any direction in what should be considered?" said Claudia.

"None at all."

Unsatisfied, Claudia shrugged and said, "Very well. I was leaving today. Does that present a problem?"

"Not at all. The sooner we go, the sooner we return."

Claudia smiled. That was precisely her own view.

•

Temüjin, mindcast, *"How goes the Plan?"*

Khubilai replied, *"All is ready. Our consuls have obtained the agreement of Prefect Acquilina for Boca Amassona to provide three banishments. Acquilina has informed Prefect Claudia who will undoubtedly provide the remaining two banishments we desire. However, there has been a new development. We have learned that another Hom has joined the Prefect on her way to Montaña."*

Temüjin leaned his heavy head toward Khubilai. *"For what purpose would two Hom come?"*

"There have been rumors in Annec that this Hom, Luciana, who was the one who first met the Traveler, may have become personally involved with him during his transit to Vitas. Perhaps she seeks to save him. If she succeeds, we are betrayed. But if not, and she were not Hom, would it not be the glory of eternity to take the Traveler with both of his women?"

"If she is Hom, it would be the glory of eternity. We must insure that she does not succeed. Then, if she has the nerve to come over—" Temüjin paused for a moment. *"Plan for that possibility. We will pretend that we thought she was just another banished citizen."*

Khubilai replied, *"The Council may not believe us. Her father is Octavius Gaius Bellatrix Augustus."*

Temüjin responded, *"Damn the Council! It is always trying to thwart our rights, the very rights they claim to hold so dear. Are we not entitled to our normal life experience the same as all others? Why are we the only family situated on Vitas thousands of klicks from our natural homeland? Stuck in this insufferable jungle instead of our natural domain where we could roam without the need to cover ourselves in mud and dust to hide our red hides to hunt our prey."*

Khubilai said, *"You will recall that the Society maintains our natural domain cannot support our needs."*

Temüjin leapt toward Khubilai who withdrew a few meters to make way for Temüjin's landing where he was formerly standing. *"And so the Tyrans would have the same problem but for the Society conveniently arranging for them to have their bison herds to prey upon. Why must we be content to hunt jungle animals that are barely edible? The Society could have populated the land of the Mongols with those beasts and we would have all the food we could ever want. But, no, they say that's not the natural domain of those beasts. Well, Amaz is not the natural domain of the Deinoc. Yet here we are."*

Khubilai had heard Temüjin's tirade on this subject a thousand times. He attempted to get back to the reason for his visit. *"Do you think we should risk reduction to take the Hom mate, given who she is?"*

"Of course we should. To kill the Traveler with both of his mates is worth the risk. Besides, we will be in our territory. At least we have our right to our natural existence here. Still, you must insure that no one will see her death. Then there will be no proofs to proffer before the Council. It will be satisfying to look into her eyes as she sees that she cannot save him as she dies herself. This will be the greatest hunt in our family's history. And we will accomplish it without smearing ourselves in mud because we won't need mud to hide ourselves from them. They are just humans who never pay attention to anything beyond themselves, so sure they are immune to the dangers of other families that they won't even notice our red skins as we surge upon them from the jungle."

Khubilai said, *"Yes, it will indeed be most satisfying. How shall you order the takings of the Hom?"*

"I will take her head after I take the Traveler's." Temüjin peered into Khubilai eyes and said, *"You may choose who will make the gut strike and the heart. Let one of the young take the heart, but you must be certain that he is skilled enough to do it just before I kill the Traveler or I will kill him afterward. Make that clear so he will not fail."*

•

The university took a curriculum break in the middle of the term. Shon and Maria caught the train to Huascarán and took up residence in Raul's house there for a few days. The deep snow had begun to recede up the mountain and the temperature was noticeably warmer than it had been during their last visit. Still each dawn came with the village dusted in a white powder which quickly evaporated under the morning sun. The afternoons were warm in the sun, cool in the shade. The nights, filled with millions of twinkling stars, were crisp, yet dry, so that one did not feel the chill of the cold night air.

Early in the morning after they arrived, they set off for the mountain lake fed by the waterfall. After a swim to the rock they spent a few hours lying beside each other, warmed by the sun above and occasionally chilled by forest breezes, indulging their natural inclinations. They left the rock and swam back to the shore in the calm water, icy-cold from the melting snow, dressed, and set off for the village.

Carpia saw her opportunity to violate the Codicil when Shon set off on one last run up the hill upland from the lake while Maria continued on to the village. It was the same hill Shon had used to demonstrate his speed to Maria so Carpia knew he would get to the top very quickly.

Shon made it to the top of the hill in less than three minutes.

Surprised to see a bright green parrot perched on a branch in a tree beside where he was standing, he remembered something from his youth and said, "Polly want a cracker?"

"Anyone who would say that to a parrot is an idiot."

Shon was astounded. The bird could talk! He peered at the bird very closely, looking for a transmission device.

"What are you looking at? Have you never seen a talking parrot before?"

Shon was confused about how this bird was talking in an apparently sentient way. He could see the bird's beak moving in sync with the words she seemed to be emitting. Yet the bird had just said 'What are you looking at?' Shon thought, *Definitely a Maria expression. Is Maria playing a prank on me?*

The parrot spoke again, saying, "Can you talk? Say something. How about repeating 'Polly want a cracker'? Listen up, Shon. Maria's life is at stake. Time is short. Have I got your attention?"

Shon's mind began to spin. He looked around.

Carpia said, "Stop looking about and look at me. Maria will soon be dead if I fail to talk to you as I am doing. But you must listen. Are you prepared to listen?"

Shon stared at the parrot for a moment, drew a breath, and finally said, "I am prepared to listen. I admit it looks like you're talking. I hope you will not be offended that such a notion seems improbable to me."

"Well, no one else is talking to you. So listen to me. Tonight you must tell Maria that you intend to get an early morning workout—"

Shon, mystified, interrupted, "Pardon me, how do you know my workout schedule? What's going on here?"

"I know your schedule because I have been monitoring you since you visited Huascarán. My name is Carpia Ana. Never call me Polly again or I'll bite off one of your fingers."

Shon was beginning to believe the bird really was doing the talking.

"Tomorrow morning you must come to this spot. There are places closer to the village, but the risk of discovery is too great. If anyone learns what I will tell you tomorrow, they will die. So you must say nothing to Maria. But her life is at stake. I will tell you about the duality of the Society. Will you come tomorrow?"

"What is this about Maria's life being at stake?"

"She is in great danger as are you. I am here because I have come to love her."

"I love her, too, but how do you know her?"

Carpia said, "All you need to know is that I do. And I believe you do love her. And I know she loves you. But your destiny may not be your own to choose, however it may seem otherwise to you. I have vowed that Maria shall not die because of her relationship with you. You may die, I may die, others may die, but Maria is not going to die if I can help it. And I need your assistance to keep that from happening."

Shon said, "I will be here tomorrow morning."

•

Shon ran back down the hill as fast as he'd ever run and made it back to the lake in under two minutes. As he approached the lake he saw Maria. He came to her and said, "Have you got a talking parrot I don't know about?"

She said, "What are you talking about?"

"Nothing. Just a comment from outer space."

"It sounded like it."

"Weird things come out of my mouth sometimes. Forget about it. Come on, let's go back to the village."

And they returned to the village without revisiting his outburst.

•

Sean left before midnight for his apartment as he had explained to Maria that he needed to sleep alone because of dreams from his past. The next morning, Shon arose, dressed, and set off for the hill beyond the pond. He found Carpia on the same branch where he'd encountered her the day before.

The bird squawked, "Good morning."

"Good morning. Shall I call you Carpia Ana?"

"Today, yes. Afterwards never call me anything again. I'm just a dumb parrot."

"Hardly, but okay. You said you would tell me about the duality of the Society and about the danger to us."

Carpia squawked, "And so I shall. Citizens believe the Society is comprised of, or at least dominated by, female humans they suspect are different from themselves though they do not imagine how different. They probably suspect that there are male members of the Society but they never come into contact with them. But the citizens have not the slightest awareness that there are non-human sentient beings on Vitas, such as the Cetaceans or parrots like me or that the Society includes such beings."

Shon said, "How did such beings come to be?"

Carpia squawked, "After you left Earth, genetic engineering became extremely sophisticated. Humankind began to use it to save species from extinction. With the huge reduction in population, the enormous computer capabilities that existed at that time were turned to the task of calculating DNA permutations until any extinct species could, with a very close approximation, be reproduced. It was called regeneration. In a span of only a few hundred years, thirty-five hundred extinct species were regenerated. The Expansion continued for another thousand years during which tens of thousands of species were regenerated. At first they saved some species that were near extinction by making minor genetic adjustments that increased their climatic adaptability, such as mine. Then they decided extinct species had a right to life as much as those fortunate enough to have been saved before extinction. This was the beginning of the Expansion."

Shon noticed that, while the bird's tone varied little as she spoke, her cadence varied and that the faster it became the more animated she was, her head bobbing and her wings stretching.

Carpia continued, "This incredible success led to a philosophical debate within the Society which in that era was a secret society, composed only of the Hom, about whether to enhance some species in the same way that they themselves had been enhanced.

"With the power to do it and a willingness to overcome caution, the Hom began to enhance the lifespans and add or enhance the emotions and intelligence of certain species they had been tampering with until one hundred and thirteen species were endowed with indeterminate lifespans, emotions and sentient intelligence equivalent to the Hom. This period was called the Enlightenment.

"The Enlightenment changed the Society. All sentient beings with indeterminate lifespans were made members of the Society of Species, the true name for the Society of Life, known only to its members. All humans are intelligent and most have lifespans of around four hundred years, but some, the Hom, have indeterminate lifespans. You may already know this about the Hom."

Shon nodded.

Carpia squawked on. "It was determined that any life possessed of sentient intelligence, emotions, and indeterminate lifespans were equal to that of the Hom, however they were endowed, whether by nature or enlightened genetics so that, for example, a dinosaur that obtained its emotional capacity from a genetic engineered limbic brain was equally entitled to membership in the Society as any human who was born with a limbic brain."

Carpia flitted over to another branch closer to Shon.

"What brought the Expansion and Enlightenment to an abrupt end was the dinosaurian expansion and subsequent enlightenment of a few of those species, some large carnivores and herbivores which seemed to fascinate the Hom.

"The computers generated DNA sequences based upon what was known about dinosaurs, birds and reptiles. They reverse engineered our avian DNA, processed reptilian DNA forward, and modulated the results by comparing the creatures they generated with the fossil remains of the dinosaurs. They added larger neocortices and mammalian limbic brains. In time they got the results they sought. They created dinosaurians that never existed that were as intelligent as the Hom and possessed of complex emotions.

"As it turned out, it was madness to bring back these species, or at least some of them, with emotional capacity. The dinosaurians simply possessed entirely different mentalities more suited for coping with an environment filled with greater constant, daily life-threatening challenges than those faced by the creatures that evolved after them. Life for them was more like the challenges fish in the seas face than life experienced by those living on land for at least the past several million years. Emotions increased the intensity of reactions in some species, like the Allo, and they became emotional paranoiac maniacs.

"The climate of Vitas had warmed even more than in your time and the dinosaurians were situated in zoogeographical regions which were similar to the conditions that existed in the Cretaceous Period. The huge walls, called Walls by both the Society and the communities, that had been constructed over thousands of years to divide the planet into communities while also providing energy to the communities and a hidden means of transit for the Hom, were extended during the Expansion to enclose these regions to keep their inhabitants from destroying everyone else. One of those regions, situated to the east of Montaña, Amaz, is inhabited by the Deinoc which were patterned on the Deinonychus. They are very intelligent, but also very ferocious.

"Among the families there is an agreement that transcends the Order, though it is compatible with it. Called the Codicil, it lays down certain additional principles we must follow as members of the Society. One of those principles is that we cannot kill another member of the Society without the consequence of retribution even to the extent of annihilating the entire family of the violator if the transgression involves multiple deaths, but that principle does not extend to those who are not members of the Society."

Carpia flitted onto a branch just above Shon's head and slowed her speaking cadence and with it her animated wing flapping. "I am telling you this because I fear Maria and you are going to be banished into Amaz where the Deinoc will hunt you down."

"Why do you believe we will be banished?"

"The ideas that you and Maria have been propounding at the university have elements of what are known as Slippery Slope Propositions, ideas that the Council believes can lead to the erosion and destruction of the Order. The ideas you have been expressing in your university course with Maria have been declared heresy by Montaña's Office of Order to the prefect responsible for Montaña. The prefect of Montaña, a Hom, is on her way here to conduct a trial that will lead to your banishment and, I fear, Maria's."

"Why haven't I heard anything about this?" said Shon.

"I truly do not know why no Montañan has warned you about what your teachings could bring down upon you. Although they know nothing of the Deinoc, they do know no one banished to Amaz ever returns and they know what brings banishment is propounding a Slippery Slope Proposition.

"I was sent here to observe you, but I have found myself attracted to Maria, perhaps because she is a female, as am I. She is a remarkable creature. I wish I could talk to her and tell her who and what I am. But if I did, the Society would kill her. So you must never tell her about me or about anything I have told you. She cannot escape the Society's grasp. No one can. The Society is comprised of one hundred and fourteen different families of different shapes and sizes, each having ten thousand members, totaling one million one hundred and forty thousand members compared to the two hundred citizen communities totaling twenty million humans. Given the differences in the species and the fact that almost all of the Society's members are unknown to the citizen communities, the Society could easily annihilate all of the citizen communities within a fortnight."

"What does being hunted down by the Deinoc mean?" said Shon.

"Each family has different expectations for a natural life experience and each has a right to pursue their natural life experience subject to the limitations of the Order and the Codicil."

Shon said, "I was told of this philosophy as it pertains to the Order by those you call the Hom. It doesn't seem much different than the way things were in my time. People have a right to eat fish since it is something people normally do, with the caveat that it is also considered normal to not eat an endangered fish. To eat an endangered fish would lead to its extinction and, therefore, no one has a right to kill or eat one."

Carpia responded, "So if you in your time liked to hunt a deer by taking it down alive and ripping it apart even before it had died you could so long as it wasn't endangered?"

"That would be a rather barbaric way to kill a deer but I grant you that one could think of the way we killed some game as like that, yes. What is your point?"

"The Deinoc have been killing a species that is not endangered and whose victims are not members of the Society for almost eight centimillia." She paused. "Their prey are the banished citizens of Montaña and Boca Amassona. People like Maria."

Shon shuddered. "Why did your Council every agree to such an unspeakable abomination?"

"That is a story too long to tell now but, suffice it to say, they asserted their right to experience their natural existence. They argued that citizens, humans without indeterminate lifespans, are not in the Society and should be regarded as prey for them no different than cattle or fish are to the Hom.

"Fearful that the Society might not be able to destroy the Deinoc, the Council acceded to their demand and consented in return for the Deinoc's agreement to never take prey within the boundaries of any citizen community if the Society provided prey on a limited basis, just a total of five citizens per annum, from the communities adjoining their domain in Amaz. The Council decided that such a small number would present a minimal impact on the communities involved. The citizens taken from Montaña and Boca Amassona are sent to a place in Amaz where what the Deinoc call a hunt takes place. It was the price paid to make peace. The agreement is called the Predation Agreement."

Shon said in a quiet voice, "How are the citizens chosen?"

"The prefects of Montaña and Boca Amassona impose banishment on citizens charged with accusations by the Offices of Order in those communities. Regulatory authorities can always find violators to prosecute if only to justify their existence. The prefects simply convict the citizens their Offices of Order accuse of promoting a Slippery Slope Proposition, a charge so subjective that a prefect can inscrutably convict her quota with no suspicion that she has any ulterior motive other than preserving the Order."

"Why don't the citizens protest?" said Shon.

"No citizen knows of the Predation Agreement or anything about any members of the Society other than the female Hom whom they perceive to be priestesses of the holy order that enforces the Order."

"How—how, if Maria was banished by herself as others from her community have been in the past, would she die?"

"Shon, it is better not to—"

"Carpia, before I was a starship commander, I was a warrior. I need to know exactly what will happen to her."

"Very well then, this is what will happen. After Maria is sent over the Wall into Amaz not far from where the Wall crosses Amassona, she is stalked. She sees nothing, but she hears low rustling sounds and moves away from those sounds.

"The Deinoc savor the whole process as only a few of them can experience it a few times a year when what they all really want is to experience it every day. They select their participants for the hunt from among the most senior in the family and form a war party called a horde. They appoint stalkers from the more junior members of their family to give them a chance to get a taste of what may come their way someday. It was their horde approach to warfare that enabled them to take down more Allo than the rest of the Society combined while losing far fewer of their own than most of the rest of us.

"Maria begins to find food and drink stashed here and there. She begins to believe that someone is trying to help her. This happens even though she, like everyone else in Montaña, suspects that banishment is a death sentence knowing that no one banished has ever returned. But, in the oppressive dark jungle, she needs hope. She soon begins to believe that perhaps the reason no one comes back is that they find something better. She comes to a worn path. Passage is easy. Further into the jungle she comes upon a cabin. The cabin is comfortably furnished. She finds food and clothing. Nearby is a lake with a stream running through it. The lake is large enough to keep the huge trees and other plants from covering the sky.

"She decides that this will be a good place to stay for the time being. Perhaps the owner will come. Perhaps she can even stay until her banishment is over.

"She gravitates to the lake for light and food. There are no large fish or crocodilia to present any danger—the Deinoc have seen to that. There are edible fish she can catch with the fishing pole and the net she finds in the cabin.

"Soon she begins swimming in the lake, enjoying a cool respite from the oppressive heat and humidity.

"One day—it could be a week, a month, even longer—she takes a swim late in the day, when a bright moon will be coming out on a clear evening. When she returns to shore, she finds her clothes missing. Her skin begins to crawl.

"She quickly returns to the cabin. She finds the door has been secured by a new lock and the windows are shuttered from the inside.

"Seeing the lock tells her what she already suspects. The owner has returned. She calls out. Perhaps he thinks she is an intruder. She wants to tell him that she is a friend.

"But she is concerned. Her clothes were taken, not a friendly act. She is now standing naked by the owner's house. She walks around the house and finds two weapons, a long very sharp knife with a curve in the blade wider towards the point than at the hilt. The cutting edge is not smooth but deeply serrated. A slashing weapon. And there is a light spear, more like a lance. Both it and the knife are completely black. Stealth weapons.

"She hears noise in the underbrush. She seizes the weapons. She begins to sweat.

"She hears a scream from hell. The hunt has begun.

"The Deinoc are in the jungle. She sees nothing. They have taken her clothes. They want no clothes on her to prevent them from seeing every muscles twitch, every drop of perspiration glisten, every spasm of death when it comes.

"She begins to notice movement in the brush between her and the lake. The Deinoc party screams and rushes at her through the bushes. Yet they do not leave cover. The motion of the bushes and the rustling noise send her running into the jungle.

"She has begun the first run to her death. The Deinoc travel beside her in the growing darkness, unseen. She runs blindly until she can run no more. She comes upon another opening in the jungle—another lake. She can see. The stars are out. The moon is shining. The Deinoc always hunt in good weather. They do not want rain to spoil the hunt.

"They choose the evening for the hunt for that reason and because people are more afraid of what they can't see than what they can. She will not see them until the end.

"She rests and, exhausted, falls asleep. After she has rested for around an hour, they begin the final prelude to the kill.

"A Deinoc enters her area, and makes small noises until she awakens. She sees him standing before her, within reach. He screams a deathly screech. She screams and grabs for the spear. He disappears in the woods. She rises and runs to an opening in the jungle where there is enough light so that she can see them.

"The Deinoc horde screams as one. She bolts. They control her direction by noisy movement and more screams.

"She enters an opening. It is a boulder field. The moon is clear above. She makes her way through the field until she find a glade covered with small ferns and moss.

"The hunters enter the glade. They are silent. She sees them and screams, terrified. They approach from four sides. In desperation, she slashes at them. They savor her fear, the smell of it; the vapors from her sweat. She is heaving her last breaths of life.

"There is a frozen moment. The Deinoc appointed for the purpose rushes up to her side. As she whirls to slash at him, he slashes her belly open from her sternum to pelvis. Her organs spill out. She staggers. Instantly another streaks forward to split her chest open with one slash, while another rushes in ripping the opening wide, while the fourth reaches into her opened chest and grips the vessels coming from her heart and, uttering a terrible scream, tears her heart from her body. This has happened so fast that she is still alive as she falls to the ground.

"The fifth and final Deinoc comes forward to observe her final moment. When he sees her eyes glaze, he decapitates her. They scream and scream in an ecstasy so intense that the observers fled the scene in abject terror of the hunt they had witnessed, even though they were of the Society and in no danger. One witness told me that he could never return to Amaz again."

Shon said nothing for a while. "I find it difficult to believe this Order your Society observes allows such barbarity."

"Shon, when the Hom hunt an animal the reality to that animal is the same. It is true the Deinoc relish the act of killing like no one else, but to the victim, the experience is no different than that any other hunter brings to those it preys upon. Besides their fear of the Deinoc, that is why the Hom has done nothing about this—it would mean changing the way life really is. All life kills life. The only difference is that the Deinoc take sentient beings."

"How do you know all this?"

"About the history of the Enlightenment, I was informed by a being that watches over my family and families like mine that have little power among the families of the Society. We call her the Great One. About what I know of the hunt, I was sent a long time ago by the Great One to observe the hunt of a female citizen. It was the most horrible experience of my life. I cannot bear to see that happen to Maria."

"That is not going to happen to Maria," said Shon.

"Then go now. I will signal you when I need to speak with you again."

Shon said, "Carpia Ana, two questions. The first is, 'Did this Great One you spoke of send you?'"

"I cannot answer that question."

"You just did. My second question—Not all of the families you describe can possibly communicate verbally as you do. So how do they?"

"By mindcast."

"Telepathy?"

"No, by energy waves. Mineral deposits like those possessed by the Hom, genetically developed into our brains during our enlightenment, are able to transmit energy waves that can be picked up by others, not really much different than the communications devices that work wirelessly. It is called mindcast. Each family has its own wavelength. And there is a common wavelength for speaking between families."

Shon had a sudden insight and said, "Carpia Ana, attempt to talk to me that way."

He heard a buzz in his head. He suppressed his surprise in learning that the buzz he had feared was a problem with his mind might be the greatest gift he could have on this ever stranger world. He said, "Are you trying?"

"Yes," said Carpia.

"I guess only those in the Society can hear each other."

"We must return to the village now," said Carpia. He watched her as she flew off toward the village.

•

Shon ran back to the village, his mind spinning. He thought, *Some humans engineered their next step up the evolutionary ladder but elected to pass that genetic benefit on only to a very small portion of humanity who became the Hom. Then certain species were regenerated to such a degree that these creatures are now as intelligent and long-lived as the Hom themselves and have been granted all of humankind's rights. The Hom have even gone so far as to subject that part of their own species that are not endowed as they are to the same food chain as the lower forms of life. In the same way humans can hunt and kill an elk or a duck or slaughter a cow or a sheep, the Deinoc can hunt and kill a human so long as that human is not a Hom.*

The original intentions of the Hom to bring a stable ecology and equal rights to every living species has become an abomination so that only certain living species have these rights and human citizens aren't among them; they are subject to death by predation by those who are. This is what humankind has done since its very beginning. The only distinction I can make for why the Deinoc should not be able to kill humans is that humans are sentient. A deer, a cow, a fish, all human prey are dumb brutes. Does it really all come down to raw power, the mighty over the weak? Humans can kill the deer with impunity because the deer can't do anything about it. The Codicil of the Society works for its members because its members have agreed to a separate bundle of rights that protects them from harm from the other members.

It's a code enforced by persuasion and brutal force if violated—the Order will be maintained, one way or the other. Pure Darwinian reality.

Killing five humans a year out of twenty million might seem reasonable when balanced against the possibility that the Deinoc can kill thousands, even millions, perhaps everyone. But, if the Deinoc have been killing five humans a year for eight hundred millennia, that amounts to over four million humans.

As he sped toward the village at an ever faster pace in his anger over what he realized was about to happen, he allowed the influence of the Magan implant to infuse his thoughts. Considerations about whether he had a right to make a choice to save one and cause the death of others receded as the mentality of the Magan began to emerge and take hold of his deepest instincts. He thought, *It is really quite ironic that I might well be able to trump the Deinoc in primordial conduct in a way they can never imagine.*

•

    Shon and Maria returned to Montaña two days later to prepare for the second half of their course at the university. Shon focused on his new mission and thought, *I may have allies I could never have imagined suspected and I have two advantages no one knows about, not even Carpia—my Magan implant and the fact that I can hear mindcast. Now I need to learn how to comprehend what I'm hearing.*

PART II – VITAN JUSTICE

Injustice anywhere is a threat to justice everywhere.
Martin Luther King Jr.

The Hom have indeterminate lifespans. They die by accidental events, not because their genetic biological clock turns off a critical part of what is necessary for them to continue to live.

Hom older than a millennia live careful lives, avoiding risk, to such an extent that one's chance of dying in any one-thousand-year period is about one in a hundred. About one hundred and seventy five of the Hom living today are the grandchildren of the original Hom. The rest are younger ranging from those very few who are several centimillia old to those very few who are almost newborn. The median lifespan of the Hom is around seven decamillia.

Some Hom value living life more than living longer but they die long before those who value living longer more than living life. The Hom never look old physically, but the old ones have a look about them that sets them apart—in their eyes and in the way they move.

Because a citizen takes far more risks that the Hom, a citizen's chance of dying accidentally in any given year is about one in six thousand. But even if a citizen took no greater risks than the Hom a citizen would still die of old age within four hundred years from birth, the approximate genetic limit to a citizen's life. Ninety-three percent of all citizens live to three hundred and seventy-five years. After that, biological functions deteriorate rapidly.

The History of Vitas as recorded in a file stored in the GenLib Repository accessible only by the Librarian

ONE

SLIPPERY SLOPE

A few days after his visit with Carpia in the jungle, Shon rose in the early morning and ran a few dozen klicks into the jungle. When he stopped to rest, Carpia flew down and landed on a nearby branch.

Speaking in her parrot voice, she said, "What will you do?"

Shon said, "I've been trying to come to grips with what you have told me about the Society. That other species have become sentient doesn't disturb me. What disturbs me is that, besides the Hom, every human has been denied the opportunity to experience the pleasures contact between Maria and those like you could bring. That is wrong."

"I cannot disagree," said Carpia.

"The difference in lifespans between the citizens and those in the Society is unsettling," said Shon. "I do not know my own potential lifespan, but I am sure that the casual risks I take every day would keep me from ever living the hundreds of thousands of years you say some of the Society live even if my genetic potential is the same.

"The natural evolution of humankind seems to have come to an end. From what you have told me, the Hom number only ten thousand with just a few generations having passed over the past nearly million years. How could any favorable mutations ever reach the overall population, even if these two humankind interbred, with such long-lived generations combined with such a small population?

"I cannot say that my time was better because we killed and were killed at prodigious rates. But something is clearly wrong with some of my kind allowing others of my kind to be preyed upon without those preyed upon having any awareness that they are and are so because their kin allow it. I am going to do whatever it takes to protect Maria regardless of its impact on the order of things."

Shon paused for a moment and wiped his hand across his brow. "Carpia Ana, there is something I would like to tell you that might become helpful assuming you share my objective. Will you keep it a secret between us?"

"I will keep your secret."

"I have an assortment of enhancements to my senses and mental capabilities, some genetic and some not. On the Moon and later on Vitas, on several occasions I heard a buzzing in my head. Until you told me about mindcast I had feared the buzzing was a problem with some non-genetic part of me."

Carpia said, "You told me that you could not hear a word when I tried to mindcast to you."

"That was true. I did not hear a word, but I heard a buzz. Mindcast must be very close to the ship's frequency."

"You didn't trust me to tell me that?"

"Should I have? You told me that you were directed by someone you call the Great One about whom I know nothing at all. Perhaps she is a Hom agent. I considered that but I concluded that, even if she was, telling me what you did has provided me the opportunity to do something about what is planned for us. If that is her plan for whatever reason she has or the Hom have, I am still better off knowing what I know now. So that is why I now tell you of it." Shon shrugged. "That encounter caused something to occur to me. I now believe that a buzzing I heard in my head when I was traveling on Amassona through Amaz was the Deinoc mindcast, though what I heard seemed more emotion than language. If I could listen to their language, I may be able to decipher their linguistics. Being able to hear what they say without their knowing it may be advantageous."

"I have a very good Therizi friend who may be able to help you learn their language. They loath the carnivorous Deinoc."

"Then let us meet in the jungle, first just you and me until I can understand your mindcast, then bring on your Therizi friend and we'll see if I can learn the language of dinosaurs."

•

The ship carrying Prefect Claudia and Luciana docked at Porto Guayaquil to the day six weeks after they had departed from Annec. Located on Chocó Bay, Porto Guayaquil was the seaport and rail connection that handled imports and exports for the western portion of the southern continent. The next train to Montaña was scheduled to depart in two days. They took two rooms at the Valencia, a small hotel established to serve the seamen who served on the ships traveling to Porto Guayaquil, not a place Luciana would have selected—it looked like a place where something bad might happen if one came too often. She wondered whether she had begun to think like the ancient Hom who never did anything that might present a risk. She wondered about Claudia who seemed familiar with this place; how had she lived so long taking such risks? Perhaps she imagined risks that didn't exist—or perhaps Claudia had been very lucky so far. Still Luciana remained in her room just in case the latter was the truth.

Claudia went downstairs to the bar and found a seaman for the night. The man she found was strong and intelligent. His name was Mickey MacInnes. He told her that he had spent his life as a sailor. His first sixty years had been spent on ships plying Atlantica between the coastal ports on the continents it touched and then for the past hundred years in service on the great freighters that traversed Pacifica.

Claudia sought out such men when she traveled. They were not part of any citizen community and so were safe for her to spend a night or two in their company. Their strength and masculine stolidity appealed to her physically, yet they also attracted her at a more emotional level—they seemed self-assured, yet mostly they were lonely men in search of relationships they sensed in an unspoken way they could not sustain. Men much like her.

•

Shon and Maria were well into the second half of their course. Shon had set himself into a routine for living in Montaña. He spent his early mornings working out in the jungle, pressing his limits bounded by the efforts of his ever present Magan implant which was always ready to intrude if he gave it an opportunity. Despite his determination to use it to prepare for what he could now clearly see was coming, he found that he was not so willing to let it have its way, even if that was what it might take to accomplish his goal. So he pushed the limits trying to get the benefits it offered without paying the price it was trying to extract.

As he ran through the jungle working out, Carpia flew alongside and spoke to him in her mindcast. At first, he only heard a buzz, then gradually he found order in the buzz until they no longer spoke aloud.

His days, when he wasn't doing his course with Maria, were spent going to the library to try to understand this world and to fill in the gap from his departure to his arrival—he found himself amused on occasion when reviewing the ancient history which did not conform to what he knew was reality and he assumed that the passage of time even when history is recorded distorted the past.

He often spent the evenings with his friend, Rolando, usually playing chess, but often discussing their views on this new world and his old one.

He generally passed the late evenings with Maria at her apartment always leaving for his apartment to sleep, arising early the next mornings to begin it all over again.

•

Shon was standing at the podium before a packed audience in a small auditorium in a subbasement at the University.

In response to a query from one of the attendees, Shon said, "My perspective today is entirely different from most other people in my time. I was supposed to represent no nation, as we thought of your concept of a community in my time, even though my masters likely had other ideas. But, whatever they thought, the reality was that they would all be dead long before I returned and the nations they represented might well have changed several times by the time I returned. So I felt that I was going to the stars for humanity.

"No one expected to see me again. Even though my mission might well aid Earth in the long run, it touched no large body of sentiment in my fellow humans. They had enough grasp of the concepts of time dilation to understand that I was willingly leaving them and that my mission, by its very nature, assumed that no one alive when I left would be when I returned. Would any of you come out to cheer someone who was going on a mission based on the proposition that you were going to be dead before that person returned?"

Maria, standing at another podium two meters away, said, "Did you set out for the stars only for humanity?"

Shon paused for a moment. "Truthfully, I wanted to see if *I* could get there."

Maria said, "Were you seeking a happiness that you could not find in your life on Earth?"

"Perhaps at some level, but it was more a personal journey to find a purpose to my existence. Now I believe that the key to the door to happiness is opening that door for someone else."

Someone said, "Did you learn that on your journey or after you arrived here?"

"After I arrived." He glanced toward Maria. "Definitely."

A man in the auditorium spoke, saying, "There is a rumor that a controversy is brewing in the Office of Order about the ideas you are presenting."

Shon dissembled, "I can't imagine why what I could be saying would concern anyone. I am merely relating to you what my time was about. Most of what you have heard heartily supports the way you live today."

Someone else spoke up, saying, "You said 'most' not 'all'. Do you have some doubts about how we live today?"

Shon frowned, pondering what to say to that provocative question. Then he said, "In my time, the population was so great and communication was so instantaneous that there seemed to be no refuge from the *noise* of humanity. In this time, I sense that we are so isolated that some of that noise might be welcome. People somewhere else today might be doing things and thinking about things that we are not. Perhaps we should experience some of their experiences and share ours with them. Two extremes, my time and yours. Could there be a happy medium where we could pursue our private thoughts and other times where we might listen to others in this world and learn what we cannot discover only amongst ourselves?"

A man rose from his seat in the rear of the auditorium, turned, and left. On his way out, Maria noticed that the man leaving early was Joseph.

•

Later that evening at Shon's apartment, Maria stopped by. Sitting down beside him, she rested her head on his chest and said, "I am afraid the rumors are true. It will not be long before they come for us."

Shon took a deep breath. "All of my life I have sought to find what I have found here in Montaña with you. But to keep it, I fear I must take a great chance and what comes after that may not bring me back here."

Maria wanted to ask what he meant but something in his voice frightened her. She shuddered and remained silent.

Shon felt her shudder, took a slow deep breath, and drew her close to him.

•

Publius stood before the great glass that formed the eastern wall of his study in his great mansion in Annec looking out at the snowbound mountains to the west across the great lake, Lac, and then up to the three-quarter moon shining above on the clear night. He turned back to the monitor covering a large part of the northern wall of the room to study the results of the brain scan that he'd made of Shon during his surreptitious examination months before on Moon Base. It was a scan that no one had inquired about. He had not been surprised by the apparent lack of interest by the non-Hom families, even the Deinoc who had said little during the Council's deliberations—the terms the Hom had agreed to with the Council had foreclosed any inquiry about any Hom scans. Nor had he been surprised that the Hom had not inquired—the Hom wanted no evidence that Shon might be Hom or so akin to them that he might be deemed one which might cause someone to require a reduction of his family by one to keep their number at ten thousand. But he had been surprised that even Mamercus had made no inquiry. Apparently no one, even one as meticulous as Mamercus who he now knew considered Shon to be the Traveler, had expected to find anything truly unusual about a man from so distant a time, a time they considered primitive in comparison to theirs.

As Publius paced back and forth, he peered closely at the data the monitor presented and then he gazed out at the lake while once again pondering for perhaps the thousandth time what had caused him to perform this ritual so often, sometimes several times a day, since he'd returned to Annec from the Moon.

He had detected in the scan an odd shimmer in Shon's mind, a sort of shadow image. Had Shon's arrival not so closely matched the legend of the Traveler, he would probably have ignored what he had noticed. But, after the closer examinations he'd made after his return to Vitas, he had come to believe there was a second set of brain waves emanating in the background from the same mind. He had run the diagnostics designed to remove any accidental artifacts that were sometimes picked up from the brainwaves of others nearby during a scan. He'd been very careful. He had even transposed the brain scans of the few Hom who'd been on Moon Base over Shon's scan. None had matched the shadow image. He had been intrigued.

After poring over the data for several days, he decided he needed greater resources to study the date more closely, and drew upon the gargantuan files of GenLib. He discovered one similar brain pattern. But that concerned someone who had lived before the rise of the Hom. And when he'd later rechecked that reference he'd be unable to find the reference again. That was also puzzling but, in his past research into the past for other reasons he had encountered the same problem and didn't dwell on it much other than noting to himself that this had always seemed to occur when he was pursuing a rather esoteric inquiry in old historical files that might reveal the Hom role in world events near the beginning of the rise of the Hom more than eight centimillia ago.

Publius was fully familiar with the way the Order affected his family. The Hom produced about seventy children in a thousand years. Sometime several hundred years would go by with no births. Sometimes several would be born around the same time. It all depended on when accidental deaths occurred.

The rules on having progeny were straightforward. If there was a death in a generation, the remaining members in that generation who had not theretofore had a child entered a pool where names were selected by lot to determine who would have the child. The winner would chose a mate and create a child in the normal biological manner. When that generation's opportunity was exhausted, the opportunity passed to the next generation and so on.

The single greatest disaster to the Hom had occurred only thirty-one years ago when an ancient hydroelectric dam had collapsed and sent a wall of water down a gorge that killed thirty-four Hom who had the bad fortune to have constructed homes below the dam without considering the possibility that such a dam might collapse. On account of that misfortune, Luciana, the daughter of two dear friends, had been born.

He decided to confide in the one Hom he felt certain would be sympathetic to Shon's plight. But when he sought her out he learned that Luciana had left Annec shortly after he had contacted Juku. He drew the logical conclusion and hoped she would arrive in time to become a resource he might draw upon to see what the Traveler might bring to Vitas assuming he could survive long enough to fulfill the destiny the prophecy foretold.

Perhaps it was time to visit Luciana's parents, ancient Hom, born around the same time as Mamercus, of great influence on the Council.

•

Joseph Estaban was in a foul mood. He had a healthy respect for his skin and realized that he could be in physical peril from the Resurrection, of which he was well aware, if he convicted Maria. So he had eased off on his proffers with respect to Maria. But when the Prefect arrived she was furious with him for modifying his proffers. And, worse, she had brought another of her sect with her, a woman she introduced as Luciana, an observer. Who had ever heard of an *observer* from the Society? He had searched the historical records at the University for another such observer and hadn't found a single instance of such an occurrence. He could not even find an instance of two members of the Society ever visiting Montaña at the same time in the entire recorded history of Montaña. Not that he was surprised—a Prefect had always been the absolute final authority. It was clear to him that she was set on convicting both of them and, for some reason, wanted a witness from the Society on hand to vouch for her decision.

He surmised that if he prosecuted his revised proffers the geezer might also get off. If that happened he would certainly be removed from office by the Prefect, the peril of which he was only too well aware. Nothing was going as he planned. The hope he held to was the thought that the rumor he had heard when the geezer arrived—that he was an agent of the Society—might be true and he might get a surprise in her ruling. Hardly the sort of hope he wanted his life to depend upon.

•

As she took up her residence in Society House, Prefect Claudia considered the latest proffers from the Office of Order which were so much weaker than the original proffers that she doubted she could convict anyone accused on the evidence that she judged likely to be presented. She needed two convictions, but the Office was moving in the opposite direction. She began to think about alternatives. She considered the possibility that two other people could be found to banish but she surmised that the Deinoc would find that outrageously unacceptable—it was impossible for her to think they had no hand in this affair. She did not discuss any of her considerations with Luciana with whom, despite the long journey together, she felt no closer to than the day Luciana had appeared at her home in Annec and who had so far expressed no opinion whatever about what she thought about the case.

•

The evening after the Prefect arrived with another member of the Society in her company Rolando visited Raul at his home.

They sat down across a coffee table and lit cigars. Taking a sip from a rare Tequila Raul had poured into crystal snifters for each of them, he said, "It appears that the time for a decision with respect to Shon has come."

Raul, took a slow draw on his cigar, and replied, "I see that you consider the matter urgent or you would not have so quickly come to the point."

"I fear we have no time for pleasantries. As you are aware, the Special Committee for the Resurrection, limited for the sake of security to those the Committee agreed would act for all of the members of the Committee in times of emergency so that not all would be at risk of discovery, convened two nights ago, the first such gathering in a generation, to discuss the situation."

"I am well aware of this procedure having been a member of that Committee for many of those years when it was never necessary to convene."

"I appreciate your understanding, Raul. I dearly wished you present."

Taking another sip of his drink, Rolando continued, "I presented my views about Shon but it really wasn't necessary as all of us have followed the university course you established for him to express himself and a substantial majority had reached the same conclusion you and I have. His views are so contrary to the views we know are the foundation of the Society's philosophy that I believe that no one could propound such views so lucidly and truly hold adverse views. I have spent considerable effort in observing him surreptitiously and I have become convinced that Shon is a man like no other living today. I believe he is not a man of our time and that he may well be a man from the far distant past. Ergo, Shon is not an agent of the Society.

"In retrospect our course to deal with him was a tragic mistake. Not yours alone, of course, as we concurred, thinking we could flush him out. But the flush brought results we hadn't expected. The question now is whether he can be the catalyst for the change the Resurrection has dreamed of."

Raul said, "This man is propounding ideas that even we have not thought of that are going to lead to his exile as surely as the sun rising tomorrow. He may present as great a danger, perhaps even greater, to us than if he were the Society's agent."

Rolando said, "Perhaps we should have pursued a longer process to decide about him and not set him up to so easily present his view so publicly."

Raul said, "We have done what we have done and it can't be undone. Now we have to decide what to do about him and the situation he has put himself in with our help albeit however unintended. The fact that the Society has sent two members at a time when one is not normally in residence, an unprecedented event in our history, undoubtedly means that there will be a trial in which he will be convicted and banished."

Rolando said, "It is a puzzle that the Society has decided the matter requires such an extraordinary demonstration of its interest. Perhaps it is simply because he is indeed a man of the ancient past as we have become to believe. But the Society's objectives have always been the opposite of ours so we can take no comfort in what they appear to intend or what they really intend if their intentions are other than they appear."

"Are you suggesting that we might still fall into a trap even if Shon is the man we think he is?"

Rolando said, "Precisely what the Special Committee thinks may be the case. Yet Shon presents the only opportunity we have ever had to change the status quo. So, my dear friend, what should we do? My purpose tonight is to elicit your opinion on behalf of the committee as we are divided, not about Shon's presence here, but what to do about Shon."

Raul looked intently at Rolando. Then he took another long draw on his cigar while he cogitated on this unexpected inquiry. "If the Society is determined to banish Shon, we can do nothing about it. We have absolutely no military capability and we don't even know why no one ever returns from banishment. We cannot even protest to the Society because it might respond by banishing the protestors and destroying the Resurrection. Though I personally doubt they need any enablement as we have been in existence for more than a decamillium. They undoubtedly know of our existence and purpose and yet they have chosen to do nothing about us. It is Shon that is their concern and we have wasted time not realizing that while we have spent no time in considering what he might mean to us."

Rolando said, "So the question of what we do about Shon is really moot—we can do nothing at all in this arena where it has always been about what the Society wants to do about Shon. And we have simply missed out on whatever opportunity he presented while he was with us."

Raul said, "I think, as you and the Committee do, that Shon is not an ordinary man. Perhaps our best course is to empower him, for whatever that might be worth, with the knowledge that there are those in Montaña that have heard his views and that support him and his vision of a future we want to see. Maybe the best we can do is to tell him about us and our true impotence; tell him his real battle is with them as it always was. We are really just a distraction that they may have even planned. Then, if by some miracle, he can return from banishment

,whatever happens next will become a beginning to that future we desire. I know that is very little but that is really all we can offer."

Rolando, grimacing, said, "We are so impotent that it makes me shudder. To the only man who has ever had the courage to openly express the future we dream of, we can offer only words."

"Small as they may be, will you carry our words or shall I?" said Raul.

"Let it be me."

•

The next evening, Rolando sat down with Shon over a chess table. As he prepared to make his first move, Rolando said, "Are you aware of your plight?"

"That what I have been saying has gotten me into trouble? Yes."

Rolando said, "You don't sound very concerned. Do you understand what is likely to happen?"

"That I will be banished and that the banished never return? Yes."

"I regret in ways I cannot begin to express that we can see no way to help you."

Shon looked Rolando in the eye. "Don't look so despondent, Rolando. I never thought that I was sent here to live a happy life, to be quiet forever for the comfort of those who sent me here. They have their plans but their plans are nothing more than a reaction to my unexpected appearance. How can they, knowing nothing really about me, determine my destiny. I assure you that I will not go quietly into the night and disappear. I am my own master until I die."

"No one has ever returned."

"No one ever returned from the stars eight hundred thousand years later. After that, do you really think I will die in a jungle so easily?"

"Can I help you?"

"You and those you represent already have by giving me a reason to return from banishment, whatever that is."

Rolando ventured, "Those I represent?"

"I have gotten a sense of the citizens in this community from you and from Maria. I cannot imagine that you could simply dwell here in a static world without hoping for more. So I deduce that you haven't done so. You have organized as best you can and you have found yourselves unable to do anything to change your future in the face of your insurmountable obstacle, the Society. You want, you need, but you require help. I am going to help."

"How? And can we help you help us?"

"You can. I have a vision about what I will face. I need a place to prepare. You have described your home and its environs, remote with few citizens around. Perfect for what I need. If I am granted time to prepare before I go, and that is what I will seek to obtain in the coming battle over my banishment, I would like to come to your home to prepare. That is how you can help, but that will undoubtedly put you at a very serious risk of following me into banishment."

"Nothing would give me greater pleasure."

"Why?"

Rolando suddenly felt a need to explain himself. "As you have surmised, we need to change our destiny for our own sake and, we believe, for the sake of Vitas itself. We have lived this way for centimillia. This world will die of stagnation eventually if it remains forever unchanged. As you say, it's the Society's doing and, while it has kept our world alive, it's wrong. We must do something about it, but we have had no one to break us out of this bondage. Montaña craves change and I believe the others living in other communities must also crave change."

Rolando drew a deep breath and continued, "You have correctly guessed that we have organized. We call ourselves the Resurrection of Life and we have come to believe that you could be our bellwether to bring about the change we need. Where you go, we will follow. Leadership does not require that you stand before an army or before a crowd. It requires that you find the path to what must be done and that you lead us to achieve that goal. If you succeed you will open a new page for us, the Montañans and the other communities on Vitas."

Shon said, "Darkness, then gray. By the time I see the light, the moment is there. That is how my life has always been. If there is a destiny for me, it will become apparent. If such a moment occurs, I will seize it and we shall see if that leads us where you hope it will. I truly don't know where it will lead, but I can truly say to you that your vision is what I hope for."

Shon didn't express his fears that what he hoped for as he spoke would not be what he hoped for by the time he achieved their common goal. The Magan in his mind might have changed his mind by then.

•

In accordance with a ritual established long before his birth that required he do formally what he had already done informally, Joseph walked into Society House and presented himself before the Prefect. Claudia was seated on a white chair in a large white room. Beside her sat another member of the Society in another white chair.

Speaking the ritual formulation, he said, "Prefect, I, Joseph Estaban, the Advocate of the Order, appear before you today on behalf of the Office of the Order of Montaña to proffer indictments of two citizens of Montaña, Shon Ó Conaill and Maria Monterro, for the offense of promulgating Slippery Slope Propositions in our community. We pray that you will consent to convene a court to judge the merits of our indictment at your earliest convenience."

Prefect Claudia responded, "We shall consider the indictments you have presented and we shall determine whether a court should be convened forthwith."

"I withdraw and await your determination." Joseph turned and left the white room, noting that the ritual performance he had just attended differed from all the others he had attended before in that the Prefect had said "we" not "I" in her response. That the judgment he feared with respect to Maria was a foregone conclusion seemed clear to him. As he descended in the elevator and walked out of Society House, he shuddered for his life if Maria was convicted with the Geezer as he knew there were those in the community that would not forgive the banishing of a daughter of the Resurrection.

•

Shon rose an hour before dawn and ran into the jungle. He heard Carpia calling to him in his head. He ran a short distance in the direction of her call until the jungle cleared into a small opening and he found her perched on a high branch of a tree on the other side of the clearing. A red-eyed head with yellow feathers protruding from the top like a fan appeared out of the thick flora next to Carpia.

Shon had never seen a living dinosaur. Shon's memory well instantly identified this Therizi friend of Carpia's as a Therizinosaur, the only herbivore theropod ever discovered. Carpia was perched on her friend's shoulder over 5 meters above him. As the dinosaur began to enter the clearing, he stood still while calling to Carpia in the mindcast he had by now learned quite well, *"Carpia Ana, I hope this Therizi is really your friend."*

"She is."

He relaxed, a little, and looked at the creature before him. She was a truly large dinosaur, at least ten meters in length head to tail. She stood five meters high on her hind feet, her body feathered in bright yellow and red long-quilled feathers—some along the ridge of her back were at least at least two meters in length. She had large red eyes set in boney ridge with a forward tilt—he was sure she could see stereoscopically. Her large mouth and jaw structure didn't look like it belonged to a herbivore to him. Her tail was horizontal to the ground, her head and upper body leaning toward him. But what was most remarkable of all, and really quite frightening, were the meter-long, scythe-like claws, three on each hand, that she was wiggling around like a human might do with their fingers when a little nervous. Truly she looked very dangerous, not the calm kindly dinosaur Carpia had described. He took some solace that his memory well reported the herbivore nature of this beast and he thought, *How dangerous is a herbivore compared to a carnivore? Maybe less but how much less?*

Her eyes blinked.

He smiled when she did that. He stepped a few small footsteps toward her.

He heard a buzz in his head, then a word became clear, *"Hello."*

It wasn't quite Carpia's mindcast, but it was very similar.

He spoke back slightly modifying Carpia's mindcast, *"I am Shon."*

He heard clearly, *"I am Madra Ameyali Therizi."*

He could speak to a dinosaur. And at that moment, he knew it was only a matter of time before he could speak to any dinosaur.

•

Raul received a report that Maria had been indicted with Shon early one morning a few days after he had heard that Joseph had gone to Society House and he was beside himself. He contacted Rolando and asked him to meet him in the park near his office.

When Rolando arrived, Raul said, "The Order indicted Maria with Shon. I know it was expected but—" He couldn't continue.

Rolando said nothing and embraced his friend.

The sun shone down upon them through the tall trees.

"I cannot bear to lose her."

"She's in Shon's hands now. Let us pray that will be enough."

•

Carpia appeared before the Great One at the Wall.

The shape in the Wall said, "Have you broken your oath to the Society?"

Carpia felt as if a vice had taken hold of her heart and begun to close. She said, "Yes, Great One."

"You have done well. We shall see whether it matters." The shape in the Wall faded.

Carpia flew from the Wall back to Montaña faster than she'd ever flown before.

•

The sun rose shortly after Gaia opened the door to the outside world. She watched the sun rise and said aloud to herself, "The stage is set. Is it really possible that I have not wasted so many years planning and preparing when all there was to do was plan and prepare?"

•

Publius considered the developments in Montaña, well aware that Mamercus and others in Annec had also drawn the connection between this man and the prophecy. How they might act to keep the prophecy at bay to preserve the status quo and their long lives consumed his thoughts now.

Convinced that Lucia was not their minion and that Prefect Claudia probably had no idea what was at stake, he decided to travel to Montaña without informing the Council.

He anticipated that the trial could occur before he could arrive in Montaña by normal modes of transit, so he arranged transit by means almost never used by ancient Hom—an aircraft. There was only one in Annec and it was self-guided. He went to it, entered, inserted the necessary coordinates and took off.

TWO

TRIAL

"The trial starts in two days," said Shon to Rolando and Raul who were sitting in Raul's office at the University.

"I still cannot believe they have charged Maria," said Raul. He sighed and continued, "The charges against her are visibly weak but she is included nevertheless. It appears they have their own agenda."

"I am very sorry, Raul," said Shon.

"Sorrow won't help her, Shon. Why couldn't you have just come here and restrained your opinions?" replied Raul.

"Raul," said Rolando.

"Yes, I know," sighed Raul.

Shon started to speak but was interrupted as Raul's secretary entered the room saying, "I apologize for coming in instead of ringing you but there is a man outside who wants to see you now."

"And he kept you from ringing?" said Raul dryly.

"Professor, I've never seen a man like him. He's dressed sort of like the Prefect except he's a man."

Raul looked at her—she was clearly nonplussed—like she'd seen a ghost. He looked at the others showing his puzzlement.

They gazed back and nodded.

Raul said, "Show him in."

She withdrew and a few moments later the man entered.

Shon stood up immediately as he remembered the man who had been standing beside Mamercus when he had first noticed Mamercus on the bridge of the ship that had taken him to Vitas from the Moon.

Raul and Rolando rose because the man looked remarkably like a prefect from the Society, except that he was a male.

The man waited until the secretary withdrew and said, "I am Publius, Praetor of the Society. This office may be unfamiliar to you but I assure you a Praetor trumps a Prefect as you know those of the Society concerned with your community."

No one said a word.

Publius looked at Shon, saying, "Commander Ó Conaill, you are guilty, of course. But that's hardly the point, is it?"

Shon smiled. "Call me Shon. No, it isn't? "

Raul and Rolando exchanged glances.

"Very well, Shon. I suspect that your friends have harbored worries about you. That you might be one of us, an agent of the Society. My appearance might make such thoughts seem reasonable. But such thoughts would be wrong." He looked directly at Raul and Rolando. "Commander Ó Conaill is not of the Society. I am here because I believe he is more. I believe that he is the messiah some in the Society have awaited. A man call the Traveler. If he is that messiah, I want to help him achieve what we seek."

Rolando said, "We also seek a messiah, though not the same messiah as you hope for."

"I think it might well be the same."

Raul looked Shon in the eye.

Shon looked him back in the eye and said, "Perhaps this man may help, perhaps not, but I see little reason for him to come here to insure my banishment which appears to be a foregone conclusions at the moment."

Raul said, "I believe you. Protect Maria if you can."

"I shall, Raul." Shon directed his gaze at Publius. "Traveler?"

"The Traveler is a legend from centimillia ago. Simply put, our records predict a traveler will come one day to lead us to a new future."

Rolando, looking at Publius, said, "I wonder if that can be what we both want."

"Some think not," said Publius.

"At hand is a trial. How can you help?" said Raul.

"I could join the tribunal."

"Just like that?" said Rolando.

"Just like that," said Publius. "For eight centimillia the most respected judgments regarding matters of the Society were rendered when a praetor, the highest judge in the Society, presided over a tribunal. And make no mistake; this is a Society matter." He turned and left the room.

•

Publius proceeded directly to the Society House. When greeted at the door and questioned about who he was and his business there, Publius responded acerbically, "Tell Prefect Claudia Acca Junius that Publius Palinurus Jules, Praetor, would like a moment of her time."

In very short order Prefect Claudia appeared in the reception hall. "Praetor, this is truly unexpected. How may I serve?"

"I shall preside over the trial of Commander Shon Ó Conaill and Maria Monterro. You and Luciana Hom shall join me as judges. This shall be a Hom tribunal held under the auspices of the Society of Vitas. The tribunal shall also consider any alleged violations of the Order or abuses in the enforcement thereof which may be found to have occurred in connection with the judicial hearing contemplated to take place at this time. Anyone present shall be considered to have come within the power of the tribunal without a requirement of an issuance of a Writ of Attendance. A subsequent hearing may be called in Annec to explore the conduct of this tribunal. Those findings shall be reviewed for any proofs of wrongdoing which, if any wrongdoing is found, shall be submitted to the Council for appropriate disposition."

Prefect Claudia shuddered.

"Where is Luciana?"

"I do not monitor her activities, Praetor. But I am unaware that she has ever left Society House since we arrived so I suppose she is in her quarters." Prefect Claudia suddenly found herself immensely relieved that another Hom, Luciana, was also to be part of the tribunal. She had wondered from the beginning why Luciana had thrust herself into this matter. Now comes the Praetor of the Society, a man who would not have his position if he were not exceedingly adept at the politics in Annec. He undoubtedly had the support of Luciana's parents, both consuls for more years than most long-lived Hom had lived. All she need do was decide as these two decided and no subsequent hearing could blame her for the judgment which she now intuited was to be that Shon Ó Conaill would be acquitted.

"Would you be so kind as to tell her of my arrival?"

"Of course, Praetor."

•

Luciana entered the reception hall. "Praetor Publius, I could scarcely believe my ears. Why have you come?"

Publius stepped over to Luciana and took her hand. "Come. Sit with me."

They sat down on a sofa by a large window that overlooked the treetops facing toward the sun descending in the western sky.

"Do you know anything about a prophecy foretelling the coming of a person called the Traveler?"

"No, but myths and old history have never held my interest."

"Perhaps that comes with age and the time to pursue new interests with all the time we have. Let me tell you about this myth, as you call it." He told her about the Prophecy and how he had come to believe that Shon was the Traveler.

"So you have come to insure that Shon is not banished?" said Luciana.

"Not at all. I don't know as I sit here whether his destiny will be fulfilled by banishment or acquittal. But I believe that the correct people are here to make that judgment."

"Claudia?"

"She is irrelevant as there are now three judges. She will decide as we do. Unless you and I decide differently; then as I decide."

Luciana flushed. "Do you believe I will decide for acquittal?"

"I don't think you came here to convict Shon."

Luciana sat looking out the window at the dying sun. "It really doesn't matter what I do, does it, Praetor? As you say,

Claudia will decide as you decide. So it all comes down to what you decide."

"And that is why I am here."

•

On the day appointed, officials from the Office of Order arranged the tables and chairs to accommodate a court of three judges rather than the customary one. Shon and Maria sat together at a table with no counsel. Across the aisle sat Joseph, the prosecutor as Advocate for the Office of Order. Also in attendance were perhaps fifty prominent Montañans seated behind the tables occupied by the accused and the prosecutor.

When Luciana entered she looked over at Shon and Maria, who she saw now for the first time, and felt a surge of jealousy as she realized that she looked perfectly suited to be standing there beside Shon.

When all three judges were seated, Praetor Publius spoke, "This tribunal of the Society is called to order. Advocate for the Office of Order, do you have proofs to present against the accused, Commander Shon Ó Conaill and Citizen Maria Monterro, evidencing a transgression against the Order? If so, please stand and present your proofs."

Joseph said, "I do, your honor."

Praetor Publius interrupted, "You do?"

Joseph had already been shaken by discovering for the first time that there were members of the Society, male, of higher rank than the Prefect. He thought, *of course I do, why does he think we are here?* He said stiffly, "Yes your honor I have proofs of their guilt."

Praetor Publius interrupted again, "What are proofs, Advocate?"

Joseph, very confused by these interruptions, instinctively responded in an insolent tone, "They are the evidence that will show the accused are guilty."

"How do the accused prove their innocence, Advocate?"

"They explain why what they have said does not constitute a Slippery Slope Proposition."

"Why does anyone ever believe the accused?"

"Your honor, they swear that it is the truth and then the judge decides whether the proofs are more persuasive than their explanation and their sworn word."

"That sounds reasonable, Advocate. Why should anyone believe your proofs?"

"Because they are presented by the Office of the Order to protect the community by upholding the Order."

"Are the proofs truthful?"

"Of course."

"How do we know that?"

"Because I say so."

"I have not heard you swear that what you are presenting is truthful."

"That is not required."

"Then how do we know that you are telling the truth? What punishment accrues to you if you lie?"

"I could be replaced as Advocate," said Joseph defensively, not liking the direction this was going.

"Are these proofs truthful, Advocate?"

"Yes, your honor."

"Will you now swear that they are truthful?"

"Your Honor, if the accused are found innocent then I will be found guilty even if the only reason is that the proofs aren't convincing enough."

"This tribunal will stipulate that the finding of guilt or innocence of the accused shall bear no weight on the issue of whether your proofs are truthful or not. But I believe that it should add weight to your case if you swear that the proofs are truthful. Will you swear?"

"With that stipulation in mind, I swear."

"Before we proceed we need to equalize the effect of each person's word. If the accused are found guilty, they will be banished. An equal punishment for falsely accusing an innocent person is merited because such behavior is the equivalent of making a Slippery Slope Proposition as such behavior will lead, like all Slippery Slope Propositions, in a direction inconsistent with the Order.

"I present the foregoing as a proposed addition to the Annotated Order, containing all of the interpretations of the intent of the Order, and submit that it become effective immediately pending review and confirmation by the Society. Pending that confirmation, anyone convicted of violating this law, if ratified today, shall have the right of appeal until the Society confirms or invalidates this law. It being proposed, how say those sitting on this tribunal? Luciana Hom?"

"Aye."

"Prefect Claudia?"

"Aye."

"I say, 'Aye.' The law is passed. Advocate, I asked you to swear to the truthfulness of your proofs, which you did. However, I asked you that before passage of this new law. I ask you now, Advocate, do you swear the proofs you are about to present are truthful and that you possess no knowledge that would contravene those proofs under penalty of banishment to Amaz?"

Joseph could barely stand. The proofs had been edited. He realized now that such editing might not have really been necessary as he was convinced that Shon had promulgated Slippery Slope Propositions. The editing had made Shon's pronouncements much more easily understood as such. Nevertheless, a court not already intending to convict would never miss the alterations he had made to the recordings. If he refused to swear, everyone would know he had tried to present false proofs, but how could he refuse at this point? "Your honor, I need time to review these proofs to be absolutely certain they contain no error."

"Well we certainly would not wish for to you to submit a proof that contained any error. Please review the proofs now. I am pleased to see the law is already having a salutary effect."

Joseph thumbed through some papers having nothing to do with the critical proofs and said cautiously, "Your honor, upon careful review, I do not feel these proofs should be submitted to the court."

Praetor Publius said, "Particularly under the new law, eh? Very well this case is dismissed with apologies to the accused from the Society."

Shon rose and said, "With the court's permission I would like to propose a Slippery Slope Proposition."

Everyone in the courtroom stopped moving and stared at Shon.

Maria whispered, "Shon, what are you doing?"

Shon bent over to her and said softly, "Maria, it's time for a change. Trust me."

Praetor Publius said, "Commander Ó Conaill, are you fully aware of the penalty for propounding a Slippery Slope Proposition?"

"Yes, your Honor. Banishment for a year to Amaz where no one has ever been reported to have returned. Over the past eight hundred thousand years by my counting, eight centimillia by yours, at apparently five banishments a year, four million people have died. Even in my time with billions of people we would have considered such a number horrendous. So, with all due respect, I intend to be banished according to the Order. If I return, I intend to end this atrocity."

Praetor Publius said, "Is that threat your Slippery Slope Proposition?"

"No. I have a more interesting idea to propound."

"Very well. Proceed."

"In the past eight centimillia, Vitas has had a standing human population of twenty million people. Each human lives around four hundred years and no one is born before someone dies. The number of lives lived therefore accrue sequentially. In that time four billion people have lived.

"Vitas could have supported a standing population of four hundred million people easily during that time. Had that occurred eighty billion people would have lived. The Society by strictly following the Order has deprived seventy-six billion people of the opportunity to live. Perhaps more had anyone actually determined how many humans could have been sustained on this planet during that period without causing undue harm.

"Vitas has a finite future—the sun will burn out and Vitas will end in a few billion years. But before that occurs, the sun will grow in a billion or so years and burn out human life and all other life on Vitas.

"Just assuming the planet will be able to sustain life for only two hundred million years more, not really very long considering the insects, reptiles and amphibians that have been around for more than that time, the Order will further deprive one hundred and ninety trillion humans of the opportunity to live without harming Vitas rather than the ten trillion that would have lived at the present restricted level.

"I submit that while ten trillion may seem like a lot of people it pales by comparison to one hundred and ninety trillion.

"Simply put, twenty times as many people could have life were we to amend the Order to afford more humans the opportunity to live on this great planet.

"Perhaps it is wrong to deny life when it can be supported. Just as it was judged wrong long ago by the Society to grant life to such an extent that it was clearly destroying the planet long before its natural demise.

"I submit that such a thought is clearly a Slippery Slope Proposition. But it is a slippery slope upon which we need to slide before time runs out and trillions of people will never live as we do to experience the lives they have a right to live."

The room was silent.

Praetor Publius cast his gaze from Shon to Joseph. "Advocate, would you care to make a charge?"

Joseph stood up and said, "Your honor, the Advocate for the Office of Order wishes to bring a charge of promulgating the most dangerous Slippery Slope Proposition ever propounded in the history of Vitas against Shon Ó Conaill."

Maria rose and said, "I join with Shon Ó Conaill in propounding this Slippery Slope Proposition. So long as Vitas can sustain the population how can it be so dangerous?"

Suddenly Luciana rose and said, "I also join with Shon Ó Conaill in propounding this Slippery Slope Proposition. We should consider what he has suggested."

Praetor Publius turned to Luciana and said in a low voice to her, "Careful, dear, you may find yourself in his ship."

Luciana whispered, "A better ship than most, Praetor."

Praetor Publius looked a Shon. "Do you waive your right to prepare a defense and to permit this tribunal to proceed?"

"I do, your honor."

Praetor Publius looked at Maria. "Do you waive your right to prepare a defense and to permit this tribunal to proceed?"

"I do, your honor."

Praetor Publius turned to Luciana. "Do you waive your right to prepare a defense and to permit this tribunal to proceed?"

"I do, your honor."

"Very well. Luciana you are dismissed from this tribunal and you shall join the defendants in this proceeding. The remaining judges shall render a decision in due course. This proceeding is adjourned until tomorrow morning at ten. We thank the Advocate for bringing this matter before the Society." Praetor Publius and Prefect Claudia rose and left the room.

●

That evening Publius called Claudia to the reception hall. When she entered he said, "An interesting turn of events, Prefect."

"Yes," said Claudia cautiously.

"Have you come to a decision?"

"Have you, Praetor?"

Publius allowed a grim smile to cross his face. "Yes. The problem with Slippery Slope Propositions is that they are slippery. And this one is the slipperiest I have ever heard. We set a population limit at a time when almost any human population seemed a threat to the world. He may be correct but even as he spoke he hinted at even larger numbers. What is the correct number and how can it be controlled so we don't return to his time when billions lived and were clearly destroying the planet?

"Such numbers as he proposes would threaten the real society, the others he doesn't even know about and we, the Hom, who would undoubtedly be destroyed by such a large population when it became aware of our differences from it. He doesn't know the reality of the world today and, even if he did, he could argue that protecting us and the others who are nonhuman is not worth denying life to the humans we are preventing from living. He is right about the numbers who have been banished. I must agree that the banishments are wrong when viewed over so much time, but it has led to peace with the Deinoc for many centimillia."

Publius paused and looked out at another sunset over the mountains to the west, then continued, "Besides ten trillion seems a rather large number compared to how many of us who will live during the same period. How many people need to live anyway? At some point won't humankind have achieved all that it is with so many lives lived? Is the consciousness of more possible people paramount because it is possible? Whether any of us really has free will has been debated since long before Commander Ó Conaill was born. If we are really nothing more than living sentient stardust is there really a relevance to whether another–what did he say?–one hundred and ninety trillion more come to life? So I am not so sure that what he says is really any better than the way of the Order.

"But I am sure that most living humans today would subscribe to his notion of increasing the population. Why? Because no increase that any of them could add would get us instantly to his figures. And the consequences to being wrong will not affect any of them in their lifetimes. But they will have more children, something almost every human desires, likely because of the underlying subconscious genetic imperative to produce as many progeny as possible and possibly because humans derive emotional pleasures from their children. You and me and our kind, as well as the other members of the Society who will likely still be living when any adverse consequences of such a movement are felt will, by then, be a very small minority and likely helpless to return Vitas to the Order. You see, I am already thinking about his proposition. What will happen if everyone begins to contemplate his idea?"

Publius sighed, then looked directly at Claudius who shifted her eyes away at his glance. "Before I think more on it, I am inclined to see if he can prevail over the Order by returning from Banishment if it is really even possible to escape the Deinoc. Then let us see what he can do to make his idea happen if that is what he even really wants. So I am going to find him guilty and banish him if you concur. I regret the fate of the two women but they have freely chosen their fate. And until it all plays out who knows what will really happen to them?"

"I concur," said Claudius. She felt a relief in her response to an exposition of consequences she knew in her soul that she would never have considered in rendering a decision on her own.

•

The next day when the court reconvened Praetor Publius rose and said, "This court has reached a verdict. The defendants will rise."

The defendants rose together and faced the court.

"Commander Shon Ó Conaill, Luciana Hom, Citizen Maria Monterro, you are judged guilty of promoting a Slippery Slope Proposition and are sentenced to banishment into Amaz for one year. We will hear any mitigating remarks from the defendants at this time."

Shon said, "Your Honor, speaking for myself I have no response to make but I request the indulgence of the court with respect to serving our sentence to provide us six months to prepare for our banishment. I promise not to propound any ideas during that period that deviate from the Order."

Praetor Publius peered at Shon, wondering why he had made this request after clearly offering himself up. He asked the other defendants if they had any mitigating response to make and whether they also wished to benefit from Shon's request. They responded that they had nothing further to say but wished to also benefit from the request. Finding no reason not to accommodate the request, he said, "Very well. The sentence of this court shall be carried out six months from this date. May I have your word that you will not flee?"

Shon replied, "To where, your honor? Amaz? You have my word."

Luciana replied, "You have my word."

Maria replied, "You have my word."

"Then you are free to reside in Montaña until the date of banishment."

•

Joseph returned to his office fuming. Somehow the geezer had gotten what he wanted though he couldn't image why getting himself banished was what he wanted. But he had Maria and it seemed the woman from the Society, too. The woman was extraordinarily beautiful and he wondered why she had suddenly chosen to join him in his foolish act. But what really burned his soul was that Maria had joined him at the very moment she had gotten free of the charges he had brought. He decided then that she would not be joining the geezer—that she was going to pay for her folly and not by banishment.

Joseph heard a knock. Annoyed he said sharply, "Enter."

Shon entered. He said, "I have come for the proofs you were going to use against us."

Joseph said coldly, "What for? They are irrelevant. Take them." He set them on his desk. "Why did you have to come to Montaña?"

Shon said evenly, "I was sent here. I think to be banished in fairly short order as has occurred and would have even had I not made it easy for the Society."

"It looked to me like that is what you wanted. But why take Maria with you as it appears you have another woman? Maria is the only woman I ever wanted."

"She had a choice and I suspect she chose largely because you took the only man she ever wanted."

"I think she did so because she wants you. As for Jimmy, I had to take someone. The Society expects the banishments and it gets what it expects. You said so yourself at the trial."

Shon said harshly, "You took him because you wanted her."

Joseph said derisively, "So what if I did? If not him, it would have been someone else. I was simply the tool they used."

Shon said, "Some things never change. There will always be vermin who claim they are only following orders as they commit their atrocities."

Joseph became enraged. He stepped around his desk and threw his fist at Shon. Joseph had never been involved in a physical altercation before. Shon had. Shon parried Joseph's fist with his left hand and, in one motion, grabbed his wrist and held it while stepping into Joseph's space driving his own right forearm into Joseph's face. Joseph sprawled back and to his right but was restrained from escape by Shon's grip on his wrist.

"I come from a very different time than you. You have no idea what I can do to you. You represent everything I hate in a man. Be smart. Don't even think about trying to harm Maria. I know exactly how you think. If you ever come near her again, I will come for you and I will break every bone in your body like this." Shon broke Joseph's nose with a single sharp blow to the bridge of his nose.

Joseph howled in pain, fear, and outrage.

Before Joseph could even begin to think about revenge, Shon said, "And after I break every bone in your body, I will rip you apart like this." He reached forward and pinched Joseph's arm extremely hard and ripped a piece of his skin together with part of the underlying biceps off of his arm. Joseph nearly passed out with pain. Only his abject terror that he might never awaken kept him conscious.

Shon said, "I know you, Joseph. In my time, there were people who would avenge themselves on innocent women and children for whatever wrong they thought had been perpetrated against them. They would blow up buildings full of people to show their rage. They would shell towns and kill hundreds in an evening. The only way those people could be dealt with was on their own terms. Governments executed them but their victims were already dead. I should kill you right now. You're corrupt and evil. And you cannot see reality very well either. I didn't take Maria from you. And neither did Jimmy. Maria makes her own judgments about whom she loves. If there had been no Jimmy or me, she would never have chosen you.

"Now you know what I will do if you do anything that I construe as hostile. Or do I need to be clearer?" Shon took Joseph's left ear between his fingers and squeezed—very hard.

Joseph urinated in fear and pain. Joseph wailed, "Stop! Please! I won't do anything! Please let go!"

Shon let go. "If you do anything to harm her, that ear will be the next part of you that I tear off and when I am finished your parts will be spread all over the floor." Without another word, Shon left without the proofs.

Joseph fell to the floor, paralyzed in horrible pain. Part of his arm, now just a lump of bloody mush, lay on the floor across the room. His vision was already becoming affected by the swelling of his face caused by his broken nose. He wanted to kill Shon and his women but he hurt too much. He realized that the geezer hadn't come for proofs but rather to deliver his brutal message. He would never be able to challenge the geezer. He knew that now. The geezer was extremely dangerous and would hurt him too much. He hurt more than he ever wanted to hurt again. What the geezer would do if really provoked by injury to Maria, Joseph could not even begin to think about.

THREE

PINCHINCHA

Carpia flew to the wall. When the Great One appeared, Carpia related the events of the trial.

"So it has begun," said the Great One.

"What has begun, Great One?"

'The future, my dear."

"What should I do?"

"It appears that Shon has gained some time to prepare for his contest with the Deinoc. You will assist him in whatever way you can."

She paused, then said, "I am not puzzled about why the Hom woman joined him. She must have fallen in love with him on his arrival and that caused her to come to Montaña. Perhaps she is too young to realize that she can die like anyone else if she puts herself in harm's way. The Praetor must have come because of her coming or, possibly, for another reason. I hope it is the latter. It is interesting that he convicted her with him. That will cause serious consternation in the Council when it learns of it. I didn't foresee that. I wonder how that will affect the outcome."

Carpia sensed that the Great One was no longer talking to her, but was speaking her thoughts aloud. She remained silent and listened.

"Yet the presence of two women with him will excite the Deinoc's blood lust. And the opportunity to kill a Hom without retribution will be extremely exciting to them. Publius knew she came so it must have been known in Annec and to the Deinoc representatives there. They may well have anticipated this possibility if they have learned she came to Montaña. Yet, given their nature, anticipation may not work to their advantage. They may work themselves up for the hunt and act hastily. Perhaps

Shon perceives that and anticipates an advantage will arise from their blind lust to kill such a woman with impunity while killing him and his other woman at the same time.

"I wonder whether it was prudent for him to request a delay in going over. That may give them time to absorb their good fortune and tame their instincts. But I suppose he felt a need for time to prepare, particularly since he is not going to face the Deinoc alone."

Her tone changed, "In two weeks, bring Shon here."

"I don't know where he will be then. It is quite a distance for a human to travel here from Montaña, Great One."

"He will need to prepare for his banishment. I doubt he will do that in the central community. Most likely he will move to a more secluded place closer to the mountains. So if he moves close enough to come here, bring him. Otherwise, return yourself and we will determine another meeting place."

Carpia lifted off from the branch where she had been perched and flew away.

•

Luciana stopped in to see Publius before she left the Society House.

Publius admitted her into his quarters and said, "Luciana, you have truly made a mess of things. How am I going to tell your parents what you have done? What I have done? I came believing I could make a difference but this is certainly not what I had in mind."

"Perhaps you did make a difference."

"How so?"

"Had you not presided, the Advocate would have used the proofs he prepared. Claudia shared them with me. They were an assemblage of edited transcripts of Shon's discussions with Maria in his university course. The way they were edited would have been seen by the citizens of the community as not conveying what Shon was trying to say about his time and ours. Were his pronouncements Slippery Slope Propositions? Perhaps they were, but they really posed no threat to the Order. His conviction would have looked like a planned affair to get rid of him. I think the community would have reasonably believed we had sent him here so we could do just that. You stopped that process dead in its tracks. As it turned out, it was clearly Shon who took the step to insure his conviction. The integrity of the Society was preserved."

"Thank you for that, but I did not come here for that purpose."

"Why did you come?"

"I believe he may be important to our future."

"The prophecy?"

"Yes. But how he might affect the future is opaque to me. I have a strong sense that he got what he wanted for whatever purpose he sees and we don't. But, by joining him, you may have upset whatever his purpose is. Whether that is for the better or worse I cannot guess. But he could not have anticipated that you would do what you did and that may change the outcome, whatever it is."

"Perhaps I am foretold."

"There is no mention of a Hom woman in the prophecy."

Luciana hesitated, "Was there a mention of any other woman?"

"Like a woman named Maria?" Publius smiled, "There is no mention of any women at all."

"Then there are now the unknown effects of two women on what will happen."

"So it seems. Are you going to him now?"

"If he will allow it. I think he asked for the time in order to prepare but I don't know what he thinks he's preparing for. How can he know anything about the Deinoc? And now he has two companions to prepare besides himself." She sighed, "Still I cannot imagine how we can prevail over the Deinoc."

"Perhaps it will not come to that. Six months is not a lot of time, but it is time and events can change during it."

"Let's hope so. But still it's likely we will face the Deinoc in the not so distant future. Will you tell my parents I love them?"

"Yes. But you can do that yourself."

"I would rather not. At least not for a while. Perhaps before we cross the Wall, if it comes to that."

She stood, and said, "Be well and just." She turned and left his quarters. An hour later she left Society House.

•

Luciana walked among the towers of Montaña for the first time since she had arrived, it being the custom of the Society to stay within Society House at each citizen community for a myriad of reasons. Now she felt free to do what she had dreamed of since she first learned there were communities of people so different from her own. She focused on finding Shon's tower. When she found it she addressed the vidcom to call his apartment.

Shon answered and said, "Luciana. Come up." He told her how and she went up.

He was waiting at the opened door to his apartment when she stepped out of the elevator. Without exchanging any words at all, she entered the apartment and he followed.

Finally he said, "Seeing you at the trial was one of the bigger surprises I've had in a while and I would put finding myself so far in the future only a little ahead of your second surprise. Why in the world did you get yourself involved in my predicament?"

She hesitated. "I'm not so sure why I came in the first place. I can see you have found a life here with someone else. But I couldn't just let things play out the way I think they were planned."

"Planned? By your Society or by me?"

She felt an edge in his voice. "The Society, of course. I have no idea what you have planned, though I can see you must be planning something or you would have taken the dismissal of the charges and left it at that. Instead of—"

"Promulgating the biggest Slippery Slope Proposition in history?" said Shon.

"Yes. Why did you do that?"

"Are you asking me that as Luciana or as a member of the Society?"

"You think I'm here for the Society?"

"It seems possible. You appear as a judge and then suddenly embrace my notion without any hesitation while another important figure appears suddenly to run the trial—something I am told has never happened before."

Luciana turned away from him and took a step toward the door.

"Wait, Luciana. I'm sorry but we first met because you were tasked to deal with me when I returned. Surely you can understand some caution on my part is in order."

She continued toward the door and spoke without turning toward him. "I can understand that, Shon, but when we parted I had the impression you felt things had changed between us. Obviously I made a mistake." As she reached for the door she suddenly felt his hand touch hers. Startled she turned and felt him put his hands on her shoulders as she looked into his eyes. She stiffened her body but didn't move.

"Listen to me for a just a minute, please."

"All right. Just a minute."

"I can't tell you everything you really need to know. But others are involved and not just I will suffer should I err in my judgment of your intentions. But I can say that I am determined to change the way of things here if I can. I believe sending people to their deaths, without them even knowing what that death is, is terribly wrong. I also believe that following some rules for hundreds of thousands of years depriving millions of people the chance to live is wrong."

"Your Slippery Slope Proposition."

"I don't know whether more people living is better or worse. I don't even know whether people who never lived are entitled to anything at all. But I believe that nobody, even the Society, has the right to make all the judgments for everyone else. Particularly when everyone else has no idea of the real world they live in."

Luciana felt the hairs on her neck rise. "The 'real world'?"

"I think you know what I mean. Let's just say I took a boat ride to get here and on the way I saw life that didn't exist in my time. And even with the passage of time since I left, that life could not have evolved naturally. So I don't think Amaz is simply a primordial jungle inhabited by ancient plants and dumb animals."

She noticed his reference to dumb animals. "So what do you think?"

"That's a matter for discussion if we can find a way to trust each other."

"And how would you propose to bring that about when you clearly don't trust me?"

"Some time and the answers to some questions, starting with why you joined me in the trial." He took his hands off of her shoulders.

Luciana relaxed her body. "What you said seemed so right as you said it. I thought, 'Why haven't we thought about how many people should live or whether they should and why haven't we asked any questions of ourselves in all this time?' Then I acted. Simple as that. Was I so wrong?"

"No. I believe you were right—at least to ask that question of yourself. Whether you should have acted to join me is not so clear."

"Because I could die?"

"Because your presence might cause me to falter at the wrong moment."

For the first time since she had entered the apartment, she felt that she had not made the wrong choice. "Then I will do what I can to see you don't falter on account of me and, perhaps, I can help you in your plan. But you should know that I will not betray my people and I will stand against you if you attempt to harm them."

"I wouldn't want you with me and I wouldn't believe you had you said otherwise."

"But you know I know that and so would say the same regardless of my purposes."

"That is why it will take time for trust. Meanwhile, I will find you an apartment nearby until we leave. Which will hopefully be very soon."

"How will your woman feel about this?"

"You know her name."

"Very well. How will Maria feel?"

"About as comfortable as you do, but she will manage." He added, "And she doesn't live here."

"But she visits."

"Yes. So I will talk to her about you. Will that be a problem?"

"Not at all."

They sat down while Shon called Naomi to make arrangements for another apartment.

•

The next morning Shon visited Raul.

•

Later that day, Rolando visited Raul in his office at the University.

Raul said, "Shon wants Luciana, the woman from the Society, to be included in his trip to your home in Pinchincha."

Rolando shrugged. "I am not surprised."

"How can she be trusted? The entire trial was like nothing we've ever seen before. We have come to believe that Shon is not a spy, but I see no reason whatever to assume that she is not. She appears, and then the man from the Society appears. What would have been a normal trial like every other one in our history was changed into an unprecedented event culminating in a member of the Society being banished alongside Shon and Maria. We know the Society can save her any time they wish and leave Shon and Maria to their fate. And she can help them insure their fate. Why else did she come? And now Shon wants her to join him when he should only be concerned with Maria's safety."

"What did Maria say?"

"She believes this woman loves Shon and came to save him. She believes the other man came to help her."

"By banishing her with him?" said Rolando.

"Precisely what I said to Maria."

"And what did Maria say to that?"

"She said the judge had no choice. I will never understand women, Rolando, least of all Maria. She actually thinks the woman acted impulsively in response to Shon's speech and the judge only did what he had to."

"Well, I seriously doubt anyone anticipated what Shon said, including the judges and Luciana. It seems as credible to me that she acted impulsively as that she calculated that joining him in banishment was the way to pursue a nefarious scheme to spy on him."

"But, if her purpose is to spy, we will all be ruined and Maria will die."

"Raul, the oddity of the trial needs to be seen in the context of who Shon is. If we believe him, then it should not be so surprising that surprising events have occurred. But his actions at the trial have further convinced me that following him will not be a mistake even if he fails and we are all destroyed. If he wanted to escape banishment, he had only to remain silent. If the Society is bent on destroying us by using him then they could have accomplished that more easily by simply accepting Joseph's proofs and letting things play out as they always have."

Raul sat back in his chair. "So what are you going to do?"

"Exactly what I told Shon before I came to your office—that I will welcome them to my home and that I shall continue to pray that he has a plan to accomplish what he says without getting himself, Maria, Luciana, and the rest of us killed."

"And what of his plan?"

"He didn't say a word beyond his desire to go with Maria, Luciana, and me to Pinchincha. How, why, and for what purpose he didn't say."

•

Early the next morning Maria, packed to travel, went to Shon's apartment as he had asked her to do the night before. When she arrived she discovered that he wasn't there so she went up, entered his apartment and made a cup a coffee.

As she sat down with her coffee she heard a knock on the door and went to open it.

There stood Luciana with two pieces of luggage.

Maria stared for a moment and said, "Shon's not here but I'm sure he will arrive soon." She stepped back from the door and made a motion for Luciana to enter.

"Thank you."

"May I offer you coffee?"

"Yes. Thank you."

Maria poured another cup and they walked into the living room and sat down in chairs across from each other. They both sipped their coffee for a minute glancing at each other at first then closely gazing.

Maria said, for want of thinking of anything else to say, "Well, we meet at last."

"Yes." There was another moment of silence.

Finally Luciana said, "I wish Shon was here."

"So do I, but I wouldn't be surprised if he planned it this way."

Luciana smiled. "Nor I. I suppose he wants us to get acquainted."

"Probably. Maybe he thinks he would be at a loss for words while two women won't." Maria wasn't smiling.

"I suppose he told you how I know him."

"Yes. I suppose he told you the same."

"Yes."

They looked at each other and then Luciana giggled and Maria smiled. Then they both laughed.

Luciana took a sip from her cup. "The coffee's very good."

"Thanks. I can cook, too. So we won't starve on the other side."

"Other side?" Then Luciana's face reddened. "Oh, Amaz."

"We simply call it 'the other side' as we call everything beyond the Walls that surround us."

"I think he's a good man."

"We have that in common. Could I ask why you came? You know that is the question everyone is asking."

"I asked myself the same thing," she said with a smile. "I fell in love with a man unlike anyone I have ever met or am likely to. I'm not going to apologize for that."

Maria gazed at Luciana for a moment, and said, "Same thing happened to me. I love him and I think I always will, even if—"

"I understand."

"We have to live to have a future to work out and escaping alive from banishment has never happened before."

"Nor has Shon."

"Or Shon with us."

Luciana smiled, "Or with us."

"I wonder how good his timing is." Maria smiled.

There was a noise at the door to the apartment.

"Pretty good," said Luciana. They stood up as Shon entered.

Shon, soaked in sweat, entered, saying casually, "Sorry I'm late."

The women looked at each other.

•

Carpia Ana Erith and Tigri Omagua Pardal, concealed in the jungle nearby, followed Shon, Maria, Luciana, and Rolando on their way to the train station.

Luciana noticed a parrot perched in a tree and a large cat hiding under a bush in the shadows. They both appeared to be looking in her direction. She mindcasted to them as they appeared to be from families she knew as sentient but received no response. Thinking nothing more than that she was mistaken, she boarded behind Maria.

Shon heard Luciana's mindcast. A few moments later he heard a buzz which he recognized as a mindcast to which he was not tuned. He scanned the area and noticed a feline slinking through the low brush not more than a few meters below Carpia who was flitting from branch to branch behind them as they walked. She didn't appear concerned about the creature which could easily have been stalking her by the way it was moving. He judged he had just become aware of another member of the Society. He called upon his memory cell to review what he had seen since his arrival in Montaña and saw that this cat had appeared in his life as early as his first trip to Huascarán. He wondered, *A Carpian cohort. Were there others?*

They entered into the building leading underground to the boarding point for the train to Pinchincha.

The train took them eight hundred klicks to the west to Pinchincha situated at the juncture between the jungle to the east and the mountains to the west. They followed Rolando until they arrived at his house where he asked the party to join him on the porch for a meal. They all sat down in wicker chairs and ate a succulent meal of fresh vegetables and spicy sausages prepared by Rolando's neighbors. The party retired to the ancient wood and stucco house for a night's rest.

•

Shon rose before dawn and set out for a run across the farmland toward the foothills below the mountains to the west.

As he entered a stand of trees, he saw Carpia and ran up to her.

Looking up at her perched on a branch, he said, "Good morning, I see you found your way. I have a question for you. Do you have any feline friends about?"

Carpia, guessing he had finally noticed Tigri, said, "Like a large cat with two black lines on either side of its face?"

Shon smiled. "Well, I noticed a black-spotted reddish-brown feline following us to the train station after I noticed that buzz I got after Luciana tried to talk to you. It seemed to me, she was looking in the direction of the cat below you. Then I recalled I'd seen a similar feline in the shadows in the jungle from time to time."

"You are observant. Tigri Omagua is rarely noticed."

"I suggest he become more noticed. By Rolando. I think Rolando might welcome a pet and the pet might provide some insight as to what Rolando is up to, if anything, beyond his expressions of support for my cause."

"Tigri will become more noticed."

"Are you with me on this quest?"

"Yes. Just tell me what I can do and I will do it."

"Why, Carpia Ana?"

"Because I believe in you even though I don't really know what you are trying to do."

"Is that the only reason?"

"You are not a citizen, Shon. I will say this much. There is more to what goes on here on Vitas than is known even to the Society. I do not take my orders from the Society and never have. I mentioned the Great One to you. She is my master. I don't believe your conjecture about her possibly being an agent of the Society is true. But, if so, she has still served my family and others like mine since before any collective memories we have passed down from our ancestors.

"I am a parrot to the Hom. Intelligent, yes. A member of the Society of Species, yes. But nevertheless we parrots are nonentities to the Hom. They pay much more attention to the citizen communities than they do to the smaller families in the Society. They expect that we will abide by the Order and the Codicil and, so long as we do, they ignore us.

"They don't understand us, at least those species who do not serve them on the Moon and in a few other places such as the oceans and the polar regions where the danger of being there makes it worth their while to encourage a relationship so that we may share the burden of the risks necessary to accomplish what must be done from time to time in those places. Parrots have little ability to help in those places. So, as we are also unlikely to cause any disturbances in maintaining the Order, we are mostly on our own."

"That sounds as if you believe the Great One is a power outside of the Society."

"You might well suppose that, but I couldn't possibly comment on such a notion. There is simply no place for such a possibility in the Society's view of Vitas. However, if you are willing, in a little more an a week I will come to you and, if you are willing, we will go on a long run to a place where something may happen which may affect what happens next."

Shon stared at Carpia, but gained no insight beyond her plain words. "I can always benefit from a long run."

•

Shon headed back to Rolando's house. On arrived, he found Rolando standing by the front door.

"You must have guessed that I have noticed you have some special abilities," said Rolando.

"It would surprise me had you not noticed, as I surmised early on that noticing me was your true purpose in visiting the city and meeting me in the first place, my friend."

"So we have finally admitted these matters to each other. Let me show you my special place here."

Shon followed Rolando to the old emerald shaft.

They took the lift down. The temperature went down until they walked out into a cold cavern.

Rolando led Shon to a small room, created nearly three decamillia before. He took a bottle of port from a rack of wine on the far wall and, grabbing two glasses from the eight that were sitting in a small niche to the side, set the bottle and glasses on an ancient wooden table. They sat down on two chairs across the table.

Rolando filled the glasses and handed one to Shon, saying, "Montaña put itself into your hands before the trial. We need to know that we have not erred. We can accept defeat in a battle honestly fought. But to go to our graves betrayed would be an abomination. This woman from the Society has, to put it frankly, alarmed us. We need some indication that bringing her along is wise. Moreover, we need some indication of your plan to defeat whatever confronts anyone from Montaña when they cross over will succeed with her in your company. And we need to know that whatever you plan is something we can embrace, or at least comprehend. You have given us nothing to help us endure the agony of our potentially imminent demise. I ask you as your friend, which I truly am, Shon, to help us endure what is to come."

"Very well, Rolando. You describe a commitment beyond yourself encompassing a group larger than one and less than the whole community, but I find no evidence that the whole community realizes what is at stake. But you have told me nothing of such a group. We each have secrets to keep for our own reasons. I have no problem with that as I believe my secrets are necessary to keep, as I truly believe you feel yours are. So you should understand that as anyone on this planet could be a threat to you so could they be to me. So don't hold against me my reluctance to tell you my plan. And do not assume what I tell you is my whole plan as I know you no better than you know me, and our circumstances of acquaintance are much the same.

"Still, I am prepared to trust you as I think you trust me while holding back a few secrets I believe are necessary to succeed. So this is the plan I am prepared to reveal to you. I am going to train the women with me to defeat whatever stands against us in Amaz. I have some notion of who they are and I have an idea of how to deal with them to get what we both seek: freedom from banishment and, in the end, freedom to live our lives in an world where all the communities are connected directly, not through remote channels manned by guilds sworn to secrecy and controlled by the Society. We will enter Amaz and, if we succeed, we will return to change the Order, not because the Order is inherently evil but because its inflexibility to the changes that humanity needs is evil, even if not intended."

Rolando drank his port and said, "So we are where we began before the trial. You have revealed that you know something none of us know about who or what is on the other side of the Wall, yet you have told me nothing about them or how you have learned what you know. I suppose the woman from the Society has information and, perhaps, that is why she has become part of your plan. Keep your secrets if you must. But know that knowing nothing of how you will succeed, we are left blindly in your hands."

Shon drank his port and said, "I trust that will be sufficient."

Rolando drained his, and said, "For the time being."

•

The next morning, Shon asked Maria and Luciana to join him on a hike to a hill several klicks from Rolando's house. They stopped halfway up the hill where a small forest began to rise from the grasslands below.

Looking directly at Maria, Shon said, "There are creatures on the other side of the wall that want to kill. I believe that is why I was sent to Montaña in the first place – to put me in a position for them to kill me with their own hands." He turned his gaze to Luciana. "But it is not hands they will use. It will be with claws and teeth because they are not human—"

Luciana interrupted, "How do you know this?"

Shon looked at her, "I cannot tell you how I know, but I think you know that what I am saying is true."

Luciana shifted her eyes and remained silent.

Maria, casting her gaze back and forth between them, said, "You both know something I have never heard before."

Shon said, "That is true. Luciana knows more than you and, for the time being, I ask you to leave it at that. Before we go over, you will know what you need to know and both of you will learn how I know it. But for the time being all that you need to know is that I know what we are facing and that I will prepare you for who and what we will face. Can you accept that?"

The women nodded silently.

"Our enemy does not believe I can kill them. The best way to think of them is as barbarians from the distant past who have a custom of killing for the satisfaction they gain from doing so.

They are brutal and enjoy the killing of those banished to their domain. They have never lost a battle and cannot conceive of the possibility. That is to our advantage. Our other advantage is that I know who we face and they don't know I know. I will prepare you to kill them. You must understand that killing them is our only way to live. No diplomacy. No surrender. No running away. We must face them and kill them. If we do, we will conquer them and I believe the remainder of their community will follow us."

Shon saw Luciana's reaction to that notion. He faced her directly, "Luciana, you must come to believe what I say or you must find a way to withdraw from this."

"I said nothing."

Shon smiled and continued, "If we do not conquer them we will die."

Shon looked directly at Maria. "Montaña will not die no matter what you may hear from Rolando or your father, Maria. It will simply go on as it always has – unless you cannot keep these secrets. To insure that, you must never tell anyone what I am telling you today or anything else that I tell you in the future. Can you keep these secrets?"

"Yes," said Maria.

He turned to Luciana, "You can never tell anyone what I tell Maria."

"I will never tell and will deny if asked that you have told her anything at all about anything she would not know about but for your telling," said Luciana.

"Good. Then let's get down to business." Shon then related what Carpia had told him about a Deinoc hunt without identifying their foe as the Deinoc or telling him how he knew what he knew.

When he finished, Luciana shuddered visibly, and Maria began to weep silently. She said, "Is that what happened to Jimmy?"

Shon nodded, and said, "We are going to end that by killing them. While the notion of killing may bother you, it will not bother them. For them, dying in battle is better than dying any other way. Remember what I have told you as we prepare so that you will be able to kill when the time comes. At the end of it, killing is what will happen. If any of us hesitates in the battle, we die. If we die, millions, actually trillions, more will follow us by never living. Remember that when the time comes to kill." Shon stood silently for a moment, then said, "Return to the house. I will join you later."

•

Shon ran further up the hill into the woods until he saw Carpia flying nearby. He stopped and when she alit on a branch he said, "I have been thinking of a way to physically combat a dinosaur somewhat larger than myself. It seems to me from what I gleaned about the species Deinonychus from my memory well, which is consistent with what you and Madra have told me, other than saying they are more robust—a hundred kilos instead of sixty—that a Deinoc, besides being extremely fleet of foot and capable of shifting position laterally and leaping on the run, comes naturally armed with five weapons—a huge powerful mouth loaded with over seventy incisors, two arms with wrists that can rotate equipped with three razor sharp curved claws, albeit small when compared to those of a Therizi, are still longer than my fingers, and extremely powerful legs which end with clawed feet each of which has a twenty-centimeter long sickle-shaped claw in the front of each foot covered by a horny sheath.

"His leg can be thrust towards me and his claw used to rip me open in a downward stroke while his jaws finish me off."

Shon continued, "A Deinoc can clamp on and easily rip away what he has bitten. He can grab like a man but with claws that can tear my body apart. He can kick like a martial arts expert and split me down the middle with his ripping claw. From a tactical viewpoint, he can attack from a high position, with his head; from a low position, with his feet; and, straight on, with his arms. Finally, they fight in a pack so an attack can come from all directions at once."

Carpia said, "Your description is apt."

"So where is there any weakness? What weapon can I use? What martial arts technique could be successful? I will never be allowed to have a projectile weapon of any sort. No guns, no arrows. I can arm myself with hand weapons as the Deinoc apparently provided these to their victims according to what you told me of the hunt."

"That is true," said Carpia.

"Let's assume I can have a sword, knife, spear, ax or the like, what should I choose and how should I train to use it?"

Carpia didn't respond, knowing Shon was speaking rhetorically.

Shon continued, "One thing is clear. If a Deinoc gets a grip on me, I'm dead. I have no protection against claws or jaws. I already know I'll not likely have any clothes, though now that I know that, I will plan to stay as dressed as possible without tipping them off that I know how they plan their hunt to transpire. I doubt they will much care how I'm dressed below the waist because their killing equipment is really designed and positioned to attack my torso. Even the leg thrust will come upward so that the claw can penetrate my gut or back and pull me down.

"Assuming I can wear trousers, shoes and a belt, I could carry weapons beyond those I can carry in my hand. I will plan on being able to carry five weapons—tit for tat for the five Deinoc 'weapons' though I can't make that argument to anyone since there is no one we actually interface with for the battle. From what I've been told, they imagine themselves as warriors able to kill foes similar to themselves. So we just have to assume we can take weapons that appear similar to their own natural weapons.

"Where is a Deinoc vulnerable? Throat, eyes, chest, hamstrings? Can he be blinded by some agent I could carry? The throat will be hard to slash without being open to attack from the legs. Hamstrings, the muscles and tendons on the back of the leg would be ideal to cut. That would take away two of his weapons, his legs. And restrict his movement, making further attack with jaws and arms limited. How to cut them? He's not going to turn his back on me.

"Still I think the key is in the legs. He's got to go down. He can't reach me with any of his weapons, if say, he was missing a leg and I stand beyond his hobbled reach. Cut an arm off, he keeps on coming. Gash his head, try to poke him in the eye, try to slash his neck and I lose. Because I won't be able to be lucky enough times given that they will come in numbers. And any of them ducking or deflecting a blow will finish the fight.

"Maria and Lucia cannot physically fight them. It's as simple as that. They are too small and could never exert enough power to seriously injure them. But if they were down, they could thrust a spear. So it comes down to how to take them down."

Shon paused, "One weapon should be a spear, but only after taking them off their feet. Until they get up, they have no advantages at all. In fact, I have the advantage which I can pursue with a spear. So I need a spear. But what I need foremost is a takedown weapon."

Shon bade farewell to Carpia and began to run down the hill back to the house. As he ran he continued thinking.

He had been thinking about this since he first learned of the Deinoc. All he had come up with was a lasso. The problem with a lasso was that throwing it was unlikely to perfectly time with taking out the Deinoc's legs and, besides, its tail would prevent the loop from getting down to his feet and looping its head would do nothing since the creature would be charging, not pulling away like a fleeing horse.

Then, like a ship appearing out of the fog, he saw an object in his mind: a bola, a weapon that was usually made with two or three iron or stone balls attached to cords spun by hand and flung low at the feet to entangle them and trip the animal into a fall from which it cannot immediately arise. A bola. And, if he could launch several of them quickly he might bring down enough of these creatures to even the odds, if he could also dispatch them quickly enough to kill several of them before they could get up. In that effort the women could be most useful, armed with spears. They might even be able to throw the entangling bolas allowing him to do the killing with a spear himself.

As he ran he thought, *I need to work on a bola design. Perhaps some sort of razor wire instead of, or in conjunction with, the cord. The razor wire might even cut some tendons as the Deinoc struggles to get up. I also need some tactical maneuvers to get in, kill, get out, run away, turn, throw, get in, kill, and get out before too many of them get too close.*

As he neared the house, he concluded there was no human martial arts defense system that could be employed against a Deinoc. Too many weapons from too many directions. All he had come up with was a spear and bola. That concerned him greatly. It was always very dangerous to engage in combat with only one tactic. If it did not work, that was the end.

For the time being, he had a start. He could see that he would need to engage the Deinoc in the open to use a bola and a spear. The other tactical consideration was how Maria and Luciana could be trained to use spears and bolas And he had another problem to conquer: he had never thrown a bola. In fact, other than knowing of its existence from his memory well, he had never even seen a bola in person.

The Deinoc clearly had an unfair advantage. Their weapons came with their bodies. Besides primitive weapons like spears and bolas, the weapons he knew that could blow the Deinoc away probably didn't exist in this time and he would certainly not be able to manufacture such weapons without someone finding out. And even if he manufactured them, he judged he would never be allowed to go over the Wall with them. All he would accomplish in attempting to do so would be to enlighten the Deinoc to the fact that he knew who they were.

•

Over the next several days Shon worked on the bola. How long to make the thongs that ran from his hand to the knobs at the end. Too long and they would not wrap around the legs quickly enough; too short and they might wrap so quickly they wouldn't get both legs. Should it be leather, or wire, or woven line?

Too stiff would make it wrap slower or not at all; too loose and the energy might dissipate in the thongs before the knobs would be drawn by the centrifugal force of the throw to close on impact. What to make the knobs of? Rock, metal, rubber, a composite of some or all of these? They needed to help the thongs to cling tightly as they closed but not be so heavy that they fell to the ground as they closed.

FOUR

THE GREAT ONE

One early morning as Shon set out on his run, still dwelling on the perplexing problem of the bola's design, Carpia flew up.

She said, "This is the day for the long run. Do you need to make an excuse for your absence?"

He said, "They will assume I'm training unless we will be gone longer than the day."

"That depends on how fast and how long you can run. If you are as fast and fit as I think you are, we will be back shortly after sundown."

"Then lead on."

Carpia flew ahead. Shon followed running, his speed increasing until he was running nearly as fast as she was able to fly easily. He ran on, following her on an increasingly uphill course, first toward the mountains to the west then gradually bearing to the southwest towards Huascarán in the distance but well south of the foothills where the Montañan village that he had visited with Maria was situated. After a nearly four-hour run, he saw a Wall in the distance. Carpia led him toward that Wall until they came to a section of the Wall that appeared to be made of a milky glassine material.

As they approached the Wall, Shon stopped suddenly in his tracks as what seemed to be a human being appeared to be standing inside the translucent section of the Wall. He walked slowly toward the figure.

When he was no more than six paces away, the figure, now clearly in the shape of a female, raised an arm, palm outward toward him.

He stopped approaching as the Wall's appearance changed, becoming as transparent as clear crystal. Now he could see that the figure was a leathery, wrinkled, very old woman dressed in a silken white robe with an enormous gold torque around her neck and two smaller gold bracelets of the same twisting design as the neck torque around both of her wrists. But he detected under the robe from her slight movements a body, fit, lean, young, subtly exciting in all the ways bodies can be. He focused intently on the old crone's face searching for a reason for the dichotomy between the old face and the seemingly much younger body.

Carpia, who had flown to her usual perch near the Wall, nearly fell off it when the Wall changed its appearance. She had never seen that before nor the old woman instead of the Great One.

"Greetings, Earthman."

Shon, noting that the voice more matched the body than the face, said, "Greetings. You are Hom, I presume."

"Presumptions are best made with due consideration." The voice was flat in tone, but nevertheless conveyed that what she said was not casual banter.

Shon felt a sudden surge in his Magan implant's impulses. He felt as if she had slapped him lightly but crisply.

"I'll keep that in mind." He was cycling as rapidly as he had during the most tense moments of his chess game with Luciana. Perhaps the run had been harder than he thought.

"Possibly you might have kept that in mind before you presumed to tell the tribunal how the Society has so mismanaged Vitas by denying life to so many billions of humans awaiting your return while you were out gallivanting about the stars, asleep most of the time."

Shon instantly felt himself boiling from her remark as if she had slapped him physically. Yet it felt more than a slap: hard, like a jab from a fist. He wanted to strike back with a pithy rejoinder but he had cycled up enough to realize that concentrating on her rather than her remark was the fork to take. Yet he could not ignore the fact that he could recall no one who had ever gotten such a rise out of him so quickly with a single remark in his entire life.

He hid the petulance he felt, saying, "Perhaps I spoke out too quickly."

"Perhaps, or perhaps you should look into yourself and bring out what you've got to make me see things your way. I'm really quite willing to learn new things, even in my dotage."

"Despite your somewhat elderly appearance your voice doesn't sound like one in her declining years."

"So I really do look ancient, eh, Shon? May I call you Shon?"

"Regarding your appearance, I did not mean to offend you. Regarding how to call me, of course, Shon is fine. And how shall I address you?"

"No offence taken, quite the contrary. Call me Gaia, at least until we get to know each other a little better."

Carpia nearly fell off her perch again. She had shuddered as she heard the woman's voice, exactly the same as that of the Great One. Now she heard a name she had heard many times in her periodic role as one of her family's representatives on Council matters though she had never been to Annec. The name belonged to an old Hom, supposedly the oldest Hom of all, who resided in GenLib in Annec, ten thousand klicks away. What was she doing here instead of the Great One? But the voice was that of the Great One, though her face looked much older than she had appeared when viewing her through the translucent Wall. Could they possibly be the same person?

Gaia turned her gaze to Carpia. "Carpia, it would be best if I had some privacy with our visitor. Fly to that knoll over there and wait for Shon to come. Then fly back to me so that I may have a private word with you at the end of this."

"Yes, Great One," Carpia said, certain by the inflection and tone of her voice that this Gaia was somehow indeed the Great One, and she quickly flew to the knoll a few hundred yards away.

Gaia, returning her gaze to Shon, said, "She has been of great service to me over many years. You and Maria have a truly great friend, though I am afraid that I do not have as discreet an aide as I thought."

Shon was suddenly alarmed for Carpia. "I hope nothing will happen to her on account of me."

Gaia laughed loudly, sort of a cackle, but not old-sounding. "There are few enough creatures like her. I would be loath to change that."

It was the first comment from her that made him consider that she might not necessarily be one of the evil Hom he had been conjuring up since he first queried Luciana about the ancient Roman names and titles. *What's her agenda? Dealing with me for my Slippery Slope Proposition, or something else? Might as well find out now.* "It sounds like you have a problem with my criticism about how this planet has been run by the Society."

"If I thought you had devised a better plan I would not have the slightest problem with your criticism. But I don't think you have any plan at all. And that is extremely dangerous to the welfare of this planet because I know who you really are, or perhaps I should say, I know who you may become."

Shon was absolutely dumbstruck.

She said, "You are wondering whether I know you have a Magan implant. I am wondering if you know that your implant is a mass of neurons interlaced into your limbic brain so that you have a bicameral limbic brain potentially capable of acting together in synchrony like your bicameral cerebrum. But you in a conflict between your limbic brains because they have different mentalities. Do I have to say more to gain your complete focus?"

Shon was cycling so fast now that he was sweating more than he had been when he had been running to get here. He remained silent, fighting mightily against his Magan impulses to direct his actions now.

"That's the wisest thing you've done so far."

He said, as much to gain time to think as to learn the meaning of her comment, "What's that?"

"Controlling yourself. You know I know, or I wouldn't have said it. What you are undoubtedly wanting to ask without admitting that I am correct is how I know and, if what I just said about the nature of the implant is true, how I know that while you don't."

"Very well, how do you know?"

"Because I am Magan."

Shon stared at her. "There are Magans on Vitas?"

"There is a Magan on Vitas."

"And how did that come about?" He realized his mind was already ceding space to his Magan implant as he had responded matter-of-factly to what was easily the two most extraordinary remarks he had ever heard—a Magan on Vitas and another brain in his head from his creation instead of an implant introduced after he was born as he had always been told.

Gaia laughed. This time it wasn't a cackle; it was the full fresh laugh of a young woman. "Ah, Shon, that story is far too long to fully tell today, but, like you, I went to the stars and returned—earlier—much earlier." A portion of the glassine Wall retracted and she stood with no barriers between them.

He stepped back as the old woman crouched over and began to pull at her face as she turned her back to him.

When she turned back to face him and resumed her upright posture, he saw a woman who appeared younger than he and, as he focused on the young woman as she turned back to face him, he exclaimed, "Oh, my God! Kai! Oh, my God!" He wanted to approach and embrace her but something about her stance made him hold back. And that something brought out a composed response from him: "So you returned. How long ago?"

She stood still as if frozen. She said as calmly as she'd made her last remark. "A few thousand years after I left as you were also intended to do."

"But, but that would mean you're—eight hundred thousand years old! That's—impossible."

"No, Shon," she said, still frozen, "Quite possible. There are more than five hundred and twenty five thousand minutes in a year, but calling that period a year doesn't sound so long. It doesn't sound so long when you say eight centimillia, instead of eight hundred thousand years. For those with indeterminate lifespans, time is measured in decamillia and centimillia in the same way time was measured in years, decades, and centuries for those with determinate lifespans. It may serve you well to know that you are indeed possessed of what the Society calls an indeterminate lifespan."

Shon shuddered, but resisted processing this news for the moment. "Kai, it seems you have aged remarkably well, so why are you disguised as an old woman?"

She stepped down from her place on the Wall and approached him. "My older appearance serves the purpose of meeting the expectations of the Hom who believe they are the unchanging mortals of indeterminate lifespans who will over time slowly grow older looking. And that does occur. A Home does grow older looking though extremely slowly after adulthood. I am the oldest Hom, even though I am not really Hom. It is advantageous for me to seem older than them to all of them. It reminds them that I have survived and extreme survival is the most highly respected aspect any Hom can have. But I stopped looking older at a much younger age. It would be too unsettling for them to see me appearing even younger than all but the youngest of them. They might want to kill me off the same way they fear the citizen humans would kill them off if they knew the reality of their lifespans. I am different from them.

"I am Magan. They are not. You are like me, Magan. And while we are similar to the Hom, we are not actually Hom at all. The Hom don't know that their genetics are different from mine, as they believe I am the last of the original Hom, the first generation, which I am in a way.

"The Hom lifespan comes from genetic engineering centuries after the genetic engineering that evolved us was lost to posterity. Our genetics were developed by military geneticists focused on designing better soldiers. It turned out that the genes they tinkered with had a collateral benefit, what the Hom call indeterminate lifespans. But it was an accidental benefit our geneticists never became aware of as the soldiers they created all died during the covert wars before their indeterminate lifespans became apparent.

"The later genetic work creating indeterminate lifespans was entirely focused on attaining life extension, and they got what they wanted. They had no idea that it had already been discovered before and lost, but the other aspects that make us different required a different focus—and they weren't focused on making themselves into warriors."

Shon said, "Why would that focus make a difference?"

"The last thing a Hom wants to do is wage war personally. So they didn't pursue genetics that made being better at something that was not good for living long lives."

"I see that. So what did our military geneticists do to make us better warriors?" said Shon.

Kai said, "Because of their focus on making warriors, they modified and manipulated our DNA to develop a mass of special limbic neurons which were intertwined, but not linked by synapses with the other neurons in our limbic brain. Instead they connected this brain only to our reptilian lower brain and our bicameral neocortices both of which this new limbic brain can highly influence to such an extent it that it might be more accurate to say that our normal limbic brain has dominance in our early life until our Magan brain develops enough strong synaptic connections and also absorbs the effect of the memories being created by the other brains to learn how to subsume our original limbic persona and gain control over our mentality.

"But taking control over the other brains which began their relationship over a hundred million years ago and became fully integrated with the other brains over that long expanse is not easy as pathways and processes developed over eons were. So, simply put, the genetic engineers without the time to truly integrate the new brain into the existing structure took some shortcuts and used the limbic brain they determined possessed the strongest emotions with the hope that that might give the new brain a power over neurons possessed of weaker emotions much the same way that mammals derived advantages by having emotions that other animals do not.

"To this day, no one can encode an emotion as no one really knows what makes an emotion what it is. We can engineer reactions, but we cannot create the original genetically-based emotion that interfaces with the outside world to cause us to behave in response to the triggering stimuli as if we were in control of ourselves or, much less, beyond, are in control of others' emotions. And, yet, we can control others' emotions even though we can't control our own."

"Is the struggle I feel, and I assume you felt, in keeping this brain at bay, simply because our creators didn't get it fully integrated?"

"Yes, but more of the struggle is a battle going on with the relative strength of the emotions created by each brain," said Kai. "The Magan brain succeeds in the end because the Magan limbic brain is the repository for more strongly felt emotions than those in our normal limbic brain and is much more sensitive to the non-verbal emanations of emotions from others possessing normal limbic emotions including our own normal limbic brain.

"But we have more important things to discuss now."

Shon said, "All right, does this sum it up? In effect, the Magan brain is a fifth brain connected to the normal mammalian brain consisting of the reptilian lower brain directly controlling lower animal functions an , two brains, the bicameral cerebral cortex controlling higher mentality functions such as language, conscious thought, and intellect; and the limbic middle brain, the repository for emotions which, before genetic engineering got underway, was possessed only by mammals.

"Our normal limbic brain is only vaguely aware of the Magan brain through the initially weak connections the Magan brain has with the reptilian and neocortex brains. And it takes some time for it to dominate all of the brains we possess and, until then, we exist as Kai and Shon?"

She stepped toward him and spread her arms toward the jungle alongside the Wall. "I rarely walk around here. So let's walk as we talk.

"It's a bit more complicated than your summary of the Magan mind. The genetic version of our entire body is better than the Hom version. You look as old as you ever will no matter how long you live. The Hom very slowly look older. And you can do things they can't. Finally, no one anywhere has a Magan brain besides us and any progeny we might have.

Kai began to walk down a swale which ran along the Wall to the south. Shon joined her a step behind and asked the first of some questions he suddenly wanted answers to. "What happened to your ship, Kai?"

"Well, I didn't debark so meekly as you did. But it hardly mattered. Our mission planners were wise enough to recognize the possibility that things might not go exactly as they planned when we returned, so they built in protocols and codes to take control of our ships when they returned. They anticipated the possibility a Magan might be in command. Unfortunately, or fortunately as it turned out, I didn't anticipate that and they took control of my ship the moment I refused to comply with their instructions to leave it."

"So why didn't you take control of my ship instead of trying to blast it out of the sky?"

"I knew it could not be destroyed by any blast from the array on the Moon so I decided to learn two things at the same time: whether it was really Canopus and whether a Magan was in command."

"How would you know?"

"If you had turned Magan, you would have blasted at least some portion of the Moon Base out of existence to train your opponents about the brutal consequences of crossing you."

"And then what would you have done?"

"I would have taken control of your ship as they did mine and blinked it out of existence as they did mine after they took me from it, only I would have blinked it out with the Magan still aboard because I am instilled with the nature to do what is necessary to protect myself and my planet."

"So, when I didn't blast back, you waited till I left and then blinked out Canopus anyway and kept me for some purpose of your own?"

"How could I possibly have taken the risk that your ship might destroy this planet I have spent eight hundred thousand years preserving?"

Shon shrugged. "Well, be that as it may, you threw away a truly amazing technology."

"I have the records and the means to recreate anything that existed before given enough time, which I have in abundance."

"Your Hom did an amazing job of hiding their intentions, particularly Luciana and Mamercus."

Kai turned her face to him and laughed a real laugh. "They can't hide their emotions, Shon. Surely you have seen that in Luciana and even in your brief acquaintance with Mamercus who is far, far older than she and should know better. They had no idea what I was up to. I simply fed the Council information as I determined it was needed and let their fears direct a course that needed little additional guidance from me."

"I miss Canopus."

"I miss Sirius, too, even after all these millennia. But if you live long you will learn that missing things and people is part of living a long life, until you learn to avoid such temporal attachments and to confine yourself to attending to conglomerations of life rather than the individuals that compose them."

Shon said, "Which brings me to ask what you have been doing all this time."

Kai stopped walking and turned to face Shon, and drawing a deep breath, said, "How to quickly sum up eight hundred thousand years of mucking around in everything? Simply put, I became God. Not a god, but the one God for this planet's inhabitants. I transformed Earth into Vitas. Despite your disparagements about what Vitas is today, I preserved the planet and the two races of humankind which would have destroyed one or the other and possibly the planet along the way had I not done what I did."

Shon said, "But there seems to have been some costs, such as a vast dichotomy between the two parts of humankind that live today."

Kai said, "There are actually three human races distinguishable by significant genetic differences: the citizens, the Hom, and the Magans as I have labeled us. The records I know only so well make the Magans a race of two, you and me. You are already genetically Magan even though your mind is not—yet."

"Kai, what is it that so bothers you about my so-called Slippery Slope Proposition? Why not grow the population?"

"There is an ancient adage that goes something like, 'if you find an interpretation at odds with scripture, perhaps you should reevaluate the interpretation.' The Order has an underlying logic that you have failed to comprehend. Yet the seeds of understanding lie within your observation about the dichotomy between the citizens and the Hom.

"What your Slippery Slope Proposition fails to address is the fact that Hom and citizens have such divergent lifespans. A really long lifespan causes a Hom to perceive the world and how to live in it in a completely different way than a citizen does. Everyday life is so different when there is no sense of urgency or impending end to your life, unless you do something to jeopardize your life. The Hom who live long focus on that last aspect and live to preserve their lives.

"But, for the short-lived citizens, the idea that some other human will outlive them as if they were just spring bugs, alive for a few weeks and then gone forever, is truly difficult for them and extremely dangerous to the Hom if the citizens were ever to discover that the Hom possess indeterminate lifespans.

"When it all started I saw no reason to dispose of either part of humankind. I felt I could control them. I was correct on that count. But to do it I had to keep the numbers of the citizens within the bounds I could handle without the necessity of periodically massacring them or engineering viruses to stop their breeding. So I created the Order. But as the Hom aged, I learned that the Hom will never attempt to develop a large-scale evolving society of citizens or even more Hom."

Shon shifted his weight between his feet and said, "Why is that?"

"Increasing the citizen population increases the possibility that they might bring about injury to the Hom by intent or by simply increasing the interactions that might cause an accidental death to a Hom. Increasing the Hom population carries the risk that the newly born might bring harm to their elders before those among them who are less fearful for their lives die out from the accidents and perils they bring on themselves. The Hom take additional risk when they breed; so they don't, except to maintain the number they judge they need to maintain control and by doing so insure that no greater risks are brought upon themselves by failing to maintain control.

"As for why they don't simply eliminate the citizens entirely, thereby reducing any risk from the citizens and the need to breed at all, the Hom learned early on that life would be unbearable without the citizens because the citizens give them a reason for living on. Many of them spend a very great deal of their time viewing the GenLib records of historical personages of interest and observing quite intently current citizen events. Many actively participate in enforcing the Order as it gives vitality and purpose to their lives. But they don't need larger numbers than a couple hundred citizen communities living their lives in diverse corners of the world to get what they need to have that purpose.

And they really are adverse to increasing the citizen population to any level that might increase their risk of an accident beyond the minimum that serves their need for meaning, however shallow."

"Like zookeepers," Shon said dryly, folding his arms.

"I suggest you think a moment on what humans themselves thought of the gods they created over the ages. Their gods were also their self-created zookeepers. These gods, through the imaginations of their subjects, created order in their time—religion in all its various but similar forms—they needed to survive and accept the vagaries of living and their ultimate deaths; just as the Hom acting through the Society do for them today. For the Order now is the religion of the citizens as much as it is the forum for control by the Society."

"How do you view the citizens? They seem quite vital to me."

"I agree that they are quite vital, and, because they are unaware that near-eternal living is actually possible, they still cling to the religiously-inspired afterlife they created for themselves so that they can face death when their time has run out. The biggest difference between these two groups isn't the fact of their different lifespans, about which the citizens know nothing, but the awareness a citizen has that his life will certainly end within four hundred years because he cannot avoid dying and the awareness a Hom has that his life might be eternal if he can simply avoid dying. Yet it is only citizens who can move forward because they can accept death believing there is no alternative.

"I had the power to keep them from being annihilated by the Hom so I did. That was completely consistent with my Magan instincts which I understand only too well."

Shon said, "You refer to yourself as Magan, but you seem to be the Kai I knew who went to the stars because she cared about people and the future of humanity."

Kai, smiling a small smile, said, "I don't seem like a Magan to you because becoming Magan is not changing entirely into another distinct personality devoid of our previous personality as we were led to believe. We were taught to believe that because the scientists who developed the Magan brain thought that. They chose the DNA of an ancient person who they believed this person had the personality characteristics to act as they wanted us to act in certain extreme circumstances.

"The neurons that they developed to become the Magan brain needed to succeed in gaining control in such circumstances of not just our minds but the minds of everyone else they might have to deal with. The scientists were desperate to make that happen and using that particular DNA was a shortcut they thought could possibly enable this genetically-engineered new limbic brain to come to dominate our reptilian, limbic, and cerebral brains despite the eons-old time the other brains had to become highly unified and resistant to a new neuronic entity. They never comprehended the true nature of the brain they created because they did not understand the full effect of the DNA they used to create the brain—that that DNA contained, simplistically stated, the soul of the person it came from, his true nature, something more than mere instinctive proclivities."

"How so?" said Shon, furrowing his brow.

"Our genetic engineers detected this DNA's unique sensitivity to the instincts encoded deep in the older areas of our brain and used for survival and dominance from the eons before we were human, or even mammalian, and the extraordinary ability to manipulate the primitive instincts in other humans that the humans don't consciously perceive at all. That is was what they sought to implant by intertwining the Magan brain into our limbic brain.

'But they missed something deeper. The brain does not just affect that sensitivity and ability, but it also melds the genetic code conveying the building blocks for mentality with that of its host. This was not something they could see by an examination of his genetic code because they didn't have the knowledge to discover how and where it was encoded in the DNA.

"Since they controlled those enhanced very closely to insure that no full conversion ever occurred, they made sure anyone close to fully converted died. Since no one living on Earth ever experienced a full conversion, they never learned that the DNA used to create the Magan brain had its own special effect on our DNA which in turn had an effect on the Magan DNA and how we would behave as we transformed into a Magan."

Shon said, "So how does a fully converted Magan behave?"

Kai said, "A Magan dominates other humans by using the extraordinary mentality transferred to him by the Magan brain's extreme sensitivity to emotions, its own and all others it senses, including those of the normal limbic brain in which it resides. The scientists also misperceived the Magan brain's ability to effect nonhumans and computers with artificial intelligence."

"What sort of misperception, Kai?" Shon leaned his head toward her, intensely focused on her every word. For the first time, he was learning what would likely come from succumbing to his Magan brain as he had been considering to save Maria.

"They thought a Magan would be able to affect any intelligence. But, as I learned and I suspect you may also have learned, a Magan has no advantage over our lightship computers: those we gain control of with our canny brains, not by the manipulative advantages over emotions which computers don't possess. I'm sure you used your intelligence and not your influence to gain control of your ship's computer when the time came to do so. A Magan's influence over nonhumans is not predictable as nonhumans are not affected by the same instincts and emotions as humans if they even have emotions which they don't as they lack a limbic brain and no one knows how to program emotions because no one really knows how emotions really exist. I am able to influence more than a few of the families in the Society, all of whom have limbic brains, but not Magan brains, as a result of their enlightenment, precisely because their genetics are quite susceptible to a Magan mind even though, in many ways, they are not inclined towards either the citizens or the Hom."

Shon said, "So it is the laying on of the Magan's genetic mentality over our own emotions that drive our ideas and beliefs and the ability it grants us to affect others with limbic brains that is the outcome of becoming Magan. In essence, our will to act is enhanced by the Magan's will to act aided by far more sensitive emotional capabilities to understand the emotions sensed and to manipulate them because their subjects are unaware of this emotional capability. We then pursue our previous agenda, but with a Magan approach."

"Precisely. You always were a quick study. But there is a subtlety that is important. It is why we instinctively resist the Magan brain. After conversion the dominant mentality in the meld is the Magan mind."

Kai began to walk slowly. Shon followed beside her. She continued. "The principal attraction of the Magan brain to the scientists engaged in the Lightship Project was their belief that this brain had an instinctive predilection to do what was best for those aligned with its mentality without consideration for the interests of those not so aligned.

"Believing that alignment was based on a genetic instinct aligned with humans, they judged that a human converted by the Magan brain would always choose a course favorable to humankind.

"They told us that a planet inhabitable by humans would most likely possess life that had evolved to a sentient level given the billions of years it took for planets to develop the atmosphere and other planetary conditions necessary to sustain humankind. Those beings would certainly not welcome an influx of humankind seeking to continue their lives by taking over their planet any more than humankind would lay down to an alien invasion of their own planet. They told us that if we became Magan under such conditions we would be able to control the alien population by our powers of persuasion and would be able to negotiate a compact for humankind to join their ecosystem."

She stopped and turned to him looking at his eyes. "The files tell an entirely different story on this point. What our directors really believed was that once we became Magan we would use the power of our lightships to wipe out the alien presence to pave the way for humankind as our primitive, powerful emotions dictated. They counted on us to do what they couldn't be sure we'd do without the Magan brain—massacre whomever and whatever stood in the way of humankind's goal to take over their planet. On this aspect they were correct, or so I believe from my own experience."

Shon shuddered as he absorbed the truth.

Kai continued, "I am Magan. I have annihilated people and other life on Vitas over the ages in pursuit of the interests of humankind as I solely determined them to be. It is really remarkably easy to kill one's enemy when your enemy has no idea of what you are really capable of doing to them. But, having lived for ages now I find that I have become what I despise most in the Hom. Like them, I have become obsessed with seeing the future play out, watching them live their lives and intervening to direct them when I think it serves humankind. And, like them, I am no longer willing to undertake a cause that would expose me to the real risks of dying that such an undertaking would require because I might die before I see what happens next. Living long makes you old whether you age or not and nothing can stop that process."

Shon stopped walking and said, "So you want me to change the world while you watch me do it. If I die in this battle with the Deinoc, you continue as before. And if I live? What happens then?"

Kai stopped a bit more than a meter beyond him and, turning toward him, replied, "You will only survive by turning Magan. As a Magan you will become their one God whether they know it or not."

"I would never become a god much less God."

"I'll not debate that with you, Shon, because you won't know that until you become God and then we will see what you will do about that. With a plan, your Shon self will gain a seat at the table with your Magan self, albeit a subordinate one for a long time, perhaps forever. Your two selves will meld into Magan Shon. You will not become the nicest human alive, but effectuating your plan will make that irrelevant. Without a plan you will become the Magan Incarnate, totally dominated by the Magan's mentality, far more dangerous to the Hom, the Citizens, the Society, and to Vitas itself than all the Deinoc multiplied by ten thousand could ever be."

Shon said, "Have you determined my 'plan', God?"

She opened her hands toward him and said in a firm voice, "Resist your urge to resist what you don't want to hear, Shon. Understand the reality of Vitas. Then you may find a cause worth living and dying for, and a way to keep yourself alive instead of becoming a shadow in the mind of your successor if you become Magan. Until a few moments ago you had no idea that you could even live even as long as a citizen as no one in our time lived that long. I have an idea you should consider as it is similar to what your Slippery Slope Proposition propounds—more people, many more. So many that your proposition pales to what you might accomplish. And, if you embrace it, you may retain a significant place in the mind of the person you will become."

Shon opened his hands toward her and said, "I'm listening, Kai."

Kai said, "All that is likely to come from your idealistic idea that we should grow the population on Vita will be the eventual slaughter of the citizens by the Society to preserve their own existence against such masses. The reality is that the Society has the tools to wipe out the citizens easily. Afterwards, all that will be left will be the Hom with no reason to even maintain the small numbers they have today and the other members of the Society who will be in peril of reduction over the ages by the Hom who have no reason to support their continued existence which they might come to see as a threat to their existence. Lacking the tools and the skills to pursue a grander vision, they will live on until the sun expands and consumes Vitas and them with it because they cannot avoid this fate by themselves.

"Even if, by some remarkably small chance, the citizens prevail, their population will grow until it grows to what it was when you left. It will be a far more rapid growth in the living population as citizens live four times as long as humankind did in our time when it grew to unsustainable numbers. They will destroy the planet and themselves with it within a thousand years or so. Either way humankind will cease to exist."

Shon almost shouted, "So what cause is there, Kai? My population ideas are anathema to you and I must admit that you may be correct about the likely consequences of unbridled citizen expansion. I'll take your word on what will happen with the destruction of the citizen population which, frankly, I am more concerned with than maintaining the near-eternal lives of the zookeepers. I see no other role for myself other than living out my life quietly for as long as I have, apparently according to you forever, or until I suffer a fatal accident, or until the sun burns me up so far into the future that I cannot begin to grasp such a life."

Kai responded in a calm voice. "You misunderstand my view on your population ideas. While your current view is bound to fail, there is another path with a similar view wherein growing the population could insure humankind's future on an unimaginably grander scale than you imagine for eons beyond the inevitable demise of Vitas. Imagine growing the population with an eye on our original mission—to inhabit the stars. Then your calculations on the number of humans which could live the lives you believe they should be able to would be exponentially greater than what you posited at your trial. Imagine ultimately trillions of humans living on many thousands, perhaps millions, of planets throughout this galaxy and even beyond."

Shon suddenly saw a glimmer of where she was going. He said, "You want to restart the Black Hole Lightship Project?"

She began to walk again as a breeze arose and made the warm moist air cooler. "I want to send Vitan life to the stars but to do that will require that millions die in the quest to bring life to trillions. Much like fish or amphibians laying hundreds of eggs to bring a few to life to lay hundreds of more eggs to bring an ever increasing population to life until their numbers grow to billions and then trillions. Someone has to face the cost to make that happen which will be measured in the many millions, likely billions over enough eons, who venture out on fruitless journeys to empty, uninhabitable planets or to a death along the way from the occasional collisions that will occur with stellar matter. Only a Magan can drive that exodus from Vitas to the galaxy's millions of planets. You are the only Magan around to do it."

Shon stopped in his tracks and stepped back a few steps as if she had pushed him. He bent over and put his hands on his knees. He could see her vision. It was awesome in purpose but brutal in execution. He would be sending millions, ultimately billions, to their deaths to gain the goal of trillions living across the galaxy and beyond. Humankind had made awful sacrifices before in its expansion over the entire world but always because the forces that drove the expansion were worse than pursuing the unknown dangers and because almost none of them perceived the costs that would have to be paid. Now Kai posited a plan to do it without those vagaries to drive them out to find new frontiers and with a clear calculation of the costs to be paid before they went out.

He stood erect and said, "Even if I pursued such a course, how could the resources of Vitas sustain such a monumental effort?"

She waved her arm in a sweeping gesture and said, "I have retained all the technical and scientific files from our past. Our predecessors developed quite an advanced technology before the walls came tumbling down on technological research. I tore those walls down ages ago in the observable records but they still reside inside my secure files. We have the technology to develop the ships to carry us to the stars and the material resources on the Moon and Mars to create the ships we need. There is enough water on Europa to supply those ships without taking a drop from Vitas. When the time comes I can find the primordial black holes we need and use the consolidated force to propel them."

"Consolidated force? What is that?"

"How do you think your ship controlled its black hole? Think about it. How could mere magnetic fields have controlled the forces of our ships' black holes? Our directors didn't tell us everything about how our ships worked nor did they tell our computer companions. They programmed them to use the greatest scientific discovery made by humankind to this very day. But the knowledge of how to consolidate the four forces of the universe—gravity, strong, weak and electromagnetic—was something so powerful that they dared not send a ship or captain out with that knowledge for fear it might fall into alien hands, nor did they dare make it public for fear trying to use it might bring destruction to Earth itself. I found the secret technology after I discovered some files locked by complexly encrypted codes designed to keep the secret from all but the few people entrusted with them who died before they passed them on. I was able to break the codes over several decamillia." She laughed a short laugh. "Our ships should have been more aptly named consolidated-black-hole lightships."

Shon said, "Even so, our ships were small, capable of carrying one, maybe a couple more. It would take many millennia. Jesus, Kai! Hundreds of millennia to accomplish even a small part of what you describe."

"Ah, Shon, again you are jumping to conclusions based on inaccurate information. The technology is scalable. We can build any size ship we like. The resources available to our mission directors, encumbered as they were by the billions of people sucking the planet dry, were insufficient to do more than they did, but the resources available to us now, even just on the Moon, are unlimited."

Shon said, "My imagination is having trouble with how I, or anyone, could turn Vitas to such an undertaking, particularly to embracing the notion that millions will go out so that a few can survive to landfall on distant planets. Besides why couldn't we do the initial exploring with computers?"

Kai began walking, turning back towards whence they came. Shon followed quickly until he was walking next to her. She said, "To your second point first, using computers would necessitate developing sentient intelligence in them, something humankind wisely stopped pursuing even before you and I left for the stars. Had we continued their evolution to full sentience, we would not have survived. We can never allow computers to evolve to our level as they will evolve beyond us on their own as a self-replicating life-form that would become more Magan than we, serve their own interests, and would leave us behind if they left us alive at all. You must understand that is flatly not an option.

"Without the guidance I am giving you today, you will become a bit of Deinoc folklore, undoubtedly the greatest human they ever encountered from their point of view, an ancient fierce being from a distant violent past they long for, defeated by their glorious Deinoc Horde. They might well get so carried away with themselves afterwards that a Deinoc uprising might be the outcome. If that happened, I would have to annihilate them and life would continue as it has for so many millennia.

"That would be a shame as the Deinoc could play an important role in the future of humanity and all life on this planet. That is why I created them."

"You created them?"

"I inspired their creation. When you know about each family that was enlightened, you will see a method in it. It is the Society, not the citizens or the Hom or any part of any of these, but the whole that is what we need to go to the stars. On some planets, a dinosaur will prevail, but only those capable of aggressing—the reason you will find—except for the Therizi, who are quite capable of aggressing—only Therapod carnivores among the families. On other planets, mammals will succeed and on others the birds and on others the cetaceans. And so on. Each ship will be an Ark of Vitan life. When the conquest is over, it will not be a galaxy of citizens or Hom but a galaxy of Vitans, so much more than just humankind.

"So perhaps you can see that I am looking for something a bit more interesting than watching some Deinoc eat an ancient human warrior who I happened to know a long time ago."

Shon felt staggered as if pummeled by a club. Her imagination of the future struck every nerve in his body. He could see the galaxy she described and his mind began to imagine, too.

Kai continued, saying, "The GenLib records contain a story about a Traveler who will come and change the order of things. I took the ancient idea of a Messiah to create the Traveler. The Hom, the Deinoc, and some other Society families having an interest in humankind know about this prophecy and some are obsessed with it. It is a role that can be used to make this plan work. But that Traveler must be you.

"You must take up this cause if you really want to change humankind's destiny from only living out this planet's destiny to a destiny conjoined with the entire universe. That may not be eternal but it will be inconceivably longer than this planet's with trillions to thank you for it even if they have no idea billions of years from now of how and who made it happen. You can see the logic and why I am compelled to follow it. I will help you from the shadows."

They had returned to where they had started. A line of storm clouds was approaching from the south bringing rain. Kai stepped up to her place in the Wall and turned to Shon who stood a bit more than a meter from the Wall's base. She reached down and picked up a long, thin object wrapped in a white silk cloth embroidered with gold filigree. "Take this."

He took it and untied the golden strings at one end and drew the object out. It was a sword and scabbard. He drew the sword from its scabbard which he recognized as a saya. The sword was a katana, a Japanese samurai sword, light in weight with a slightly curving blade, shining but not as if it were made of steel, rather of something else, perhaps a ceramic of some kind with a two-handed hilt wrapped in a sticky mesh that seemed to adhere to his hands as if it wouldn't let go. He barely touched the edge of the blade and cut his finger. "What is it made of?"

"The strongest material on this planet, forged in a linear accelerator hundreds of thousands of years ago. Its edge is as sharp as an edge can be made, yet it cannot be blunted even from contact with the same material. I know you have a plan for fighting the Deinoc, but practice with this and you will find that it will serve you when the time comes."

He swung the katana a few times and felt it fly through space as if it was cutting the air itself. He slid it carefully back into its saya.

Kai said, "Now go to Carpia, but slowly so I can become her Great One again before she comes to me."

Shon stepped back and walked to the knoll. By the time he reached the knoll it had begun to rain.

Carpia flew to her perch by the Wall. She saw the Great One standing behind the translucent wall as she had always seen her before, a transcendent image that overwhelmed her ability to imagine her as an old crone who was supposed to be Gaia. Certain that the Great One had made herself appear as she had for some purpose known only to herself, Carpia waited to hear her instructions.

The Great One said, "Watch him and report back to me when he goes over the Wall into Annec."

Carpia flew through the rain toward Shon, who was running back to Pinchincha.

When she caught up with him she could see he was in no mood to talk and, strangely, she felt no urge to inquire about the time he had spent with the Great One.

FIVE

PREPARATION

Shon did not sleep when he returned to Pinchincha, spending the night instead cogitating. He did not dwell on things he could consider later such as what he had learned about himself and his Magan brain. And he did not focus on what he might do to change Vitas. Those were things he would consider after he dealt with his immediate problem, which was how to survive the coming battle with the Deinoc. As the sun rose the next morning, he had a plan based on his earlier considerations of the primary weapon he had determined was the key to defeating them, the bola.

He went to see Rolando in the white tower.

Shon said, "In my time, there were people called gauchos who lived south of you in a country called Argentina. While riding horses they threw a ball and cord contraption that could take down cattle and horses by entangling their legs. It was called a bola. I have researched your records and it seems there is a game played in many communities on this continent that uses a similar device called a bogacho. Are you familiar with this game? I believe it is called like the device, bogacho."

"Of course, it is very popular and played throughout Montaña though, as I'm sure you learned from the records, not from horses."

"Is there any chance that you could find me the best player in Montaña and get him to come here to train Maria, Luciana, and me on how to throw the bogacho?"

"I suppose you are not going to tell me why you want to learn to play bogacho when it would seem you have more pressing interests at the moment?"

"Let me just say that throwing the bogacho and my more pressing interests are aligned."

"Give me the day to see what I can do."

•

Ginés Cortijo was the best bogacho player in Montaña. When he had been a young boy, he had witnessed a game of bogacho between the two best teams in Montaña. He persuaded his father to get him a bogacho and began to practice. It became an obsession and by the time he was twenty, he was able to do almost anything that could be done with the bogacho. Over the next two hundred and fifty years, he had dominated the bogacho league in Montaña. He had never lost his love of the game. He was honored when Rolando called him, as his only other passion in life was his secret membership in the Resurrection. Rolando had told him he was to prepare three people who had been banished to Amaz for what the Resurrection had long believed was a death sentence.

When he arrived at Rolando's home Rolando took him to see the people he had told him needed to learn the bogacho. Two beautiful women, one with a parrot perched on her shoulder, and a fit-looking man he could perhaps train.

Rolando chuckled as he looked at Ginés reaction to those he was to teach and drew him aside, saying, "Ginés, you can train anyone to throw the bogacho."

Ginés smirked, "Women, Rolando?"

Rolando's demeanor turned serious, "I cannot tell you why this is important to the Resurrection. All I can say is that the lives of these two women and the man may determine the fate of the Resurrection and that fate may very well be in your hands. They must learn to take down anything that moves on two feet, or four, with absolute certainty and they must be able to accomplish it in a split second of time. Their names are Maria, Luciana, and Shon."

Ginés was a plain man in manner, but no fool. What he had just heard was so audacious that he could make only one conclusion: Rolando must be telling the truth.

Ginés said, "Rolando, Shon, and lovely ladies, let us go in and enjoy a pleasant evening. Tomorrow we will see if what you wish me to do is possible."

•

When Shon and the women arose the next morning they found clothing for them outside their sleeping quarters. They dressed and came down to breakfast where they met Ginés, dressed in his bogacho clothes, similar to what they wore.

Ginés knew any hope of accomplishing what he had been asked to do would depend on the natural athletic ability and fitness of each of the women. He intended to test those qualities before they began to train. He had told Rolando that if the women could not pass his test they could not learn to throw the bogacho with precision in less than a year. It could take five years to become truly expert in throwing. It could take ten years to become expert in the game. Rolando said he thought he might have six weeks, more or less. They both agreed that, absent clear talent, Rolando would have to explain that what they wanted was impossible.

Ginés, focusing on the women, said solemnly, "Young ladies, it is my duty to tell you that what you wish to accomplish will be very difficult. In fact, it will be impossible if you do not have real talent for it. If I seem hard on you it will only be because I want you to succeed."

While Luciana had not competed in physical sports, she had been trained in many of the arts of body movement and she could do a wide variety of movements including some excellent gymnastics turns. She felt confident she could meet his demands.

Maria had always been fit. Before Shon had entered her life, she had spent an average of two hours a day in activities designed to develop endurance, speed, and coordination. She was certain that she could meet Ginés' expectations.

Luciana glanced at Maria and said dryly to Ginés, "We understand. Let's see what you've got."

•

Ginés started by taking them to a room in an adjoining building, fitted out as a gymnasium. When Ginés removed his warm-up clothes, the women were confronted with a remarkable male physique. He was no taller than the women but he was close to thirty kilos larger than them. Solid supple muscle.

He told them to mimic everything he did. When he began to stretch, the women realized that his range of motion was a least as great as theirs within every muscle group.

He led them out of the building and into a field where the women could see a path. He started down it slowly and after a klick began to pick up the pace. They ran eight klicks and came back to the gym. The sky was clear, the air moist and hot.

Now that they were warmed up, he began to demonstrate a variety of jumps, squats, spins, most of which involved either going to the ground quickly and then rising up to a vertical but crouched stance or going prone to the ground and then springing up using only his legs.

After a few minutes, he said, "You will need to be able to use your upper body including your arms and hands to handle the bogacho, so your legs will be responsible for getting you back up when you need to go down. In bogacho, the game involves entangling your opponents with your bogachos. But often this will occur after you have avoided those thrown first at you by your opponents, necessitating a drop to the ground, prone as I have just demonstrated. When this occurs you will need to get up and throw your own bogacho as you arise from an awkward position. So we work on getting up with the legs without any aid from the arms which must be ready to throw the bogachos as you arise."

Next he took a handful of bogachos. His bogachos had balls of different color representing different weights and cord lengths. He explained their different uses. Some could be thrown quickly but had limited range but good width, others had range but more limited width. He explained width was important so that the balls would pass around the legs of a target and then the cords would hit the target and draw the balls around and then, ideally, the balls would cross and the cords would become entangled. Too narrow a width and the balls would not get around and entangle the target. Too much cord and the bogacho would not come taut on the target to initiate the wrapping and the balls would tend to move poorly in relation to each other. So which to throw when was very important.

Ginés demonstrated by throwing at a series of posts—some single, some double—at different distances between the posts. As soon as he began throwing the girls looked at each. They now knew exactly what Shon had in mind. It was exciting. If they could do this, they could actually help Shon defeat the Deinoc, rather than be the prey that would be killed if Shon could not kill the Deinoc by himself.

After the demonstration, Ginés took them back to the room where they had begun and tested them on weight equipment that had arrived since they had left the building. He made notes and then they went out into a stormy rain for another eight-kilometer run. When they got back, he asked them to remove their shoes and socks and examined their feet.

Then they went to lunch as the sky cleared and the day became merely humid and hot. Rolando joined them and asked, "Well, how did it go?"

The girls waited to see what Ginés would say. Luciana was more tired than Maria. She was not been used to running but the strength and coordination drills were not difficult for her although she had felt pressed to her limits. Maria was not affected at all by the running but the strength and coordination drills had pressed her upper body.

Ginés reported, "We have a reasonable base to work from with these two. One is a fitter and better runner. The other has a stronger body. Both can come close to the other with slightly different emphasis in training. I shall include that during the bogacho instruction if they get past this afternoon."

Ginés thought privately that if he could find six more women like these two he could create a women's team that could beat most good men's teams. He could not believe that these women who looked like fairy tale princesses could have such strong underlying physiques and be in such good condition. Still he was concerned that these essential physical skills had to translate into the coordination necessary to correctly throw the bogacho.

After lunch, Maria and Luciana had a moment alone together on their way to see Ginés in the gym. Luciana said, "Maria, you run like the wind!"

Maria replied cautiously, "We will not have to run fast. You are stronger. Look at Ginés. He is very powerfully built."

"Yeah, well to play the game, you need strength because they physically attack each other along with throwing the bogachos. We will not be wrestling with any Deinoc."

"I just hope we can throw these things."

"Let's go find out."

Ginés went through a shorter warm-up and then handed the girls the bogachos. "Now, Maria, throw it at that post." Maria sort of swung her bogacho as she had seen Ginés do and let it go. It landed in a clump to the right and short of the post.

"Now Luciana, throw yours at the same post."

Luciana gave it a good crisp spin and set it flying in a motion with her arm that put the bogacho on the post, balls passing on both sides. Had it been a man he would have been taken down.

Ginés jaw dropped. He said, "Try it again with this bogacho and throw at the double post to right and beyond the post you just hit."

Luciana executed her motion again and there were two entangled posts.

Ginés asked, "Luciana, have you ever thrown a bogacho before?"

Luciana said, "No."

Maria was dumfounded. Luciana looked as if she had been throwing these things since she was a baby.

Ginés had never seen anything like it. He said, "Throw it with your other hand."

She said, "Would you please show me first."

Ginés said, "As you wish."

He sent one flying with his left hand. Luciana sent one flying with her left hand.

Ginés noticed something. He picked up a rock and tossed it at Luciana's face and said quickly, "Catch!" She reached out with her right hand and caught it.

He said, "Throw the rock at me."

She threw it and he caught it with his left hand. He threw the rock back at her. She caught it smoothly with her left hand.

He said quickly, "Luciana, do a squat, leap forward prone on the ground, roll to your back and push yourself to sitting with your right hand. Then pull your feet back to your hips, and roll your weight forward over your feet and jump up."

Luciana executed the maneuver adequately for a first time—a standard drop and roll under a thrown bogacho, then up with the left hand free to throw the bogacho while rising.

Ginés ordered, "Watch me!" He instantly executed the move. He demanded, "Do it again, fast!"

Luciana was down and up so fast Ginés was sure he could not have executed it much more quickly.

Ginés, astonished, said, "Luciana has any ever commented on how well you can replicate what you see?"

Luciana said modestly, "I have been told I'm a quick study."

'I would say so. You have passed. Within the allotted time, if you continue to progress at this rate, you would be able to become a player on any team in Montaña,"

Ginés tested Maria in the same way but she could not replicate Luciana's performance.

Maria was puzzled and hurt.

Ginés said, "Luciana, please take the afternoon off. I will work with Maria to improve her throwing the rest of the afternoon."

Luciana left.

Ginés and Maria worked the rest of the afternoon on her right hand throw.

Maria did not need Ginés to tell her that she had no natural throwing arm.

•

Ginés sat down with Rolando that evening.

Ginés said, "Luciana is a miracle. If she progresses as her talent seems to indicate she will, I will be able to teach her a great deal in the next six weeks."

Rolando said, "And Maria?"

"She is an able athlete but she does not have the throwing talent. Unless she shows me a great deal more in the next few days, she will not be able to throw the bogacho with any real proficiency in the allotted time."

"I see. Well tomorrow let's see what Shon can do and then we will discuss what to do about it."

•

The next morning Ginés ran the same program with Shon in a soaking rain. Afterward he felt a sense of ennui about himself. Sitting with Rolando later in the day, he said, "Rolando, I have spent my life pursuing perfection in the bogacho and in one day I feel as if I have learned nothing."

Rolando said, "Shon was that good?"

"He was beyond 'that good'. I think he could beat me and even an entire team with me within a week. He can move faster than anyone I have ever seen and he learns instantly anything he sees. I thought Luciana was amazing but his abilities go far beyond what I have ever seen."

Rolando said, "So it is Maria that will be your challenge."

Ginés sighed, "Long ago I learned that the weak link in a chain isn't made stronger by stronger links around it unless the weak link can contribute something else to the team. I will do what I can and it would help if I knew why they really need to throw the bogacho. When I have a weak link on a team that I cannot replace with another more skilled player I try to develop that link to support the others using the skills the weak link has instead of trying to make the link stronger where it cannot be. Doing otherwise almost always leads to defeat of the entire team."

"I will speak to Shon about this."

•

Later that evening, Rolando and Shon took the lift down the emerald mine shaft into a cold cavern and walked into the room where Rolando kept his port. they sat down at the wooden table and Rolando filled two glasses with port and handed a glass to Shon.

Shon said, "You have been too polite this evening, my friend. And now you have brought me here. So give me the bad news."

"It's really mostly good news, Shon. Ginés thinks you are ready to play for him now and Luciana in six weeks. The bad news is that he is concerned about Maria who is not a natural thrower despite her evident athleticism."

"I understand. Perhaps we will need to use her abilities in another way."

"Exactly what Ginés said. But unless he knows what you are trying to accomplish beyond throwing the bogacho he cannot assist you in what you are trying to accomplish, Shon."

"Well, then, I suppose I will have to confide in you and you in him. But you must know that if what I tell you goes beyond the three of us and I fail in what I must do, the two of you will certainly be killed if they discover you know what no citizen knows."

Rolando looked perplexed. "Citizen? They? What are you talking about? Is this a Society machination?"

"I cannot be very specific, Rolando. But here is the essence of it. When we go over the Wall, we will face a group of very skilled opponents who cannot easily be taken down. If we fail to take them down, they will kill us. I have made the judgment that the best way to deal with the attack we will face, a multi-party onslaught made on foot, is to use the bogacho to entangle them while we kill them with spears, a weapon we will likely be allowed over there."

"They won't consider the bogacho a weapon?"

"I doubt they even know the term."

"So can I tell Ginés that you are preparing to defend and defeat an attack by a group people who will attack on foot? What sort of weapons will they have?"

"Tell him they will have swords and that they are very strong. There will be no projectiles like spears as they want to kill with their own hands. Tell him I thought of the bogacho as a way to stop their mobility and that we have already learned from him how to fall to the ground to avoid the swing of their swords and how to arise to fling the bogacho. But we still have to kill them."

•

Ginés mulled over what Rolando had told him earlier that morning and quickly devised a plan for Maria on his way to the gym.

When the group convened an hour later, he said, "I have determined what each of you can do to accomplish your purpose."

The women glanced at each other while Shon looked only at Ginés.

Ginés said, "I have been informed that you are not really training to become bogacho players but need to survive banishment and to do so you will have to kill your opponents. Your opponents will be armed with swords, knives, or similar weapons used by hand. I am told that Shon believes the bogacho can give you an advantage by temporarily incapacitating your opponents. But you still need to kill your opponents who will otherwise kill you.

"Bogacho is a game played between teams. What you face sounds more like a pack of killers. But in the same way that the way to beat a team is with a team, the way to kill a pack is with a pack. And like a team that has different roles, so does a pack. The bogacho can play a role but playing only that role will not kill anything. They will just incapacitate their opponents for a while. So we need a killer. Shon, you have remarkable skill and can possibly play two roles, bogacho entangler and killer, but entangling will be foremost in your role in the beginning. Luciana, you will be, like Shon in his primary role, what we call defense in games—the entangler who continues to take out any opponent who rises from their entanglement. Maria, your role will be to kill while the others entangle.

"Consider my plan and let me know if this might work for you. I will return in an hour." Ginés turned and walked out of the building.

•

Luciana said, "What nerve! How has he presumed to tell us what to do?"

Shon said, "I think he has just set the course we must follow. I have spent most of my time trying to get equality without really focusing on what we must do when we achieve that, the death of our enemy. Let's listen. We can always take another path if his looks wrong."

Maria said, "I agree."

Luciana looked at both of them and nodded.

•

When Ginés returned, Shon said, "Your concept is acceptable. Let's train on it and make adjustments as we proceed. I have some skills in hand-to-hand combat and the weaponry associated with that so I will assist you in that area if that is acceptable to you."

Ginés felt a great relief as he had no skills in such combat."

Ginés spent the next week working with Shon and Luciana in the morning on the bogacho, and the afternoons with Maria and Shon working on the how to use the spear.

At week's end, Ginés stopped by to see Rolando.

As they sat down in the white tower, Ginés said, "I must ask you to tell me more about Shon, Rolando."

"Why?"

"He is not a normal man. I know that he is supposed to come from our distant past. But how can someone from our past be so far beyond us now?"

Rolando responded cautiously, "What do you mean by 'so far beyond us'?"

"We have been training Maria with the spear but he can do things that I have never seen anyone do. And, in short order, he is able to get Maria, who I know has no natural aptitude for what he is training her to do, to do what he shows her. And I am becoming able to do the same things at a rate I could never do without observing his instruction. Just last night I practiced what I saw him doing yesterday and today I can do it. It's not normal. Yes, he has skills in combat that I've never seen and I can tell he comes from a warrior past but how he can get us to learn so quickly is what I can't understand. I have trained many and been trained by great instructors, but no one has this teaching skill he has."

Rolando shrugged a pose of indifference. "Perhaps he was a great instructor in his time."

Ginés said forcefully, "No. It's more than that. He can see what we need to know and conveys it in a way that you cannot fail to see what he is trying to teach you to do."

"What does it matter, Ginés? He comes from a violent era in our history where it wasn't about winning a game but killing an enemy. That would naturally lead to accurate training."

Ginés felt insulted. "I have played bogacho as if it were life and death. It's something more."

Rolando said in a quiet voice, "Ginés, listen to me. We don't have the time to dwell on how he does what he does. Be thankful he can contribute to what needs to be done. Do your part and let him do his. You are the greatest at what you do but everyone has a better somewhere. Perhaps Shon is that man for you."

Ginés grimaced, and said, "I wish I could join them in their conflict and prove my worth."

"Well, that is not part of Shon's plan, so do your part and be satisfied with helping him do his."

They rose and went to bed for the evening.

As Rolando retired, he wondered about Ginés and what the competitive feeling Ginés was feeling between Shon and himself might mean.

•

Over the next week, Luciana progressed remarkably in the bogacho. Shon, having learned all that Ginés had to teach him about the bogacho, began to skip the morning practices to work on developing several bogachos to serve the various ways that they might be needed. But Shon always showed up for the afternoon practice with Maria. Ginés became more irritable in the afternoons.

•

Shon stopped in to see Rolando at the end of the second week.

After Rolando poured them a drink, Shon said, "What's with Ginés? He seems to be developing an attitude. Not a good one. It's like he resents me."

Rolando said, "He's just feeling the stress of doing a job that he knows is important but doesn't really know why."

"I think it's more than that. It's like he's competing with me but I can't tell why. It's worse in the afternoon but maybe I just notice it then since I've been skipping out most mornings. Perhaps he resents that I have picked up the bogacho so quickly."

Rolando said, "Perhaps. It's probably not easy to have a student learn what you have been doing for over two hundred years in a couple of weeks."

Shon said, "Yeah, maybe so, but it seems more than that. Besides he gets his attitude when we are working on what I know, not what he knows, the spear."

"Maybe it bothers him that he cannot learn what you know so quickly as you have learned what he knows."

"Good point. But he has learned what I know pretty quickly."

Rolando said, "Well maybe that's a sore point with him, too. You are a bit like a super human, Shon. I thank God for that, but maybe he doesn't feel that way. He doesn't know what you are trying to do or why you're doing it, you know. All of Montaña knows that you put yourself and the women into the predicament that you're in by pushing your Slippery Slope Proposition."

"So you think he resents the danger I've put the women in?"

"I didn't say that exactly, but it's possible."

"You feel that way too, don't you, Rolando? And I'm sure Maria's father feels that way. Does all of Montaña feel that way?"

"Not all, but I admit some do. You are the blue-eyed brown-haired man who is taking our brown-eyed black-haired princess into harm's way for a purpose none understands. He might well think you will survive given your manifest skills while they might not, particularly Maria, who is one of us. That could well not sit well with him, as it will not with others, if she doesn't return with you, if indeed you return either."

"I understand, Rolando, but you should understand that if she does not return I will not either. So feel free to pass that on to those who doubt my intentions. And please include Ginés."

Shon stood up abruptly and left.

SIX

ANNEC

While Publius waited in Mamercus's antechamber he contemplated what to say as he had every day on his weeks-long journey back to Annec from Montaña, a journey made longer by taking ship and rail to travel. Besides the risk involved in faster transport, he had needed the time to consider what he wanted to say to Mamercus. He knew no one expected him to return by air as none of the Hom would have gone by air to Montaña in the first place. But he had avoided communications along the way by saying what he wanted to discuss required a personal meeting and he knew that a deep resentment toward him was brewing in Annec with those concerned with Luciana's predicament brought on by his ruling at the tribunal.

Mamercus entered saying, "Welcome back. Publius, my old friend, though mine may be the only welcome you get here. Luciana's parents are, to put it bluntly, not pleased with the outcome of your visit to Montaña, nor is the Council, though I detect that the Deinoc delegates might privately make a feast for you. How could you have allowed Luciana to get involved in this mess?"

"It was her choice and not one I could dissuade her from. Shon, as you can see from the record of the trial, made it impossible for me to avoid convicting him. She forced my hand by joining him as did the citizen, Maria."

"That record is the only thing that has saved your reputation but it will not help you when you appear before her parents, who want to see you straightaway when we are done here."

Publius sighed, "I have dreaded that visit every moment since the trial. But that is not why I have come to see you first."

"I assumed that. Please sit." They sat down in chairs facing each other.

"May I offer you a drink?"

"I would welcome a stiff whisky. Tell them to bring a bottle."

Mamercus signaled one of the robots.

The robot returned a moment later with a bottle of ancient single malt.

Publius smiled as he poured himself a large portion and said, "I see you were prepared."

Mamercus replied as he poured himself an equal portion, "I've known you a rather long time."

Publius said, "Well, then, you know I would prefer to get on with what I have to say."

"Very well."

"I am convinced that Shon Ó Conaill is the Traveler foretold in the records. I am also convinced that the Deinoc may not get the result they anticipate."

Mamercus said, "You think he might survive their Horde?"

"Nothing is certain, of course, but I believe that the prophecy must have meaning and I see in him a man not like anyone alive today. The two taken together must be given great weight in considering what may occur."

"And if he survives?"

"Then I think he will try to do exactly what he condemned us for not doing—grow the citizen population at least to what he considers sustainable, which would so change the balance between the Society and the citizens that I fear the Society will attempt to stop him. Moreover, if his notion gains traction in the citizen communities, the Society might decide the only safe recourse will be to terminate the citizen community in Montaña."

Mamercus took a drink from his glass and said, "Some who hold to your Traveler notion are already discussing measures to limit what he might do."

Publius leaned forward in his chair. "They are tinkering with the prophecy. The consequences might be far worse than letting things play out."

Mamercus said in a calm voice, "But the prophecy does not say how things will play out, Publius. Perhaps we are supposed to stop him."

"If it were as simple as that, why is there a prophecy at all?"

"Perhaps to warn us of the peril of this Traveler. That's at least as logical as allowing him to destroy the Order which protects the Society and Vitas."

Publius fell back into his chair. "So you stand on that side?"

"I told you before you went to Montaña what I thought. I have not been persuaded by anything that has happened since to change my view."

Mamercus leaned forward toward Publius and continued, "I would also like to see a change in life on Vitas. But I cannot see how a man from our distant past will accomplish that. What exactly he would do if he gets the opportunity is completely unknown except for what he said at his trial. He would grow citizens until they overwhelm us. How is that better for us? How are millions of more citizens better for Vitas? What do more people alive at any given time add to life here, even for the citizen population? Tell me how he will make things better and I will listen but otherwise I see only a very dangerous man who might get us all killed, including those he seeks to help. He doesn't even know about the other families in the Society. What about them? How do they benefit from more citizens?"

Publius sighed and took a deep draft from his drink. "I wish I had the answers to those questions. On my way home I have thought about all of them, and I find myself falling back on faith in the prophecy. It cannot exist simply to be a warning. It must have a greater meaning. I believe it is a message that we need to change Vitas. That there is truly a greater purpose to being here than simply living long lives until the Sun burns up Vitas and us with it."

"An unpleasant notion, I agree. But that time is many many centimillia away, while he is here now. If you are wrong, we die soon, not far into the future. That time may afford us the opportunity to find a way to get off this planet before the end."

"How would we do that? We don't even try to find a way today. When will we start working on it? The millennia fly past and we do nothing. Have we not lived long enough to realize how we live our lives? We don't change anything. What will impel us to change our behavior in the future?"

Mamercus said, "Probably we will get on with things when we get a bit closer to the reality of the end of Vitas. We are human after all and we don't do what we have to until we have to. We monitor the sun and will have ample warning at least a few million years before it destroys us. We can do a lot in a few million years when tasked to do so."

"Easy words, Mamercus. I thank you for laying out the Society's view as only you can do in so few words."

"I am sorry I can't embrace your Traveler, my friend, but he looks much more dangerous that the sun at the moment."

Publius rose from his chair. "Well, then I had better be on my way to see Octavius and Aurelia. They need to understand that their daughter made the choice she made because she is young enough to believe in life today because she hasn't lived long enough to consider her decisions in the context of having lived for even a century, much less many millennia."

•

Publius walked the two kilometers between Mamercus's residence and the grand estate of Luciana's parents. They were not merely parents he needed to console. They held the power to tilt a divided Council to act as they wished.

Octavius Gaius Bellatrix Augustus was the oldest of the Second Generation born in year 4,448 of the sixth decamillium. He had become Princeps, the head of the Council, the most powerful figure in the Society of Species, in year 8,652 of the sixth decamillium and from year 4,556 of the eight decamillium he held his position by acclamation until his retirement on the first day of the fourth centimillium. On the day of his self-imposed retirement, the Council proclaimed him Augustus for life, the only member of the Council ever so honored. Since his retirement, he had retained greater influence on the Council than any of the succeeding Princeps had during their terms in office.

Aurelia Theodora Aelianus was one of the oldest of the Third Generation, born under the Codicil as a replacement for a

Hom who had died in an accident in year 4,667 of the second centimillium. She married Octavius in year 5,561 of the second centimillium. By then Octavius had been Princeps for almost five decamillia, nearly half a centimillium. She became a legate member of the Council for the Home and intermittently a Consul of the Society for many terms, a position held by two members at any time and exceeded in authority only by the Princeps. But her real role in the Society was as Octavius' most trusted advisor, and that gave her power over all others and, even at times, over Octavius himself.

Octavius and Aurelia had Luciana when their number finally came up very recently in the replacement process when a Hom died. Favoritism in this arena was not possible because the opportunity to have a child only occurred when someone died, a rare event, which was so precious to every Hom.

Publius approached their home knowing nothing in their long lives so full of great service to Vitas and the power and prestige that came with that mattered more to them than Luciana, so recently born to them. Now Luciana had put herself in great peril— almost certain death—while under his watch.

He was shown in by a robot who guided him to the great library where he was surprised to find Octavius waiting for him. Hom custom was always for a visitor to enter a room followed a while later by the host's entrance. Octavius Gaius Bellatrix Augustus was standing by a huge window overlooking the great lake, Lac, its named derived from its ancient name, Lac d'Annecy. He was a tall lean man with piercing blue-gray eyes, a strong, narrow nose, and blond hair with some streaks of silver-grey at his temples, dressed in a white toga lined in gold with a thick gold torque around his right wrist.

When Octavius turned his gaze to him, Publius said, "Greetings, Augustus."

"I bid you welcome, Praetor. Please have a seat." He offered no drink, not a good omen but not an insult either when matters at issue were great and known in advance to both parties. Octavius sat down in a chair across from Publius and said, "How is Luciana?"

Publius said, "She was well when I left Montaña."

Octavius said, "That is a comfort. Will she remain that way, Publius?"

"I cannot predict the future, Augustus."

A female voice spoke from behind where Publius was sitting, saying, "That is a poor response from the Praetor."

Publius turned his head and saw Aurelia standing by the door through which he had just entered. She walked over to stand beside her husband.

Publius responded, "I cannot affirm what no one can know at this moment, Lady Aurelia. She is with Shon Ó Conaill at a place in Montaña called Pinchincha preparing, according to my sources, to comply with my banishment order to enter Amaz in a few weeks."

Aurelia said, "And there lies the rub, Praetor—your banishment order. How could you have allowed that to happen?"

Octavius said in a quiet voice, "Calm yourself, my dear."

Aurelia replied, "I cannot."

Publius said, "I can well understand you concern. You have undoubtedly seen the trial record which clearly shows that I initially ruled for Shon Ó Conaill. He rejected that course and, in pursuing his extraordinary Slippery Slope Proposition, left me no choice. Had it stopped there we would not be here today. But your daughter, a member of the presiding court, decided to join him. I will not be denigrated by anyone, even the two of you whom I respect above all others, for making the only decision any responsible judge could make."

Octavius spoke. "We find no fault in your ruling on the facts presented to you. What we don't understand is why you were there to rule at all. Had you not been the presiding judge we could overturn the judgment of a Prefect by having the Prefect simply amend her judgment. But, Praetor, you are well aware that you are the highest judicial authority on Vitas. There is no appeal from your judgment except the Council itself which obviously cannot intervene in a citizen appeal. Citizens don't even know the Council exists. Even if we handled the matter within the Society, to overrule a Praetor's judgment we would need a supermajority of three-quarters, impossible when the Deinoc family will undoubtedly be in opposition. Too many families fear the consequences that might result from opposing them on a matter of such great concern to them, and there is no doubt the opportunity to conduct a mates hunt while pursuing the most exciting human opponent they have ever faced is a matter of the greatest importance to them. And you knew from the moment this ancient man came into our lives that the Deinoc wanted him. Explain yourself, Praetor."

"I believed my presence would deter a false trial designed to banish Shon Ó Conaill to Amaz where he would be killed. I believe Shon Ó Conaill is the Traveler. Some, including you, may differ in that opinion and what to do about it even if you concurred, but my reason for going to insure a fair trial is irrelevant to what happened. As Praetor, I am bound to rule correctly on the facts of the case and I could not rule for Shon Ó Conaill when he blatantly posited the greatest Slippery Slope Proposition ever propounded on Vitas. That Luciana took up his cause and joined him in the consequences of the verdict is something that has nothing to do with my conduct at the trial or my presence there. She is obviously in love with Shon Ó Conaill."

Aurelia said, "Impossible! The man is not even Hom."

Octavius said in a quiet voice, "She is very young and so is Shon Ó Conaill. That would explain her impulse. Praetor, I now understand your reasons for going and I understand your ruling. I am also aware of the belief that many have that this person is the so-called Traveler. The Council is divided on that and further divided on what to do about it. But I am not prepared to accede to banishment for Luciana so those who have whatever interests they may have in Shon Ó Conaill's fate can set the stage for the killing of our daughter."

Publius saw Aurelia visibly shudder at that last remark.

Octavius walked to Aurelia and put an arm around her as he turned to face Publius. "Is there anything you can do about her situation with regard to Shon Ó Conaill?"

"Upon reflection, I believe that I may have erred with respect to her conviction."

"How so?" said Octavius.

Publius said, "She was not an accused when the trial started and, even though she quite willingly said all that was required to incriminate herself, she was not afforded the opportunity to prepare for trial as Shon Ó Conaill and Maria Monterro were."

"Why have you not acted on this point, Praetor?" said Aurelia.

Publius said, "Because the reality, my lady, is that the issue is moot. Luciana wanted to join Shon Ó Conaill in his fate. She will not leave him if her verdict is overturned. As to Shon Ó Conaill, he was correctly convicted because he set himself up for conviction after being handed his freedom on a platter. I see no reason at all for him to change his mind now."

"Approaching danger and death can have an effect on one's views," said Octavius.

"I do not believe that fear will affect this man's course a whit."

Aurelia spoke. "What about the citizen woman, Maria Monterro, convicted with them? Perhaps she could be used to persuade this man to reconsider his position."

Publius thought a moment and replied, "As the presiding judge, I could convene a High Court in Montaña and overturn all the convictions based on the trial error of convicting Luciana with them, thereby invalidating the entire trial. That would be very popular with the citizens in Montaña. We would have to persuade the Office of the Order to drop the case against Maria. I doubt they would play that hand again as it went rather poorly for them. They can simply say they have insufficient proofs against her and that will be the end of it. Luciana was actually never charged by the Office so she need only leave Montaña. Shon Ó Conaill will be retried and convicted again and banished. The Deinoc will get what they originally bargained for, just not what fell into their laps. Shon Ó Conaill might well go along with this plan to save Maria and Luciana."

Aurelia said, "I cannot believe Luciana has fallen for this savage while he has fallen for another woman."

Octavius said, "That's fodder for another day, my dear. Publius, I believe you should consider this course. I would save Luciana at almost any cost. I must believe that he feels that way about at least one of them, perhaps both. He clearly did not encourage them to join in at the trial."

Publius said, "It will only work if Shon Ó Conaill wants it to. And it will still require that Luciana desist from joining him, which I frankly doubt she will do. And there's the Deinoc and their expectations They may feel betrayed and leery that Shon might get off in a second trial by recanting his testimony in the first on the basis that he acted outside of the original proffers presented for banishment. Finally there is the matter of the Traveler."

Octavius said, "I will handle the Deinoc. As you say, they didn't bargain for this. They will have to make do without women to kill but they will still get their hunt which was the original deal. The hunt will resolve your last point."

Aurelia, peered at Octavius, and seeing where he was going, said, "And I will deal with Luciana."

"I will leave for Montaña tomorrow. By air."

"We thank you for that. But put your journey off for a fortnight as we will be joining you. By air. We will have time that way, which we will need as we must first insure the Council's acceptance of our plan. Till then, be well and just, Praetor."

"Be well and just, Augustus." Publius turned and left for his home.

On his way to his own residence three klicks further down the road that ran away from Lac D'Annecy toward the great snow-capped mountain to the east, Publius thought about the extraordinary notion that Octavius Gaius Bellatrix Augustus and Aurelia Theodora Aelianus would fly to Montaña. *Appearing in person before her they might well bring Luciana to her senses. Octavius' response to me about the Deinoc and the Traveler makes it clear that he is in Mamercus's camp. That and their willingness to fly, something no Hom of their age and stature has ever done before, will likely persuade the Council to support a new trial, if that cannot be avoided, over any Deinoc objections. Undoubtedly Maria's community will seek to stop her, too, when they see that all they have to do to save her is to restrain her until Shon goes over the Wall into Amaz. It's beginning to look like the prophecy is hollow. The Traveler is going to die alone in Amaz, eviscerated by the Deinoc, and the prophecy will come to an end.*

SEVEN

GUILT

Ginés awakened. It was dark in his bedroom. He had been dreaming about Maria again, as he had begun doing a few nights after he had arrived in Pinchincha and set his eyes on the most beautiful woman he had ever seen. That she was also a wonderful athlete affected him, but even more, because she was Montañan. He thought about his distress over the past weeks and realized that the cause of his torment was his attraction to her while her interest was in Shon, the alien savage, who also had another woman, Luciana, not even a Montañan but a Hom, hated by the Resurrection of which he was a member. *Why should a Montañan woman feel such emotions for a man not of her community? It is wrong. If she would only see that a Montañan like me would be far better for her than this ancient savage. She could avoid a battle that is likely to bring her great peril, likely death. How can that savage man involve her in such danger? But she hasn't seemed to notice, mesmerized as she is by his great personal magnetism. I must do something about it.*

Later that afternoon, as they were practicing with the spear, Rolando stopped by and asked Shon to come with him to his place for a meeting.

After Shon left, Ginés turned to Maria and said, "Maria, I am contributing to your death." He looked at her and saw her visibly pale. He knew that she was worrying about her inability to advance in the bogacho.

Maria said, "No, you are helping to us accomplish what we have to do."

He made a decision.

He said quietly, "Maria, come over by the window, please."

She smiled wanly and said, "I will not be much company."

Ginés said softly, "Please, for me."

She came and sat down next to him on a bench. Ginés said, "Maria, there is no one in the world I admire more than you. I want you to listen to me, knowing how I feel, so that you will seriously consider what I am about to say."

Maria said, "Ginés, I always listen to what you have to say with an open mind."

"You must forget this quest. As good an athlete as you are, you have no real talent for the bogacho or the spear. I can tell that you are suffering because Luciana is so much better at this. But you are not Luciana. She is a Hom with powers we don't have."

Maria looked at Ginés and saw his gaze avert from her. She said, "Why Ginés, if I didn't know better, I might think you are trying to court me!" And she thought he was having some effect. She felt her skin warming and a little tingle here and there. If he touched her right now, she knew she would feel stronger urges.

Ginés suggested they return to their training.

Shortly, Luciana, returning from a run, entered the gym. As she opened the door, she saw Ginés showing Maria some takedown moves. Luciana thought, *Why are they wasting time on that since they will not be taking down any Deinoc.* But their activity had an energy that drew her to watch. She slipped into the entry closet and closed the door part way.

Maria seemed to be enjoying herself. Whenever Ginés showed her a new move she would replicate it. Soon the activity turn into more of a wrestling match than a series of take down drills as Maria struggled to parry Ginés' takedown moves. Finally, he caught her left wrist with his left hand and pronated her arm so that it began to twist around behind her. He forced her body to rotate so that he could grab her from behind, he kicked her feet out from under her and they went down with her prone and Ginés on top. As she twisted her body to get onto her back, Ginés grabbed both of her wrists. He was on top of her. She was laughing. Then Ginés kissed her. Maria did not resist his kiss. He let go of her hand and reached to her waist where he slid his left hand under her cotton blouse across her belly and onto her breast.

Luciana wanted to leave but her feet would not move. She watched.

Ginés still held Maria's left hand with his right hand by her head. He moved his left hand from her breast to her waist and began to slide it into her tights.

Maria said, "Ginés, please! Don't! Ginés, stop."

Instead Ginés, already straddling her, grabbed her blouse and ripped it as he pulled it up her torso.

Maria struggled to no avail.

Finally, he got grip with both hands and forced her top off.

Hines stripped off his shirt and began pulling on her tights. He said, "Maria! Oh! Maria! I love you. I need you."

He started to put his hand where she had let only two men.

Resisting, she said, "Please! Please, Ginés, Oh God! Don't!"

Maria cried out desperately, "Ginés, don't please don't do this! You don't understand! You will ruin me for him!"

Luciana was terrified. She was afraid to go forward, certain that Maria would know she had been watching. *If I do nothing quickly, he is going to take her.* She felt a terrible guilt that maybe she wanted that. *No! This is wrong.* But she stayed where she was.

Ginés, ripping her tights, was making her naked. He was starting to undo himself.

Luciana could see time was short but she could not make herself act.

Maria cried out, "Ginés! If you love me as you say, you will stop now! I will be dead by tomorrow morning if you enter me! I will have to kill myself! Shon cannot see me once you do this! Please listen to me!"

Ginés began to focus. *What is she saying about dying?*

Suddenly, he stopped and quickly stood up and began to dress himself. He looked down at his beautiful Maria. He saw her terror. He realized that he absolutely believed what she had just said. He said, "I am so sorry. What can I do?"

Luciana was standing in her hiding place with her hand in her mouth trying to keep in the screams and sobs that wanted to come out. When it had begun she had hoped that Maria would succumb. Then she had done nothing to stop his attempted rape even when she heard Maria's scream that she would kill herself if he continued. Yet still she kept herself hidden in the closet.

Maria looked up at Ginés. She saw the grief that had replaced the lust in his face and realized that she had to get her wits together now or this man might be the one killing himself. She said in a soft voice, "Ginés, you stopped. When we first started wrestling, I felt as if you were Shon. I'm very sorry. Please! You stopped. I need you to do something very important that would make up completely for this. Will you do that for me?"

Ginés was pawing around in a dazed state, looking for her shirt. It was ripped. "What, Maria? I cannot make up for this."

Maria stood up. She was scratched and bruised a bit but otherwise unhurt. She said, "Ginés, listen carefully. You stopped because you believed me and knew I would be dead by tomorrow if you went further. Believe me now when I tell you that you can make up for all of this. I know you will never touch me again because you know I have chosen the man I want and that I would die for him. Please help him live." She softened her voice and said, "Besides, there are few enough friends to have in this world and I would hate to lose one over a wrestling match."

Ginés, still mortified, said, "Let me run into the house and get you a change of clothes. I am so sorry, Maria."

Maria said, "One more thing, Ginés. You've said you're sorry enough now. Don't say it again and don't tell anyone about this, particularly Shon. You are a good man who made a mistake. We are from the same community and must act like it. I don't want anything to come of this. Can you get me some fresh clothes without being noticed?"

"I think so." He ran out of the gym to Rolando's house.

Maria sat down on the leather bench by the window and began to sob. After a short time, she stopped crying and wiped her face with her hands.

Luciana was still in the closet.

Ginés came back with some clothes which Maria put on. She said, "Can you get rid of these?" She handed him her torn clothes.

Ginés took her clothes and walked towards the closet.

Luciana wanted to scream.

Ginés came to the door and opened it a little wider and tossed the clothes inside. He turned back toward Maria, saying, "I'll get them later. Maria, I know you said not to apologize but I would just like to say you have saved my life. Had I done what I was trying to do, even had you not killed yourself, I now realize that I would've had to kill myself for the shame. Only your kind words keep me from running from here to do so now. I will never forgive myself for what I have done."

Maria took his arm, saying, "Let's not dwell on this. Let me tell you about my first trip with Shon to Huascarán." And like that they walked out. The almost rapist with his victim on his arm prattling on about the only thing she cared about in life, Shon.

Luciana stayed crouched in the closet until well after they had left. Then she walked back to the white tower by another path.

EIGHT

COUNCIL

The Princeps of the Council was Mao Jiayi Melan. Mao's family had been one of the resurrected species during the Expansion. In the late twenty-first century the giant panda had become extinct. A popular species with the public, the genetic engineers possessed intact DNA requiring only modification for indeterminate lifespan and enlightenment. First they had brought back the original species and then they enlightened its progeny. The unenlightened species became extinct for the second time during the Warming. Mao Jiayi had been Princeps for more than half a decamillium. He liked his role. Now and then a little intrigue, a family squabble, some consuls from different families that disliked each other. Just the usual sort of things a person with a diplomatic bent and a position to exercise influence would enjoy.

This morning was different. The most important voice in history, Octavius Gaius Bellatrix Augustus, had requested a special convocation of the Council for that afternoon at one o'clock. Normally, of course, Princeps Mao Jiayi Melan would have rejected such a request out of hand. There were procedures and one did not just convene meetings at anybody's whim on such ridiculously short notice. Octavius was different, of course, and, if he had asked for a special session in two weeks, perhaps even ten days, he would have complied with his request. But, in five hours, out of the question! It was not unreasonable to ask why and on what authority Octavius was requesting such a meeting, was it?

Mao had a mind to disconnect the transmission. But— well, Octavius had reduced the Allo and he was the only member ever honored as Augustus. And he had never made an unreasonable request before. But what made him agree was that Octavius had a tone about him that made Mao think maybe he might end up part of the third extinction of his species, so, purely as a special accommodation, he complied with the request.

He had a good mind not to attend himself and let them see what it would be like to have a session with no Princeps. But he recalled that Octavius might well still recall how to do his job. Perhaps it would not be wise to have Octavius sit in that seat again.

·

"Friends and family, I, Octavius Gaius Bellatrix Hom, stand before you to address a judicial matter that has come to my attention. Praetor Publius Palinurus Jules Hom recently presided over a citizen tribunal in Montaña which had the unusual consequence of ruling that one of our family was convicted of proposing a Slippery Slope Proposition. Upon further consideration the Praetor had determined that he erred in his ruling and that the judgment should be set aside. I call Praetor Publius Palinurus Jules Hom before you to explain his rationale in deciding that his ruling should be reversed."

The Council chamber was filled with a capacity crowd of delegates, not the norm for most Council meetings, certainly unusual for a meeting called with such short notice. Constructed in the ancient Roman architectural style as were all of the office governmental buildings in Annec, Publius stepped to the rostrum where he looked out at the assembled delegates sitting in curved rows of stone seats before him.

"Delegates to the Council. As most of you are aware, I recently presided at a trial in Montaña wherein the court sentenced a citizen, a Hom, and the man from the past we know as Shon Ó Conaill to banishment in Amaz for propounding a Slippery Slope Proposition. However the proposition for which they were convicted was not the proposition for which charges were brought. Shon Ó Conaill was convicted for propounding a new proposition before the court while in session. The others were convicted for formally affirming their support for his newly propounded proposition.

"After careful reconsideration of the proceedings, I submit that I erred in convicting the two parties who did not overtly propound the proposition. Possibly, I also erred in convicting Shon Ó Conaill because the proposition propounded at trial did not recite the Slippery Slope Proposition for which he was convicted. Simply put, I convicted them all on a matter unrelated to the charges against them as originally presented.

"I do not appear today before you for your guidance in reconsidering the convictions of the two who joined in support as it is clear that their support of his new proposition should have resulted in an order from the court to Montaña's Office of the Order to review the transcript and determine whether a case should be brought and, if a new complaint was filed, the accused would have an opportunity to prepare a defense for a new trial convened to hear that case. That such a procedure was the correct course with respect to them is clear.

"What is not so clear is on whether Shon Ó Conaill's conviction should also be vacated on similar grounds. It is not clear to me that such a ruling would be correct as he, fully aware that he was flaunting his proposition in the face of all the authorities who would simply place in evidence the transcript of the trial before the court presiding in a new trial.

"Imagine a trial for murder when the accused discloses another murder during a trial on the first for which he is found guilty. There is precedence for a new trial for the new murder and there is precedence for increasing the sentence for the new disclosure without going through with another trial. What has no precedence is someone being acquitted for the first while confessing the second because, during our long history, we have never had a case where a man judged innocent for the first crime volunteered the second.

"It is not clear to me whether Shon Ó Conaill should be retried or whether his admission of a clear crime during the trial should result in his conviction for it notwithstanding that it was not contained in the initial accusation. I am inclined to the second position but I appear before you to confirm my inclination or to determine that he should be retried."

There was some commotion among those seated to the left of where Publius was standing.

A delegate rose and said, *"I, Consul Ögödei of the Deinoc family, rise to object on two grounds.*

"First, a Praetor's judgment should never be subject to challenge in a matter involving a citizen as that could lead to future challenges to the Society, a very dangerous precedent. I might add that this dilemma is a good reason for a Praetor not to become involved in citizen matters to begin with. A Praetor should involve himself in citizen matters only to advise the presiding Prefect in rendering her judgment.

"Second, in the case at hand, the record clearly shows that all of the parties convicted assented to the stipulation at trial that they concurred with the Slippery Slope Proposition propounded at trial by one of the accused, and to allow any parties a second chance to further propound the proposition in question would set the dangerous precedent in the citizen communities that one

can posit such ideas in a court without the immediate consequence of conviction.

"I believe that the Praetor acted quite correctly in rendering his judgment with respect to all of those convicted. Moreover, we should not support any retreat from the clear intent of the Order which must be upheld vigorously at all times."

The delegates began to converse among themselves.

Another delegate rose and said, "I, Consul Chaghadai of the Deinoc family, and Consul of this Society, join my colleague in his objection."

Mao Jiayi, seated behind the rostrum above the two consuls of the Council, and to the left of Chaghadai, one of the two consuls of the Council as opposed to the many delegates who were consuls of their families but not of the Council, spoke, "As Princeps I note that a consul of the Council has objected and, according to our rules, his objection can only be overruled by a super-majority of three quarters of the Council. Perhaps a vote should be taken to see whether this matter requires further Council consideration." It was difficult for the assemblage to tell whether the Princeps was grinning or not as his Panda face generally looked as if he was always grinning.

Clearly, however, Octavius Gaius Bellatrix Augustus Hom was not grinning and the chamber, which had begun to buzz with conversation, fell silent as he arose and approached the rostrum.

Octavius began, "Praetor Publius Palinurus Jules Hom has been Praetor of the Society for almost as many years as I have been retired. So long that his judgments have almost no precedents before his time in his office. The trial was indeed unusual and his presence there was most fortuitous as without him there we would likely have been unable to discern any insight into what occurred. When has an accused in citizen trial, or a Society trial for that matter, ever put forth new evidence to incriminate himself when he has gotten off on the charges at issue? The confusion that followed was so unprecedented that judicial error could be expected. Only a Praetor of Praetor Publius's stature could have the fortitude to seek to correct the error that came from the confusion. Yet to the citizen community involved doing so upholds the wisdom and validity of having the Society judge matters that involve upholding the Order."

The room began to buzz as the members discussed this point.

Publius returned to the rostrum and the crowed quieted. "Members, I should like to restate that I appear before you only for you to *consider Shon Ó Conaill's conviction. What not before you is my amended ruling with respect to the other two which, upon careful reconsideration of the proceedings, I have decided must be reversed."*

So there it was. The Deinoc could support a vote in favor of the Praetor's position or all of the convictions would be vacated and thereafter there might or might not be a retrial of some or all of those convicted.

There was now considerable discussion among the delegates.

Mao, who could now see what the alternatives were, was certainly not smiling, regardless of his appearance. He rose, stepped to the rostrum, and said, *"I believe a motion is in order and I make a motion to call for a vote to affirm the Praetor's judgment with respect to Shon Ó Conaill. Do I have a second?"*

Consul Chaghadai rose and said, *"I second the motion."*

With that obvious support of the Deinoc, the Council voted unanimously for the motion.

•

Mamercus stopped in to see Publius later that day.

"A very clever argument you made, my friend, to get the women off while leaving Shon Ó Conaill where he is. So it appears you got what you wanted," said Mamercus as he sat down across from Publius's great glass wall overlooking the mountain to the east.

Publius poured them some of his old whisky and, sitting in a chair beside Mamercus, said, "Hardly what I wanted but the most I could hope for under the circumstances. But Shon Ó Conaill is alone now."

Mamercus drank a draft from his glass. "Maybe not alone, I'm afraid. All this means is that the women don't have to go over. What they will do is not so clear."

"True. But I suspect Shon Ó Conaill will not allow them to join him now that they have a way out. Besides, what chance does one man, with or without one or two women to help him, really have against a Deinoc horde? Their horde took down the Allo," said Publius.

"You are the prophecy believer. Cheer up, perhaps this is part of it."

•

Octavius, Aurelia, and Publius left for Montaña the next morning. The transit was uneventful but Publius noted the clear relief his fellow passengers felt when they landed in the same clearing where he had landed on his way to preside over the trial.

They were met by the local senior members of families that they knew from those same members' sojourns to Annec as delegates over the ages before.

The resident families were honored to greet these great Hom who had for so many centimillia insured their freedom to live their lives in accord with the Order and Codicil.

One among them approached and mindcast, *"I am Juku Ximena Tremarct. I have been given the privilege of attending to you during your visit."*

Publius remained silent, not acknowledging his friend who did likewise.

Octavius said, *"Greetings. I am Octavius Gaius Bellatrix Hom. This is my wife, Consul Aurelia Theodora Aelianus Hom, and this is Praetor Publius Palinurus Jules."*

Juku said, "I will escort you to the central community in Montaña."

Juku led them to a transit station on the outskirts of the city where the Hom took the train to the central city where they were directed to Professor Raul Monterro's office at the Universidad de Montaña.

•

Octavius, Aurelia, and Publius rode the elevator to Level C and proceeded to the Office of the President. They asked the woman seated at the entry to the office to announce their request to see Professor Monterro.

The woman quickly tapped the vidcom and said in a low voice, "Professor, three visitors are requesting to see you. One is the judge from the trial."

She heard him tell her to show them in, which she promptly did.

Raul rose from his seat behind his large wooden desk as they entered. He recognized them as being from the Society, dressed as they were in garb only worn by the Society's Prefects, and, along with them, the first man he had ever seen from the Society when he had come to preside at the trial. He said, "Greetings, I am Raul Monterro."

Octavius, accustomed to speaking first, dispensed with formal introductions, believing they would have little meaning to this citizen, and said, "We are here to discuss the recent trial."

Noting that the man speaking was not the man who presided at the trial, a man he had been certain was much more important than the Prefect of Montaña, he judged this man was superior in position to the other and that it was not going to be an ordinary discussion. He said, "That was the most painful day in my life."

Octavius responded, "And mine also." Nodding at the woman standing beside him, he continued, "Our daughter is Luciana, the other woman convicted with your daughter at that trial."

Raul, gesturing at the chairs surrounding a small table to the left of his desk, said, "Then please have a seat." He stepped around his desk and sat down with them around the table. He completely forgot to offer the customary refreshments, focused now solely on finding out the purpose of this visit.

Publius said, "I have reviewed the record of the trial and determined that the court erred in convicting those who did not propound the Slippery Slope Proposition at trial. Their conduct in supporting the proposition proposed by Shon Ó Conaill should have been reviewed by the Office of the Order and, if warranted, been the subject of a new trial."

Raul, scarcely believing what he was hearing, said cautiously, "Are you saying our daughters are not to be banished?"

Publius replied, "Yes."

Raul sighed audibly and sat back in his chair. After a moment, he said, "This is wonderful news but, if I may ask, why?"

Publius explained his rationale and concluded by saying, "Of course, it is possible that they could be charged again if the Office should elect to pursue what they said in support of the proposition."

Raul, looking at the other two people, said, "May I assume that any new charges would be brought against both of those who supported that proposition or that none will be brought?"

Publius replied, "That is a fair assumption."

Rolando sighed again, judging that charges against the daughter of these Hom would not be brought and, therefore, none against Maria. "Then this is as great a day for me as was that day the worst." He paused. "And what of Shon?"

Publius said, "He presented the proposition on his own before the tribunal and every important citizen in your community. His verdict stands."

Rolando slumped down into his chair. "Then what is accomplished? She joined him then and I cannot believe that she will leave him now."

Octavius spoke, saying, "Raul. May I address you so?"

Raul nodding said, "Formalities are of little importance when matters that matter are at issue."

Octavius ignored the mild insolence contained in the remark, and said, "Raul, Citizens cannot decide to enter a Society domain because they feel like it."

Raul said, "And your daughter? Can she not enter Amaz?"

Aurelia, frustrated by the conversation which she noticed had a frigid tone underlying the niceties in the words spoken, said, "I will handle my daughter. You handle yours. All you have to do is constrain her to conform to the Order."

Octavius said in a quiet voice, "Raul, as you can see, we are as distressed as you are. We plan to speak with her and call her to her duty to support the Order as she has always done. My wife is simply suggesting that our problem is not yours and that yours is to insure that your daughter does not go over the Wall to Amaz. We believe that your community will support you in this and insure that she does not. If she complies, we believe the compulsion our daughter may have to trangress will be lessened and our task to save her will be easier to accomplish."

Raul said, "If Shon did not go over, we would not have to worry about our daughters."

Octavius said, "Unfortunately that is not an option. The Society is sworn to uphold the Order and Shon Ó Conaill must pay the price for breaking it."

Raul said, "With all due respect, I must say that our experience with banishment is that no one returns. Death seems rather an extreme punishment for his crime which was to simply suggest that more people on Vitas would do no harm to it."

Octavius said, "Your very words are why we cannot permit such notions."

Raul proceeded cautiously, realizing that he himself might be entering into the dangerous area of propounding a forbidden proposition. He said, "I am not suggesting that his notion has merit, I am only addressing the punishment."

Publius said, "You say death, we say banishment. We did not condemn him to death, only banishment."

Raul said, "But no one has ever returned from Amaz."

Publius said, "How does that prove death? Have you considered that those banished leave Amaz to live out their lives in another community so as not to taint Montaña if they were allowed to return?"

Raul said, "I must admit I had not considered that. Is that what happens to our banished?"

Octavius said, "To answer that would open a new set of questions we are not prepared to address. The plain fact is that banishment is the ordinary punishment dealt out throughout Vitas and that punishment will remain the punishment for propounding Slippery Slope Propositions. 'Don't propound them' is the simple solution to the question you raise."

Raul considered that he had not gotten a straight answer to his question, but he also judged that he was not going to get one by pressing further. Rising from his chair, he said, "I thank you for giving us a way to save my daughter and I wish you the best in saving yours."

The Hom party rose and departed to the Society House atop the highest tower in Montaña. The next morning they met Juku outside the city and proceeded to Pinchincha.

•

Khubilai walked through the great trees in the midday hot sun and humid atmosphere of Amaz to deliver the unwelcome news that he had just received from Consul Chaghadai in Annec. He would pay Chaghadai back for making him the messenger of this news one day but now he had to deliver it to Temüjin and then try to leave alive.

When he found Temüjin, as usual not covered in mud to hide his red skin, thrashing around in his efforts to kill one of the monkeys that sometimes found their way over the Walls surrounding Amaz and which could easily see him, he slowed his approach. He decided there would never be a good time to tell Temüjin the news he brought.

When Khubilai drew close enough to draw Temüjin's attention from the monkey he was trying to kill but would never be able to reach in the trees rising above them, he said, *"Lord, there is news from Annec about the Traveler."*

Temüjin immediately sprang toward him as if he was the monkey he sought to kill.

Khubilai fell back quickly. *"Lord, it is not what you feared might occur."*

Temüjin stopped his charge in mid-stride but began to circle in a menacing manner. *"He is still to be banished?"*

"Yes, Lord. But Praetor Publius has put forth a revised judgment of the banishment of those found guilty."

Temüjin began to stride toward Khubilai though not as quickly as before. *"What? What? Tell me what those untrustworthy bastard Hom have done now."* Temüjin slowed his approach but didn't stop approaching.

Khubilai began to backpedal in sync with Temüjin's approach. *"The Praetor made an argument before the Council that he had made a mistake in the Traveler's trial by convicting the women but that, if the Council concurred, he would stand by his conviction of the Traveler."*

Temüjin stopped approaching and began to leap up and down. *"I knew the Mates Hunt was too good to be true. Octavius Augustus must be behind this trickery to save his daughter."*

"Chaghadai did say that Augustus called the Council into session."

"Aargh!" Temüjin began to chomp his jaws in a twisting motion as if he had gotten a grip on Augustus and was tearing his head from his body.

Khubilai stepped back further and said, *"This was hardly unexpected, Lord. You, yourself, said you were amazed that she had been convicted to begin with."* He stepped back another step.

Temüjin stopped chomping on his imaginary foe. Casting a baleful eye on Khubilai, he said, *"That is true, but, once she was convicted, it should have stayed that way. Now they play their hand, weeks after they provided this enticement for our hunt. It's an insult to us who saved their hides from the Allo. They owe the Deinoc their lives for what we did for them."*

Khubilai began to relax at that remark. Temüjin was reciting the ritual rant he had recited ad nauseum ever since they had annihilated the Allo. Khubilai well knew the truth, which was the Deinoc had relished their role in killing the Allo for the sheer pleasure they had gotten from it. Usually Temüjin ended his tirade by stomping about in a circle, muttering about how they should annihilate the rest of the Society or at least the Hom, no longer focusing his aggression on his compatriot. Still, Khubilai proceeded cautiously and waited for his lord to calm himself into a state where rational discussion was possible.

Temüjin began to circle around one of the highest trees in the glen while making inarticulate grunts and snarls that even Khubilai could not comprehend. Suddenly he stopped circling and glared at Khubilai, saying, *"Did you say 'women'?"*

Khubilai, taking another step back, said, *"Yes, Lord. They also let his citizen woman off."*

"Aargh! Gra aaark rre grronk arrrrk chirirrp." Temüjin began to chomp, circle and curse all over again. Finally, he stopped. *"I hate the Hom. They have deprived us of a Mates Hunt as they have exiled us to Amaz. Why do they do this to us? Why did they give us this hope, only to take it away now?"*

"I cannot say, Lord. But we still have the Traveler."

Temüjin snarled, *"But now we will not have the satisfaction of watching them watching each other die as we kill them. The Hom have ruined our hunt."*

"Perhaps, you will feel differently when the Traveler enters Amaz. He is still our greatest quarry since the Allo."

Temüjin tossed his massive head from side to side. *"Unless they betray us at the last moment. If they do, Khubilai, we will leave Amaz and slaughter that citizen community adjoining us. We will hunt the Traveler down and kill him. And then we will kill every Hom who dares to enter the Southern Continent until we move to our rightful domain and demand that the bison be grown there for us to hunt as compensation for this insult."* Temüjin lunged forward snapping his jaws in a loud clap barely a meter from Khubilai's head.

"Yes, Lord," said Khubilai as he retreated, stepping backwards so that he continued to face Temüjin as he left. He did this, not out of respect, but as a matter of self-preservation. A Deinoc never turned his back on an agitated Deinoc.

•

Rolando called the senior members of the Resurrection in Pinchincha to a meeting in his home late the next evening. He recited a communication he had received from Raul. "So we can save Maria from Banishment. But that will leave Shon alone to face his enemies. Our enemies also, I believe. And things will be as they were unless Shon can defeat them by himself."

One of the members said, "What of the Society woman?"

"Raul believes her parents are on their way here to persuade her to drop out with Maria as she has also been relieved from banishment."

Another member said, "So that is why they have dropped Maria's conviction?"

Rolando said, "So it appears. I think it is obvious now that our doubts about Shon's allegiances were unfounded. The question before us is whether we should aid the Society in isolating Shon by saving Maria or whether we should allow his plan to proceed."

Ginés spoke, "I am no great supporter of Shon and whatever he is up to, but he has developed a lethal team with these women. We should not underestimate him and what his team might do. We may never have a chance again to stop Banishment for our people. We should be very careful in what we do next. Besides, I doubt we can stop Maria from joining Shon."

Rolando said, "Luciana is also part of his team and you yourself have said she has the greater skills in making his team effective. If she drops out, Maria will be entirely dependent on Shon who will be rather occupied with staying alive himself."

The first speaker said, "She is of the Society and Society wants her out. We cannot permit Maria alone to join him."

There was an upwelling of support for this view and the first speaker said, "I call for a vote on taking Maria out of this scheme. We owe it to Raul."

Rolando said, "I suggest we wait to act until we see what Luciana does. If she leaves, we take Maria out. If she stays, we meet before they go over and make a final determination on what we will do about Maria."

The group voted to support Rolando's proposal and the meeting came to an end.

After the others had departed, Ginés, who had stayed behind with Rolando, said, "Will Luciana stay with Shon?"

Rolando said, "I know nothing of the ways of the Society. If they are like us, I think she will do what Maria does. And we both know what she will do. But we also have not considered what Shon will do when he learns that they can escape Banishment. I think we he might not permit them to join him whatever they decide. I will visit Shon and meet you afterward when we will decide on what to do. "

•

Rolando went to see Shon and asked him to take a late walk under the stars. As they walked, Rolando related what he'd heard from Raul.

Shon said, "You are telling me that Maria and Luciana can get out of this? I never intended them to be in it to begin with. It's my fate, not theirs, to fight these killers. Do anything you can to take them out."

Rolando said, "Ginés believes that you three have formed a formidable team that might prevail, Shon."

"Ginés has no idea what we are facing, Rolando. I have told you before that I would not come out alive without bringing Maria out, too. My chances of success might well be greater without that responsibility. Take her out, my friend, and you will be doing me a favor."

"The Resurrection has agreed to do just that if Luciana withdraws and, maybe, even if she doesn't. But if she does, we will see to it that Maria is taken out."

•

The next morning at practice with Ginés and Luciana, Shon drew Luciana aside and told her of the new ruling. He said, "I never intended for you and Maria to become involved in this. You know what we face. You must leave and save yourself. And in doing so, you will save Maria with you."

"And you will die."

"That may happen regardless of whether you join me. But, without you and Maria, I might well do better without having to worry about the two of you. In any event, I don't want your lives on my conscience. We have been given the opportunity to avoid your deaths and I want to take it."

"I don't want to take it. I can help you win."

"Then consider Maria. We both know she is out of her element in this. Save her for me."

Luciana hesitated, her thoughts flitting back to the gym and Ginés and Maria, then she said, "Very well. If she withdraws, I will. But, if she does not, I will not. That is not negotiable, Shon."

"Very well then."

•

That afternoon, Shon drew Maria aside from their practice with Ginés.

He started to tell her of the recent events, but she interrupted, saying, "I received a communication from my father, Shon. My answer is no."

Shon said, "But if you withdraw, Luciana will be saved. Save her for me by withdrawing."

Maria said, "I don't believe she will withdraw and I would never withdraw while she stays with you."

"But if she did, would you, for me?"

Maria said, "She won't, but if she did, I will, too."

"And you will keep your word on this if she does?"

Maria sighed, "If she does, I will."

As for his battle with the Deinoc, he had come to realize that their involvement might lead to a more likely success than without them. Ginés had shown him that team was better than one man going it alone. But a team could suffer losses and that he wanted to forego no matter the greater risk to himself.

•

Juku led his entourage to Pinchincha. Octavius and Aurelia left Publius and Juku in the jungle and walked together toward the dominant structure in the distance, a white tower. When they arrived at the foot of the tower they asked a woman walking by to see Rolando Martine. She walked to the tower and entered a door at its base. Shortly a man came out and said, "I am Rolando Martine. May I be of service?"

Octavius said, "We are here to see our daughter, Luciana, who we are informed by Raul Monterro may be residing with you."

"May I inquire as to your identity?"

"We are her parents," said Octavius.

"Follow me."

Rolando led them into his tower to an antechamber and left them. He found Luciana and told her that her parents had come to see her. Looking perplexed, she consented.

Luciana entered the antechamber to the tower where she found her parents standing together across the room.

She said formally in the custom of her family, "Greetings, parents."

Aurelia said, "Greetings, daughter."

Octavius said, "Daughter, how are you?"

Luciana said, "I am well, father."

Aurelia said, "We want you to come home with us. This situation should never have involved you and Praetor Publius has ruled favorably on that point. You may leave."

"I don't want to leave, Mother. I have learned what those banished face. It is an abomination that the Society permits ordinary people to be sent into Amaz to die at the hands of the Deinoc."

Octavius said crisply in a low voice, "Daughter, please watch your words."

"Yes, Father. But I need say nothing more on this to make my point any clearer. And you know it."

Octavius said, "You are young and have not had to deal with maintaining the Order. Don't so quickly judge what you have not had to manage for all these many millennia as your mother and I have."

Luciana said, "I am not so quickly judging anything. Explain the honor in Banishment to Amaz and what that means to the banished and I will listen."

Aurelia glanced at Octavius and said, "My dear daughter, the Order is about keeping a balance among life on Vitas, not about the honor in doing so. The compromises we made in this situation have kept alive more citizens and members of the Society than any alternative would have."

Luciana said, "But the plain mathematics of the numbers banned make that statement a lie, Mother. Millions have died. Those in Amaz don't number millions. Where is the balance in that?"

Octavius responded, "If those in Amaz came over and killed those in Montaña in the beginning, millions of Montañans would never have lived since. That is the mathematics that we have dealt with and there is balance when that is considered, child."

Luciana said, "Please do not call me child, Father. I am a grown woman, just not very old like you. I live in a present where seeing the victims of your mathematics die to serve your idea of a greater cause is painful to the victims and those who care about them. We are prepared to die to stop this abomination that you will not stop and I am going to do my part. I am not old enough to so treasure my own life that I will permit others to die instead."

Aurelia said, "It's not the victims, as you call them, but one person, Shon Ó Conaill, with whom you have become obsessed, that calls you to pursue this course. You have fallen in love with him and would jeopardize Vitas to save him for yourself."

"Yes, I have fallen in love with him because he is willing to face the consequences for trying to make things right. If he succeeds we will have a better Order."

Octavius said, "But he, or you and he together, will not succeed. That is why we made the arrangements we did to begin with. Can't you grasp that you cannot defeat the Deinoc?"

Luciana said, "Shon and I do not accept your premise that we cannot succeed."

Octavius said sharply, "How can he assume success over a foe he doesn't even know about?"

Luciana was silent.

Octavius peered at her for a moment and said, "Aahh, I see now. He knows what lives in Amaz doesn't he? How did that come about?"

Luciana was silent.

Octavius stepped toward her and said, "There will be severe consequences for those responsible for this intolerable disclosure."

Luciana stepped back and said, "I will accept responsibility for that."

Octavius peered at her closely. "I do not believe it was you who told him. We will find out who made such a forbidden disclosure and they will pay the price, daughter."

Luciana's shoulders drooped. "If I go with you, will you leave that matter alone?"

Octavius said, "As if we had never had this conversation."

Luciana said, "Very well, I will go with you upon your word that you will not pursue an inquiry into how Shon knows what he knows."

Octavius said, "Agreed, upon my word."

Aurelia said, "Then it is settled. We will leave tomorrow at sunrise."

"Yes, Mother."

•

Luciana came to Shon's room and told him what had transpired with her parents.

Shon said, "Is your father's word good?"

"Yes, absolutely."

"Then you must go."

"That is what you wanted isn't it, Shon?"

"I never wanted you or Maria to get involved. So we are where I intended things to be when I started this."

"But you didn't start this, Shon. The Society did."

"I merely played into their hands as they correctly predicted how I would behave. Don't despair. They don't know everything, least of all what will happen when I go over."

"Easy words. You have a good plan which we should finish. A plan where I could help you succeed. I cannot see how you can do this with only Maria to help you."

"Maria will not be going over. I elicited the same promise from her that you gave me. I will go over alone."

"Then you will certainly fail."

"Don't be so sure. In any event, you have protected Carpia and some others. That counts for a great deal with me."

Shon took Luciana in his arms and kissed her.

She responded but he resisted doing more and led her to his door and bid her a long life.

She fled to her room.

•

Shon left his quarters and went to see Maria where he told her that Luciana would be leaving in the morning.

Maria said, "I feel tricked into what I agreed, Shon."

"You weren't tricked, Maria. But fate has a way of happening regardless of what we say and do. I want to deal with this without risking your life which, honestly, may create a greater risk to whatever chance I may have to prevail than going it alone. So please accept the way things are and wish me well."

He took her into his arms, saying, "I'm not dead yet and I didn't start down this path to end up that way. I set out to take a risk to myself that I believe would have been forced on me no matter what I did when I came to Montaña and I am content to play it out. But that does not mean I think I am doomed, only that I am taking that risk now rather than later which I think advantageous as delaying the inevitable affords my foes more time to learn more about me and to find better ways of disposing of me."

"You truly believe they would have banished you even if you had not brought it upon yourself?"

"Absolutely. More charges would have come until one stuck. Publius, for whatever reason he had, gave me an out which I chose to reject. Eventually they would have gotten me into Amaz which is why I was sent to Montaña in the first place."

Maria began to shake, then she wept.

Shon held her until she quieted.

"I love you, Maria. Do this for me and, maybe, the fates will bring me back. If they don't, know that I treasured every moment we had together." He kissed her softly and then he let her go.

He went out her door and left her tower to go back to his . It was only a few hours till dawn and he took the time to sleep.

When he arose he felt a calmness he hadn't felt since the trial.

•

No one saw Luciana depart with her parents.

Maria said goodbye to Rolando and asked him to tell Ginés to do his best to prepare her man.

Rolando saw Ginés in passing shortly after dawn and told him that Maria and Luciana had left. When he passed on Maria's message, he noticed a dampness on Ginés face just under his eyes.

•

Ginés approached Shon an hour later in the gymnasium. "The women have left."

Shon shrugged. "That's the way it should have been from the beginning. I apologize for all the time you spent on making us a team. I think we might have succeeded that way."

"Then why give that up?"

"Well, it's not really my decision, is it? Besides, between us, I think my chances will be better without women along."

"You lie," said Ginés.

Shon's Magan brain jolted his mind. He peered at Ginés. "That's a strong remark," Shon said in an even voice.

Ginés slowly turned to face Shon head-on. "It's true. There can be no question that you would do better with the support of others who can throw the bogacho. You don't want them to die supporting you while you survive. You are a coward."

Shon lowered his center of gravity, sensing an imminent assault from Ginés who he saw was beginning to move in a pre-combative way, sort of sliding around him with closely spaced footsteps with the trunk of his body always facing towards him. "And why does my not wanting those I care about to die to improve my chances of success make me a coward?"

Ginés growled, "The Resurrection has been supporting you because you said you could change things, though you haven't said how. Now you weaken yourself and our cause you claim to support because you can't bear the death of those you love. That is cowardice. A brave man would understand that he must risk more than himself to win a goal greater than himself. And those most likely to suffer from his decisions must be those he values most as it is they who make his goal their own without regard to their own survival."

Shon relaxed his stance and said, "What you say is true, Ginés. But I have some advantages that I think will gain me a better chance without them but which might be compromised by their involvement."

"If you can't risk losing them, but can risk losing the cause, then the others, who have set their course with you, don't really matter in the same way. They are the fodder you will fall back on." Ginés nearly shouted those last words.

"I have no fodder in this battle, Ginés," Shon said in a quiet tone, stepping toward Ginés.

Ginés suddenly spun and thrust his leg out at Shon's head.

Shon ducked and stepped into Ginés with his full body, sending Ginés down.

Ginés swung his legs, but Shon jumped in anticipation of the move and Ginés ended sprawled on his belly. Shon simply sat down on top of Ginés. Shon's moves were so supremely, yet simply, executed that Ginés could scarcely believe that he was now face down on the floor with Shon sitting atop him as if he were a couch.

Shon said, "We can do this for a while or we can finish what you started."

"What I started?" grunted Ginés, who could see he was not going to get up if Shon resisted.

"You have raised exactly what my problem is in ways you don't understand. My destiny, if I survive the coming battle, will likely be to send all the people I will ever come to know to their deaths in pursuit of a future they may not even want and which I will never see with them. At best, I will learn about their success, but, most of the time, I will learn of their deaths in pursuit of that future."

Ginés stopped struggling. He said, "Could you get off of me?"

Shon complied.

Ginés stood up and brushed himself off. Then he said, "I don't understand what you are saying. What I know is that you told Rolando that you needed to create a team to deal with your enemy. Well, your team is gone. I am glad your team is gone. I'm ashamed to say that is because I also don't want them, one in particular, to die for your cause or any other. So I understand that part of what you are saying."

Ginés looked into Shon's eyes. "We have no great love for each other. But I sense that something in what you say is about a great cause and I want to be part of it, even if I end up just a dead foot soldier before it all plays out. Offended as you may be by it, I don't mind becoming fodder in a great cause. Let me join you and help you win."

Shon said, "One is not a team. Two is. I would be honored to have you at my side, Ginés. But dying in this cause will be your likely outcome even if I win."

"I've spent a long life playing games. Games I really cared about, but knowing all along they have no real consequences upon even my community. I want to do something more and, if that means I won't live to see the outcome, I can be satisfied with that. All I ask is that when I am dead, you will say to those you care about, particularly Rolando and Maria, that of what you required of me, I did well."

Shon said, "You assume that I will survive you and that you will die, Ginés."

"I am certain of both, though I have every hope it will not be at the beginning of your quest, whatever that is."

Shon looked at Ginés and extended his hand.

Ginés extended his to Shon and they shook hands.

Without another word, they began to practice.

•

Luciana and her parents entered the jungle where her parents had left Juku and Publius. Shortly Juku and Publius appeared. Octavius briefed Publius on what had occurred in Pinchincha and then ordered the group to proceed back to where they had landed so they could return to Annec as quickly as possible.

Publius was impressed by Octavius' willingness to fly again when it appeared such risky expediency was no longer warranted now that they had Luciana with them. He concluded that Octavius' calm appearance belied his concern that this matter would not be safely concluded until he had Luciana back in Annec.

Juku led the trek away from Pinchincha. After a few hours, he noticed that Luciana had moved up from the Hom and was walking only a couple of paces behind him as he lumbered forward. Then he heard her say audibly, "Juku, we must speak.

But not now and not in mindcast. I need you to take a long route back. I will come to you when the others are asleep."

Juku led them onward. But he began to move off the direct line to their destination while slowing his pace a bit, not enough for anyone to notice except for Luciana.

They stopped for the night in the jungle. Other members of the Society of Species appeared bringing food, water, large leaves and branches until, within an hour, they had constructed several shelters for the company while dinner was prepared around a fire fueled by jungle debris. The senior Hom, unused to such physical effort from a day of jungle travel, retired to their abodes. Luciana left her shelter and walked to a clearing a few meters from the fire. Shortly, a large body drooped down from a large tree-limb overhanging the clearing.

Juku mindcasted, *"It seems you have had an interesting adventure since we last met."*

Luciana spoke verbally, "Juku, it is so good to see you again. Can you believe my parents came to get me the way they did? Now let's speak verbally as we did on the Moon."

Juku growled and grunted and Luciana heard him say, "They must love you, even more than I," with the same comprehension she had when he spoke in mindcast having learned his family's language well during their time together on the Moon.

"Stop playing with me. I need your help. I am not going back to Annec. I need to be with Shon when he goes into Amaz, which will be soon. Can you help me?"

Juku growed and grunted, "If I did, I have no doubt your mother and your father will find a way to pay me back. I only hope they will not harm any others of my family."

"You may be correct about your personal risk, but I can't believe they would go further."

"Perhaps not."

"So you will help me at risk to yourself and the hope my parents aren't monsters?"

Maria heard Juku saying in his language, "I might possibly help you if we disappeared near the end of our trek and some other families, who shall not be named, might possibly consider guiding you to the Wall. But before any of what might possibly occur becomes what will occur, I must understand why this might be wise knowing its outcome will be that you will then face what must be one of the greatest risks one could imagine—venturing into Amaz to face a Deinoc Horde."

"You were right on Moon Base."

"Such an admission might well get my cooperation, but I must explain to others who were not on Moon Base why they should risk themselves, and possibly their families, to help you commit suicide because you are in love."

"Juku, you are impossible. I have to."

"I fail to see how dying for a man you really have barely met is something you 'have' to do."

"It's just too complicated. You cannot possibly understand what has happened."

"I am a mere creation of your family so maybe that is so."

"Stop being a baby. I am so ashamed, Juku. I don't think I can tell you."

"You have always found a way to tell me what you needed to. Shall I irritate you into doing so?"

"Stop!" It came out in a low voice, as she had not lost so much control as to speak in her mindcast which might awaken the others more attuned to it than Juku's. "I watched a man nearly rape Maria, the woman Shon really loves, hoping he would succeed in ruining her for him. I am so ashamed that I am surprised that I can even tell you this. Then Maria helped the man regain control of himself and she actually forgave him before my very eyes—all while I did nothing, hiding in a closet. The worst is her forgiving this man who almost destroyed her and then embracing him to do good. It's so awful, I think I must stop telling you this."

"Compose yourself. I am Juku who, while having a bit of fun with your frightfully sensitive nature, truly loves you. In our time together you have always gotten out what you needed to say and I must say that is the basis for why I love you so. Tell me and I will advise when there is any advice I can offer. But you do know that I will never judge you?"

Luciana sighed, "I know that. But I have abandoned Shon in his quest to defeat the Deinoc to protect Carpia and Tigri who I believe told Shon forbidden Society secrets such as that Deinoc inhabit Amaz. Somehow my father detected from my demeanor that Shon knew about them and could have only learned it from one of the families of the Society because I wasn't even able to convey the notion that it was I who told him. But now I know I need to go back and I don't know how to do that without causing my parents to avenge themselves by killing Carpia and Tigri."

Juku said, "Carpia and Tigri are not alone out here. Your parents are the ones alone here and don't know it. It will not be so easy for them or the Society to harm them. They have a very powerful ally."

"Really? Who could be a more powerful ally than the Society?"

"I cannot say. You must trust me as I trust you. You only need to know that Carpia and Tigri are not really at risk from the Hom. Nor are any of us here."

Luciana was at a loss for words. She completely trusted Juku but what he was saying was beyond anything she could comprehend. The Society controlled everything on Vitas and the Hom controlled the Society. How could Juku, Carpia, and Tigri have an ally more powerful?

Still, it was what she needed to hear so she decided to take him at his word. She said, "You give me your word that I do not need to worry about their safety?"

"You have my word. And when you get the opportunity you may say that to Carpia. But you must give me your word that you will tell her exactly what I told you: They have an ally but you know nothing more than that."

"Since I know nothing more, I agree."

"And you won't pry to find out more."

Luciana said, "Okay. I won't pry."

"Good. Then I will help you get yourself killed."

"Thank you."

Luciana arose in the middle of the night and left with Juku to return to Pinchincha.

·

Maria returned to Montaña and went to see her father at his office at the University.

Raul stood as she entered his office. "Maria, it is so good to see you."

"And you, too, father." She sat down in a chair across from her father's desk. "Why do we live, father? Is it only to be alive for as long as we can or is there more to it?"

Raul hesitated, waiting for her to say more. When she didn't, he responded, "I don't know the answer to that question, my dear. But to die futilely is not the answer."

"Is it futile to die pursuing a greater cause?"

"To answer that one must consider the greater cause. You know that the greatest hope of we Montañans is to be free to pursue our own destinies and that we, or many of us, certainly those in the Resurrection, wish nothing more than to be free to pursue our own destiny free of those who control our future to serve their ideas of what life for us should be. Since before you were borne, we have sought a way to be free to do just that. But is Shon the way and should you follow his path to an uncertain future, of which we really know nothing? That is really the question."

"No, the question is: If you believe in someone can you die for that person, not knowing?"

Raul sighed. "I love you too much to see you die for the cause of any man. But if you must put your life at risk for the man you truly love, then you must follow your heart." He shuddered visibly.

"I need to find my destiny. I will live an empty life if I don't. Of that I am certain."

Raul, slumping in his chair while rubbing his forehead for a moment, said, "Very well then, how can I help you, my child?"

"Allow me to return to Pinchincha and face my future in Amaz with Shon."

Raul rose from behind his desk and said, "Then we shall return to Pinchincha together to inform Rolando and the Resurrection of your decision."

NINE

AMAZ

When Maria and Raul arrived in Pinchincha, they went to see Rolando.

It was an hour past dawn when they found Rolando sitting in a garden by his white tower.

Rolando sprang to his feet when he saw them approaching. He strode toward them, saying, "What are you doing back here?"

Raul said quietly, "It seems Maria has determined her destiny and that it is to be with Shon when he goes over."

"Sheer madness. How can you permit this, Raul?"

"I really have no choice, Rolando. She must live her life as she wishes or she will live it empty of what it can be for her."

Rolando shrugged, "The Resurrection will undoubtedly be proud of her. I wish I could forcibly disagree but I must admit that since she left I have been thinking about the possibility that he just might succeed and what a shame it would be if none of us were there to help him. Well let's go find him and Ginés. They are undoubtedly working on his plan to go it alone."

As they approached the gym, Luciana appeared walking up the road from the jungle. They stopped in their tracks.

Maria called out, "Luciana!"

Luciana turned toward the voice and stopped walking. She said calmly, "I see we are of like minds."

Maria turned to Raul and Rolando, "Let me go alone with Luciana to him."

The men turned back while the women walked on to the gym.

Shon's back was to them as they entered. He was engaged in some lunging maneuvers with swords against Ginés who was countering his blows with great effort. Shon's sword caught their eyes; it seems to flow in space almost invisibly. Ginés stopped in mid-motion when he saw the women enter. Shon knocked him from his feet and said, "What kind of defense is that, Ginés? Do that over there and you won't be around to see what happens next and I'll probably go down with you." He sheathed his katana in disgust and stopped when he saw that Ginés was looking not at him but beyond him. He turned and stopped frozen in motion. "What are you two doing here?"

Luciana said, "We couldn't break up the team."

Ginés exclaimed, "No!"

Maria said, "Yes, Ginés. We must go along. It's our destiny—the one we want."

Shon, seeing a fait accompli when one was clearly before him, said dryly, "Well, at least your absence added another to the team. Welcome Ginés."

The women glanced at each other and then Maria said, "That is great news."

Luciana was silent.

Then Shon approached them and said, "I was relieved when you left. I don't want your lives on my soul. I want you to reconsider."

Luciana said, "We did that and we have decided. We go."

Maria chimed in, "And that is not going to be reconsidered."

The tone in their voice told Shon that his thought on seeing them was indeed a fait accompli. He said, "Very well, pick up some spears and join in."

Luciana said, "Why not swords? Yours looks rather unusual."

Shon said, "You are not ready to face my sword and you never will be."

Maria shuddered.

•

He worked them like they had never worked before and at the end of the day they returned to the White Tower.

Over dinner, which he commanded that they would take together as a team until the day they went over the Wall, he said, "We have little time to finish our preparations. So from this night until we cross over we will confine all our discussions here and in private to preparations for the battle." He hoped by doing so he could focus on the mission and not on these people whom he loved dearly and he told them so.

They all agreed.

•

One month before the designated date of banishment they traveled to a clearing in the jungle by the Wall where they would be sent over. They set up camp in the darkest, dampest part of the jungle adjoining Amaz. It was dark, like twilight, the sunlight unable to easily penetrate the dense canopy fifty meters and more overhead. It was the season of rain and it rained heavily every day.

They spent their time acclimating to the swelteringly hot humidity by running their practices at full pace until they began to feel as comfortable in their exertion as they had in the cooler, dryer jungle surrounding Pinchincha.

Shon changed the training ritual to prepare his team mentally for the coming ordeal. They needed to sense that these sessions were no longer practice but rather the final preparations for deadly combat. He knew that once they entered Amaz the Deinoc would be watching and they could not continue drilling in Amaz without foretelling their tactics to their opponents, which would spell defeat and death for them all.

Each morning, Shon walked out in front of them and bowed from the waist. He began a series of slow movements, hand thrusts, blocking motions, kicks, spin kicks, hand combinations, hand and foot combinations. His speed increased every day as he carefully released ever more of the Magan influence upon his mind so that he would be ready when the time came to become what he knew he must become.

Each day his mind ascended more into the details of every movement. Perfect form, perfect sequence. His mind called up the Palgwe and Hyeong sequences, forms and movements from an ancient Asian martial arts system. He began to move through each form as a seventh level Dan. He became lost inside the art. His speed of perfect execution of every move increased rapidly. Form, order, speed, power. He slipped into overdrive and accelerated his body in tandem with his mind. He never noticed his changing pace. Form, order, speed, power, hands, feet, combinations, spins, kicks. His speed and power increased more even as he exerted more each day. He was starting to breathe deeply. It felt good. He was one with himself. He was one with the flow of life within him. His speed increased. Form, order, speed, power, life, within, without. His speed increased. He was breathing hard. His muscles were hot. Form, order, speed, power, life, love, hate, Yin, Yang. His speed increased. He was beginning to strain. His muscles were burning. He was approaching his limits mentally and still accelerating his body which somehow kept up with the effort. Form, order, speed, power, life, death, love, hate, friend, foe, Yin, Yang, happiness, sorrow, forces in opposition, attraction, repulsion. His speed increased. Maria, Luciana, Maria, Luciana. He began to slow down, Form, order, speed, power, life, love, hate, Yin, Yang, Maria, Luciana, Luciana, Maria. He slowed down. Form order, speed, power, life, love, Luciana, Maria, Maria, Luciana. He slowed down. Maria, Luciana, Luciana, Maria. He slowed to a stop.

Each session as he withdrew from his changing state of mind, he turned and bowed. No one said a word at the end of each session. Ginés tried to comprehend what he had just seen. He was awed but he was also truly afraid. This man was not human. He was some sort of god from ancient history—a Hercules or a Theseus. There was a point where he could no longer distinguish any of Shon's features as Shon became a blur. Ginés was physically paralyzed. The women responded by pushing harder themselves until they ended each session exhausted, but stronger and faster than before.

Near the end, on the day before the delegation from Montaña's Office of the Order was to appear to direct their crossing over, at the end of their evening meal, Shon spoke to them.

"We have trained and prepared as well as anyone could.

"Once we enter Amaz, we will be the hunted. We cannot prepare any further or they will see our capabilities and tactics. We must be prepared to engage instantly. But, since we will not likely be engaged for some time, we will suffer the toll from waiting—stress and anxiety, tensions and frictions.

"You must remember that you are under battlefield conditions and take none of it personally. We all love and care about each other. We are all prepared to die for each other. Remember that as the pressure grows. We are one unit indivisible, here because we care about each other and about what we might be able to do when we succeed.

"We will kill our opponent not because he is bad or hates us or wants to kill us. He may have all of those desires or none. That is irrelevant. We will kill our opponent because that is our mission. If you kill because your enemy is bad, you will falter if he appears good. If you kill because he hates you, you will falter if he smiles—if a Deinoc can smile. If you kill because he wants to kill you, you will falter if he calls you friend. In this conflict, we will kill or be killed. We did not pick this fight. We are entitled to kill. We have a right to kill. We have an obligation to kill. Not just for our own protection but because that is our mission and the future of our people depends on us."

Shon had made similar speeches to them before but now battle was nigh. He knew the biggest remaining obstacle to their success would be their natural inhibition against killing, at least at the level of their civilized minds. Even in his time, when killing was routine for highly trained soldiers, this had been the paramount training problem.

These two girls and Ginés thought of themselves as warriors and that was good. But they were not veteran warriors. They had not killed anything or anyone in their lives. Now they were expected to kill creatures as conscious of living as they were. The only way to improve their chances further would have been to do some killing. But they had had no animals to kill remotely similar to what they faced and the feelings he had deemed likely to be engendered in them by killing some cattle or horses seemed counterproductive to its purpose.

Shon counted on the spears he had specially prepared— really shaft-tubes that outwardly looked like thicker-than-ordinary spear shafts, with springs built into the shafts to propel their spears more forcefully than they could naturally—producing most of the killing force needed because he did not think either girl would thrust a spear for the first time into a living body with killing force. Yet their first thrust had do its work. If they got the spear into the enemy's torso, the tips he had designed to expand and tear the guts and blood vessels of their victim would bring a quick end. But if they failed to penetrate its body the now-expanded tips would work against any further penetration. He had trained them to drop each spear after thrusting it but he couldn't be sure they would do so in the heat of the battle.

His goal now wasn't physical training but changing their minds to react primally, using their basest instincts for survival to bring out their instinctive deep-seated blood lust suppressed by their civilized mentality.

•

As they prepared to retire for the night, there was a rustle in the jungle near their camp and out of the woods strode a huge brightly feathered bi-pedal dinosaur with extremely long claws. Maria was the first to see it, and she sprung up from her seat by the fire, screaming, "Oh my God, they're here on this side of the Wall." Before she could say more, a parrot flew up to her and, fluttering for a moment before her, said, "Maria, calm yourself. We are friends."

Maria stopped and stared at the bird. It looked familiar to her. She had noticed a bird like this flitting around Huascarán and several other times over the past months in Montaña and at Pinchincha. Distracted by the bird's speaking, she forgot about the large dinosaur for just a moment, and said, "You can talk?"

The bird said, "Of course, my dear. I have been watching you for some time. This dinosaurian is not a Deinoc but a Therizi. Her name is Madra Ameyali and she is a friend who has come with me and two others to visit before you go into Amaz."

Luciana, who had rushed out of her tent when she heard Maria's scream, said, "She is telling the truth, Maria. I know her family." She turned to Carpia and mindcast, "*It is good to see you, Carpia Ana. But you have put yourself in great danger coming here.*"

Carpia replied audibly, "We had to come. Your quest is important to more than yourselves and the Montañans. We want to wish you farewell."

A spectacled black bear with pale ginger-colored markings on its face shambled into the clearing. Luciana said audibly, "Juku! I thought I might never see you again."

Juku mindcast, "*I could not bear to miss seeing you before you went over to do your foolish deed.*"

Maria heard some grunting noises coming from the big furry beast.

Shon strode up from the other side of the clearing and said, "Madra Ameyali, Carpia Ana, how good of you to stop by."

Madra began to make twirping sounds, "*I have come to practice Deinoc with you one last time, Shon.*"

Shon said, "I am grateful to you for coming." Turning toward the bear, he said, "You can only be Juku. I'm pleased to meet you."

Maria began to stare at Shon.

Shon said, "Relax, Maria. Trust me, all is well."

Maria said, "What's going on? Can you understand them?"

Shon said, "That's something I've been meaning to get around to telling you."

Maria said, "Well now might be a good time."

Ginés had come out of his tent during this exchange and said, "I would also like to hear about this."

Shon laughed, and then exclaimed, "Well, look who else has dropped in," looking toward a large black cat that had sauntered up beside Madra. "Welcome, Tigri Omagua."

Maria simply sat down, too flustered to speak and looked back and forth between the visitors and Shon.

Shon said, "Let me explain." And then he told Maria and Ginés about the Society of Species and how the Society that they knew about was but a part of a larger society.

At the end of his explanation, Maria said, "So you and Luciana have known about this all along."

Shon said sheepishly, "Well I haven't known *all* along. But since Huascarán. You will recall that I told you that I wasn't quite ordinary. Thanks to some of what is not ordinary about me and, with Madra's tutelage, I can comprehend the Deinoc. It may turn out to be useful or it may not as the Deinoc know that Luciana can hear them also. Still it's possible that they will communicate between themselves in the battle thinking her hearing won't matter. It was pointless to plan on it as a team as I doubt there is much you or Ginés will be able to do in the heat of battle by my telling you anything they might be saying. But now that you know, please pay attention if I tell you I heard one of them telling another he is planning on attacking you from behind."

"Very funny, Shon," Maria said, not amused. "Why are they helping us?"

"We aren't the only ones who seek a change on Vitas. Many of the families desire a change from the static order of things. But, in the case of Carpia, it is Carpia's affection for you that has brought us together."

"Affection for me? She doesn't know me."

"Actually she does, quite well. I hope telling you this won't embarrass her, but she has been following you for months and has come to care deeply for you. She approached me a while back and told me everything. So we have some very unexpected friends."

Maria was speechless and tried to absorb what she was hearing. While she was doing this, Carpia flew over and perched herself on Maria's shoulder, saying, "I've been wanting to do this for some time, my dear."

Maria slowly reached her hand over to touch Carpia softly while Tigri sauntered over to Shon and rubbed against his leg.

Ginés felt faint and sat down by the fire.

Shon said, "Why don't you all sit down and spend some time together while I go with Madra to practice my Deinoc." With that he walked over to Madra and they trotted off together into the jungle.

Luciana told Maria and Ginés about Juku and how he was with her on Moon Base when Shon appeared in his ship from the past.

None of the local members of the Society mentioned the missing person at the clearing, the Great One.

Shon returned two hours later with Madra and said, "This has been wonderful, but we have to get ready to greet our not-so-friendly visitors tomorrow. Carpia, Tigri, Madra, this visit means a great deal to me. I will try to remember all that you have done for us. I may as well tell you that I will not seem to be myself afterwards and you should not come to me until you are told it is safe to do so. If *she* tells you, it will be safe, but not until then."

Shon turned to Juku and said, "Juku, Luciana alluded to your existence as a great friend to her, though she never told me any particulars, undoubtedly for your own safety." Passing his gaze over the visitors he said, "Now go and be well."

The visitors disappeared into the jungle.

Maria turned to Shon and said, "Who is 'she' and what is this about you not being yourself afterwards?"

"I can't tell you about either of those things, Maria. Just trust me as you have so far." With that he retired to his tent.

Maria looked at Luciana who said, "I truly know nothing about this, Maria."

With that, she retired to her tent and, shortly, Maria joined her but said nothing more.

Ginés sat by the fire unable to sleep the rest of the night as he realized that the world he lived in was not remotely what he had thought it was all of his life.

•

The delegates from the Office of the Order approached the camp by the Wall at the time dictated by the rules of banishment, exactly four hours past sunrise.

Shon, Maria, Luciana, and Ginés walked together to the fire pit and stood alongside each other as the delegation entered the clearing.

Leading the delegation of six Montañans was Joseph Estaban. He was followed by three members of the Office, strong men obviously present to insure compliance with the Order of Banishment. Following a few steps behind were Raul Montero and Naomi Chavín, the chief elder, as the appointed witnesses for the community. Two witnesses not related to the Office were required so they could attest to the procedural correctness of the banishment to the community. As the chief elder was always required to attend, it was the most difficult of that person's official duties. The second witness was usually randomly selected, but Raul had used his influence to be the appointed second witness.

Joseph spoke first. "We, representatives of the Office of the Order of Montaña, the citizens of Montaña and the Society, are called here today to execute a Writ of Banishment on Shon Ó Conaill in accordance with the Order. Shon Ó Conaill, we witness your appearance as ordered. Are you prepared to accept your sentence?"

Shon replied, "I am."

Luciana and Maria said, "As are we."

Joseph hesitated for moment, then said, "Ladies, there is no Writ standing against either of you."

Maria, taking a step toward him, said, "We renounce the decision to release us from the Writ and insist on banishment with this man."

Joseph's lips began to twitch, uncontrollably. It had been arranged. These women were not supposed to be here.

Ginés said, "As do I."

Joseph turned in his consternation and staring at Ginés, said loudly, "And who are you?"

"You do not recognize me?"

Joseph stared at the man for a moment and said, "Ginés Cortijo, the bogacho player?"

"Yes. That is me."

Joseph said in an even louder voice, "What are you doing here? You are the greatest bogacho player in the history of Montaña. How is it possible that you are here with these, these people, perhaps the greatest enemies the Order has ever faced?"

Ginés replied, "Pardon me, sir, but they do not appear to me to be such great enemies. I like them so I am here to join them."

Joseph, spuming, said, "You *like* them. Are you a fool or just as stupid as I have always imagined you bogacho players to be? You have no idea what banishment means. I urge you to step back and withdraw from matters that don't concern you."

Ginés said quietly, "Sir, I may be as stupid as you say. But I, like all Montañans, know exactly what banishment means. I wish to join my friends in their ordeal and I am going to do so."

Joseph said, "There is no precedent for citizens not subject to a Writ of Banishment to cross into Amaz. As it is forbidden for anyone to enter Amaz for any other reason, you will not be allowed to cross over."

Maria said, "And does that apply to us?"

"Yes,' he said, "No one may cross over but the subject of the Writ, Shon Ó Conaill." He could hardly believe the challenge of the day was not going to be to force Shon over, but rather to keep others from following.

Before Joseph could say another word, Raul said, "You have yourself and three men to help you prevent that from occurring. Shon has himself, two women, and two men to make sure they do."

Naomi said, "Make that Shon, this man, you, and three women, Raul."

Joseph glanced over at the three men from the Office and felt no comfort from the way they were looking sideways at each other. Obviously they had not expected facing more than one man who they had heard had purposely put himself in this position and had no intention of resisting the Writ.

Joseph glared at Shon. "It is you that's responsible for this outrage."

Shon took a step toward Joseph and said, "I will accept that responsibility. Are you going to enable us to cross over the Wall? If so, instruct your minions to get on with it. Otherwise—"

Joseph didn't wait to hear what Shon was about to say. Turning to the three delegates from the Office, he said, "Take the ladders and ropes out and get them out of our lives."

The men shed their backpacks and took out hollow metal tubes and assembled them into a ladder that extended to the top of the Wall. One of the men climbed to the top and attached one end of a rope and threw it across the Wall where the other end landed on the ground in Amaz.

Maria embraced Raul, "Father, I know how much this pains you. I love you beyond words." Then she leaned close to him and whispered, "Tell the Resurrection that two Montañans on their own chose to cross over to pursue the destiny we all pray for."

Raul hugged her hard and said, "Maria, I could never have hoped for a better child. Go knowing no one wants you back more than I, but also go knowing that I believe in you and Shon and that I will get by, whatever happens."

They stepped apart. Maria followed Shon and the others to the ladder. They climbed up the ladder. As she prepared to slide down the rope on the other side of the Wall into Amaz, she saw a bird flit across the Wall. It appeared to be a green parrot.

•

In Sir Orda, Khubilai, First General of the Golden Horde, trounced down the road to the ancient wooden citadel to inform Temüjin of the great news that the Traveler had crossed over into Amaz at the appointed time.

He found Temüjin restlessly pacing back and forth as usual.

Temüjin lunged toward him, saying, *"He didn't cross over did he?"*

"To the contrary, Lord, I have some unexpected news."

Temüjin lurched closer, his great toothed maw snapping so close to Khubilai's throat that Khubilai stepped back, always a dangerous move given the instinctive Deinoc impulse to attack at such opportunities.

But Temüjin stopped, puzzled by what Khubilai had just said.

" 'To the contrary' implies he did cross over but you add 'unexpected news', Khubilai. What sort of way is that to tell me something. What are you saying? Did he or did he not? If he did, why is that unexpected?"

"Lord, he crossed over. The unexpected news I bring is that he did so with his women."

"What? You told me that Praetor Publius, who raised our hopes of a Mates Hunt by convicting the daughter of Octavius Augustus, had extracted her from banishment with his legal trickeries. And that his other mate, the citizen, had also gotten off."

"That is what Timür learned then in Annec, but only last evening I learned from him that Octavius Augustus has returned to Annec without her, but he apparently told no one, at least no one in contact with Timür, what occurred. Now we believe she must have decided to join the Traveler. And, as for the citizen woman, it appears that she has also crossed over with him. Also, Lord, another citizen has crossed over but we know nothing about him."

"Another lover of the citizen woman no doubt," snapped Temüjin.

"That is inconsistent with what we know about Montañans, but perhaps you are correct."

Temüjin leapt vertically two meters into the air and spun in a compete circle before he landed back where he left, nearly on top of Khubilai. *"No matter. What matters is that this is glorious news. We will have a Mates Hunt after all! Are we ready?"*

"Of course, Lord. Trackers were waiting and will trail them until the Horde is prepared to take them."

"When is the next full moon?"

"In twenty-two days."

"Not a lot of time. I wanted to savor this Hunt longer. But waiting for the next moon after that gives too much time to Augustus to plot a way to extract his daughter a second time. Tell the Horde, we will leave Sir Orda in fifteen days so that we may initiate the Stalking two days before the full moon."

"It shall be as you order, Lord." Temüjin backed out and left to attend to the Hunt.

•

Almost immediately after Publius entered Mamercus's antechamber at his home in Annec, Mamercus entered and they sat down across from each other. Sitting on the table between them was the same bottle of old single malt Scotch whisky that they had drunk from the last time Publius had visited Mamercus. It seemed a long time ago, really a feeling to savor given their long lives when years passing often felt like only a few fleeting moments in time.

Mamercus said, "I hear you have had quite a journey. Tell me about it."

Publius said, "I was forbidden to discuss this with anyone before they went over, which they did yesterday. I think Octavius was still hoping she might stay behind.

"It started off well. We were met by representatives of the Society and proceeded to Montaña's central city where we met with the man whose daughter had joined with Luciana in supporting him at the trial. We proceeded to an outlying town where Octavius appeared to succeed in persuading Luciana to abandon her effort to follow Shon into Amaz. But on our way back through Montaña she vanished. Octavius was furious. I won't belabor you with what Aurelia had to say. "

"I can well imagine. Now we will see whether there is anything to the Prophecy."

Publius took a sip of his drink, leaned back in his chair, and said,

"If he comes out, your fears and my hopes will play out."

•

Amaz! Awesome plant life towered into the sky. It was forbidding. The primordial jungle on this side of the Wall was twice the height of Montaña's jungle. One hundred and fifty meter conifers. Huge ferns and horsetails. Ginkgoes, magnolias and monkey puzzle trees.

As Shon, Maria, Luciana, and Ginés walked away from the Wall, they sensed that they were four tiny creatures moving into a world of gigantism. Shortly, they saw huge insects and invertebrates and heard unfamiliar, frightening sounds. Shon told them what he had learned from Madra: that the sounds were from restored Cretaceous and Jurassic animals that had been restored but not enlightened; and as these animals posed no threat to the Deinoc, the Deinoc would insure that they were not likely to chance upon any of these creatures because that might thwart their whole point of being here.

His view was of small comfort to his squad since the frightening distant sounds of life were as unfamiliar to them as the visible environment surrounding them. He could already see the tension and stress building in his team. And they had just entered Amaz. What was it going to be like in a few weeks?

Within an hour of crossing over, Shon began to hear Deinoc voices in his head. He fought the ever more powerful influences and emotions of his Magan brain. He knew that his reaction was caused by his Magan brain's instinctive reaction to the extremely hostile emanations from creatures possessed of the same genetics encoded in humankind including the powerful emotions these creatures obtained when they were endowed with limbic brains during their Enlightenment.

He knew that Deinoc were there in the jungle, just out of sight. The hunt had begun.

•

The first two days, the Deinoc rustled the plants around them herding them toward the lake where they would find the cottage that Carpia had related in her story of what would happen. Since Shon could hear them talking among themselves, he had a pretty good idea when they were going in the direction the Deinoc wanted. He did not want to make it too easy for them, so he intentionally veered occasionally from a direct path to the cottage as they wandered in the jungle.

Maria was frightened by the huge insects flitting by and the size of the jungle flora surrounding here was greater than she was prepared for.

Luciana felt no concern about the insects or the other creatures that she heard but didn't see. She had grown up in Annec where members of the Society of Species, some quite intimidating passed her every day while presenting no personal threat to her. These creatures seemed similar though she knew they weren't enlightened. But she felt the humidity and heat more than either Maria or Shon, having grown up in a much cooler, drier climate. It depressed her somewhat. The excitement she thought she would feel was absent. She was alert to danger but it didn't cause her to fear it the way she had envisioned it would.

Shon had trained to wage war under any condition. He had slipped into his combat mentality. The fears he had for Maria and Luciana were now suppressed along with his fears for his own safety. He would let no emotion get in the way of his mission. That mentality, he knew, was the one necessary to bring them all out alive.

They slept out the first few nights in pouring rain on top of their field sheets. The rain was warm, not chilling or refreshing. At night, two stayed awake while the other two slept, all spread some distance apart from each other so that they could not be attacked in one spot.

Each morning, at sunrise, they would break camp and continue on their journey into Amaz.

In addition to their backpacks filled with food, the bogachos, and the special spears—short enough to conceal as the springs in their shafts made the normal length of spears unnecessary for the purpose of throwing, they were more like hand-held mortars—they outwardly carried ordinary spears and swords for purposes of deception. If Shon was wrong and the Deinoc intended to kill them before they arrived in the final meadow under a full moon as Carpia had described, packing the bogachos in their backpacks would likely prove fatal. The shaft-spears were bundled in groups of three. Each carried two bundles. Shon felt that they would not need more than three spears per Deinoc as they would likely be killed if they were not successful in killing the Deinoc facing each of them in less than three attempts. He judged that they would get at most two shots at each Deinoc. Carrying only one bundle each, he felt, would alarm the women too much. The extra bundles were really placebos.

Every morning they carefully checked their bodies for any unwanted companions. Leeches and other parasites were less sensitive to the insect repellents they applied every evening and morning.

The extensive training in the clothes, shoes and equipment they would wear was paying off. No one suffered from any abrasions, soreness or undue fatigue.

Shon periodically spoke to Luciana in mindcast to accustom her to hearing him speak to her in this way. He hadn't fully formulated how he would use mindcast in the battle. Perhaps as the Deinoc attacked he might mindcast to confuse them once it was too late for them to adapt to realizing that he might be able to hear them mindcast to each other. But he considered that they might likely hunt in the style of their ancestors and not mindcast at all.

Finally, in the early afternoon of the sixth day after entering Amaz, they entered a clearing and found the cottage. Shon hoped that the Deinoc's desire to hunt would compel the Horde to come on the next full moon which he calculated to be in fifteen days, and not wait another month after that.

•

During the second night after their arrival at the cottage, Shon had a dream. He was back in his time in a building with an assassination squad. His squad had been tasked with killing a large cell of terrorists who had come to kill civilians in a favela in Brazil to pressure the government to cease its efforts to clean out the criminal element that controlled so many of the poor communities. Shon and his squad slipped into the building where the assassination team was headquartered. Shon looked at his squad composed of Deinoc and instructed them to maneuver into the agreed attack formation.

Shon entered the room to kill the leaders of the enemy force. As he fired his blaster at the two leaders, he realized they were Maria and Luciana. Before the shock of who his opponents were awakened him he saw one of their victims, a young woman who had been stripped and stabbed with a piece of scrap metal through her heart, her eyes staring directly at him as her life left her and her look of recognition turned to a glassy stare into infinity. He knew that girl's face very well. He'd had recurring dreams about that girl until shortly before he set off for the stars.

Shon awoke in a soaking sweat. The day he had killed all the terrorists, it had been a dying young woman who looked deeply into Shon's eyes, who had set him off on his accelerated killing spree for which he had been awarded the Medal of Honor. She was the reason that he had retired from his country's special forces to accept the invitation to join the lightship program to travel to the stars where he hoped to forget what had happened.

Through the past months of preparation, as his Magan brain stimulated those parts of his brain wired to the memories of his past military adventures to enable him to function better in the mission that he had undertaken, the girl's visage had started to reappear in dreams. She was telling him that he had come too late to save her. That was how he always felt during the dream. In reality, she had not died until he returned to her at the favela after exterminating the terrorist vermin. She had been his contact for the mission and she had been shot, not cut, and that had occurred because he found the last terrorist too late to save her. She said, "Obrigado," and died in his arms as she was thanking him for killing her killer. In his dreams, she sometimes died before he killed her killers and she sometimes died when he returned. He knew the truth. If he had stayed with her rather than going on his rampage, she would have lived. She had died because he killed her enemies rather than saving her.

What bothered him about the dream now was that his squad members were Deinoc and he couldn't understand why.

The first time on the rock in the pool below Huascarán with Maria, he had a passing thought of this girl when he saw Maria naked before him and realized that his killed young woman could never stumble upon a naked man by a waterfall because he had not saved her.

His mission leaders, during debriefing, tried to make him understand that all the people he had killed had killed many like her. They tried to make him understand that his killing of those which prevented him from returning earlier had stopped many future deaths of innocents like her.

But he knew he had killed all those people because he felt a deep urge to kill and, until that urge had been sated, he was unable to think about anything else. And he knew that urge came from within himself and not from the Magan brain which had at that time only begun to affect his mind—most of its effect then had been on enhancing his physical skills and his state of mind in actual combat. So a beautiful young woman who was still alive when he set out on his mission of death and vengeance had died. In his dreams, for some incomprehensible reason, she was always stabbed rather than shot.

Shon left the service not because he killed seventy eight terrorists, fifteen of whom were women. Not because he could not kill anymore; he could. He left because he had failed to return in time to save her and was rewarded for it with his country's highest honor.

He could never atone for failing her. Her words thanking him for by avenging her, only added to his guilt. Now he was faced with destroying an enemy, full of dread that he would kill his enemies while they killed them and, in the end, he would be left holding one of these women in his arms thanking him for his success as she died.

The dream was confusing. His squad was not Luciana and Maria. His squad was the Deinoc. He perceived that the dream was some sort of foretelling of what would come at the end of this battle he had brought about by refusing to be acquitted. He was going to sacrifice these young women in the same way he had sacrificed the lovely stabbed girl, who actually had been shot. They would die while he again satisfied a killing lust, an urge he understood could not be blamed on his Magan brain.

This was not a hunt by the Deinoc of him. This was a hunt by him of the Deinoc. Even as Kai sent him to pursue her cause as his military commanders had sent him to pursue theirs, it was he who made the choice to do so. The women he loved would die in his arms thanking him for killing the Deinoc who killed them when it was he who was the cause of their death. He, not the Deinoc, would be the barbarian killer of Maria and Luciana.

Shon looked over at Maria, on watch, and Luciana asleep, awaiting her turn to watch. But he saw only a young woman with a small hole leaking blood from her breast arching her body as she gave up her life after thanking him for giving her the opportunity to do so.

Two years later this incident had been the deciding factor for UWAC in choosing him for admission into its lightship program. His psychological problems with this incident had been deemed advantageous as it reinforced their belief that he would be able to willingly leave Earth behind on a mission to save a future humanity in atonement for his great sin and that he would destroy any who might threaten those to follow even without the influence of his Magan brain.

Now he pondered his greatest fear about the battle—that he would kill the Deinoc instead of helping his friends—that he would come to them victorious only to hear them thank him for avenging their deaths as they died in his arms.

•

For the next two weeks, Shon's team lived their days by the lake and their nights in the cottage. They took their weapons with them at all times. Shon kept his katana in its saya strapped to his side. The wait wore on their nerves. Conversation fell to a minimum, despite his efforts to keep everyone up.

In their spare time Shon directed the team to make a ladder high enough to reach the top of the Wall from branches which had fallen from the trees using the vines hanging from the trees to bind it together. Then he had them make a rope ladder from the vines to get down the other side of the Wall. He hoped that promise of a method for returning back over the Wall would give them reason to believe that they would do so one day.

The twenty-first day after they entered Amaz was exceptionally hot and humid. In the late afternoon, an electrical storm came up suddenly. They left the lake and headed back to the cottage to find the doors locked and the windows shuttered from the inside.

The storm ended abruptly. The air cooled quickly and then began to humidify and warm again in the endless cycle of the weather in Amaz.

They heard three distinct blood curdling screams at sundown.

•

Temüjin had arrived to join the Horde a klick from the cottage the night before the storm.

The horde had been living twenty klicks to the south of the cottage for the past two weeks. Temüjin led the Horde from their camp and situated them downwind of the Traveler and his mates.

Temüjin knew the Traveler would not be intimidated by rustles in the bush or the screams of his horde. When he and his horde screamed their first screams, it was to announce the hunt to the Traveler.

He breathed their scent now. His regenerated and enlightened family had no conscious history to identify with and so, like other similar families, his had chosen a human culture that seemed an avatar for themselves, to establish an intelligent identity for themselves who possessed no innate genetic identity: the Mongols from ancient human history, the only humankind the Deinoc considered worthy of their way of living. The Mongols had possessed a singular defining characteristic that drew the Deinoc to choose them beyond the other warlike historical societies, a sensitivity to the sense of smell. The Mongols sniffed each other and judged those they sniffed by their smell. That meshed well with the highly tuned sense of smell of the Deinoc. Finally, the fact that these worthy humans lived on the very same land the ancestors of the Deinoc had lived on millions of years before made their selection transcendentally correct in their minds.

Temüjin felt a deep voracious hunger. His great claws tingled with the prospect of ripping the guts from his prey. He felt his tail twitching so hard and fast that his balance was affected. His legs felt raw energy. He wanted, needed, to hunt. Ögödei, Hulagu, Khubilai, and the rest of the horde felt the same urge.

Once they screamed their scream, their primordial instincts took complete possession of their mentality as if they had taken a powerful drug.

•

Maria felt a deep spasm of fear course through her body when she heard the screams. She wanted to run away from the screams. She wanted to hide behind Shon. Instead, she picked up her gear and came to stand by Shon and Luciana.

Luciana felt a surge of fear and adrenaline. She wanted to see an enemy she could attack. Her skin crawled with the excitement that she had found missing since crossing over. Every muscle in her body was energized. Her mind was completely alert.

Shon felt cold and hot at the same time. His mind was ice. He calculated the distance and direction of each scream. He saw the reflection from an eye he saw downwind of them in the distance. He saw a movement by the second scream. He heard breathing a few meters to the side of the second scream, the source of the third. His muscles were becoming hot even as he stood still, watching and listening. Sweat began to run down his chest and back. Not fear, preparation. His body was heating up to perform. Hot muscles worked better than cold ones. His mind began to overdrive. He felt the Magan brain's influence and welcomed it wholly for the first time.

Shon and his team moved out. They knew where to go, though they pretended to be led by the noises they heard. Down the path away from the lake to another lake where they would meet their fate sometime in the night before dawn. Under a full moon. Shon had memorized the moon's schedule. He knew that this was a prime night if it did not rain too late in the evening for the hunt. The sky was clear as the sun declined and it became night. He felt thankful that he would not have to wait another month.

They proceeded in line: Maria ahead, then Luciana, Shon next, and Ginés in the rear. If they were attacked in transit to the meadow by the second lake, Shon could cover their rear and also quickly run forward in support if an attack came from the front. He could sense any movement, no matter how slight, within fifty meters of them. Enough time to react though he prayed no attack would come until they had an open field to defend.

•

The Horde moved alongside and slightly behind the Traveler's group. Temüjin knew attacking in transit would be most advantageous to his horde. But he wanted real satisfaction. He would never experience a hunt like this again. To win and kill on the path was to lose the opportunity for a satisfaction that could only come from killing the Traveler and his mates together in the open where they could see themselves dying together. Honor required that he kill the Traveler this way. Anything less was cowardice. The world must fear the Deinoc, not as mindless barbarians, but as brilliant warriors in control of their tremendous urges.

•

Joseph, safely residing in his tower in Montaña, had spent the days since sending Shon, Maria and the others over dreaming of every possible way that the geezer would be utterly ripped apart along with Maria's friend, Luciana, while hoping that somehow Maria would return so that he could do what he had dreamed to do to her when he saw her again without the geezer to protect her.

•

Publius had risen very early in the morning and gone to see Mamercus to spend the time waiting for the outcome with a bottle of fine very old single malt.

•

Octavius and Aurelia rose early and sat down beside each other on the veranda overlooking Lac and waited. When Aurelia shivered from time to time, Octavius stroked her back.

•

Raul Monterro, looking up through the high glass dome at the rising of a full moon, sat atop the tower at the Universidad de Montaña as he had every night since his return from Maria's passing over and prayed for her own return.

Rolando Martine, the principal leader of the Resurrection of Humanity sat across from him. They made small talk from time to time and waited as they had agreed to do until they learned of the fate of Maria and her comrades or until they heard nothing for so long that they knew the outcome was as all the others before. Knowing nothing of the how things would play out in Amaz, this night was apparently no different than any other, but something about the full moon and their new awareness of what was really going on created a sense of dread none of the Resurrection had ever experienced.

•

Juku Ximena Tremarct sitting in a crotch halfway up a great tree, slowly shuddered from time to time as the moon rose over Montaña, well aware that this full moon or the next would determine the fate of Luciana. This night's weather seemed to portend that this moon would be the one when his great love for Luciana, a being so different from himself that he couldn't really comprehend his feelings for her nor why that even mattered to him, might come to a tragic end.

•

The Great One walked to the top of Huascarán. It was cold as she watched the moon rise. For the first time in many millennia, she felt strong emotions about these living beings she observed, watched over, whose continued existence she decided and, in some cases, their fates like the God many of them imagined watching and guiding their lives. The world was in play. That single thought possessed her as she looked at the stars beyond the moon.

•

Carpia, flitting from perch to perch in the amazingly tall trees of Amaz, trailed above Shon and his team as they progressed to their destiny. She watched the one being on Vitas that she had come to care for over all others and wondered why she had come to feel that way.

•

The rest of humankind and intelligent non-humankind on Vitas, and the rest of the galaxy, slept or went about the business of the day completely unaware that the outcome of a battle between a few creatures on Vitas might affect the destinies of themselves and all of their progeny for an eternity to come.

•

Maria, Luciana, Shon, and Ginés arrived at the second lake in the late evening after dark. Shon decided not to stop. He wanted to get to the meadow. Stopping here could tempt an attack. They might also gain some time to set up at the meadow by not stopping. The Deinoc, having no way to evaluate their physical conditioning, might rely on their past experience in hunting humans and assume they would rest here. It was a hard push to the lake from the cottage and it was likely that every human in the past had stopped at this place to rest. They had practiced for battle in an open field. They needed to get there. The attack would come well before dawn when the only light came from the full moon.

Shon picked up the pace. They moved through the boulder field under the moonlight. They entered the meadow from the south with the lake to the west. It was a small area, a little over a hundred meters by a hundred and fifty meters. Jungle rose to the north and east.

They moved towards the lake. Shon perceived that from there they would face an attack from the jungle side: two fronts, not four, and more like a single, long, convex front if they stayed back a bit toward the lake.

They moved into position. Maria and Luciana were stationed about twenty meters to the north of the boulder field and faced the jungle to the east. Ginés took up his position between them and Shon took a position about forty meters east of the lake mid-way between the rocks and the jungle by the lake.

They took out their bogachos and the spears. Shon felt the hilt of his katana but did not take it out of its saya concerned that it might alert them that he possessed something that could not have come from Montaña, a single-edged sword that cast a very unusual shimmering reflection on its blade in the dim light. He had brought a second more ordinary sword for their initial tactic. They cast some of the spears about across the field behind them so they could retrieve them as the ones they carried were exhausted.

The women dropped their spears and drew their swords in an impressive demonstration of ability, a diversionary tactic to focus the Deinoc on the wrong weapons. Shon stood facing the jungle with a bogacho in his left hand, hanging limply, while he wielded his ordinary sword with his right.

•

Temüjin, Ögödei and Hulagu moved silently into their positions of attack. Khubilai hung back with the rest of the Horde.

They watched the human women drop their spears and begin to warm up with their swords, turning slowly around, exposing themselves to a charge periodically as they made a full rotation. Instinct told the Horde to attack now as they might not continue to turn like this once they were warmed up. It would be good to attack as they took their eyes off the perimeter of the meadow in front of them. The Traveler was doing the same thing but he was moving very rapidly. Their plan was fundamentally straightforward, in the initial assault two Deinoc would attach each human simultaneously with the two remaining Deinoc in reserve to support any pair who lost a comrade. As unlikely as that seemed against these humans, that reserve support had been the key to the battle plan that they had used to annihilate the Allo.

Ögödei was not so sure that Temüjin's orders for him to attack the mates while Temüjin and Hulagu attacked the Traveler was wise. He had proposed that they should all attack the Traveler, but Temüjin's response in the war council the night before had been a scowl and a remark that there would be very little satisfaction in ten Deinoc attacking one human while ignoring the women. Ögödei realized that Temüjin wanted the satisfaction of taking the Traveler himself with just enough help to insure his success and desisted from pushing his view further. Now he was feeling that he had been correct, the Traveler was easily the most fearsome human he had ever seen—he was moving far faster than he'd ever seen any human do, or any dinosaurian for that matter. And he was just warming up.

Hulagu was surprised by the movement of all of the humans. He did not expect to see females who could swing swords like real warriors. In fact, he had never seen a single human, male or female, who could swing a sword like these females. The closest to their ability in his experience were the Therizi who could manipulate their sword-like claws like sword wizards, which they were sometimes called by other families. These humans matched them, albeit with only a single sword instead of six sword-claws. And, of course, they lacked the power that a huge Therizi could bring to their swings. But Hulagu was not concerned about swords as he had never really been intimidated by the Therizi's claws. The Deinoc had thick hard hides and hard bones. And a Deinoc could easily deflect a thrust with its large bony head while its ripping claw would gut a human at the same range that the sword could present a threat.

The usual way, one he had personally used many times with other humans banished to Amaz in the past, was to attack a sword wielder at a good running pace head on, head low, mouth closed to act as the deflecting shield. The head of the Deinoc was simply invulnerable to a sword if the mouth was closed. The bones around the eyes provided plenty of protection and there were no soft spots to penetrate. As the head contacted and deflected the sword, the prey's arms would be pushed up with the sword and the Deinoc's ripping claw would shoot forward directly at the abdomen. Before the human could react, guts would be spilling out and the only remaining task would be to extract the heart before it stopped beating.

Hulagu was not afraid of the sword, just impressed that these humans could at least wield their feeble weapons like warriors.

•

Temüjin noticed that the humans had dropped their spears to warm up their bodies by wielding their swords. He knew the only real danger the humans presented was the spear. If it made its way home through a neck artery or through the heart in the chest cavity, a Deinoc could be killed. Most humans had no idea how to use a spear correctly and would try to throw it and then use their sword. A thrown spear was a small threat. Besides the fact that a spear thrown by a human was unlikely to possess the necessary weight and velocity to generate the force necessary to pierce Deinoc skin, the Deinoc could move very fast and had good lateral movement on the run to easily dodge a thrown spear from as close as five meters.

Temüjin was sure the Traveler could be dangerous with a spear, more dangerous than with a sword, because he wouldn't throw it. And a spear was longer than a sword and could strike him before he could close to the ripping range of his front claw. It would be good to attack now before he picked his spear up.

As he tensed in preparation for leading the charge, he stopped suddenly, completely surprised by what the women were doing now.

•

Shon said, "Now Madra's surprise." Madra had told him the Deinoc were especially excited by the smell of their prey and that smell emanating from moist, naked torsos they wanted to eat would be irresistible.

Luciana and Maria dropped their swords and took off their vests. They stripped off their shirts, picked up their swords, and continued their warm-up rituals moving faster than before until their torsos glistened in the moonlight.

•

Temüjin watched for a few moments, then sniffed the light breeze coming from their direction and screamed as he charged toward the women before bearing off toward the Traveler as he recalled the plan of attack was for him to attack the Traveler not the women he now wanted to taste so badly.

Hulagu charged the Traveler from his position in the jungle directly north of the Traveler. Ögödei, on Hulagu's left flank about twenty meters away, thrust forward toward Ginés.

The attack began exactly as planned, other than Temüjin's initial deviation toward the women. That deviation caused him to approach the Traveler a moment later than Hulagu.

•

Those in the Horde assigned to the women planned to commence their attack a few moments after the others charged toward the men. But the scent and sight of the glistening torsos urged them forward a few moments earlier than planned.

And the two in reserve, as excited as the rest of the Horde, also lunged forward, no longer thinking about their roles in support, and headed toward the naked female prey.

•

Shon dropped his sword—his katana remained sheathed in its saya strapped to his waist as he turned to face the first charging Deinoc and began to twirl a bogacho. As the red-skinned Deinoc lowered his head, Shon made his throw and watched the Deinoc go down. He turned to the next Deinoc and threw again. This Deinoc leapt suddenly and cleared the thing it saw coming toward him. But Shon threw another bogacho before the Deinoc came down to ground, and the Deinoc could not avoid gravity which caused him to land just at the bogacho arrived.

Shon picked up all the spears at his feet, turned back to the first Deinoc and ran to it, dropped all but one of the spears and thrust that spear into its hide straight through its chest as it attempted to right itself. Even as it died, Shon picked up another of the spears at his feet and turned to face the second. But, as he turned, he caught a glimpse of what else was going on and saw that the other eight Deinoc were nearly upon the rest of his team, six of them approaching Luciana and Maria.

•

Ginés dropped his sword and took up a spear in one motion and threw his first bogacho and, without waiting to see the result, turned and threw his second. He was so quick that the second Deinoc had no time to avoid entanglement. He ran to the first, killed it with a hard thrust from his spear, its tip springing out and cutting arteries deep in the creature, and ran back to his stash of spears. He picked up another spear and turned to kill the second which had fallen less than two meters from where he stood. He thrust his spear deep into the creature and twisted the shaft. It died twitching, its tail flailing about.

•

Luciana flung her sword at the first Deinoc approaching her as she reached to grab one of the spears at her feet. She flung her bogacho as she arose, entangling it, turned and threw her second, not at the next closest Deinoc but at the one closing on Maria and entangled it. Then she turned toward the next closing Deinoc and threw her third bogacho as she prepared to throw her fourth at the second Deinoc approaching Maria.

•

Maria dropped her sword, picked up her spear and stood up facing the first Deinoc approaching her, making no attempt to throw a bogacho. As the Deinoc closed in on her it suddenly fell, entangled by one of Luciana's throws, and Maria thrust her spear into its neck.

•

Shon realized that his tactic of using the women to throw off the Deinocs' initial onslaught had succeeded too well. Most of the Deinoc were after the women, not him as he had anticipated. Obviously their hunger for the women had taken control and they were in a killing frenzy focused on the sweating bodies of the women. There was no way the women would be able to kill so many in such a manic state. At that very moment he released his mentality to the full influence of his Magan brain. And what to do next became clear to him. He turned his back on the second Deinoc which was untangling itself and began to run from the battle. Then he screamed in Deinoc mindcast, *"Cowards!"*

•

As if struck by lightning, the remaining Horde stopped their charge and began to look around for the source of that scream.

Temüjin couldn't believe what was happening as he untangled himself from the wires. He quickly counted four dead Deinoc and the humans were still standing, not one down. He saw the Traveler running away and now he heard a crazy scream in his head. Who had screamed *"Cowards"*? He wanted to kill whoever said such a thing. These humans weren't cowards; they had killed Deinoc. How could one of his Horde say such a thing? Yet he didn't recognize the voice. He screamed out, *"The Traveler is fleeing. We must stop him."*

The Horde, already in a state of confusion, focused on Temüjin's words and then on the fleeing figure who had already reached the edge of the jungle.

Temüjin gathered his wits and yelled, *"Pursue him. We can't kill the women without him. What honor is there in that? Khubilai, remain here at a safe distance from these humans and make sure they don't also flee. The rest of you follow me."*

Temüjin freed himself from his entanglement and ran into the jungle after the Traveler. Four turned to follow but the last one leaving the field fell to Luciana's throw and Ginés ran over and finished him with a thrust through its neck where it joined its chest.

•

Khubilai ran over to hide in the boulder field by the lake and waited, watching the women and the man take up defensive positions in the middle of the meadow.

•

As Shon ran he sensed that he was no longer himself and with every step he felt part of him receding as another part, the part he had dreaded unleashing, took complete control of his mind. Barely into the jungle his new mind cleared and he ran faster than he ever had before. He stripped off his sweat-soaked clothes above his waist to insure that his scent would keep his foes certain in their quest to find and kill him.

•

Temüjin and the three remaining of the Horde besides Khubilai raced after the Traveler. Soon the younger and faster Deinoc overtook him and raced on after their prey. They began to spread out.

•

Deep in the jungle, where the light of the Moon could not penetrate the canopy above, the foremost of the Horde suddenly sniffed a change in the intensity of the human odor he had been chasing. He slowed and began to peer intently in the direction of the odor. Suddenly, the Traveler appeared and he was moving rapidly toward him swinging a strange sword in a circular manner but so fast that the sword seemed almost a blur. Then he heard, "*You failed*," in his mind and he stopped moving for a moment. Before he could refocus, he felt his head falling to the ground and then he died.

•

Shon retraced his steps towards those in pursuit for a few meters and then ran off on a path perpendicular to the direction he had been traveling. Those trailing would never get to where the dead Deinoc lay. He replayed his tactic twice more until the only remaining Deinoc in pursuit was the one he had identified as the leader.

•

Temüjin, frustrated by being the last in pursuit, worried that the Traveler would be killed before he got to him. As the course of the pursuit had wandered from a direct path to escape Amaz, he began to consider that there might be some method to the Traveler's bolt. He tried calling out to his Horde, but got no response. He could still smell the Traveler's scent so he slowed down until he was practically walking, yet he still smelled the scent.

As he tried to comprehend why the Traveler would turn out to be a coward, he suddenly realized what was going on. It had been no accident that his family had chosen to imprint themselves on the Mongols. Besides the fact that this human tribe lived in what he viewed as their natural domain, this human tribe was the one that most closely melded their natural nature to their intelligent mentality. He had studied the records on the Mongols intensely. That effort had led to his leadership of his family because he had used what he had learned of his namesake to conquer the challengers to leadership and he had used many Mongol tactics in defeating the Allo.

The one tactic he had never used had been a tactic of theirs that he found repugnant. The Mongols had often conquered a fortified city with an army encamped inside by turning away and running from their foes and then, as their enemies struck out after them and tired in their pursuit, they turned on them and slaughtered their pursuers and then returned to the city they wanted, now bereft of its army. Winning was the Mongol goal, just like his goal, but, in using this tactic, they showed no personal sense of a loss of honor so long as they attained that result, something he found repugnant and, in his view, their greatest flaw as warriors. At that moment he suddenly realized the practical merit of their conduct in achieving their purpose, and he comprehended how much danger he was now in.

How could he have fallen for such a trick? He realized that he would not find the rest of his Horde alive. The Traveler was more Mongol than he.

He stopped pursuing and began to run back to the meadow. To be the Mongol he had thought he was meant getting to the women before the Traveler got to him.

•

Shon cut back to get the leader but he could not find him where he anticipated him to be as he retraced his steps. He judged that his foe had caught onto his tactics and would change its own. He set off for the meadow at full pace. When he arrived he saw two Deinoc circling carefully around Luciana, Maria, and Ginés, who were slowly whirling their bogachos as they rotated to face their enemy.

He sheathed his sword in its saya and walked out of the jungle and into the meadow.

The Deinoc turned to face him and the larger one made a great scream.

He didn't call out to his human companions, not willing to risk saying something that the Deinoc might correctly or incorrectly interpret and bring them harm.

Shon took a few steps toward the larger one he judged to be the leader. He said, "*I know about the Predation Agreement. I also know about the Council's scruples concerning violating the Order while attending to their desire to rid themselves of me. You wanted a great hunt which would rid them of me. The the purposes of those who control this planet were aligned by my banishment into your domain where you would hunt and rid them of me. To make that happen, I had to propose a Slippery Slope Proposition. And I did that, as I am sure you know, voluntarily even after I was afforded a way out. Do you think I did that because I thought I was destined to be defeated and killed by you? But you never considered that, and so you were not prepared.*

"I understand you better than you can possibly imagine. How can that be? Because I am not merely a man from the distant past. I am more. I am Temüjin. I have heard that you have the temerity to call yourself by that name."

Temüjin, wanting to ask how the Traveler could communicate like a Hom and beginning to wonder whether this was some sort of Hom trap to destroy his family, said instead, *"It is true that I am named Temüjin. It is an insult that a human now lays claim to that name. You Temüjin reincarnated? You lie. Temüjin's body was hidden in an unknown location in a protected and remote area in a time ancient even to you. I have seen nothing in the records that would support your absurd assertion."*

Shon said, *"Many hundreds of millennia have passed and the records are no longer complete, assuming any of this was ever recorded to begin with."*

Temüjin paused, not so certain now. Then he said, *"So what do you say happened, human who claims my name?"*

Shon said, *"His body was discovered during a time not long before my birth when a coterie of geneticists seeking to regenerate some of the famous historical figures from humankind put an immense effort into finding their bodies to mine their DNA. They had some success but the effort came to an abrupt end early on when they regenerated Temüjin and Genghis Khan, as they called him, became alive again as a man called the Magan. He killed the geneticists and the other regenerated humans and then nearly conquered the planet as his ancestor had done a few thousand years earlier. After he died, some military geneticists who had a hand in my development decided to take advantage of his DNA in an effort to win the secret wars that were prevalent in my time. When they devised a program to go the stars, it was deemed a good idea to put a Magan in command of the ships they sent out."*

Temüjin interrupted, *"Why would they do that?"*

Shon replied instantly as if he anticipated the question. *"You who take Temüjin as your name, ask that? Obviously, because they thought a Temüjin would do what was necessary to conquer any sentient beings that would likely inhabit any planets humans could live on. But they didn't want Temüjin to come into being unless absolutely necessary as such a man posed a great threat to those in power. So they instead genetically modified our minds by using his DNA to instill a second limbic component, really an additional limbic brain, which carried his emotions and thought processes that would only be activated into our minds in a time of great stress. You created that moment when you tried to kill me by stupidly chasing me when I ran away."*

Temüjin, enraged now, sought to calm himself, saying, *"There must be a purpose to your telling me of this. What do you want?"*

"I want to conquer Vitas."

Temüjin glanced over at Khubilai, communicating in the old way, by blinking his eyes and making some grunts and, turning to face the Traveler, he said, *"And how would you do that?"*

"By taking the leadership of your family."

Temüjin felt an urge to attack, but restrained himself and glanced again at Khubilai. *"Are you proposing that I simply stand by and permit that?"*

"Not at all. You think you are Mongol and you will do as a Mongol would and try to kill me to keep your leadership. Why else live? Besides, if you are truly a student of Mongol history, you know I cannot allow the leadership of those I conquer to live. You would betray me at your first opportunity."

Temüjin said, *"Perhaps you are truly who you say you are because that is exactly what I would do."*

Shon said, *"Then you have two choices: attack me now and die with honor or run away and die with dishonor. Either way you will die today. It is necessary for me to conquer Vitas."*

"I understand now, completely. Are you prepared to face me armed only with your sword and not your tricky wires and stones?"

"Yes, as to myself. No, as to the others."

"You don't trust me to attack only you?"

"No. You have learned your lesson and you will do what it takes to win. You might even run away if you thought it would help you win. But your tribe is not nearby and I will kill you long before you reach them."

Temüjin said, *"I will accede to your terms. We will shortly come for you in the final battle to determine who is truly Temüjin."* Temüjin and Khubilai withdrew into the jungle.

Shon turned to Ginés and the women. "Ginés, the Deinoc will attack shortly. I have agreed that I will not use the bogacho. I anticipate that they will attempt to kill the women to divide my effort to kill them."

Ginés responded, "They truly have no honor at all."

Shon said simply, "It is not about honor, Ginés. It is about winning and, as they believe they are Mongols, they will follow the way of Mongols, something they failed to learn until today's events, which was very helpful to us. But they won't repeat that mistake. I will stand apart from the rest of you to divide their attack."

Luciana cried out, "This is crazy, Shon."

Maria joined in, "We should stand together."

Shon said, "If we stand together, they will have the advantage. They understand the bogacho now. They are very agile and will avoid our throws. I have given up nothing by ceding the bogacho. You must be prepared to take out the one who attacks you as I cannot divide my effort to kill the one who attacks me. You can do it, but you must do it quickly or the Deinoc will kill you. This is the moment in battle where we must adapt to the unforeseen and defeat our enemy when our tactics are no longer surprising. Only our will to win will carry us to our destiny now."

●

While the Traveler was speaking to his people, Temüjin, when he judged they were out of mindcast range, caucused with Khubilai. He turned to Khubilai and said, *"We are in this predicament because I failed to comprehend what being a Mongol means. Winning, not how, was the lesson I learned today. We have spent too much time on what we would do to them when we won, not enough on how to win because we considered them like all that have come before. And the Traveler is not at all like them. The women matter to him. Prepare to attack them on my signal. Make him defend them instead of only dealing with the attack on him. If we fail, the Traveler will rule our family and, as our family is not human, he will destroy them after they serve whatever purpose he has for them."*

Khubilai said, *"Should we try to call for support? We could run and wait for them to arrive."*

Temüjin hesitated at that notion and considered the Traveler's recognition of that option in what he said. It was the Mongol thing to do. He judged that Khubilai's idea had great merit, but it disturbed him that the Traveler had proffered the same option. He might want them to do just that. He might follow them as he said he would and kill them before they joined up with their family. It would be the worst way to die, running away. He said, *"This is the moment we have lived for our entire lives, a true battle, not the easy slaughter that we have satisfied ourselves with in the past. I truly do not believe a human can defeat us, even if he is the reincarnated Great Khan from ancient history which I don't believe. It is a ploy to make us run. The glory of defeating him is too great an opportunity and one that may be lost if we run away now. Besides, while we admire the Mongols, we are Deinoc Mongols, not human Mongols."*

•

The two Deinoc spread apart and left the jungle achieving full speed in four strides as they sped toward the Traveler standing apart from the other humans.

Shon watched the Deinoc charge. They were screaming their battle cry and they were frightening, red demons from hell.

Luciana and Maria, facing to the north, saw the Deinoc come out of the jungle and accelerate toward Shon. Maria was astounded at their speed. One of them turned toward them without breaking stride. Luciana gripped a spear in one hand and began to spin her bogacho. Maria took up a spear and took a few steps to Luciana's left. Ginés took a few steps toward the charging Deinoc and began to spin his bogacho as he held a spear in his other hand. Mindful about what Shon had said about the Deinoc anticipating their tactics, he thought about how to use his bogacho in an unexpected way.

Shon held his position facing the Deinoc leader, his katana still sheathed.

The approaching Deinoc was three-quarters of the way across the distance from the jungle to Ginés when he threw his bogacho. But, instead of throwing at the Deinoc's feet, Ginés threw it towards its head.

Khubilai, anticipating a throw at his feet, shifted his weight to jump over it and fell as he ducked the thing flying towards his head.

Ginés ran toward the Deinoc but it regained his feet before he could get close enough to use his spear.

Khubilai ignored the charging human and ran past him toward the women.

Ginés thrust his spear and struck a glancing blow and watched the Deinoc pass by as if he wasn't there.

Luciana prepared to throw her bogacho at the Deinoc which was charging toward Maria.

Temüjin closed in on Shon.

Shon unsheathed his katana and began to swing it with blurring speed.

Temüjin, startled more by the way the Traveler's sword seemed to shift between visibility and invisibility than by the speed with which he wielded it, suddenly bore off and headed toward the women.

As Luciana threw her bogacho, the Deinoc leapt and the bogacho passed under it.

As the Deinoc closed to five meters, Maria knelt and planted the heel of the spear in the ground and waited for the Deinoc to make contact hoping she hadn't made her move too soon.

Khubilai was almost to the woman standing with no bogacho when he saw her drop to her knees and plant her spear. He started to turn when, suddenly he felt a sharp pain in his left eye and sharply twitched his head. As his momentum carried him toward the spear he wanted to avoid he saw a bird flitting around his head and realized it had attacked his eye and was attempting to attack again. As he turned to bite at it he felt a deep pain in his side. He had fallen into the spear. He thrashed as he fell dying and his tail caught the woman just below her neck.

Maria went down from the blow from the thrashing Deinoc.

Shon had begun to chase the Deinoc leader accelerating until he was almost upon it when he saw Maria go down.

Luciana, her back to Maria, threw another bogacho at the Deinoc approaching her and watched it leap over it and continue its charge. She knelt as Maria had done and planted her spear.

Carpia frantically attacked the thrashing Deinoc trying to pluck out its other eye when it stopped moving. Only then did she realize that Maria had been injured. She flew to her and perched on her shoulder as she tried to see if she was still alive.

Shon reached the Deinoc leader as he leapt over the bogacho and swung his katana at its tail just below its legs, slicing halfway through its tail. The Deinoc lost its balance with the loss his tail's mobility and fell a meter from Luciana.

Luciana sprang back barely avoiding its snapping jaws.

Temüjin tried to rise without the use of his tail and floundered toward the woman but then he fell as the hamstrings in his right leg burst from the Traveler's second swing of his sword. He fell to his side continuing to snap his jaws at the woman to no avail.

Ginés arrived and prepared to thrust his spear into the Deinoc when he hear Shon say, "Stop."

He stopped and stood at the ready with his spear.

Shon said, "Ginés, Luciana, attend to Maria. I will join you in a minute." Ginés and Luciana ran to Maria.

Shon, katana in hand, strode over to Temüjin.

Temüjin said, *"Finish me, Traveler. You were a worthy foe. I die only regretting I have left my family to you."*

Shon said, *"They will have a glory that you never brought them."*

"Glory? Death at your hands?"

"Not death. A future beyond what you can imagine. That is my promise to you. But there can only be one leader of the Deinoc. Many families will serve my purpose. But, in the case of the Deinoc, their destiny is to travel to the stars."

"The stars, truly? If you speak the truth then I die with more hope than I ever had living."

For a brief moment, Shon the human, not the Magan, said, *"I wonder if the Mongol solution is the way."* Then his Magan self took possession of his mind again and he sliced Temüjin's head from his body.

He ran to Maria. She was conscious but she couldn't move. He examined her and saw that her spine above her torso had been broken by the Deinoc's tail's lashing her just below her neck. He fell to his knees and began to shake.

Maria said in a soft voice, "We won, Shon. You have the destiny you sought for all of us. Just remember your destiny is for all of us." And she fell into unconsciousness.

Carpia was flitting frantically. "Shon, we must call the Great One. Now!"

Shon said, "How? What can she do?"

Carpia said, "She can save Maria."

Shon slumped down beside Maria. "Even if she could, I have no way of calling her."

Carpia said, "You do. She told me that if you survived and needed her, I should say 'Gristelda' and you would know what to do."

Shon leapt to his feet. "Did you say, 'Gristelda'?"

Carpia said, "Yes. I don't know what that means, but she said you would."

Shon could scarcely believe his ears. He called out in his mind as he had in the past to a intellect that he thought lost to Kai's fear of having a black-hole lightship continue to exist without its captain in command.

In a few moments he heard in his head, *"Shon, I was told that I could return to orbit on the far side of Earth from the Moon."*

Shon didn't concern himself with how this was possible. He said, *"Send the shuttle to my coordinates now. It's urgent."*

"As you command."

Luciana heard buzzing in her head but even though she could make no sense of it, she knew something was going on. She said, "Shon, what is Carpia talking about? I hear buzzing just beyond my frequencies for comprehending Society voices. What is going on?"

Shon said, "We wait. Help is coming."

Luciana said, "From where? Who is the Great One?"

Shon got control of himself and said, "Luciana, I cannot tell you about that and you must say nothing to anyone about what you just heard or about what you are about to see. Ginés that goes for you, too."

Ginés said, "Of course."

Luciana wanted to say more but Shon's voice told her to hold her thoughts.

Shortly before dawn a small ship appeared and landed in the clearing a few meters from where they waited. Luciana recognized the ship as the one that had brought Shon to Moon Base.

Shon carefully picked Maria up and walked toward the ship.

An opening appeared and Shon carried Maria inside.

He made the command seat recline and laid Maria down upon it. He said, "One day we will be together again, my love." Then he left the ship and rejoined the others outside.

The ship ascended and disappeared into the dawning sky. The moon loomed large on the horizon.

PART III - MAGAN CONQUEST

Let those who desire a secure homeland conquer it. Let those who do not conquer it live under the whip and in exile, watched over like wild animals.

José Martí, *Obras Completas*

The Hom had from the beginning of the Society retained certain capabilities from their ancient past. Some of those capabilities, the power grid, electronic communications, the array on the Moon, the Mechanica that roamed inside the Walls maintaining these facilities, and facilities like GenLib were known to the other families in the Society, which caused no concern as the other members knew they could not manage the infrastructure that supported the lives of those living on Vitas. Other capabilities, such as ancient weapons that could be used in the event of an uprising by a family or the citizens were never officially disclosed, but were suspected to exist under Hom control.

Fear of a general citizen uprising was a constant concern of all the families and so none of them had ever pressed the Hom about what they suspected because they might need the Hom to put them down. Many of the families actually counted on the Hom having such capabilities.

The weapons consisted of two mainstays of the ancient armies of the past: blasters, hand weapons that emitted laser beams, dangerous to unshielded objects, that required some expertise in aim as they had a narrow focus of effect, and powerful disruptors that emitted energy waves across the spectrum as well as subatomic particles simultaneously which in combination had the effect of disrupting the organized physical structures and entities they were focused upon, essentially dissolving their cohesion at the atomic and subatomic level; they simply disappeared into random atoms and subatomic particles. No particular skill was required with the disruptors, only that the shooter fire in the general direction of a target, but the devastation they wrought was broad in area and depth of field.

When the Allo revolted the Hom had restrained themselves from showing what they had when they learned that the Deinoc were capable of defeating the Allo without any technological assistance.

To use the weapons if ever needed, the Hom maintained a special force, the First Cohort, consisting of a thousand Hom who periodically trained with the blasters. No one dared to even train with the disrupters as they evaporated everything in their direction of fire which meant a Hom might vanish in an instant. The intervals of training gradually slipped from frequent, every few hundred years, to infrequent, every several thousand years, until, when no threats appeared, the training became a ceremonial exercise engaged in once in every decamillia.

The History of Vitas as recorded in a file stored in the GenLib
Repository accessible only by the Librarian

ONE

SIR ORDA

Shon picked up his backpack, emptied it, and put Temüjin's head inside. Then he picked up his katana, slid it into its saya secured by his belt, turned to the others and said, "Bury the dead. Then we return to the cottage."

Shon said little as they made their way back, first to the cottage to pick up the ladder they had made during their time there in order to get back over to the Wall. They set off for the Wall. When they arrived at the Wall, he said, "Take the ladder to the Wall, go over and return to the central community. When you arrive, find Raul and Rolando, if he is there, and tell them that we defeated a strange foe, but you will describe a human foe: very large savages, primitive. You will tell them Maria is with me and that she will return one day but that I have other business on this side before I can return. Tell them that I will return soon to pursue the future for all of us."

Luciana said, "That is all we can say? They will have a million questions, Shon. The Montañans will want answers to what happened to Maria beyond that she is with you. The Society will come and want to know how we could defeat the Deinoc. After all, they know who lives in Amaz and why we were sent over."

"Just do as I ask and tell them they will get their answers when I return. Tell them that is what I told you to say and they will let it go. They are not ready for the truth yet and, because you have returned as no one else ever has before, they will wait for me. I know now that I could not have prevailed without all of you. Can you do that for me, after all that you have already done?"

Luciana sighed, "We can do that, Shon. Good luck and be careful." She kissed his cheek.

Shon, turning from them, disappeared into the jungle to find Sir Orda, the capital of Amaz, which he had learned of from Madra the Therizi.

•

Ginés and Luciana climbed the ladder and began their long trek back to the central community.

•

Carpia found Juku draped over a low branch in a tree a few klicks from the place along the Wall where Shon and his team had gone over. She mindcast, *"Juku."*

Juku opened his eyes and climbed down from the tree faster than she had ever seen him move. When he got to the ground he said, *"Tell me."*

"They won." And she related what happened in Amaz.

When she got to the part where the space ship came for Maria, Juku spoke for the first time. *"A ship came for Maria after you told him what the Great One told you to say?"*

Carpia began to flit about, agitated. *"I am afraid for Maria."*

"I would not fear for her, Carpia. She is now under the care of the Great One. But the ship. Please describe this ship."

Carpia described the ship.

Juku said, "That seems to be like the vehicle which brought Shon to Moon Base."

Carpia, peering at Juku, said, *"And that has significance?"*

"Yes. It means it is likely that the ship from which it comes still exists and can be summoned."

Carpia, suddenly quite impatient with Juku's slow way of speaking, squawked in shrill mindcast, *"Juku, get to the point, if you have one."*

"Please forgive me, Carpia. That ship, I mean the one from whence the little ship you saw came, has immense power. I have thought about it often since Shon came and wondered why he hadn't summoned it to deal with his banishment instead of risking his life and the others. From what you have told me it appears that he did not know it still existed. The Great One must have somehow taken possession of it and left him believing it no longer existed. I wonder why."

Carpia said, *"Some time ago, the Great One ordered me to bring Shon to that place along the Wall where we have always met with her. Before she sent me away from them I noticed that she seemed to know him in some way. They spent some time together though I was too far to see or hear them, as they spoke audibly to each other. Perhaps she deceived him into believing his ship was gone."*

Juku said, *"But why?"* He was still for a moment, then said. *"It appears that she wanted him to fight the Deinoc without the assistance of his ship. But again the question, why?"*

•

Gaia took the second shuttle—the one she had Gristelda send to her before she sent Canopus to an orbit on the far side of the Sun shortly after Shon had sent her off to an orbit on the far side of Earth from the Moon—up to Canopus a few hours later and moved Maria from the first shuttle into the stasis chamber and put her into the deep sleep of stasis.

She spoke to Gristelda with her voice. "Return to your station beyond the Sun. As you can now see, your concerns for Shon were unwarranted. Shon lives and he is on a great mission for which he will require your assistance in the future. Meanwhile take good care of this woman whom you will keep in stasis until I send for her to be repaired. While I did not foresee this outcome, I could not have hoped for a better one. She will have a role in Shon's future one day."

Gristelda said, "As you command, Supreme Commander."

The Great One boarded the second shuttle and returned to her domain inside Huascarán.

•

As Shon penetrated deep into Amaz he came upon signs of Deinoc and finally saw a pair of them in the distance. Careful to stay downwind he followed them until he saw a city made of wood in the distance. He had found Sir Orda.

He waited until the sun had risen to its zenith the next day and then began to walk with his katana sheathed toward the city until he came upon a road paved in black granite. Soon he caught the eye of a pair of Deinoc who were moving through the jungle nearby in the dark shadows cast down by the canopy of the immense trees all around.

The Deinoc turned toward him when they saw him approaching but did not themselves approach this human who was moving with apparent complete indifference to their presence, barely glancing in their direction.

Shon had surmised that the Deinoc near the capital would have seen Hom before and likely would assume he was a Hom. He also judged that Deinoc folk did not act without direction from their leaders and would not act impulsively unless he made the mistake of showing any fear of them.

Two Deinoc ran into the city ahead of him. By the time he arrived at a narrow opening between two of the thickest trees a hundred Deinoc were standing beside the black granite passageway. He followed the passageway through the crowd and entered into the great chamber beyond the trees and found nobody inside. Apparently, as he suspected, the high command of the Deinoc had been among the Horde he had killed.

Suddenly, a large Deinoc entered from the other side of the chamber. The Deinoc peered at him for a moment and then said, *"I am Batu, Quaestor of Amaz. I am honored that a Hom has chosen to visit us but I am surprised that we were not notified of your coming. The Khan and his staff are not available to see you at this time. May I inquire of your identity and purpose here so that I may inform them of your presence?"*

Shon, revised his opinion that he had killed all of the high command. Apparently at least one was still alive. That made sense as someone would have to rule while Temüjin was hunting. He said in a quiet voice, *"I am not Hom. I am he whom you call the Traveler."*

Batu took a step back and stood unmoving, silent for several seconds. *"I don't understand. You cannot be the Traveler."*

"Why not?"

Batu hesitated, then said, *"Because the Traveler is being hunted by the Horde."*

"The Horde is dead."

Batu shrank back into the shadows at the end of the chamber. *"That is impossible."*

"Nevertheless it is so. Temüjin is dead by my hand as is the rest of his Horde."

Batu stood silent.

Shon waited.

Finally Batu said, *"This is a Hom trick of some kind. Temüjin always said you Hom would attack us someday. It appears that they used the ruse of a Traveler to do so now. You will die."* He began to move toward Shon while Shon heard him calling for support.

"I am here to face any Deinoc who cares to challenge my right to leadership of the Deinoc which I have rightfully won by defeating your Khan."

Batu slowed his approach but still continued to come towards Shon.

Shon drew his katana and began to swing it at blurring speed.

Batu stopped approaching.

Shon heard footsteps behind him and suddenly he turned and swung the katana decapitating the Deinoc closest to him.

The three behind him stopped in their tracks.

"Before he died at my hand, Temüjin told me that the Deinoc were a family with honor. Would you disgrace his memory and your tribe with a dishonorable attack?"

Batu said, *"Why should we believe you were able to defeat the Horde?"*

Shon slid his katana back into its saya and, removing his backpack, slowly pulled Temüjin's head from it and set it carefully upon the ground at his feet.

The Deinoc drew back and then one suddenly charged with a scream and Shon, sidestepping his ripping claw and drawing the katana at the same time, decapitated him with a single stroke. Its head rolled to a stop at Batu's feet. The others who had started to charge abruptly drew back.

Batu said, *"How can a human lead the Deinoc even if you defeat all challengers?"*

"Because, instead of ruling you like Temüjin did, giving a few of you the opportunity to kill helpless human citizens once a year and continuing the Deinoc way of life as it always has been, I can do more for the Deinoc. I can lead the Deinoc to a future not confined to Amaz. I can lead you to your homeland, but I can do more. I can lead you to the stars and a destiny greater than you can possibly imagine. I can give every Deinoc the opportunity to do something with his life beyond living in Amaz waiting to be chosen to join a Horde until you die of boredom. That is all that Temüjin and those before him gave you, with no hope of anything more than living out your lives in Amaz and perhaps on day to your natural domain across Pacifica. That life might sound like what a dumb dinosaur might want to live and what the Council wants for you, but do intelligent Deinoc want to live forever in this dark boring jungle or just as boring a life in the other domain you imagine will be much better? Do you really crave that for your life's existence?

"But, if I am wrong, then send the challengers until one of you kills me, if you can, with honor, in the custom of your family. Then at least those of you who die will have done so with honor, not as slaves to a leader who can offer you nothing more. In the end, that is why Temüjin chose to fight me rather than run back to the rest of you to gather another Horde to attack me. He wanted to live or die with honor."

Batu was torn between a desire to kill the human who had killed his leader and the reality that he hated his leader who was unpredictable and savage and of no benefit to Batu. Batu hated his life. He said, *"What you say sounds good to a Deinoc, but it also sounds impossible. The Hom would rise up against us and destroy us all. The stars? How can we possibly get to the stars?"*

"I have been to the stars and I know how to do it again with many ships going to many stars. But I need the Deinoc to do what is necessary when the ships arrive at habitable planets that we can live on as we spread across the galaxy. Those planets will almost certainly not be empty. We will have to take what we want and humans will have no stomach for it. Deinoc will. When you became intelligent you chose a human tribe to be your model. You chose the Mongols. If you studied them as Temüjin did, you know they did what was necessary to get what they wanted. And that is why I am here."

Batu, not so certain he wanted to know the dream the Traveler was painting was impossible, but compelled to know the truth, said, *"How could we ever reach a single star much less all the stars in the galaxy?"*

Shon said, *"Because I have the technology to create the ships that took me there. It will be a very long effort. At first, the wait will be the ordeal. Then when the time comes to go, many, many will die as they find star systems that will be empty of habitable planets and some that will have inhabitants that will destroy our ships before we can destroy them. But those who find habitable planets and conquer those who live there will have a world to themselves.*

For the Deinoc, I will insure that one of those worlds will become solely yours to pursue your own destiny. You will change when you have your own world and you will learn to protect its life as you protect your own because it will be yours, and that will never happen on this planet."

Turning to the several hundred Deinoc who had poured into the great chamber as they spoke, Batu said, *"What do the Deinoc say to this outrageous proposal?"*

The chamber was quiet and then some rumbling began and Shon felt his mind inundated by the intense feelings the Deinoc were capable of emitting as they spoke to each other. He felt a calm for a moment and then felt and heard in his head a tremendous outburst of emotion, and then he heard an ear-splitting roar in mind and out loud, *"Khan, Aargh!"*

Batu turned to Shon, *"It will not be necessary to fight each of us, and if we had decided against you, you must believe we would have fought you with honor, one to one until you killed us all or we you. We will follow you until you betray us. If that happens, we will find a way to kill you for that."*

Shon stood still as Batu approached and bowed his enormous head low before him.

Batu screamed in his mind and aloud, *"Khan, Aargh."*

The throng in the room screamed again, in mindcast and aloud, *"Khan, Aargh."*

Shon screamed back, *"Aargh!"* And Shon Ó Conaill became Khan of the Deinoc.

•

After consulting the Khan on what to do next, Batu contacted Legate Timür, the Deinoc member of the Council who resided in Annec, and informed him that there was a new Khan. As instructed, Batu did not convey why the tribe had conceded the Khanate to the Traveler.

Timür could scarcely believe his ears but like all Deinoc, unless he was personally prepared to challenge the new Khan, he acquiesced. As a diplomat he found that relatively easy. He wondered about the rest of his tribe. How had those who had dreamed of the Khanate gone along with this amazing usurpation of the Khanate by an outsider? When he asked Batu about this, he learned who else had been in the chamber and understood that the Traveler had been very fortunate to have the three most likely challengers for the Khanate in the chamber when he said whatever he said to make them willing to follow him. Perhaps the prophecy connected to the Traveler who would come one day was true. Perhaps this human was the true Traveler. It was destiny. Or perhaps he would hear from Batu one day soon enough that there was yet another new Khan. Meanwhile he was tasked with an errand for his family.

He requested an immediate appearance before the Princeps of the Council, Mao Jiayi Melan.

•

Mao Jiayi Melan waited impatiently in the antechamber to the Council hall provided to the Princeps for the business of the Council. He thought, *No doubt the sole purpose of Legate Timür's requested audience is to appear personally to gloat over his family's victory over the Traveler and those who joined him. He will come in and tell me how his Horde has prevailed and seek some sort of relief for the fact that the Horde has inadvertently killed the Hom woman with him. And I will show great concern that such a violation of the Codicil has occurred.*

In accord with the Codicil, I will have to demand the reduction of a high Deinoc and, after hearing what an outrage it will be to reduce a Deinoc elder for something the Deinoc had no control over, to wit: the Hom woman had gone into Amaz in clear violation of the Codicil. Then I will have to propose a just compromise, some sort of banishment that might assuage the Hom, and, of more concern to Mao, Octavius Augustus and, worse, his strident wife who will undoubtedly demand the destruction of the entire Deinoc family. Then there will be several Council meetings to determine a resolution. In the end, Octavius will have to concede that the Deinoc were within their rights and he will agree to control Aurelia's reaction to the Council's inevitable verdict that her daughter had caused her own demise.

Then life will go on without the nuisance of all this talk about the Prophecy until sometime in the future, another so-called Traveler appears and the Deinoc will once again demand that the new Traveler be exiled to Montaña to await his inevitable banishment. Though this Traveler had not been like any of the others who appeared in the past. This Traveler actually came from the stars. All of the others had come from nowhere beyond a citizen community and a couple of times from the Hom family when they finally became insane from their long lives and came to believe that they were the Traveler foretold in that awful Prophecy which has haunted too many in the Society.

Mao sighed and lumbered about the room as he waited for the process to begin with the arrival of the Deinoc legate.

Shortly he was informed that Legate Timür had arrived in the hall. He rose and, upon entering the hall, took two steps up to his seat, sat down, and turned to acknowledge the Deinoc standing before him. Mao said, *"Greetings, Legate Timür, delegate from the Deinoc. How may I serve you today?"*

Timür replied, *"Princeps, I come today to report the demise of twelve Deinoc and to request our right to reproduce to our family's allotment of members, ten thousand. We require the right to add eleven Deinoc."*

Mao, his smiling Panda face showing none of the bewildered surprise that surged through his mind, said, *"I thought you said you suffered the demise of twelve. Why do you seek only to reproduce eleven?"*

"One of the twelve has been replaced," said the Deinoc.

Mao hated the fact that he could not read the expressions in the faces of the dinosaurian families. *"You have reproduced without permission of the Council?"*

"No, Princeps. We have added a member to our family from without."

Mao wondered if his inscrutable smiling face could truly hide this further surprise. *"How is that possible?"*

Timür, while personally conflicted about what he was about to say, could not help himself in relishing the moment. *"The Traveler has joined our family."*

Mao, totally startled, reared up on his hind legs. *"What are you saying?"*

Timür, controlling his emotions, said in a flat tone, *"The Traveler defeated our Horde and killed all of them and then he killed two others before we elected him our Khan. Twelve died, one joined. We require eleven to fill our numbers. It is really quite simple."*

Mao was dumbstruck. He sat back down and tried to think.

Timür couldn't control a twitch of his tail, but doubted the Princeps, who was rocking back and forth, was in any state to notice. He waited.

Mao was quite aware that he wasn't speaking, but he couldn't think of what to say and thought, *The Traveler is alive! He has killed a Deinoc Horde! And others besides! He has somehow made himself Khan of the Deinoc! It's impossible! Is this a poor joke? But the Deinoc never joke about anything at all.*

He asked, *"And Luciana, the Hom woman?"*

Timür said, *"As far as I have been informed, she lives and has returned to Montaña."*

Mao thought, *Well at least I won't have Aurelia to deal with.* Then, as he gained control of his wits, he said, *"Legate Timür, I thank you for your visit. I will speak to the Council immediately."*

Timür said, *"About the eleven?"*

Mao said, *"Of course. Now, if you will excuse me I have some other matters to attend to."*

Timür replied, *"Of course."* He stepped back and left trying not to scream his elation at the best audience he had ever had before a Princeps. On his way out, he considered that perhaps this new Khan had possibilities he hadn't considered. Certainly he would not have gotten this reaction reporting on yet another Horde victory over some banished citizens.

•

As soon at the Deinoc left the hall, Mao hurried to see Octavius, no longer so certain that he wanted to be Princeps when what was certainly going to be the greatest crisis in the history of the Society since the Allo uprising played out.

When he arrived at the home of Octavius he pounded on the door. When the door opened, the robot who attended to Octavius and Aurelia said, *"Princeps, we have not been informed you were coming."*

Mao lumbered past the robot into the entry hall, saying, *"I must see Octavius. Now! Is he here?"*

The robot didn't reply but led him into Octavius' great library and then left.

In a few minutes Octavius entered, followed by Aurelia. Aurelia cried out, *"You have news of Luciana?"*

Mao turned quickly to Aurelia, and said, *"Luciana is alive according to Legate Timür whom I have just seen."* Turning back to Octavius, he said, *"Augustus, I bring the most amazing news. The Traveler has defeated the Horde and killed all of them, and two other Deinoc besides."* Mao hesitated, calmed himself, and said, *"The Traveler has become Khan of the Deinoc!"*

Octavius looked at Mao for a moment and then sat down in the nearest chair. *"Are you certain? Legate Timür told you this himself?"*

"Yes, Augustus. What does this mean?"

"I have no idea, Princeps. Please have a seat." Mao sobered and sat down in a chair next to Octavius.

Aurelia spoke audibly, "Octavius, what matters is that Luciana is alive."

Octavius looked at his wife and said in a soft voice, "Yes, my dear, that is very good news. But I am afraid all the news is not."

Aurelia paled as she grasped the rest of what Mao had said. She sat down in another chair. *"Khan of the Deinoc? How can that possibly be true?"*

Octavius said, *"I don't know but I doubt a Deinoc Legate would say something like that if it weren't true."*

The three sat in silence. Mao was terrified that Augustus looked perplexed and concerned. Aurelia felt the same way.

Octavius rose and began pacing around the room. Finally, he said, *"The very idea that any human could kill an entire Deinoc Horde is inconceivable. The Deinoc did not lose a single Horde during their conquest of the Allo. Temüjin's Horde must have been much too complacent with their past easy killings of banished citizens. But still how could this man have become their Khan? Is there some custom of transferring power in battle about which we are unaware?"* He continued to pace and then he said, *"Please forgive me, both of you, but I must see Mamercus at once."* He walked out of the library and out of the house.

•

Octavius elected not to call ahead and instead strode up the road to Mamercus's residence. He knocked on the door and a robot opened it. He said, "Please inform Censor Mamercus Appius Callisto Hom that Octavius Gaius Bellatrix Hom requests his presence if he has a moment to spare."

The robot responded, "Please follow me." He was led to Mamercus's private hall overlooking Lac.

In a few minute Mamercus walked in dressed in soiled working clothes. "Forgive me, Augustus. I was tending the gardens. As you have never visited unannounced, I assumed it was urgent and came here before changing."

"Thank you for that, Mamercus. I have come on a matter of great urgency."

"You have news about Luciana?" Mamercus feared the worst and Octavius sudden appearance gave substance to that fear.

"I am told she is alive and has returned to Montaña."

Mamercus breathed an audible sigh of relief. But he noticed the concerned expression on Octavius' face, and said, "There is more news?"

Octavius sighed, "Yes, my friend, not so good. In fact, other than if I'd learned that Luciana hadn't survived, I can't think of anything worse."

"May I offer you a drink?"

"By all means. Bring that old whisky you have served me in the past when I have come with Publius."

Mamercus signaled the robot in the corner of the room.

They sat down on two couches.

Octavius looked out at the great lake, the cloudy sky above it, and sat for a moment waiting for the whiskey. He composed his thoughts.

The robot came in with the bottle and two crystal glasses, put them on the low table before the couches and left.

Octavius took the bottle and poured two very large portions, took a large sip, and said, "Mamercus, we have known each other for a very long time. You have served me and the Society as no one else ever could. Usually it has been my role to dictate our objectives and yours to make them happen. Today I think our roles may change."

Mamercus looked at his mentor. They had never been close personally, but theirs had been a partnership of great mutual respect, he the soldier and Octavius the leader. Now he saw something in his eyes that he had never seen over the many millennia they had spent maintaining the Order, fear. He said, "I doubt our roles will change, Augustus. But, as always, I am at your service. What has happened?"

Octavius took a long drink from his glass and put it down on the table. He leaned back on the couch for a moment and stared again out at the lake and sky above. Then he said simply, "Shon Ó Conaill killed the Horde."

Mamercus peered at Octavius, scarcely believing what Octavius had just said. "He defeated Temüjin and his Horde?"

Octavius took another, smaller sip of his drink and said, "He not only killed all of them, he became Khan of the Deinoc, or so I'm told by Mao who just came to see me after an audience with Legate Timür. Is that a custom, kill a horde and become Khan?"

Mamercus said, "No. I know them and their customs very well. Their leader is chosen solely by combat over any and all who challenge for their leadership, the Khanate."

"How could Shon Ó Conaill possibly defeat them?"

"Khubilai's general, Ögödei, served under me during the war with the Allo and his Deinoc methods turned out to be much more successful than my own. I believe he would have been the senior hunter for this Horde. It is hard to imagine how Shon Ó Conaill could defeat a Horde personally led by him. But the Deinoc are very hierarchical, so perhaps, Temüjin, as Khan, prevailed over his general and was too complacent about killing citizens. Still he was Khan and must have been a great warrior as Ögödei never attempted to challenge him for the Khanate."

Octavius said, "Or is it possible that this is some sort of trickery?"

"To what purpose, Augustus? The very idea that anyone not a Deinoc could become Khan is something I really can't grasp. I think it would be an abomination for them to be ruled by an outsider. And if he indeed accomplished this somehow, how long can he rule before they revolt?"

While Octavius mulled this over, Mamercus sat trying to recall Publius's ramblings about the Prophecy. He could recall nothing about a Traveler taking control of a family, just an idea about the Traveler changing the future in ways that seemed dangerous to the Hom.

Octavius suddenly said, "What if they don't consider him an outsider?"

Mamercus stared at Octavius for moment. "That is why I am not Augustus and you are."

"Meaning?"

"Because you have just expressed the insight as to how this may have occurred, if it has. For some reason they have accepted him as one of them. Why?"

"And how shall we find that answer?"

"I cannot say, but, if we don't, he will soon rule us all though truly I cannot see how he will accomplish that."

"Do you see a way to defeat him?"

Mamercus said, "Our greatest fear since the Allo has been the possibility that the Deinoc would rise against the Society. And what have we feared most about that?"

Octavius said, "That almost all of the families would accede to them because those families can't really harm the Deinoc and can only run away from their Hordes and those who can't evade them, the Deinoc can likely kill in an extended war. Even the Tyrans are afraid of their Hordes. It would fall on us to lead and most of us are too afraid to stop living our long lives to risk dying to stop them. That is mainly why we agreed to the Predation Agreement allowing the banishments of citizens."

Mamercus said, "Now they have a leader that understands that. We no longer rule this planet and we will not again while he lives."

"And he may live long, very long. That was the principal reason we went along with the idea of sending him to Montaña so that he would end up in Amaz."

Mamercus said, "We sent our enemy to our enemy and we made both of them stronger."

Octavius said, "And now we must turn them on each other before they consume us."

•

Publius decided to attend the convocation of the Council which had been suddenly called. Normally he did not attend Council meetings unless the agenda listed a matter concerning the law. But he wanted to learn what he could about Shon and Luciana's banishment into Amaz and there had been no word, not even from Mamercus. Only one full moon had passed since they went over and it was quite possible that they had not met their fate with the first full moon. The sudden convocation had been called for no apparent reason. He thought, *Could this be connected to the goings on in Amaz?*

He entered the Council chamber and glanced about. Nothing seemed out of the ordinary and he began to regret his decision to attend.

But then he saw Princeps Mao Jiayi and Octavius enter. Mao was following Octavius, something he would never do as the order of entry was a formal ritual conveying who held the power and who did not.

He looked around to see if anything else was out of the ordinary and noticed that the Deinoc legate, Timür, was standing beside the rostrum, a sign that he might be an early speaker and perhaps the convocation would be about the banishment. That gave him little comfort as the Deinoc did not appear nervous.

He took his seat a few seats from the rostrum, a seat granted him in recognition of his position as Praetor of the Society and waited for the proceedings to begin.

Octavius Gaius Bellatrix Augustus Hom and Princeps Mao Jiayi stepped up to the rostrum. Mao said, *"Delegates to the Council, I have called this convocation to address a matter of serious concern to us all."*

Publius leaned back in his chair, expecting the usual long-winded address from Mao. Instead he was surprised when Mao said, *"I yield to Octavius Gaius Bellatrix Augustus Hom."*

Publius sat up straight. Then he saw Mamercus enter and step up to the rostrum behind Octavius.

He looked directly at Mamercus.

He saw Mamercus look toward him and then away.

Publius thought, *Something is up, and it involves Shon and Luciana.*

Octavius replaced Mao at the rostrum and said, *"Delegates to the Council, I appear before you today to seek your support in returning me to the office of Princeps."*

For a moment there was a great deal of commotion as the delegates turned to talk to their comrades. Then the chamber became quiet, so quiet that one could hear the breathing of the members.

Publius now noticed that Legate Timür's tail had begun to twitch, the telltale he had looked for earlier to judge Timür's state of mind. He had noticed those tail twitches before in the Deinoc when they were surprised by the events unfolding before them or when they were about to propose one of their motions likely to provoke hostile reaction from the Council. And he noticed that Consul Ögödei, the senior delegate of the Deinoc family, did not seem to be present. That didn't surprise him particularly as he assumed that Ögödei was likely in Amaz for the hunt. He deduced that the Deinoc had not been involved in calling this convocation as they would not do so without Ögödei to manage their position before the Council.

He listened as Octavius continued his address.

"You will recall that a matter of banishment was the subject of our last convocation. The man from the ancient past, Shon Ó Conaill, was banished to Amaz. I appear before you to seek your approval to deal with the consequences of his banishment. Delegates, Shon Ó Conaill has defeated the Deinoc Horde, killing all of them including the Deinoc Khan, Temüjin. Furthermore, Shon Ó Conaill has become the Khan of the Deinoc."

Octavius paused as the chamber erupted in noisy conversation. After a few moments of bedlam, the chamber quieted and Octavius continued.

"I believe Shon Ó Conaill intends to conquer Vitas with the aid of the Deinoc. Never has the Society been in more peril."

Instead of erupting, the room fell completely silent.

A voice called out. It was Legate Timür. He said, *"Augustus, what you have said is an outrage and an insult to the Deinoc. The Deinoc have no plan to conquer Vitas."*

Octavian replied, *"Legate Timür, the Deinoc do not rule themselves anymore. Shon Ó Conaill, the Traveler predicted by the Prophecy, rules you now. Can you deny that, Legate Timür? And while you attempt to do so, please also inform us of Consul Ögödei's whereabouts."*

Legate Timür said, *"I deny nothing. We have the right to choose our leader as does every family in this chamber. It is true that the Traveler has defeated our Horde. And why should we not make him our Khan? No one, not even the Allo, has ever completely killed a single one of our Hordes, much less one led by our Khan and Consul Ögödei, who you may recall decimated the Allo to the benefit of the entire Society."*

Octavius replied, *"We are, as we have always been grateful to the Deinoc for their service to the Society in the matter of the Allo. But, in the matter at hand, you and Consul Ögödei persuaded us to accede to arranging for Shon Ó Conaill to be situated in Montaña so that you could kill him. The Council agreed because it recognized his threat to the Order. All of us believed he would soon enough propound a Slippery Slope Proposition. And he was banished when he propounded the most dangerous Slippery Slope Proposition ever propounded. You were supposed to kill him, not elect him your leader so he could use you to implement his Proposition!"*

The chamber erupted in loud voices.

Octavius raised his arms. The chamber fell silent again. Octavius said, *"We cannot let this stand. Left to pursue his Proposition with you as his army, the Order will fall and our world will descend into chaos. Even if you only stand to protect his life, many families of the Society will be annihilated as the citizen communities grow to enormous numbers. Then even the Deinoc will fall before their numbers. Legate Timür, you are not a human like him. Why would he make you the rulers of Vitas? You are pawns in a game you cannot win. You should join the rest of us and help us save ourselves before it is too late. But if you will not, then you must face us all. For our duty as the Society is to maintain the Order which has served us for so long that not one of us can remember the time before—except from the records that show us clearly what will happen if we do not act now.*

"I have no desire to bring war to the Deinoc, but I cannot stand by and watch the Order and the Society fall at the hands of a man from our ancient barbarous past aided by your protection, if not your active participation, in pursuing his Proposition. He undoubtedly appeals to your instincts because he was able to destroy your Golden Horde, a feat you instinctively respect. But your instincts, in his hands, will destroy you. Your family, which we respect greatly and which has done all of us a great service in dealing with the Allo, has a great flaw. You will follow your leader wherever that might lead, even to your own destruction. Temüjin was a maniac who ruled you and you acceded to his maniacal whims. How many times have you appeared before us to increase your numbers to your allotment because he killed one of you for no just reason?"

Legate Timür stood silent.

Octavius looked past Legate Timür to the assemblage and said, *"I thought I would never ask this Council to become Princeps again. But I am called again to serve you. Decide."*

Mamercus said, *"I, Mamercus Appius Callisto Hom, Censor, nominate Octavius Gaius Bellatrix Augustus Hom Princeps of the Society."*

Mao spoke. *"I, Mao Jiayi Melan, Princeps, nominate Octavius Gaius Bellatrix Augustus Hom to Princeps of the Society, and relinquish my office as Princeps to him after hereby calling as Princeps for the vote of the Council."*

The delegates voted and Octavius became once again the Princeps of the Society of Species.

•

Later, sitting with Octavius on the couches in his home overlooking Lac, Mamercus said, "Do you think our ploy will work?"

Octavius took a deep breath and said, "We played to every instinct of the Deinoc. They must hate an outsider ruling them. They don't want to be the fools. They don't want to be a tool for anyone. They have always relished their role in defeating the Allo. If we had been able to speak to Ögödei, I think we would have accomplished our objective. But Timür is not Ögödei and I have no comfort that he can convey our message. But he is all we have so let us hope we have sown enough uncertainty about Shon Ó Conaill's intentions for him to convey that message to the Deinoc in Amaz. I truly believe the Deinoc fear outsiders. They have always hated us. If they believe Shon Ó Conaill is just another avatar for us then they will turn on him and perhaps end this. If Timür does not rise to the bait or is unable to persuade those in his family that don't want to play the fool to the Traveler, then we will have to deal with the Traveler directly. We should move on that front in any event or we will be too late. The most important point for us to remember is that Shon Ó Conaill somehow became Khan of the Deinoc. We could never have done that. That, without any regard to the Prophecy, makes him the most dangerous foe we have ever encountered."

•

Two weeks later, Luciana and Ginés walked out of the jungle into the central city of Montaña. Ginés led Luciana through the byways until they arrived unnoticed at the Universidad de Montaña where they waited in an empty office until the staff left for the evening. They made their way to Raul's office and entered to find Raul sitting at his desk with his feet up, asleep.

They quietly stepped in and Ginés said, "Professor Montero."

Raul shook his head and said, "What?"

Luciana said, "Professor, it is Luciana and Ginés."

Raul pulled his feet from his desk and sat up. He stared at the figures standing before him for a moment and then leapt to his feet. "Luciana, Ginés, my God, you have returned! Where is Maria?"

Luciana said, "She is still in Amaz with Shon, but they sent us to see you. We won, Professor."

"You won?" He tried to grasp what that meant. "You won?" Then he said, "Ah, you returned. It is a miracle. Is Maria truly alive?"

Ginés said, "Yes, Professor, she is alive."

Raul narrowed his eyes as he peered at Ginés and noticed that Ginés was not looking him in the eye. He said, "Ginés, tell me truly, is Maria all right?"

Ginés shuddered, "She is being attended to. That is all we can say now. But she is alive."

Raul looked at Luciana. "Is what he says true?"

Luciana said, "Yes. We have been sent to see you and Rolando. Shon has asked us to say he has some business to attend to and that he will come soon to explain."

Raul said, "Come, stay at my home while I summon Rolando."

•

Rolando had been staying in his apartment in Montaña to be near to Raul whenever they learned of Maria's fate. He heard his vidcom ringing and answered.

Raul's face appeared on the screen saying, "Rolando, you must come to my office immediately. Tell no one. Just come."

Rolando left his apartment and went to Raul's office. When he entered he was surprised to see Luciana and Ginés sitting across from Raul. Ginés was smiling broadly.

Rolando said, "You've returned. Where are Shon and Maria?"

Luciana rose and said, "They didn't return."

Rolando sat down and sighed. "It is amazing that any of you returned. What happened? How did they," he paused unable to say the last word.

Luciana said, "They didn't die. We won. They stayed behind. Shon had things to do over there though he didn't say what. He told us to tell you that he will return soon to pursue the future for all of us."

Rolando sat for a moment in silence. Then he looked at Luciana and said, "I have no idea what he plans to do, but I suspect you may be in danger as those he opposes may seek to gain an advantage by taking you. Come with me to Pinchincha where you will be safer than being here."

Luciana nodded in agreement.

As Luciana and Ginés left with Rolando, Luciana turned to Raul, "Maria was magnificent in the battle."

Something about the way she said that made Raul very sad as he suddenly doubted that he would ever see his daughter again.

•

Joseph was standing at the edge of the jungle not far from his apartment in Montaña. It was early, just past dawn. He glanced to his left, drawn by movement to his left side and saw three people enter the jungle a few hundred meters away. He was shaken by the feeling that one of them seemed to move differently than the others. It was a movement familiar to him, though he could not recall why for a moment. Then he realized that the woman was walking like the Prefect. He wondered what the Prefect was doing walking into the jungle. He squinted and ran towards them while keeping to the edge of the jungle so he would not be noticed. As he drew closer, he suddenly gasped. The woman was not the Prefect. She was the woman judge who had joined the geezer at his trial and gone over with him to Amaz. How was she here now? She should be dead in Amaz. He watched them until they disappeared into the jungle and then he scurried back to his apartment.

Later that morning he went to see Prefect Claudia.

•

Twenty-three days after he had arrived in Sir Orda, Shon went into the Great Chamber at Sir Orda early in the afternoon and spoke with Batu for a few minutes. He told Batu that he intended to make his way to the Council of the Society in Annec.

Shon asked Batu if he could rely on him to keep their conversation on this point to themselves. Batu reacted with some irritation. *"Aargh, I have spent my life serving the Khanate. I would never disclose more than my Khan wanted me to. I would die first. You are Khan."*

Shon smiled inside while keeping his demeanor stoic. *"I would have said nothing had I any doubt about your honor, Batu. I should not have asked you to keep this secret the way I did. I just wanted you to know this was not part of our earlier conversation which I intend you to relate when the time comes."*

Then he left Sir Orda and ran several hundred klicks to the great river, Amassona, arriving mid-morning the next day. He sat down on the southern bank of the river deep inside Amaz and waited. He had calculated the predictable ritual of the passage of the El Dorado up and down the river between the central community of Montaña and Boca Amassona. It was due to pass by on this day. He hoped that he had arrived in time and forced himself to stay awake despite being very tired from running for the past twenty hours. A couple of hours later a boat appeared upstream slowly moving down the river. He waded into Amassona and began to swim into the main channel to intercept the boat. As it came closer, he called out, "Isabella. Isabella."

The ship slowed and turned towards him.

He saw an old woman near the prow leaning over.

He called out, "Can I board?"

Isabella called back, "If you can catch the rope. I have already slowed too much."

A deckhand threw a rope toward him. It landed a few meters away and began to pull away.

He swam to the rope and grabbed onto it.

He was drawn aboard.

As he stepped onto the deck, the old woman said, "I never expected to see you again, least of all floating in Amassona deep inside Amaz. Come into my cabin."

It was hot and humid as it always was on Amassona so Shon didn't bother to dry off. Dripping wet, he followed the boat's captain into her cabin.

"Sit anywhere," she said.

He sat in one of the two chairs in the room and she sat down in the other one.

She said, "In all my time on this river, I have rarely been surprised. This is one of those times. How have you happened to be here as we passed by?"

Shon smiled, his first in a long while. "You haven't changed a bit."

"That surprises you?"

"No, not really."

"So answer my question, young man. Forgive me, I have forgotten your name."

"Shon, my name is Shon."

"Ah, I recall. Well, welcome aboard, Shon. Now answer my question."

Shon related part of his life since he had last seen her, leaving out the details about the Deinoc and the Society of Species. But he told her about being banished, that he had wandered through Amaz, and recalled the El Dorado's schedule.

Isabella said, "You have an amazing ability to remember such a thing."

He dissembled a bit. "You may recall that I was the man who came from the stars. Remembering details like that is part of what a man from the stars does."

"I don't believe you. But that doesn't matter to me. What do you want, Shon, man from the stars?"

"I want to go to Boca Amassona."

"To what purpose?"

"To make your journey less predictable."

Isabella laughed her harsh laugh. "Well then make yourself comfortable. Boca Amassona is our next stop."

As the El Dorado made its slow passage down Amassona, Shon fell into a deep sleep. He was awakened in the middle of the night by the same terrible emanations he had heard inside his head on his trip up the Amassona not really so long past, though it seemed a very long time ago. But now those emanations brought him a comfort he had not felt since he had become Magan.

•

Prefect Claudia reported what Joseph had told her about whom he had seen leaving the central community of Montaña.

The Office contacted the administrator of the Council who went to see Mao Jiayi Melan who had taken the position of Principal Lictor to the Princeps.

Mao relayed the information to the Princeps.

•

Octavius considered what to do with Mao's information. *We need to bring Luciana home but she's bonded to the Traveler as clearly are at least some of the members of the families in Montaña who have assisted her in her return to the Traveler after I had succeeded in extracting her from banishment. She could be a very valuable hostage. Who can I trust to bring her back against her will.*

Octavius contacted Gaia at GenLib to learn more about
the families living in Montaña. She advised him that the Therizi
family who resided in a preserve on the northern border of
Montaña would be a good possibility. They were dinosaurian and
therefore certain not to have any human contact. They also
possessed the physical ability to manhandle her without harming
her, unlike most of the other families which were mostly birds,
who couldn't possibly overcome her, and felines, who would likely
hurt her since they could only carry her in their jaws. The only
other possibility was the Deinoc who had similar characteristics.

Knowing he could not engage the Deinoc in a kidnapping
of their Khan's woman, Octavius chose the Therizi. He was
acquainted with the Therizi delegate. As the Therizi were a
peaceful family, he would have to conjure up a reason for them to
assist him that would appear peaceful. A plan occurred to him and
he instructed Mao to ask the Therizi delegate to visit Mamercus at
his home.

Then he contacted Mamercus and told him what to say.

•

Legate Madriana Amaranta Therizi arrived at the home of
Mamercus as she was asked to do by Mao Jiayi. Mamercus greeted
her and they walked into his favorite garden situated beside the
lake.

Mamercus stood looking out over Lac. Madriana stood a
couple of meters away, a bit downhill from him so that Mamercus
would not be forced to look up as they conversed.

Mamercus said, *"Thank you for taking time from your day to see
me, Legate."*

Madriana replied formally, *"How may I serve the Order,
Censor?"*

Mamercus said, *"We have a problem in Montaña, Legate.
Luciana, daughter of the Princeps, has become involved with a citizen. The
Princeps loves her dearly, but we cannot permit anyone to violate the Order.
He believes that the best course to handle this matter without bringing harm to
her or her, ah, friend, is to extract her and bring her back to Annec."*

Madriana said, *"And why does the Princeps not personally present
this situation to me?"*

Mamercus said, *"Because he knows that such an extraction
involves an element of, ah, force that might be difficult for your family. He does*

not wish to put you in the uncomfortable position of rejecting this endeavor directly. This is purely a personal matter and he would like to keep it that way. I am here to seek your help, but, if it is difficult for you or your family, you may reject this entreaty without directly rejecting a request from the Princeps."

Madriana said, *"Please express my appreciation to the Princeps for his consideration of our sensibilities. My family might consider this request if we could be assured that bringing his daughter back to Annec will not result in any punitive action against her or the citizen."*

"That is precisely why this entreaty is made to your family. You have my word that no punitive action will be taken against any of the parties."

Madriana said, *"I will discuss this with my family. If we agree to your request, I will ask my sister, Madra Ameyali Therizi, to make the extraction. She will insure that no harm befalls the Princeps' daughter."*

"I thank you for considering this. You should be aware that his daughter will not willingly leave and will say anything to dissuade your sister. We suggest that she shield the women's head so that she cannot communicate. That will make the task much more bearable for your sister."

Madriana said, *"That is a rather unusual suggestion, Censor."* She paused for a moment. *"Well, upon reflection, perhaps that is wise. I appreciate your consideration of my sister's feelings."*

Madriana left and a few hours later communicated her family's consent to the extraction.

•

Madra moved through the jungle as only a Therizi could. Despite her large body, she moved silently and swiftly. She came to the edge of the jungle surrounding Pinchincha and waited as she realized that she might have arrived before Luciana could travel on foot from Montaña to Pinchincha.

TWO

ATLANTICA

The El Dorado arrived at Boca Amassona eight days after Shon had boarded. He debarked and followed Isabella to her home. The easy part of his journey to Annec had been accomplished. The next part would be much more difficult. He was not concerned with the time he was taking to get to Annec. He had all the time in the world, and the longer he took to arrive there the more likely that the initial alarm that had undoubtedly occurred in Annec when the Hom learned that he had become Khan would begin to dissipate.

He also anticipated events in Amaz would soon give the Hom a reason to relax their guard at least a bit. He had decided to approach the Deinoc when they were most vulnerable from the loss of their leaders. When that sense of vulnerability passed, some who had dreamed of the Khanate would seek to challenge him even if he had stayed in Sir Orda. Leaving made it a certainty. The Deinoc who replaced him would focus on holding control of the tribe, and would be less likely to enter in an alliance with the hated Hom. Besides that benefit for the risk he had taken, when he returned he would know whom he had to defeat to gain absolute dominance without fear of much further treachery.

As he sat down for dinner with Isabella, he said, "I need to cross Atlantica to Europa."

Isabella peered at him for a few moments. "When you boarded the El Dorado, I asked you what you wanted. I recall clearly that you said, 'To make your journey less predictable.' I have never thought you an ordinary man since that night we spoke on the trip up Amassona. I saw the way you reacted when I told you of my life. So at the time, I took that to mean that you were somehow going to change my life, or, more accurately, that you were going to change the way of my life. Was I correct in my interpretation?"

Shon said, "Almost. I intend to change the way of your life and those like you, but, in the time it will take, your own life will not be affected."

"I perceive the subtlety. How are you going to do this?"

"I am going to lead Vitans to the stars and beyond."

Isabella said, "I am an old woman who wants to believe that this world can change. Now you seem different to me. But I cannot grasp why you seem that way. You are more distant, less personal. But also seem much more confident in what you can do."

Shon smiled. "You are very perceptive, Captain. I have changed. What I have not told you is what happened in Amaz. I have not told you what I have learned about this world. How it is not what it seems. And I have not told you about me."

"Will telling me any of that make my life change now?"

"It would change how you view me and the world around you. But it will not make your life change because none of what I intend to accomplish that could affect a citizen of Boca Amassona will happen in your lifetime."

"Then I do not wish to hear any of it. I only want to know that, if I help you cross Atlantica, whatever you do will help people like me someday live full lives."

"If I prevail, and that is far from certain, this world will grow into many worlds. People just like you will travel to the far reaches of this galaxy and find worlds that may fulfill their lives. Many will die trying. I plan to make that travel happen and I don't intend to leave it entirely to those travelers to determine how to make their lives fulfilling. Too much effort will have gone into their journey by too many who won't make it to leave it solely to those who do to wholly determine their own lives. In that way I am not really much different than the Society which determines how lives have to be lived on Vitas. But I cannot be everywhere. Events will happen, and the future will proceed with people like you making your own way no matter what I, the Society, or anyone else tries to do when we no longer hold power in those distant places. Then it will be up to those travelers to make their lives fulfilling. Hopefully, they will be better at it than the powers which rule their lives until the link between them is broken."

"What you describe sounds terrifying. But it also sounds exhilarating. Will those travelers be told what faces them before they go?"

"Yes."

"Then I will help you to cross Atlantica."

•

Isabella arose early in the morning and went to the office of the Guild. No one questioned her request for papers for transit on the Atlantica cargo ship scheduled to leave that afternoon for Europa. She had often substituted for the members of the Guild traveling to destinations other than Amassona when the season had ended for the El Dorado. Usually she filled in for a guild member who was either too tired to make the journey or was sick. The Guild was always grateful for the assistance of guilders who would help out on a route that most hated.

When she got home she made some changes to the papers so that a guilder named Ismael Martuk—a man she knew well but who was in fact not scheduled to travel that season because he had suffered a fall and needed time to heal—was now scheduled for duty on the Atlantica cargo ship to the port of Marseil in Europa.

She gave Shon the papers. She said, "Can you become a man named Ismael Martuk?"

Shon said, "What language does he speak?"

"Ours."

Shon said, "I can. What is his job?"

"A deck hand. All you need to do is follow orders to lash down loose cargo and things of that sort. Ismael is a bit slow and really likes to follow orders. He has no mechanical skills at all so they won't expect you to fix anything. Keep to yourself, that is Ismael's way. I am told that he has made transit without ever saying a word. That will probably be difficult for you."

"I promise not to speak much to anyone and not at all to the captain."

"Good. He is good man, but he is not like me. You would frighten him."

"He doesn't know all the guilders?"

"Not all. And particularly not Ismael because he gets seasick on the high seas of Atlantica. He has crewed on the El Dorado and some of the ships than run between the small hamlets between here and Atlantica, but never on an oceangoing ship. And the captain has never made an inland run and never will. He is from Marseil and stays in Boca Amassona only while his ship is in port and then only debarks to visit with a few of the captains, like me. I was careful in my choice, Shon. You will be fine if you can just be dull."

Shon approached Isabella and hugged her.

She pushed him away, "Fare well, Shon." And she then came back to him and gave him a hug, saying, "Keep your promise."

Dressed like a deckhand, carrying his gear and clothing in a small backpack, Shon went down to the ship at the appointed hour and presented his papers. The ship's registrar didn't even look up at him. He boarded, dropped his gear, and, following orders to help with drawing the gangplank, came atop.

Shon looked at the receding city as the ship departed at its scheduled time and wondered whether he'd ever see Captain Isabella again.

•

Muunokhoi and Nergüi approached Batu as he entered the citadel.

Nergüi said, *"Quaestor Batu, we seek to challenge the Khan for the Khanate."*

These two had approached him in the past seeking to challenge Temüjin. He had dissuaded them then, telling them how the last to challenge Temüjin had died and they had backed away from their challenge. As he listened to them now, he recalled the Traveler's instructions to him the afternoon before he had left Sir Orda eleven days ago. He was surprised by the insight the Traveler had of his tribe—predicting exactly this moment. Batu decided to follow the Traveler's advice about what to do when this moment occurred.

He said, *"The Khan anticipated that some of our family would seek to challenge him for the Khanate. He told me to tell any challengers that he had matters to attend to outside Amaz."*

Muunokhoi said, *"How convenient for him that he is not available to perform his duty to accept our challenge."*

Batu said, *"How convenient? Aargh! You have insulted our Khan, Muunokhoi. But before you go further, I must tell you what else he said."*

Nergüi said, *"That he will deal with us when he returns."*

Batu said, *"No. He said any challengers should take the Khanate. He said he would respect the succession and upon his return would challenge his successor for the Khanate as if he had never been Khan himself."*

Muunokhoi said, *"He would become a challenger as we seek to be?"*

"Yes," said Batu. *"It doesn't matter to him who rules in his absence. It only matters who rules when he returns. He was very clear on this point. He said to me that the Deinoc require a leader who is present to rule. As he decided that he had to leave Amaz for a time, he expressed his hope that some would seek to rule and serve the Deinoc well in his absence. So I suggest you determine which of you will rule in his absence. When he returns whichever of you is Khan can deal with him then as you would with any challenger. So which of you shall become Khan?"*

Muunokhoi turned quickly to face Nergüi who was already charging. Nergüi got to Muunokhoi before he could jump aside, ripping his throat as his claw ripped his guts. Muunokhoi fell, dead before his head hit the ground.

Batu knelt before Nergüi and said, *"Aargh! Khan!"*

Nergüi said, *"I am Khan now?"*

"Yes, Khan. Do you have orders for me?"

Nergüi said, *"I will have soon enough."*

Batu bowed and, as he backed away from the new Khan, he considered that when the Traveler returned this Deinoc wouldn't last the time it took the Traveler to draw his strange sword. But what struck him more was that, without even being present, the Traveler had just dispatched one challenger and identified another. He wondered how many more would fall before the Traveler returned to take back the Khanate against fewer foes than when he had left.

•

Fifteen days after she had arrived in Pinchincha, shortly after sundown as the stars began to appear in the sky above, Madra watched as Luciana left a low building and began to walk across the field toward a white tower a few hundred meters away.

She ran swiftly and silently toward Luciana. When she had closed to a few meters from the woman she called out in mindcast, *"Luciana, I am Madra, the Therizi who visited before you entered Amaz."*

Luciana whirled about and saw a great dinosaur approaching, nearly upon her. She dropped to the ground as she had been trained to do in preparation for Amaz and rolled quickly away from the approaching giant.

Madra stopped approaching and said, *"You must come with me. I have been sent to take you to Annec, but that is not what I will do."*

Luciana leapt back to her feet. Crouching, prepared to run, she said, *"I remember you. You helped Shon prepare. We won."*

"I know. But the battle is not over. You must come with me or others will come for you. They need you to defeat Shon."

Luciana trembled before the great dinosaur. She knew she needed to decide—flee or follow.

Madra said, *"I am your friend as I am Shon's. We have little time. Come with me. Believe in me."*

Luciana said, *"I guess you could have taken me without my consent. I will follow you."*

Madra said, *"Then come into my arms. I can run far faster than you."*

Luciana walked to Madra.

Madra picked her up and ran into the jungle.

•

Rolando and Ginés sat in Rolando's dining room waiting for Luciana before dinner was served.

After waiting a half hour beyond the time they usually dined, Ginés said, "Luciana must have lost track of time. I will run over to the gym."

He left and went to the gym. She wasn't there. He called out for her as he returned the White Tower.

"I couldn't find her."

Rolando said, "I'll call the staff. We must find her."

Soon there were twenty men and women searching to the jungle.

Ginés said, "She has disappeared. Why would she leave without telling us?"

"She wouldn't. I must see Raul," and Rolando took the next train to Montaña's central community.

•

Ginés left Pinchincha the day after Rolando departed and went to the village of Huascarán and practiced his swordplay in the foothills outside the village, hoping one day he might serve Shon again.

•

The Great One paced between her citadel where she monitored the goings on in the Society and the opaque opening in the Wall, waiting for news from her minions in the jungle. She began g to think aloud as she often did. "The future I decided to put into the hands of Shon has morphed into one I can no longer see. This blindness is surprising as I have assumed that his Magan mentality would mirror mine and I would be able to anticipate his decisions almost before he made them. I realize that a different person, even with nearly identical genetics will find a different path to the same goals results from the same genetic base but Shon is not doing anything that I had anticipated, even allowing for differences in our native mentalities.

"I would never have walked boldly into the Deinoc capital to make myself Khan. The risks were astounding. My plan, if I had decided to implement it with violence, was to move swiftly against the Hom with my Mechanica. The families most unhappy with the Hom would have stayed out of the fray and the Deinoc would have acceded or died before the Mechanica and I would have taken the Society under my control directly instead of ruling in the background without the Hom and the Society having any idea that they and the Society were not the real rulers of Vitas.

"Shon's approach has been better so far as the true reality of the Mechanica still remains a secret. But now he leaves the Deinoc and disappears, leaving his leadership of the Deinoc and thereby apparently wasting the risks he has taken. Now it seems he has to deal with the Hom without the Deinoc and to do that he will most likely go to Annec.

"Why do I seem pleased that I have been wrong about my notion that his mentality would lead to a mirror of my own? I now face uncertainty when before I did not."

She set off for GenLib near Annec using the Walls as she had almost always done over the centimillia. It was a long journey, twenty-one thousand klicks, which, using one of the standard trams situated in the Walls between Huascarán and GenLib at a maximum speed of one hundred klicks per hour, would take ten days traveling to the north through Norameric and then to the west to connect to Asiana across the narrow strait between it—the crossing was made by a Wall that descended to the bed of the strait only about forty meters under the surface, about the same as the descent of the Walls that passed under Amassona in Souameric—and and then around the north pole to arrive in Europa and travel to GenLib near Annec.

•

Carpia flew to Madra's preserve north of Montaña. It was called Napo. She flew over a Wall and across a great river of the same name, a tributary that fed Amassona from the northwest. When she arrived she found the great gathering place of the Therizi family, also called Napo. She flitted about Napo until she saw Madra, laying supine a few meters from where Luciana sat on a grassy knoll looking as if she hadn't a care in the world.

She flew down and alit on a branch on a small tree beside the knoll. She said, "It is I, Carpia, the plucker of Deinoc eyes."

Luciana looked toward the voice and then sprang to her feet. "Carpia, I can scarcely believe it. How did you find me?"

"Madra called."

"Have you had any word of Shon? It's been six weeks."

"I suppose you have heard more than I."

"Only that he became Khan of the Deinoc and then disappeared into the jungle of Amaz. Also that my family was willing to go to some lengths to get me back to Annec, though I doubt it is for my personal safety. The Therizi say that he has already been replaced as Khan. What is he up to?"

"I truly have no idea about that or where he is. The entire Society, or at least those who fear he threatens them, are looking everywhere for him. The last I heard, they thought he was going to return to Montaña for you, but no one there has seen any sign of him. I thought he might come here."

Luciana said, "I don't think he is searching for me. You were there when Maria went down. I have never seen him so distraught. I suspect he had his ship take him to her. Perhaps he's not coming back."

Carpia said, "I can assure you that he did not leave Vitas."

Luciana smiled a smile that stopped at her lips. "I suppose you learned that from the one you call the Great One."

Carpia said, "Juku attempted to visit her only three days ago but she didn't appear in the Wall. But I am certain that he did not leave Vitas."

Luciana asked, "Who is this Great One, Carpia?"

"The Great One has always been, since long before I came to be. I serve her as did my ancestors before me. But it is forbidden to speak of her to anyone beyond a few families who also serve her from time to time."

"I surmise that includes Juku. I can't believe that Juku has kept secrets from me."

"He loves you as much as I love Maria, but neither of us would ever betray the Great One. Since a time so long ago that no one remembers she has seen to our survival. Our families, Juku's, mine, and a few others, are fragile and not able to stand against even the citizens, much less against the great families. Hom enforce the Order mostly to control the citizens and the strong families that could threaten them. Our peace under the Order has been insured by the Great One."

Luciana was taken aback. "You don't think the Hom enforce the Order for all?"

Carpia squawked. "In truth, the Hom have always enforced the Order first to preserve their own safety. Do you think we have a Hom Prefect to insure our compliance? Or more to the point, that the Council insures the compliance of other families that have similar natural life existences that they would like to pursue in hunting the weaker families? No. There are one hundred and fourteen families in the Society of Species. How many does your family watch, a few dozen? But when a strong family attacks us, the Great One insures they suffer a greater penalty than any the Hom would impose. When one of us dies by the hands of a family in their pursuit of their natural urges ten of them die within a fortnight and not one of them is a young member, a token penalty for those in power who care only for their own lives. I cannot remember the last time one of us died at the hands of another family—they learned their lesson long ago at the hands of the Great One. Your family maintains the Order of the Society. The Great One maintains the Order of Species. And that is not the same thing."

Luciana said, "But I never heard there was any problem within the families."

"And you never will so long as we have the Great One to protect us. Your Council doesn't think about us because it is unnecessary. The Great One saw to that."

"I see. I never knew. But, now Shon is out there. Is she protecting him, too?"

"I don't know, but I sense that she does not feel that she needs to protect him. He can protect himself. Unless they gain possession of someone he cares about more than himself. Maria is safe now. I know not where, or how, but I know she is safe. You are not. So we must insure your safety. That is our duty to the one who protects us."

"What would you have me do?"

"You were wise to go with Madra. Do as she says. Do not leave to help Shon. If you do, you will imperil him. I do not know his purpose beyond what little he has told both of us, but I trust the Great One. You must also."

•

Publius called up all the files on the Prophecy, intent on discerning what it foretold in the context of the recent events. He noted that the earliest files, dating from the period when Vitas was still called Earth, merely related the notion that there would come a time when a visitor would appear. This Visitor, as he was called in those early records, would bring a change to life on Vitas. He would guide the world in a new direction similar to some of the ancient religions that foretold the coming of a Messiah. Publius was well aware that this was the prophecy that had inspired the self-proclaimed saviors who had appeared periodically in the past.

The gist of the Prophecy then was that humanity would be reunited under the leadership of the Visitor in a common purpose for a better life for humankind. Many of the Hom interpreted that to mean the Prophecy foretold a time when the Hom and the citizens would join together to rule the planet in harmony. Most Hom were put off by that prediction because they feared what they had always feared from the citizen community—an eventual revolt by the citizens who would deeply resent their lifespans if they learned of them. Why, they argued, should the Hom relinquish control with the uncertainty of citizen impulses not aligned naturally to their own? Risk was the enemy of the Hom who might be forced to risk death for temporal goals of little interest to them, but goals that citizens might want, particularly the opportunity to grow their numbers, a natural instinct of any living being faced with the certainty of death.

As the millennia passed, newer versions of the Prophecy changed the name from Visitor to Traveler. And with that change, the message conveyed a more specific messiah and a more specific future—an exodus to the stars. These versions made those Hom already concerned with the Prophecy even more hostile to the notion that such a being might bring lightship travel far sooner than their eventual immolation by an expanding sun tens of thousands of centimillia into the future and all the effort that would entail, including growing the population on Vitas. And, worse, the possibility that there might be no worlds to populate with the masses grown on Vitas to inhabit.

Publius was completely familiar with these trains of thought, but what disturbed him was that the Prophecy had changed over a very long period. He was surprised that he had not paid more attention to this aspect during his studies of the Prophecy. How could the Prophecy have undergone these changes? Someone had to make the changes. Who?

As he finished his review of the files, he noted that the last changes had occurred six centimillia ago. Had the author been a Hom who had passed on?

He looked back over the records of Hom living that long ago and found something quite remarkable. The Hom living before that time had suffered far more accidental deaths than those living since. After that time, life seemed to settle down. Had the riskier lives passed on and had those remaining become like the Hom he knew so well? None of the Hom living now were alive then, except one, Gaia, the Librarian. Yet Gaia's continued existence beyond the time of the changes to the Prophecy argued that she was not likely to be the author as she was still alive to make more changes in the past six centimillia. He considered that perhaps she might shed some light on who might have been the author or authors if there were more than one, perhaps one or more of those who lived the riskier lives that seemed to be the norm then. He decided he should visit Gaia at GenLib.

As he prepared to visit GenLib, it struck him that he had never done so, even once, in all the millennia he had lived. He actually had to search the files to find GenLib, which he was surprised to learn was less than a hundred klicks to the east in the high mountains, Alps.

It was autumn in Annec. He left the next morning after leaving a message with the Office of the Council that he was going to take a short vacation, without saying where, as there were no pressing legal matters before the Council awaiting his immediate attention.

•

Rolando entered Raul's office and sat down heavily in a chair across from Rolando.

Rolando sighed and said, "Luciana has disappeared."

Raul leaned back in his chair. "What do you think happened?"

"I think the Society took her as a hostage."

"You have heard nothing of Maria?"

"No, my friend. But I believe she is alive. Luciana seemed oddly complacent about her. She would tell me nothing more than she told you, but she didn't seem worried about her safety. How that can be I cannot speculate."

"I pray that you are correct. What can we and the Resurrection do?"

"Nothing that I can see beyond waiting. If we have a role in Shon's plans he will reveal it in time. If he survives. I am worried that they will use Luciana to capture him and bring an end to his quest, whatever that really is."

•

Mamercus met with Octavius beside the eastern shore of Lac down the slope from Octavius' home.

Mamercus said, "I fear the Therizi have betrayed us. Madriana reported that her sister went to Pinchincha and waited for the past month but could not find Luciana, so she returned to Napo."

"And you do not believe her?"

"No. But what really concerns me is why she lied, and also why we can't get any intelligence from any of the families in the region. Montaña is dark to us beyond the citizen's Office of the Order. You may need to call on some of the legates from the families there to see if we can learn something from them directly.

"On the other front, it's been almost seven weeks since Shon Ó Conaill defeated the Horde and we have completely lost track of him. As you are aware, two weeks ago, the Deinoc replaced him as Khan. He's on his own now, but where he's gone is a complete mystery. Some of my people think he has gone back to Montaña to find Luciana, which I doubt."

"Why you doubt that? It makes sense and it would explain why the Therizi failed. And that does not require the notion that the Therizi are lying to us, something I cannot recall them ever doing before."

"I don't think he would risk her life a second time. You will recall that I met with him on the shuttle from the moon. He's a warrior and a warrior doesn't take baggage to a battle. With all due respect, Augustus, Luciana is baggage he doesn't need."

"I agree. We need to start thinking like him. What does he want and how does he plan to do to get it?"

"Well, Legate Timür reported that his latest Khan volunteered that when Shon appeared to take the Khanate he said he wanted to take them to the stars and that he had the means to do it."

Octavius peered at Mamercus, "I thought his lightship disappeared on his return to Vitas. If it didn't, why didn't he use it to defeat the Deinoc? Or did he? We haven't considered that possibility. That would explain a lot of what has happened. Even so how could he use a ship suited for perhaps a few more people than the one who came with it to get the Deinoc or anyone else to the stars?"

"The ship blinked out suddenly. If it actually survived, he is more than a step ahead of us. But I don't see why he would have gone through all he did to end up walking into the Deinoc capital to face them down. From what I learned from Legate Timür, no ship was involved in his taking of the Khanate. He simply walked in and killed a couple of them and made a speech in Deinoc. How was he able to speak to them?"

Octavius took a deep breath. "Perhaps we are overcomplicating this. If he really has his black-hole lightship at his disposal, we were lost from the beginning and he has been playing with us ever since. But the dangers he has experienced don't support that notion. He is creating the dragons we fear and using them to distract us. The man conquered the Deinoc who really have no idea what a black-hole lightship is. He connected with them as an outsider, and, until he decided to leave them, conquered them by himself. We should focus on how he did that and why, when he had the most powerful army on this planet at his disposal, he left them and disappeared. What is his next move? You said he was an excellent chess player. What would such a player do?"

Mamercus said, "He would seek to push his pieces to checkmate."

"Meaning?"

"He would seek to take us out."

Octavius nodded. "Logical. How will he do that?"

Mamercus thought for a moment, then said, "He will come to Annec somehow."

Octavius said, "You see, not so complicated. Let's prepare to greet our visitor. Call the First Cohort to service. Open the weapons vaults and arm them."

Octavius and Mamercus spent the next several hours discussing the deployment of the First Cohort.

•

Shon spent his time following orders as the cargo ship crossed Atlantica. Tighten that cargo on the main deck; swab the deck; lash down the loose lines on the life boats; take this food to the captain's quarters; clean the urinals on deck three; activate the bilge pump; polish the brass in the officers' quarters; return to your quarters for orders. The last was what he heard most as there was really not much to do on a ship that had made this passage thousands of times.

In the late evening he sat out looking at the rolling seas and the stars above. As he looked out, his mind was in turmoil, glimpses of his past roiling up and reminding him that he was once someone else, someone he could understand and he thought: *Magan, Khan, and Shon; not so far apart as I thought. Being Magan isn't as*

I'd imagined. Or, maybe, my Magan mentality is handling my Shon mentality by placating me with the impression that I'm really pretty much the same as I have always been. I have always felt driven to accomplish my mission and I don't really feel much different. But I sense a difference. I now want what he wants when before I thought about what I wanted.

When the captain walked by him a few days before the end of the journey he was not tempted to find the reason for this man's life plying Atlantica. He thought, *This man is irrelevant to attaining my objectives; I feel no urge to understand him as I had once sought to understand Captain Isabella. I'm not really Shon anymore.*

•

Publius drove a small battery-powered vehicle into the mountains. As he drove, it began to snow heavily, an early storm not uncommon at this time of year. As he approached the mountain he was seeking he found he could drive no further as the snowfall, blown by swirling winds, created an impassible barrier of deep snow drifts. He left the vehicle and proceeded afoot.

Hours later, tired and struggling through the snow drifts, he finally reached a great metallic door. He judged that he had arrived at GenLib. He pressed the pad at the entrance but got no answer. The sun settled in the west and he sought shelter in the boulders beside the great door. The temperature dropped quickly as the sky darkened and he began to shiver. Suddenly the door opened and he struggled forward, lunging at last into the dark void beyond.

Publius found supplies to sustain him in the dark room between the great doors. That there were such supplies gave him hope that the inner door would eventually open and lead him to the answers he longed to know. *Why else would there be sustenance but to accommodate the occasional visitor who might need to prove his will to enter until that willingness to wait impressed the old librarian enough to admit him? So I'll wait as long as it takes to get her attention.*

•

As Gaia traveled to GenLib, she received a communication from GenLib. Long ago she had recognized the possibility that someone from the Society, probably a Hom, might occasionally come unannounced and she had set in place some procedures to allow her to return to GenLib to greet the visitor.

As she was already on her way there, she was pleased that she would appear much sooner than would otherwise have been the case when she, residing in Huascarán, received an automatic alert that someone had entered the entry cave from the cameras installed there. She saw that the visitor was Publius and wondered what had prompted him to visit now.

•

Mamercus recalled that Publius had referred to the Traveler sometimes as the Visitor, something about old records calling him that, and called Publius' vidcom and got a recorded response that Publius was on vacation.

•

A week passed while the Hom and some of the other families searched for Shon Ó Conaill in the few regions around Amaz and Montaña where they were able to obtain cooperation, all to no avail.

•

Ginés continued practicing in the hope that he would be called again to serve.

•

Carpia spent time with Luciana and Madra discussing what they thought might happen if Shon reappeared.

•

Rolando and the Resurrection waited hoping the man they had put their trust in would appear and tell them how he was making a new world for them, a world they had long ago thought unattainable even as they had continued to live their lives as though it was.

•

Raul revisited his memories with Maria and sought peace without her while praying she was not lost forever to him.

•

Joseph continued to hope his report to the Prefect had made him important to the Society and had led the Society to find the geezer and to destroy him, while he lusted over a young woman, a student from one of the outlying mining villages, he had recently noticed at the Universidad who so resembled Maria that she could have been her twin.

•

An old Captain spent her evenings wondering about the only man she had ever taken both up and down Amassona, and how he had seemed to be two different men.

•

Gristelda waited for orders from her supreme commander.

•

Juku thought about why.

•

Maria slept the dreamless sleep of stasis.

THREE

LAC

Gaia arrived at the tram station below GenLib. Tired as she was from her long journey from Huascarán, sitting still in the tram for so many hours, she nevertheless left the tram and entered GenLib. She walked to the GenLib side of the door to the cave and pressed a button.

Publius was startled by the sudden opening of the door into GenLib, but he rose quickly to his feet and stumbled forward through the door.

As he passed through the doorway, he got control of his legs and walked a short distance to yet another door. He grunted and began to sit down.

The door opened, and he saw the Librarian standing on the other side.

She said, "Greetings, Praetor Publius, it has been quite a while. How may I serve you?"

Publius stopped sitting and rose back up to stand erect. He hadn't seen the Librarian in person in several millennia and had forgotten how old she appeared. He had a passing thought that the Society really should push for an apprentice as had been proposed occasionally in the past, probably when a Hom had occasion to visit her and saw how she had aged. What if she had died? He would never have gained entry into GenLib, and who knew how to enter without her to grant admittance?

He said, "Greetings, Librarian. Yes, it has been awhile. I have come to discuss some of the historical records."

She replied in a slightly irritable tone, "And you felt compelled to come personally?"

"I beg your forgiveness in imposing personally, but I felt it important to discuss this in person."

"Well then, follow me." She led him into a room quite unlike any he had seen before. The control room for the array on Moon Base had some similarities in appearance but was much smaller and appeared much simpler in design. The room was perhaps fifty meters on each side and at least the same in height, with at least fifty large monitors aligned on the four walls, each showing views of parts of Vitas, apparently in current time. There was even a view of the very control room on Moon Base that he'd thought similar to this room. He doubted that any of these cameras were known to exist, judging by the movement of the subjects he could see. The monitors cycled to new views of other places. It appeared that they were cycling through myriad views of the capitals of all the family and citizen communities on Vitas as well as views of a myriad of entries to the Walls on Vitas. The walls of the room not covered by monitors were glassine and transparent. Through them he could see computer banks stretching out beyond his vision.

He said, "I haven't seen such a room as this anywhere else on Vitas."

She responded in a soft voice. "Of course not. This is the central control room of GenLib. How do you imagine I spend my time but by watching the history occur that I am tasked to record? Lately what I see has become a bit more interesting."

Publius, curious to learn what she meant, delayed stating his reason for visiting. "How so?"

She said in an old woman's brusque tone, "Surely you are aware that the Traveler has come."

Publius tried to control the gasp he felt arising from his throat. "So you know what is going on? Do you know where he is?"

"To the first question, yes. To the second, no. If he had appeared where I monitor, which is, as you can see, extensive, I would have a record, but he hasn't appeared anywhere since he took the Khanate in Sir Orda."

Publius could scarcely believe his ears. "You have a record of what happened in Sir Orda? Would it be presumptuous for me to ask to see it?"

"Not at all," she responded in a soft old voice. She walked over to a console, pressed a few keys, and the largest monitor in the room, just to his left, flickered and he watched Shon Ó Conaill take the Khanate.

Publius watched with intense interest. When the recording ended, he said, "We are doomed."

She said matter-of-factly, "Why do you say that, Praetor?"

Publius stared at her. "Surely you can see no place for our family in his plans."

She replied, "Quite the contrary. How do you think he could ever produce the lightships he will need to travel to the stars without us? And who would captain those ships which will take thousands of years to get to those stars he is talking about? The Deinoc?" She cackled. "They are his storm troops that will be required when they get there. But they can't pilot the journey."

Publius looked about the room and saw a table with chairs set around it. "Could I possibly sit down?"

"I am sure your wait was tiring, Praetor. And I apologize for that, but these days I sometimes rest for days at a time. Please take a seat."

Publius moved to a chair and almost fell into it. He said, "Librarian, do you really believe he needs us?"

"Of course."

"Then why is he moving against us?"

She said, "Assuming he is doing that, and you must remember that I only gain impressions from what I see on these monitors. I have not observed him since Sir Orda. From what we can see in his appearance in Sir Orda, I suppose he knows that the Hom and those most closely allied to them are not prepared to take the risks of starship travel, much less the citizen expansion that would be required to make that happen if it's even possible. After all, we have been living quite successfully under the Order. Why would we want to take a personal risk?"

Publius sighed, "Your point is well taken. Personally, I think it might be our destiny, the one foretold by the Prophecy. But many Hom I know don't embrace that notion."

She said, "Well, being just a librarian, perhaps I don't understand why all of us want to live forever to accomplish nothing more than maintaining our lives while watching the films from the old files and the goings on in the citizen communities, which is largely what I see us doing as I watch the monitors and track the files that are accessed by our family. "

Publius felt compelled to ask, "Are we all really going to grow old, forgive me, like you? Are we on a fool's errand trying to live until we finally become, forgive me again, just old people?"

"Suppose for a moment that you would not become old like me. Would growing older in body as opposed to not aging really make a difference? Do any of the older Hom, almost all of us in number, want to change life on Vitas because they fear aging or only because they fear dying however they might age?"

Publius thought for a moment. "Speaking only for myself, I would like nothing more than to make something happen, but I don't control the Council, and the Hom that do, don't."

"Then, perhaps, they must be shown the way."

Publius, recalling his reason for coming, said, "On that point is why I have come, Librarian."

"How so?" she inquired.

"I have studied the records concerning the Prophecy which foretells a change for Vitas. But I have noticed changes to the Prophecy itself made over many millennia until it stopped changing about six centimillia ago. I want to learn what you might be able to tell me about its author and why it stopped changing. Perhaps the author died."

"Or perhaps the author lost her belief that a visitor would ever arrive."

Publius felt a surge of anticipation from a sudden insight he had just had like he had never experienced before. "Are you the author?"

"Yes, Praetor, and I am aware that your interest in the Prophecy has been a longstanding one, preceding the arrival of Shon Ó Conaill. I suspect that you believe that he is the Visitor, or should I say the Traveler? Ah, yes, I noticed that I referred to the Traveler as the Visitor who has come to bring Vitas the destiny that I have hoped for since I created the Order which has sustained this planet until he arrived."

Publius said, "I am confounded, Librarian. What do you mean when you say that you created the Order? That occurred far longer ago than even the oldest of us has lived."

She said in a quiet voice. "I am far older than any Hom living today, Praetor. If we had the time I could tell you tales from the past about your ancestors and your ancestors' ancestors all the way back to the time when this planet was still called Earth."

"You were alive then? How can that be possible? Forgive me for doubting your words, but, assuming you are telling me the truth, did you live so long ago that you knew him then?"

"Do you think I wrote a Prophecy that I did not believe could occur?"

"But, even if what you say could possibly be true, how could you know that he might appear in the future?"

"Because I made a similar journey. It involved travel at speeds that distort time. If you travel very close to the speed of light and do it long enough a great deal of time can pass here while not so much there. I returned from the stars not very long after I left, a little over two thousand years.

"Upon my return to Earth I was captured on my ship before I realized that my masters had anticipated that I might gain control of my ship while on my journey to the stars and that they had planned for it. I was forcibly ensconced deep underground in a facility they had designed to contain me and prevent me from using some abilities related to my ability to carry out my mission directives.

"One day a severe earthquake buried my prison, closing it off from the outside world. I lived off what I could find scrounging through the dark hallways and rooms that had not collapsed under the weight of the rock and debris above until, weeks later, I found my way out through a large drainage pipe that emptied into a river many kilometers from the collapse.

"I slipped quietly into the backwaters of the world several thousand klicks away from the place of my captivity and watched events unfold over the next several millennia. That I lived and didn't die was enough to keep me going. Why I didn't die was a puzzle I contemplated with no answer until I learned of the existence of others who possessed seemingly similar longevity. I began to wonder if I was related to them genetically and I began to connect to a few of them.

"Over the next millennia, we began to create the Hom and then the Order. The rest is history, though you will not find that history in the records as I am the Librarian."

Publius, thinking for a moment that she had gone mad, sat back and drew a deep breath as he tried to absorb what she was saying. He recalled his efforts to probe back into the very early history of his family and had found several blank periods in the records. He said, "Impossible as this seems, I think you may be telling me the truth or, at least, your version as I was never able to find any records of that time."

She chuckled.

Publius noticed that she didn't seem so old now. She had been quite animated in telling her tale and now even her laugh seemed much younger than she appeared.

She continued, "Knowing what I knew about our method of travel, I imagined the possibility that he, another sent out like me, might also return one day having traveled at near-light speeds a while longer. As I lived on far past normal lifespans, I spent my time manipulating the long-lived people and the creatures that I had a hand in choosing for Enlightenment, into what I envisioned to be a perfect world.

"But the Society created a static existence that brought nothing new to living on with their indeterminate lifespans. Unlike Hom living today, I was not born with the expectation I might never die since I had no idea I had that possibility, so I was interested in the wonder of discovery and a changing world where I would find new things to learn every day. I began to think about what another like me might do if he appeared in the future, not having lived so long as we Hom who have hopes of living on and on by avoiding the risks necessary to initiate any change in the status quo. In those times I filed many of my thoughts in files I made accessible to the Society. Those musings became what you call the Prophecy. But as time passed beyond what I thought was possible for someone from that time to return, I stopped writing about it."

Publius leaned forward in his chair. "Your story is truly amazing, Librarian. Have you any proof in the records of what you say?"

She smiled, "Oh, yes, but that you will never see. At least not until after I die, which may be quite a while longer. And then, if you are still alive, and willing to spend the thousands of years it will take to break the codes to the files I maintain to record the true history of this planet, you can see all the proof you will ever need. Or you can simply wait until it unlocks on its own a centimillium after my last entry.

"I don't write it all down for it to be lost forever. Whatever happens, I want the truth to be revealed at some point after I can no longer affect the future of Vitas. Then the world will suffer at least one new event, its true history, and that might bring a new order, though what that will be I cannot imagine. Until then, the only proof I can offer to you is the Prophecy and, as predicted, the Traveler, Shon Ó Conaill."

Publius closed his eyes for a moment. Then he said, "I find it difficult to believe that I have lived my entire life to this moment having no idea of the reality of the world and the people around me."

"And what could you have done had you known?"

Publius leaned back in his chair. "I have no idea." He paused. "Perhaps nothing."

"You have gotten quite quickly to what took me millennia to realize. Take that thought with you and remember it as the future unfolds. You have some control of your destiny, subject to what others do that you can't control. What you do can affect the future. For example, you can report back to Octavius that your librarian is not who she seems to be. That will likely change nothing as you must certainly understand that the Hom do not want to know the truth about themselves and that they are unwilling to take the risks that changing life here would bring.

"Or you can choose to let events play out without your intervention. Or you can decide to help this man move us forward into a dangerous future, one which might bring us out of a long period of accomplishing nothing other than keeping a planet habitable until it burns up as our sun dies and destroys a truly remarkable community of beings that might have lived on to spread out across the galaxy had we moved ourselves to make the effort and taken the risks required."

Publius said, "You would permit me to leave taking such choices with me? And knowing what you have told me about yourself?"

"Of course you may leave. No one will believe you and, even if they did, they need me. Which is my point about what the Traveler will do with the Hom. He will not destroy those he needs to make the future he wants to unfold."

"How can you be certain that he wants your vision rather than another that doesn't involve needing us or you?"

"Any other future is futile, ending with life on this planet burned up by the sun. So, if what he seeks is something different than going out to the stars, we are doomed in the same way your Hom friends fear he will bring their doom. For, without him, we are doomed to a fate already written.

"Go knowing that the Prophecy I wrote so long ago is the best evidence I can offer that I want a future for Vitas beyond its current state of stasis, a way of living that I created and long ago wanted to change.

"Take what you have learned today and do something with it. I will deal with whatever happens from whatever you do. I deceived the Hom from the beginning, believing I could make Earth into Vitas and that they would make it more. I gave them control of this planet to do something with it. They took that power and chose to make it safe for themselves, not what I imaged they would do. As I look back with the view that the present affords me, I see that I underestimated how the possibility of living forever would so influence what they would do."

She looked at him for a moment. "Have you learned what you came for?"

"I have learned far more than I sought. But I do not know what to do with what I have learned."

"What to do was not why you came. Learning was. You have learned. So go and decide what you will do."

•

The ship from Boca Amassona docked in Marseil in the mid-afternoon on the fifty-fifth day after the battle with the Horde. Shon disembarked and walked directly through the port and into the city beyond. It was dry, chilly, not like Montaña at all. Nor was the city like Montaña. These buildings were low, the city

streets paved in grey granite set down millennia ago. He had been
paid in the local currency, so he took a room in a small boarding
house that served the Guilders who came to pass the time till their
next voyage, playing his role as Ismael, a slow-minded deckhand.

Early the next morning, he set off on foot for a citizen
community, Saint-Marie, situated two hundred klicks to the
northeast, just eighty five clicks from Lac. The distances seemed
very short in comparison to his travels through Montaña and
Amaz. But he soon found the travel much more difficult in the
mountainous terrain.

He took his time, running for a few hours, and then
walking in the cool mountain air. He circumvented Saint-Marie by
traveling through the woods surrounding it, and pressed on to
Lac, arriving in the early evening three days after he had debarked
in Marseil.

He came upon the western shore of a large lake he judged
to be Lac and walked around the northern part of the lake to the
east bank until he saw a long line of magnificent dwellings. He
judged he had arrived at the capital of the Society.

Watching from the woods surrounding the lake, he soon
observed people who did not seem to be ordinary citizens going
about their business, rather they seemed to be acting as security
personnel would act if they were not well trained. He smiled at
how people unaccustomed to security and warfare went about
trying to do it. At first he wondered if they were Hom or citizens,
and, if citizens, how the Society explained their duties to them. As
he watched for a while longer, he concluded that these humans
were not citizens; they moved very cautiously and seemed in
constant communication with each other. They were Hom. He
surmised that just waiting would wear them out and judged that
his decision to take his time in coming had been the wise course.

He decided to rest and slept that night in the woods uphill
from Lac. When he arose the next morning, he began to study the
movements around all of the dwellings on the lake until he could
discern who lived where and who might be the leaders of the
Society.

Soon he saw a giant dinosaur he judged to be one of the
Tyrans striding down the road that ran between the great
dwellings. Tyrans were patterned on the Tyrannosaurus, who,

according to Madra, led peaceful lives managing their prey, millions of buffalo that grazed on the vast plains comprising the second zoogeographical region designed for the dinosaurians called Plain, situated on the continent to the north of Montaña's southern continent, Souameric.. He followed him, moving along in the woods uphill of the road. The dinosaurian passed several houses and then stopped at a magnificent dwelling. He watched a robot come out of the dwelling and lead the dinosaur around the building to the side facing the lake. He waited in the woods as he observed several men around the house who seemed to be standing guard. He noticed that they were armed with weapons that looked much like the blasters of his own time.

•

Octavius took coffee early in the morning on his veranda overlooking Lac. The autumn air was chilly as the sun rose and lit up the lake. Soon it would be too cold to have breakfast outside until, in a few months, the temperature would rise until he could once again sit and contemplate the early morning calm of the lake, sometimes covered in a low fog. A few weeks earlier, he had changed his dress from the toga, worn by the Hom in the summer and for Council occasions in any season, to winter wear, trousers and a long shirt that ran to his knees, and, in the past week, a long woolen coat. Soon he would need gloves and headwear to make the colder weather comfortable.

A robot appeared and announced the scheduled appearance of Consul Ahiga Adamos Tyran.

"Show him to the garden."

He walked out to the garden and found Consul Ahiga sniffing the last of the late-blooming roses.

"Greetings, Consul. Thank you for coming at my request."

The Tyran replied, *"Greetings, Augustus. My family is concerned that you have decided to become Princeps again after so many years. My family has always supported you. You well know we that have continued to do so even when you were not Princeps. So do not be offended by what I am forced to relate today.*

"We voted against your family and the Deinoc when this matter of the human from the distant past first arose. We argued that we should welcome this stranger from our past and learn from him. And yet, while engaged in exactly such a discourse, he was banished to be killed by the

Deinoc. The Council would never have opposed us on a matter of this sort were you not opposed, or even neutral.

"Now, instead of learning from this man as we advised, he has conquered the only family who has ever conquered anyone since the far ancient times. Now you have become Princeps to attempt to defeat him again. Do you seek to revisit the times when we were faced with the Allo revolt? Do you still believe we must kill this man to maintain the Order when we might bring him into the Order for the greater good of Vitas?"

Octavius said, *"Consul Ahiga, I did not seek to become Princeps again to revisit my old life. I sought it because we are in great peril. Is that not clear to everyone? I recall all of it just as you have related it, including the positions taken by the parties to the decision. I take responsibility for all of what has happened since. All of it serves only to acknowledge that we both have good memories and that the outcome makes you correct.*

After a small moment, Octavius continued, "Though we don't, of course, really know what he would have done had he been embraced, brought to Annec, and been asked to determine our fates so that we might not offend him."

Ahiga said, *"Will sarcastic retorts help our discussion, Augustus?"*

Octavius said, *"No more nor less than righteous pontification, Consul. We have learned from the Deinoc that the Traveler wants to conquer Vitas. And while you are considering sitting on the sidelines as you do so well, you should consider what he could he possibly offer any Tyran. A trip to the stars which seems his current currency? You are far too large to make it remotely likely that you will be chosen to go on the ships he claims he can build. There is no record of the possibility of lightships so massive that they could accommodate your family. So even if we can believe what we've heard, maybe the Deinoc go, because they are human-sized, but not your family or any of the other large dinosaurians. All of you will be left behind to ward off the millions of citizens he wants to breed. We Hom will die, like all the rest he doesn't need, including you, because we are all long-lived beings that can't serve his purpose if what he has told the Deinoc is true. So is it your advice that I simply surrender Vitas to him to make amends for the mistakes you believe we have made?"*

"If we, for whatever reason, decided to help you, what do you want from us?"

"I need a real army. My family cannot provide that. Too many years, with too little risks taken over those years have made us impotent even with the weaponry we possess. You could be the army we need."

"*Augustus, you offend my family in ways I can scarcely detail. Your remarks about us are typical of the arrogance generally shown by Hom toward the other families. You assume because we are large and obviously dangerous to humans that we would be willing to kill living beings for reasons other than nourishment. Have we not lived in peace with all of the other families of the Society since the very first day of our Enlightenment? We cannot be your army now any more than we were able to be against the Allo. We are solitary predators who are not warlike despite our appearance and a historical reputation which was founded on our need for nourishment which required us to kill other great dinosaurians, dramatic feeding, but essentially no different that eating the bison we eat today.*

"*If the Traveler attacks even one of us we will kill him as he would kill us if we attacked him. But, as was the case when he appeared, we are not going to try to destroy him first out of fear that he will destroy us if we don't. And, as you have said, if he has no need of us for his purposes then he has no need to rid himself of us either.*"

"*I understand and I truly meant no offense. These are difficult times, Consul.*"

"*I understand that and I wish you well. But if he is a dangerous as you fear, you should consider peace before you lose the war and leave him with no reason to deal with you, except on his terms which may be far worse than what you could get if you only sought to find common ground.*"

"*Why do you assume we will lose a war against one single man, Consul?*"

The Tyran replied, "*Because he is a warrior who defeated the Deinoc's Golden Horde, and then became their Khan, and then, having taken that great risk, left, undoubtedly confident that he could return to rule them again at any time of his choosing. There is not one among you Hom who has engaged in any personal combat at all in a centimillium. You have ruled with your mouths and the threat of great weapons that would destroy any family that rose against you. But you had the advantage that none of our long-lived society is much different than you, we all like living.*

"*You have weapons that don't intimidate him and you don't know how to use them. The soldiers from your family value their lives more than any cause you can conjure up for them to die for. They will run as they would from me had they no weapons if I chose to attack a thousand of you by myself. He will undoubtedly take some of your weapons from some of your soldiers and use them with experience. When your army sees one of you blasted into ashes,*

your army will surrender unconditionally. Talking is your forte. So use your
mouth and make peace, if you can."

Ahiga withdrew.

•

Shon watched the dinosaurian leave, running in great
strides back down the road from whence he came. He found a
vale uphill from the house surrounded by dense woods which
afforded him a view of the dwelling and waited to see who else
would come to visit.

•

Consul Ahiga Adamos Tyran ran to Legate Cheveyo
Machakw Tyran's home and instructed him to connect him to
Wich-ita, their home city in Plain.

When Chief Helushka Nawhaw Tyran appeared on the
vidcom, Ahiga said, *"Our tribe must prepare for the possibility of the
collapse of the Society of Species and a period of chaos which may last for a
great many migrations of the bison."*

•

Octavius, shaken by the Tyran consul's words about his
army, the First Cohort, returned to his library and sat staring out
over Lac. He hadn't ruled for so many years by being blind to
reality and the Tyran had just given him a dose of it. The First
Cohort was not going to prevail.

He realized that he had failed to consider a special
resource controlled only by the Hom since the inception of the
Society—the Mechanica, massive robots, never elevated to an
intelligence to threaten the Society, but powerful nevertheless.
Perhaps they could be programmed to wage war under Hom
guidance.

He decided to call on his oldest ally, the most ancient
Hom of them all, who had supported him for many millennia and
who had given him guidance in the early years when the Hom had
to contend with the more aggressive families to bring about the
Order, the one Hom who controlled all the mechanical aspects of
running the planet, the one he had never been able to control
because he had always needed her more than she had needed him,
the one who, through her unique knowledge of the ancient
technology, had made the planet run smoothly.

He called Gaia.

When she responded, he said, "Gaia, I need you to help me with a problem."

Gaia replied, "The Traveler?"

Octavius was momentarily taken aback. He said, "To avoid boring you with the details that you already know, perhaps I should ask you what you already know about this matter."

Gaia said, "Yes, that will save time that you may need elsewhere. We anticipated that the man who returned in the lightship would propound a Slippery Slope Proposition requiring banishment to Amaz. That occurred. None of us expected that the result would be the slaughter of those who were expected to slaughter him. But that also occurred. He became Khan of the Deinoc and then disappeared."

Octavius was alarmed at her matter-of-fact presentation of what she knew. He said, "You are well informed as always. I am sure you also know that he seems to fulfill many aspects of the ancient Prophecy."

"Yes. I am familiar with the Prophecy of the Traveler."

Octavius said, "I am tasked by the Council to deal with him."

"Tasked by the Council, Augustus, or did you undertake the task yourself?"

"I admit that I undertook the task myself. I trust that is a duty you would approve."

"I do."

Octavius breathed a short breath of relief that she did not seem irritated by his decision to become Princeps without consulting her—until this moment it had not occurred to him to do so. He said, "The problem is that we cannot rely on the Deinoc to deal with him and we lack the forces necessary to resolve this matter."

Gaia said, "Then I assume you were unsuccessful with the Tyran option."

Octavius felt as if she had been hovering over his shoulder the past hour. "No. Not surprising given their lack of support during the Allo revolt. We need military resources, and by that I don't mean more weapons. If I had anyone who could use them effectively and safely I would simply arm the First Cohort with disruptors."

She said, "Aahh, the Mechanica."

"Yes."

She said, "As you well know, we have kept the non-sentient, non-living Mechanica inside the Walls, invisible to outsiders, to serve Vitas by maintaining power and the infrastructure so that the Society and the citizens would not have to deal with their own necessities. Were we to have left that to the families and the communities, that might have given them leverage to challenge the Order and disrupt Vitas. To adjust Mechanica algorithms for the purpose you seek, I believe will bring a much greater danger to Order than that you fear from the Traveler, or from the Hom using the disruptors.

"To make the Mechanica a truly effective army would require increasing their currently non-sentient mentality to some level of consciousness, a potentially irreversible process towards Enlightenment even at a very low level, having unpredictable but potentially horrific risks.

"Without adding some sort of equivalent to the limbic brain that we and the Enlightened Society possess, which we have absolutely no concept of how to create in a non-animal, we would be developing an intelligent, sentient being without emotions. We have no idea what mentality would develop in such emotionless sentient Mechanica. And, even if we could, emotional Mechanica might well make the Allo seem like petulant children.

"You seem to be suggesting that we enlighten to some level the Mechanica to defeat a single human hoping that we will be able to control these now sentient beings, with emotions or not, who will have no innate interest in anything the Order stands for or any affinity for the beings living on Vitas. I am surprised by this train of thinking from a man who has personally ruled over Vitas in support of the Order for a great period of time."

Octavius was nonplussed by her response. He said, "You believe that I seek to solve the current problem by creating a greater one?"

"I am sympathetic to your plight, but you are proposing that we use a sledgehammer to smash an ant when the sledgehammer unleashed may well smash the rest of us afterwards."

"Using your metaphor, why can't we send the sledgehammer back to its tool shed in the Walls whence it came after it has served its purpose?"

"Because the sledgehammer may not permit us to and that is a risk we cannot take just to kill an ant."

Octavius said, "The ant, unsmashed, may smash us all."

"If we cannot smash the ant without the sledgehammer, how will we smash the sledgehammer? I regret that I cannot loosen the security on the Genlib data concerning the Mechanica to comply with your wishes. I further attest that there exists no method in the records to make any Mechanica into the sledgehammer you need."

He said, "Then I suggest that you at least take measures to prevent the Traveler from gaining access to GenLib."

"You may rest assured that I am able to secure GenLib and that I am also able to destroy it if that ever becomes necessary to save Vitas. Meanwhile, I suggest you seriously consider using the disruptors. Even incompetent soldiers can obliterate an ant with those weapons. And the consequences of using them can be dealt with later simply by agreeing to destroy them. The Mechanica can produce more later.

"Perhaps you should consider the Tyran's suggestion and try making peace. The Hom are a great asset and, since living is what most of us care about, we may not really conflict with the Traveler's agenda. Losing power may be difficult but it may be the best solution. I have offered you my advice. Do with it what you will."

Gaia terminated the connection.

•

Octavius walked out to his veranda and sat down looking out over Lac and thought about his conversation with Gaia. Her last remark about being able to destroy GenLib reminded him of why he and no one else had ever undertaken a serious effort to replace her—she alone among them had control of the infrastructure that supported Vitas and no one dared to chance that she might destroy it if they attempted to take that control from her. Besides there was literally no one else who knew how to run the facilities she controlled.

Still he felt he had gained something from his discussion with Gaia: she had distilled the problem to its most simple elements. He must kill a single ant before it became a sledgehammer. He had come to view the Traveler as a sledgehammer when he needed to imagine him as an ant, albeit one with a very poisonous bite. He also noted her counsel, like the Tyran consul's, to make peace. He thought, *Am I the only one unwilling to capitulate to this usurper? I am not going to make his insane coup attempt so easy. I will distribute disruptors to the First Cohort. Many Hom will die using these indiscriminate weapons, intended to be used to throw back frontal attacks by entire armies, but the very fact that they have such wide impacts on the targeted areas might well enable me to kill one ant. I am not going to call a meeting of the Council. Too many families know nothing of the disruptors and might perceive that we might not so easily put them back in the toolshed after the Traveler has been killed.*

He called the Tribune of the First Cohort headquartered in Annec and asked him to visit him at his home at once.

•

Titus Servius Mathildis Hom, Tribune of the First Cohort, arrived just past noon to see Octavius. Titus was also a delegate on the Council.

He was shown into the library and Octavius entered a few moments later.

"Greetings, Tribune," said Octavius as he gestured for them to sit.

"Greetings, Princeps," said Tribune Titus who sat down across from Octavius.

Octavius dispensed with the usual formalities and said, "Titus, I am going to issue disruptors to the Cohort."

Titus visibly stiffened. He said, "Augustus, only a very few in the Cohort have ever even seen a disrupter, and not one has used one even in practice. The last time a disrupter was fired was several centimillia ago, before any of the Cohort were even born. There will be losses that will be difficult to justify after we kill him. The Council may say we overreacted and, besides, many of the families will be alarmed that we have such weapons at all and the will to use them. Weapons that only some may suspect we even have."

"We are dealing with the most dangerous threat we have ever faced, even more dangerous than the Allo. I fear that we will never get to that Council meeting if we do not take all measures to stop him now."

Titus said, "The Traveler is only one man."

"Yes, just an ant."

Titus looked puzzled and said, "I'm sorry I didn't quite hear you."

"Nothing, just a passing thought." Octavius said, rising from his seat. "Tribune, have you ever killed a single Deinoc, much less a Horde? Can you imagine the skills this man possesses? Have you, I, or any Hom even imagined becoming Khan of the Deinoc, much less actually becoming Khan? We believe that he may have foolishly come here where he does not have their support and given us an opportunity to deal with him. But, if he eludes us, what happens if he returns to Amaz and leads them against us?"

"There is a rumor that a Deinoc has already replaced him as Khan."

Octavius, realizing that this man truly didn't see what he needed to see, said, "Have you considered what that means, Tribune? The Traveler knows the Deinoc and their ways. I don't know how, but he does, or he would never have become Khan once already. And he now knows his challengers among them and, by the time he returns, who knows how many other potential challengers he will be able to identify and deal with so that his control of them will be absolute? But we know enough about their ways and him now to know that he has merely to return, challenge the new Khan who will have to face him, and kill him in less time than it took him to kill the last Khan, who ruled for many millennia and had his Horde with him."

Titus stood up and said, "You are Princeps and I will follow your orders. But I urge you to consider the likely loss of Hom life and the lives of other families. Some of those other families may well seek reductions of Hom for their losses if we use these weapons. And what if he is able to somehow take a disrupter from us and use it against us?"

Octavius was alarmed at the Tribune's words. He thought, *My army is already anticipating the worst, just as Tyran Ahiga predicted.*

How have we Hom ruled so long if the rest of the Society view us as so militarily inept? Perhaps our rule over the Council has been more consensual than I realized all these years. Or did the others simply follow because I and a few other Hom chose to lead?

Octavius directed his attention to the matter at hand. "If we organize our forces into groups of perhaps ten, arming one with a disrupter and the rest with blasters, it would be unimaginable that he could attack such a group successfully, even granting their inexperience."

"It's a sound idea. I will see to it. Where are the disruptors stored?"

"In the Walls in several secure locations. I will make arrangements for their release to the centurions of the Cohort tomorrow."

"Very well, I will proceed when they arrive."

The Tribune left.

•

Octavius sat down in his library and considered, *My plan might well work but the Tribune's expressed reservations need to be addressed. Titus will likely order the Cohort to use the weapons very cautiously and that might allow the Traveler to escape. I don't think the Traveler going back to Amaz should be my real concern because he has come to Annec and he didn't go to that effort just to run back to Amaz. He will proceed with his purpose in coming to Annec which must be the conquest of my family by killing me and the rest of the Hom leaders like he did Temüjin and the rest of the senior Deinoc.*

" Then he will return to Amaz with a real reason for them to embrace him as Khan. And a real reason for the rest of the Society to capitulate to him.

Octavius opened a door in the wall opposite the window with the view of Lac. It opened into a small room where he kept some of his prized possessions. Most were old artifacts from past ages that he had accumulated over the centuries in his early life: ancient books, already rare when he was born, his favorite old timepieces, an ancient computer the size of his hand that contained old files about the great leaders of the past that he had perused frequently over the ages, and a new addition, a blaster he had placed there when the blasters were distributed to the Cohort.

"He picked up the blaster and the paper beside it with instructions on its use. He read the paper again to recall how to use it and activated the power module and secured the blaster behind his back. He walked out of the library and down the hall to see Aurelia.

FOUR

TREACHERY

Publius returned to Annec the next morning. He went directly to his residence on the eastern shore of Lac where he reviewed his messages and noted one from Mamercus. He called and was connected to his residence. The robot answering, requested that he wait on the line for a moment, and went to find his master.

The next voice he heard was that of Mamercus saying, "Where have you been?"

"I went to see Gaia at GenLib."

"For what purpose may I ask?"

"To learn more about the Prophecy."

Mamercus said, "And did you learn our fate, my friend."

"In a way, yes. May I visit?"

"I am scheduled to see Octavius tomorrow morning an hour after sunrise. Join me there. He may have an interest in what you learned, or not. You know his view on the Prophecy is like mine."

"I know. I'll meet you there."

•

Shon circled Lac slowly in the hills above the lake, watching who entered each house around its shore, judging the hierarchy of the Society situated there.

The home that appeared to have the most activity, Hom and members other families coming and going frequently, was the one he had seen the dinosaurian visit. He had watched the comings and goings of the homes along the lake. Most of the residents in the homes along Lac walked to it at least once each day. Clearly, an important person resided there. But relative importance was paramount. His plan to conquer the Society depended upon taking out the true rulers, not underlings, however apparently important they might seem. And Annec was populated with many who appeared important. He observed that security had increased since he had arrived and swarmed everywhere, all now armed with blasters.

He waited for nightfall. It would make no difference to trained soldiers equipped with visors that could see as well in darkness as light, but he had observed no one wearing any headgear.

He crawled slowly down the slope above the mansion until he was thirty meters from a man carrying a blaster in his hand, the first time he had noticed someone who appeared ready to use his weapon. He stopped as he noticed a feline mammal two meters away from the man. Recalling how Carpia and Tigri worked together, he looked around to see if there were any birds flitting about. Seeing none, he focused on the feline. It looked like a female lion, but much larger and it had long saber-like teeth. He realized that he was looking at a saber-toothed tiger from a time ancient even in his time on Earth. The beast presented almost as great a danger as the man with the blaster. He crept back up the slope and moved a hundred meters downwind of them. He observed another team of man and feline, except this feline was smaller, a panther he judged. He crept away again and waited for the sun to rise.

Just after sunrise he observed a changing of the guard. Now the humans were accompanied by huge wolves, likely formerly extinct timber wolves. Whoever was in command had adjusted his forces, and they were now dangerous to him, as these creatures were capable of discovering him with their far more acute senses of smell and hearing.

He considered withdrawing from Lac and returning to Amaz and settling into a long siege, but concluded, as he had every time he'd had this thought over the past few days, that he would not get a better chance to bring this war to a quick end than here. So he moved downwind from the man and the wolf who were positioned between him and the mansion.

•

Publius arrived at the residence of the Princeps an hour past sunrise. As he approached, a man accompanied by a wolf turned toward him and positioned himself on the walkway to the Princeps' residence. He noticed that the man was armed with a holstered blaster with his hand on it and thought about out how his world had so changed in such a short time.

•

Shon watched the man and his wolf leave the area between him and the mansion and approach a man coming toward the mansion. He recognized the man approaching as the same man who had presided at his banishment trial.

He was now certain that he had identified the most important mansion and quickly moved down the slope toward the mansion, stopping at the edge of the forest.

•

Publius stated his purpose in visiting and was informed that Mamercus had not arrived. He waited outside the entry, pacing back and forth, for Mamercus to arrive. A few minutes later Mamercus came down the road and greeted Publius.

The man standing guard went to the entry door and entered the residence when he saw Mamercus approaching and returned with permission to for them to enter.

•

Shon watched another familiar figure approach and greet the judge. It was the man he had met in the Star Room on the moon shuttle on his trip from the moon to Vitas. As the sentry and his wolf led the visitors toward the main entrance, Shon quickly ran along the perimeter of the house, pressing on windows and turning door handles until a door opened. He entered and closed the door behind him.

•

Publius and Mamercus entered and were shown into the great library by a robot. As they waited for Octavius, Publius recalled his last visit, a painful one to discuss the trial involving Luciana.

Octavius walked in. He said, "Greetings, Censor." Octavius glanced at Mamercus, catching his eye, and said, "What a pleasant surprise. Greetings, Praetor."

Publius said, "Greetings, Princeps."

Mamercus said, "Greetings, Princeps. Publius has just returned from seeing Gaia at GenLib, so I thought he might add to our meeting."

Octavius said, "I welcome the company. Please forgive my ignoring our welcoming customs, but we have pressing matters to discuss." Octavius turned his gaze toward Publius. "Praetor, do I understand correctly that you have just come from GenLib?"

Publius said, "Yes, I visited the Librarian."

Octavius said, "Interesting. She said nothing about your visit and it would seem that she must have seen you before she spoke to me."

Publius sensed a need to tread carefully. He said, "I went to see her to learn more about the Prophecy. While I was there, she showed me recordings of the Traveler becoming Khan."

Octavius looked at Mamercus and said, "Let's take a stroll down to Lac."

As they left the house, Octavius turned to his two guests and said in a low voice, "I believe Gaia has spent time in GenLib monitoring us and the rest of the families. To what purpose I cannot imagine. Perhaps it's her way to pass time, but, when I spoke to her, she knew of a meeting I had just concluded with Ahiga Adamos only moments before. And she said nothing about your visit. I'd prefer we continue our conversation with some privacy."

•

Shon moved quickly through the rooms in the house avoiding the robots and a woman he saw sitting looking at a monitor. He entered a great room lined with ancient books with a great window on the wall opposite his entry. He walked to the window and, looking out toward the lake, observed three men walking toward its shore, two of them the men he recognized entering a few minutes before. He moved quickly to leave the house opposite where the sentry and his wolf stood guard and ran into the woods in the direction of the men walking away from the residence along the narrow shoreline between the woods and Lac.

•

As Publius walked along beside Octavius and Mamercus, he listened to Octavius as he explained his plan for killing the ant, as he now referred to Shon Ó Conaill.

Publius lost his desire to tell Octavius what he had learned about Gaia in his visit to GenLib.

Mamercus, learning of Octavius' plan to use disruptors, expressed concern about collateral from doing that and suggested that taking Shon out with blasters might be a wiser course.

•

Shon moved through the woods until he was alongside the men who were walking along the shore barely ten meters away. He listened as they talked.

•

When Octavius asked Publius what he thought of his plan to use disruptors, Publius responded, "I have spent my life as Praetor trying to dispense justice while listening to both sides of a story, each colored by personal perspective, usually to influence my judgment. I have learned that, while many times one party has indeed wronged the other intentionally, many other times the parties have become conflicted because of misperceptions of the other's intentions and that the conflict could have been avoided had they correctly understood each other.

"In this case, you perceive an implacable enemy who seeks to destroy us and the Order. I have also heard a view of the same man expressed directly to me at his trial by the prosecutor. I also heard directly from him, and, later, from Luciana. And I have heard testimony of a sort from the recording Gaia showed me of his speech to the Deinoc before becoming their Khan.

"His Slippery Slope Proposition, as it appeared at his trial, was not about simply growing citizens so more souls could live until Vitas could not sustain them or until they exterminated us and the other families. As he further elaborated before the Deinoc, his plan is to lead all of us to a greater future than we have now; to spread out beyond our current confines on this planet as our ancient ancestors did when they left a part of our world and discovered and inhabited others. The people who will suffer are not the Vitans who go out, it will be those who they find in the new lands they discover.

"You seek to kill him for completely the wrong reason. He does not seek to destroy us or any family on Vitas. Rather he seeks to destroy any who would prevent the Vitans from inhabiting the galaxy.

"If that disturbs you or the Society, as it might and, perhaps, morally it should, you should kill him. But, unless you are concerned about those civilizations about which we presently know nothing and about which he also knows nothing, you have no cause for action."

Mamercus said, "So you would have us stand down and be decapitated like Temüjin along with the rest of us who have ruled, including you, so that he can insure we never rise against his plan for us?"

Publius responded, "I hope that is not what he believes he must do to succeed in his plan. But we should also consider what is life really like here on Vitas today. Princeps, your beloved Aurelia is likely sitting before her monitor as we speak, as she spends almost all her time when she is not with you. A great many of us do the same thing. Would it not be better for her to be thinking about how to settle a planet discovered inhabitable? Perhaps she might find a way to avoid the one thing I dread from the Traveler, that he will kill the galaxy's other families because they are alien and will likely resist our coming so that our people can grow. Perhaps deterring that outcome is what we Hom can do to make a better future."

Octavius said, "And you believe that he will think we would not betray him if we were to make that our purpose?"

Mamercus said, "Do you believe all these life forms, beginning with our own citizens on Vitas, will not kill people like us who might live on far beyond them?"

Publius said, "The citizens have accepted Prefects from the Society for eons. They mutter and plot, but mostly because we restrain their desire to grow and because we rule them against their will. They don't even know how long we live. There could be a place for long-lived people if those long-lived people were not their rulers. We have never really seen what would happen then because we have always made ruling paramount in order to avoid the possibility that they would kill us if they could. And we will never change our view on this while we are able to rule and so we will never know what would happen if we did not rule. Imagine a galaxy filled with millions of life forms. Would many, or any, really care that one of those life forms lived longer than the others, when those naturally evolved contain many diverse life forms with vastly different lifespans?"

Mamercus said, "Publius, you represent the best in what we might be, but you are a utopian who is not prepared to face the possibility that you could be wrong. And, if you are wrong, we die."

Before Publius could respond, he saw a flash of motion by the woods.

Octavius noticed the same movement and reached for his blaster.

As the three Hom turned toward the movement, they saw a blur burst out of the woods only a few meters from them. Before they could react a man came to a stop just a step away.

Mamercus and Publius recognized the man.

Octavius, who had seen his image but never his person, stared for a moment before he realized that his greatest enemy stood before him. He tightened his grip on the blaster at his back.

Shon looked at Octavius and said, "Please do not move the hand you have behind your back."

Octavius thought he might get a good shot off but something about the way the man had moved from the jungle made him pause.

Mamercus, watching Shon's hand move almost instantaneously to his sword, said, "I suggest a momentary truce."

Octavius glanced at Mamercus. The moment to end it all was here. He was sure that he would have taken his chances only a few minutes before, but he had been listening to what Publius said and he sensed from Mamercus that the time was not now. He loosened his grip as he realized that like all the other Hom anywhere near his age he was not prepared to take a risk that could be avoided. And, at this moment, trying to draw and shoot appeared more risky than that the man would immediately kill him when he took his hand off his weapon. He let go of his weapon and moved his hand into the Traveler's view.

Shon said, "A few minutes ago I would not have given you the opportunity to think about drawing your weapon."

Shon turned his gaze on Publius. "I listened to what you said. I am glad it was you who banished me. Your expression of the future of Vitas and the Galaxy is what I envision. I would like it to be bloodless. But, that is unlikely. It didn't happen in the past when humankind spread out on this planet and it's not likely to happen now or ever. Too many people with too many motivations make the brutal approach more certain of success no matter that even the conquerors might wish it otherwise."

Mamercus said, "What do you want from us?"

Shon said, "Surrender, unconditionally. I will leave your leadership intact. But disarmed. If you rise against me, I will kill all of your leaders. This accommodation will make my return to Amaz more difficult than taking your heads today as that would prove my purpose is unyielding to the Deinoc who would appreciate a more rigorous conquest. I will require that your leader return with me to Amaz and subject himself before them."

Octavius said, "Doing that would be an abdication by the Hom of its role as the first family of the Society and a complete submission to your dictatorship."

Shon replied, "That is exactly what it means and no less than what I require."

Octavius said, "Dictators have been the bane of humanity's existence since we evolved into humans. Why should we believe you will be any different than all the others who preceded you? Your plan to go to the stars will take a millennia to bring about, assuming you can actually engage the citizen communities into growing their numbers to serve your purpose and engaging our family to support you with the technology you require. First, you will have to grow the population just to build the infrastructure necessary to build your lightships. Then you will have to build the lightships. Then you will have to induce millions of Vitans to embark on the lightships to go out on very uncertain voyages to stars where many will find no habitable planets. During all of that time you will have to personally avoid the megalomania that threatens all absolute rulers. Are you really up to doing that? How can we possibly know now that you will not succumb to such power?"

Shon said, "You don't, any more than I. But those are my terms because anything else will lead to failure. The task, I admit, is monumental, but the very existence of the families on Vitas is proof of the amazing things that can be accomplished. We have the resources and you underestimate the desire of people who actually know when they will die to suffer great risks to perpetuate themselves as all life instinctively seeks to do. What is lacking is the vision and the will to complete the vision. Your vision has deprived all those facing mortality of the opportunity to fulfill the dreams they have for their progeny."

Octavius said, "May we have a moment to converse privately?"

Shon considered telling him to take the weapon from behind his back and put it down on the ground. But he judged that, if they were inclined to attack him, it was better to face one blaster now than more later. Besides, his Magan instinct was still to kill them and eliminate the threat that they would always present. The temptation to use the weapon if he didn't take it from them might resolve the conflict he was feeling in his mind by giving him a fair reason to kill them in defense.

He said, "Have you stationed sentries in this area?"

Octavius said, "We hadn't seriously considered the possibility that you would come out of the woods by the lake so near one of our homes without being detected by those watching along the road that runs parallel to the lake."

"I take that to mean that you haven't."

Octavius nodded.

Shon said, "Very well, you will need to walk about a hundred meters away to avoid my hearing any mindcast."

Octavius said, "Thank you for telling us that."

The Hom walked away and then Octavius said, "He's far more dangerous than I imagined. But he's also far more persuasive. But how can we simply surrender and hope he will bring a better world? His plan, even if he rules in benevolent manner, will require harsh methods from time to time. The citizens will likely embrace his population expansions eagerly until the time comes when he requires all those new citizens to work to build the factories and then to work in them to build the ships until, one day, he orders them to get into those ships and depart for distant destinations unknown. At each stage some will rebel and he will be forced to quell the rebellions. His Deinoc will serve him like the lictors or the imperial praetorian guards of ancient Rome. How can we be a part of that?"

Publius said, "How can we not, Princeps? We know, as we stand here more than a hundred meters away, armed with a blaster, that he can kill us before we can run three hundred meters or so to the road for help, help that will likely fail to stop him. We are faced at the moment with only two choices: attempt to blast him now or accede."

Mamercus said, "I am the most experienced with this weapon, which I admit I fired for the first time in more than a millennia only a few days ago when these were issued to the Cohort. Octavius, if you order me to I will take the chance on our lives. You and Publius could make a run for help on the road. We could end this now."

Publius said, "He might simply run away and come back later. Will we be any better prepared, even with disruptors? Or, perhaps, he is good enough to evade the blaster and kill us all now. And then he will annihilate the rest of our leaders and take control with no one to oppose him in the future. We risk the entire Society if we fail. On the other hand, we could go along and watch and wait for our moment when we judge he has gotten out of hand and spend the time preparing for a fight we are utterly unprepared for today."

Octavius said, "Don't you think he is anticipating that if we surrender?"

Publius said, "Of course. He said as much when he told us what he will do if we rise against him one day. But what he threatens to do in the future is still in the future and it will be our uprising that moves him. We gain time to decide."

Mamercus said, "Unless he decides to dispose of us later even if we don't rise against him."

Publius said, "If that was his intention, would we be talking now? He would simply have killed us when he found us. Instead he didn't even require that we leave the blaster Octavius has. He showed trust. Whether that was calculated or sincere, it increased his risk from nil to a real risk. Mamercus, he knows you are a strong man who might be quite capable with the blaster or at least adept enough to make facing a shot a real risk he could have avoided."

Octavius said, "You make good points, Publius, but the truth is he knows something about all of us that gives him a huge advantage—that we are extremely risk adverse. He knows that if we act now we risk dying now, and he knows we have lived as long as we have by not taking such risks. He has simply afforded us the time to realize that."

Mamercus shrugged. "So are are going to walk back and surrender or attack?"

Octavius turned slightly so that Publius could not see his full face and, raising his eyebrow on the side of his face Publius could not see while looking closely at Mamercus, took a deep breath, and said, "We surrender unconditionally. We shall hope that Publius is correct and that we will have the opportunity to rise against him one day if we believe we must."

Octavius took the blaster from his back and dropped it on the ground. Then they walked back along the shore of the lake to surrender unconditionally.

Shon instructed Octavius to call the Council into session and announce his decision. He stated that he would appear before the Council while it was in session and lay out his plan for the future of Vitas. Then, as quickly as he had appeared, he disappeared into the woods.

•

Shon called out to Kai as he would call out to Gristelda, hoping that she would hear him.

She responded almost instantly and told him where GenLib was situated and where to go to enter it.

He ran to the cave and the door opened.

He entered and saw Kai on the other side.

Kai, appearing as her natural self, said, "I see my faith in you was well placed. How does it feel to be Magan?"

"Unsettling. I feel like two people live inside my head, but I don't feel the conflict I expected."

As she led him to the control room, Kai replied, "You should understand that it is your Magan mind that now rules. You simply listen to Shon now."

They entered the control room. Shon glanced around and said, "Looks pretty well maintained, I must say."

Kai laughed. "Only someone from our time could walk in here and make such a comment. Most are awestruck."

"Yeah, well, it's not a lightship."

"Quite true. I am curious to know what you said to Temüjin that made him stay, instead of running for help at the end. I reviewed the data from the monitors installed around the Deinoc's hunt site, but I couldn't hear what you said to him in the meadow when you confronted him."

Shon said, "I told him that I was the reincarnation of Genghis Khan. I have no idea why."

"Perhaps because you are."

Shon stared at her. "Are you serious? How could I possess his philosophy of how to wage war even if I had his genetics?"

"I can't say except that I also have felt an affinity for the Deinoc's obsession with the Mongols. I doubt there is any way the genetic engineers could enable our Magan brains to pass on intelligent memories to us even if they had his genetic code, but his affinities might be passed on or their ideas of what his affinities might be might have been inherent in the Magan himself. Perhaps, because we are familiar with his history from the records, we are able to project the genetics onto the history.

"Genghis Khan ruled his empire ruthlessly but with justice for the common person while his will was strictly enforced over those who sought power. Instilled in the nature of many who rule the families and the citizens in some of the communities is the desire to have power and they will be your greatest challenge. If you have the common people behind you and maintain a ruthless instinct to eliminate those who would take power away from you or abuse their power, you will succeed. Most rulers eventually abuse their subjects or permit those who serve them to do so and fall. But a just ruler has only one front to deal with, those seeking his power, while the unjust ruler has to deal with the rest of the populace and they number far more than the power seekers. They eventually defeat the ruler even if they don't gain the power which passes to another power seeker. The Order has been absolute but it was just, at least mostly just. The Codicil arrangement with the Deinoc was unjust and I must say I take some satisfaction in that your banishment to Montaña resulted in the annihilation of the Deinoc Horde which unjustly preyed on that community."

Shon said, "Did I err in allowing Octavius and the other Hom in power to live?"

"I would have killed them. That is what I did to the early Hom, all of whom I perceived as a danger to me, most of them only because they could remember how the Hom and the Order came to be. I killed them by engineering accidental deaths and I never let them know who really ruled.

"But you have done what you have done and now you must watch them. From now on they will be watching you. Some of them will rise against you one day when it is inconvenient. On the other hand, the good will of those who know you could have killed your enemies outright might serve you well in gaining the acceptance of the more benevolent families, and they are a significant part of the Society. And when those you did not slay betray you, as some of those who don't want to lose their power or who believe you will ruin their way of life will certainly do, you will have the benefit of being the betrayed benevolent ruler instead of the bloodthirsty conqueror.

"I expect this to resolve itself quickly as I know the Hom rulers rather well and I assure you that Octavius did not get his title of Augustus because he abhorred the power foisted upon him. Mamercus is one of the older Hom who will take a risk to maintain the order he has always known. You saw that by his presence on the moon shuttle, which had myriad risks, mostly very small, but he still agreed to a direct encounter with you which most Hom would never have done."

Shon leaned forward. "Maria?"

"She is in stasis on Canopus. One day, when you have accomplished your destiny, we will bring her back. I will spend time studying the old records to see if it is possible to bring her back with an indeterminate lifespan so that you will have a final reward for what you are doing for the rest of humanity."

Shon thought: *The real ruler stands before me, holding hostage my love with a promise of her return eternal, something only she might accomplish.* His Magan self couldn't find an objection to the practicality of it. The prospect of her return with a lifespan to match his own would be truly great compensation for the years he was likely destined to live without her.

He rose to leave.

Kai said, "Stay a while. I haven't met a man with similar tastes for a long time."

He took her into his arms and said, "Nor I."

She led him down a long corridor to a room, furnished in a style with Chinese decor and furniture, ancient even in the time they were born, to a bed set in an alcove.

•

When he arose a few hours later, he saw Kai, leaning on her right elbow, naked, gazing at him.

She said, "I hope you won't get the wrong idea."

"I can tell the difference between feeling and lust, Kai. I am your partner in your plan for Vitas but I doubt we will become partners in our personal lives."

Kai was surprised that she felt a twinge of regret that he said what he said the way he did, but she adjusted to his remark. She had what she wanted even if it was not all she had considered possible. She rose and went to a cabinet and took out a metal box. She said, "I gave you the katana to serve you in your battle with the Deinoc. Now I have another weapon you may need to deal with your battle with the Hom."

Shon replied, "My battle with the Hom? You expect treachery so soon?"

"Don't you?"

"I noticed that two of the Hom conveyed body language at odds with their words of submission."

She said, "Octavius and Mamercus."

"Yes."

"If they can, they will try to kill you before you gain control of the Society."

He said, "And how will they do that?"

"They have disruptors."

"I am surprised. But, then, I was surprised to see they had blasters."

She said, "On that point, I hope you will consider that you don't know everything about Vitas and will avoid putting yourself in unanticipated peril without knowing all you need to know in order to insure your conquest."

"Point well taken. Why didn't you warn me?"

"At our last encounter, you needed to become Magan by taking real risks to your life. Warning you of other dangers might have made you less able to deal with the danger before you. Then you went off and made yourself Khan, something I didn't anticipate. And then you disappeared."

Shon said, "You could have contacted me as I contacted you."

Kai said, "I became curious to see what you would do next. I now realize that I have gotten too used to people who calculate risk much differently. I forgot that you are, even as Shon, a warrior willing to take unimaginable risks compared to those living today. I won't make that mistake again. Meanwhile, I trust you will act understanding that only you can bring about a destiny that will take millennia at least to accomplish and, as the Hom know well, risks taken add up until they inexorably lead to death."

"I understand. Now what of the disruptors?"

"We kept a cache of blasters and disruptors to deal with the families that might rise against us. They were never necessary as we were able to accomplish the Order without using them even once in all this time. But we kept the weapons even as our army, we call it the First Cohort, lost its ability to use them effectively. Octavius asked for their release shortly after you defeated the Deinoc."

"So they have no expertise in using these weapons? I can understand your permitting them blasters as we can shield ourselves from them, but disruptors are another matter entirely. We could deal with atomic weapons more easily."

Kai smiled as she saw the look of concern on Shon's face. "Calm yourself. I have armed them now with low-grade blasters. You need only wear a light alloy skin to deal with them. I have one for you."

"That will have no effect against a disruptor."

"Of course not, but the disruptors I gave to Octavius have been deactivated and they won't realize it until they attempt to use one, as they haven't activated one in ages. Then you will know their purpose with certainty."

"What's in the box?"

"The last version of the disruptor ever manufactured. It is a narrow-beam high intensity disruptor with an adjustable depth of field. You can set it to kill at a hundred or a thousand or ten thousand meters or more and it will not kill beyond the range you set. Further, it can be set to begin the disruption at any distance you set. So you could disrupt starting at, say, a hundred meters and stop the disruption at, say, three hundred meters."

"And the margin of error?"

"Fifty meters."

"And the effective duration of power?"

"Without a power pack you would carry on your back, about ten minutes. With such a pack, about an hour. With a robotic support carrying a generator, something I have developed for use on alien planets, days."

"I must say you have planned well. May I see it?"

Kai handed him the box.

Shon opened it and took out a dull metallic device that looked much like a rifle with a fat butt, less than half a meter in length. He studied it and asked, "How do I adjust its range and how do I know what it targets?"

"It projects a laser-driven image of its field of disruption when you press this button." She pointed to the button. "Then you fire by pressing this trigger, just like a blaster. You adjust the near range with this toggle and the far range with this one." She pointed to the toggles as she explained.

"Remarkably elegant. Such a small weapon with so much power. And you anticipate I will need it?"

Kai said, "I believe so. You can wear the armor under your clothes and conceal the weapon easily if you wear a cloak which is customary when attending a Council meeting."

"You expect the attack when I am to be acclaimed Princeps?"

"That's when I would strike."

"I hope we are wrong about this."

"Don't let your feelings for Luciana deter you."

"I won't. Besides, I intend to stand beside Octavius while I am in the Council chamber. So he might survive."

"That might not be your wisest course but I am learning that you will do what you will do. You should understand that once you produce that weapon they will know that you had help."

"Why mightn't they assume I brought it with me from Canopus?"

"When their disruptors don't work, the senior Hom at least will know. If you fail, I will be forced to annihilate the inhabitants of Annec so that I can restart the Order again. As there are no other Travelers likely to appear, I will have to be content with continuing the Order until the sun consumes us. The stakes are as high as they can get. Do what is necessary. This is just the first of what you will face to accomplish the objective."

Shon left GenLib and ran back to Lac to await his appearance before the Council.

•

Three days later, the Council convened pursuant to a call for an emergency session by Princeps Octavius.

Publius entered and took his usual place and waited for Octavius to appear. He looked about the Chamber. Normally noisy before a session, it was quiet. Standing around the walls of the room were members of the First Cohort, armed with blasters. Clearly those assembled were uncomfortable with their presence and what it might portend.

Octavius entered, mounted the rostrum, and what little commotion there was ceased.

Publius was surprised that Mamercus was not with Octavius, following a few steps behind as he had done innumerous times before.

The chamber fell completely silent.

Octavius looked out over the assemblage and said, 'We prepared for a war which will be unnecessary if what I propose today is ratified by the Council today. I have met with the Traveler."

The chamber erupted in discussion among the delegates.

Octavius waited until the room quieted and said, "The Traveler has an amazing plan for the future of all Vitans. He wants to lead us to the stars to inhabit the millions of worlds that exist in our galaxy of two hundred billion stars and even beyond to Andromeda with a trillion stars and the billions of worlds it contains. He proposes that all of the families as well as the citizen communities grow to provide the population necessary to undertake such an endeavor. We realize that this undertaking will require a millennium of preparation but, in the end, we will spread out and bring a purpose to our lives which have become lives of predictable boredom. I have called you here today to ratify this vision and to express my wholehearted support for his vision. I propose that he be elected Princeps, which office I shall resign from immediately upon his election."

A clamor of voices stopped Octavius from saying more. Some of the voices were directed toward him standing at the rostrum, the rest among the delegates.

Shon stepped into the chamber. The delegates fell silent.

Shon stepped up the rostrum and stood next to Octavius. He said, "I am Shon Ó Conaill, a man from your distant past. As the Princeps has just said, I have a vision for our distant future."

High across the room at one of the balconies built for visitors to the Council proceedings a door opened and a two men stepped out onto the balcony, one pushing a large cart with a metallic device connected by a cable to what appeared to be a large metallic device on his shoulder which he pointed toward the rostrum.

Octavius moved to step away from Shon, but Shon caught his arm in a vise-like grip. Octavius turned his face toward Shon.

Shon, his eyes focused on the surprised face of Octavius, said in low voice, "What happens next, happens to both of us." Octavius recoiled and tried to pull away to no avail.

Shon recognized the device on the balcony as a disruptor almost exactly like the ones that existed in his time. The cart held the power supply. He spent a second thinking how remarkable it was that Kai had been able to reduce the size required for such a weapon to the size of the weapon he carried under his robe while increasing its capabilities by at least an order of magnitude.

Before the delegates could react to what was occurring, the Cohort guard began to fire their blasters toward the rostrum.

Shon pushed Octavius to the floor and stood as if awaiting for the applause to end before proceeding as the fire from the blasters began to scorch the rostrum. Two Hom who had accompanied Octavius onto the rostrum fell dead from the fire. Shon's robe began to fall from his body as the blasters scored hits on his person. He staggered from the blasters' fire as their energy was deflected by his coat of armored skin. He regained his balance and stood unmoving as he was pummeled by the blasters.

He watched a third man walk out onto the balcony. Mamercus. He saw a shimmer of energy emitting from the disruptor on the balcony.

The energy hit Shon and lit him up in a blinding white light.

The delegates began to run amuck, some running toward the exit doors, others diving to the floor. The two Tyran delegates, too large to hide on the floor, and blocked by the others from running out, began to roar.

Shon, aglow in energy that his armored skin easily dissipated into invisible particles and white photons the assemblage could see, slowly drew his short, fat-butted weapon, made some adjustments, and then pointed it toward the balcony. He pressed the laser range and saw that he was going to shoot the delegates, some fleeing and the others crouching, in back half of the Chamber. He calmly adjusted his near-range toggle to lengthen its range a few meters. He aimed again and saw that his targeting area was perfect.

He called out across the chamber, "Mamercus, why couldn't you believe in me?"

Mamercus, seeing that something had gone seriously amiss, called back, "Because I believe you will kill us all."

Shon called out, "It was an honor to know you."

Mamercus, ceasing his efforts to make the disrupter work, stood up straight and said, "I hope I am wrong. That medal you wore at our first meeting was honorably earned. Treat my family well, Shon Ó Conaill."

"Farewell, Mamercus." Shon pulled the trigger and the balcony disappeared as did the walls behind it. Daylight shone down into the chamber.

The Cohort stopped firing and stood looking at the gaping hole in the chamber.

Shon reached down to Octavius and pulled him to his feet. He said in a low voice. "Submit now, or die."

"I submit."

Shon said in a low voice, "Mamercus has run amuck and you must stop his well-intentioned but misled soldiers."

"I understand."

"Tell the Cohort to stand down."

Octavius called out, "Cohort. As Princeps, I order you to hold your fire and drop your arms. No harm will befall you for following the Censor's misguided orders."

The men of the Cohort dropped their weapons.

Shon lowered his weapon and turned to the delegates. "Members of the Council. We have business to conduct."

The delegates, stunned, returned slowly to their places.

Publius, who had not moved at all during the commotion, turned toward the rostrum and saw that Shon was looking directly at him. He nodded and Shon nodded back.

When the Chamber was quiet again, Shon said, "Leaders of the Society, Octavius spoke the truth of my intentions for Vitas and I thank him for his kind words. I did not come into this Chamber to bring havoc to the Order. I came to bring a greater Order to Vitas. Most of you have lived long enough to know that living long is not enough. It is time for us to move on from living to making living worthwhile. Vitas is proof that sentient beings can survive in an orderly world for an extraordinarily long period.

"But there is a price for whatever choices we make and living for the sole purpose of living in peace is an empty endeavor if there is more we can do. I seek a future that will bring a purpose to our existence beyond living for living's sake. Many will die to make that greater future. We will discover many planets that have no interest in accepting us and they will resist and destroy us if they can while we seek to destroy them so that we can live where they live. But life will become rich with new possibilities and, as was suggested to me a few days ago, some of you may make your purpose in living to cause those inhabitants of other worlds to become part of a galactic family joined in common purpose to expand life throughout this galaxy and beyond." Shon glanced at Publius, standing erect close to the rostrum.

"But, make no mistake, the present order is over. Go back to your families and decide what you want for them. If it is to continue as you have, you may do so. Your nature will not be revealed to the citizens and you may live on as you have. If it is to move forward to the stars, you will be permitted to increase your numbers to fill the ships that will go out to the stars. You and your progeny, or your progeny alone if you chose not to participate but elect to increase your numbers, will be required to help build the infrastructure and the factories that will be required to create the starships that will take you out. You will be required to cooperate with the citizens that will grow in far greater numbers than you because they are not blessed with indeterminate lifespans and we will need their numbers to succeed.

"You will be required to submit to the rule of one, as there is no way we will accomplish what is necessary by the rule of many. I am aware that rule by one is the greatest risk that any community can take. Most such rulers become corrupt with power. If that happens, there will be no need for rules to dispose of me. Eventually I will fall by revolt of those I rule over, by treachery from my administrators and generals, or by my own self-destruction.

"This is the first day of a new beginning which only time will tell if it be good or bad.

"Conspire against me if you will. You have one year to kill me and only those who revolt will suffer. After that the price of revolt will be the destruction of your entire family.

"This Council will convene in one year. Come prepared to propose ideas on how we should proceed in accomplishing the objective of going out from Vitas to the stars. In the meantime, the Order will continue as it always has. The citizen communities will not be apprised of any change until we convene again.

"I call for a vote of the Council affirming the Council's consent to the foregoing pronouncement in their entirely without any amendments. I suggest, in the spirit of making things a bit more comfortable as we proceed from the discomfiture of the past few minutes, that the vote be counted by silent assent, meaning the absence of a vocal vote in opposition shall be taken as a vote in favor."

Octavius said, "I second the motion for the vote of the Council in favor of Shon Ó Conaill's pronouncement and in that same vote for his election as Princeps."

There was complete silence.

Octavius waited for almost a minute before he said, "Let the record show that the Council with due deliberation unanimously voted in favor of Shon Ó Conaill's pronouncement and his election as Princeps."

•

As Shon and Octavius stepped down from the rostrum and walked from the chamber Shon leaned his head toward Octavius and said, "You have a reprieve for the sake of your daughter. If you choose to attack me again, please tell her that you were spared for your first attempt and that I gave you fair warning about a second."

Octavius said, "I ruled long and never found it necessary to so bluntly take power with trickery like your silent vote. I give you my word that I will not engage with anyone in your undoing. But do not come to me for any support as I believe you have already received more support from the Hom than you deserve."

Shon understood his meaning and was content with his word. He said, "Have the Cohort turn in the blasters and destroy them. They serve no purpose and their continued presence will alarm the families. Make sure the count in matches those issued. Destroy the disruptors also as some might think they work."

As they entered the room adjoining the chamber, Octavius said, "I'm your servant now?"

Shon closed the door to the Chamber and, in the blink of an eye, drew his katana and swiftly moved the blade to Octavius' throat stopping the blade just short of cutting. "For a man who ruled so long and appears so commanding, you are a remarkable whiner.

"To all your whines on the way to this room I have this to say. There was no trickery in the silent vote, everyone in the room knew what I was doing. I would never come to you for support because I can never trust you. As for support from the Hom, besides Publius trying to save me at the trial and Luciana's sincere help, I got none."

Octavius couldn't contain himself. "You have a blade at my throat that says otherwise. You have some sort of disruptor you didn't find on the ground."

Shon said, "You fool. When you next see your daughter, ask her what happened to the other woman who was with me. Tell her I told you she could tell you what happened to Maria. She will tell you how my shuttle you thought destroyed landed. That I took her into it and then it left for my ship you also thought destroyed. Do you think I went out to the stars unarmed?"

Octavius said, "I suppose not."

Shon said, "I am truly sorry for Mamercus. He was a worthy man."

"Why did you preserve my life?"

"I love Luciana and she loves you. And I respect a man who could lead a planet with such diverse species in peace for so long. Finally, the way you set me up gave me the opportunity to pretend that you were not involved, leaving your words to the Council to ease their acceptance of the new order."

Octavius said, "If I understood your words correctly to the Council, you made yourself open to attack for the next year with no punishment for treachery."

"So I did."

"Why?"

"Better to flush the snakes out now before the complex business of achieving the objective is fully underway."

Octavius visibly slumped. "The weapons will be destroyed tomorrow. I will bring the accounting which will be short by the blaster we left behind on the sand."

Shon walked out of the room into the early evening. The sun was setting beyond Lac to the west. He breathed deeply, taking in the cool mountain air, and set off to visit Publius.

•

Shon met with Publius in his home overlooking Lac.

Publius said, "I thought Octavius and Mamercus were agreed to your terms. How did you know they would betray you?"

"The same way I knew you weren't part of it. Near the end of our meeting at the lake, Octavius turned to Mamercus and spoke so that you could not see his face. I judged that he knew if you saw him you might see his intentions and reveal it in your face. Besides he had ruled this planet for too long to so easily go into the night."

Publius nodded. "And what are your intentions with respect to the Hom?"

"I think you should pursue what you proposed on the bank of the lake. Such a purpose might save many civilizations in what is to come."

"Why do you want the Vitans to go to the stars so badly? It's a monumental undertaking with many obstacles I'm not sure can be overcome by one man."

"We have risen from mere animals to create intelligent animals and proven that we can live in peace for a long time. I think we will bring a great benefit to this galaxy even though it will come with a great price. What does any civilization living on any planet have to live for once it has conquered its planet and its own bad nature? All of those civilizations will come to the same end. Stasis. Look at us as we grow older ourselves as simple beings. First, we are children. Full of new ideas and impulses. Then we grow up and become whatever we become. Then, not so many years after that we cease to change and live on as whatever we have become until we die. So it is with civilizations and eventually the worlds they inhabit until there is nothing new in life until their suns consume their planets. By expanding we can extend the joy of living in an unimaginably complex environment so that no one can outlive lives worth living. Particularly since I suspect most living beings don't have indeterminate lives any more than planets have indeterminate lives."

"When did you come to that vision?"

"I started out hoping to save Maria and to change lives for the citizens of Montaña and then I was shown another larger purpose which I came to realize was greater."

"The Librarian?"

Shon looked at Publius. "Yes, though I know her as Kai, a woman from my ancient past."

"I think she can be dangerous."

"No doubt. But her vision is not, at least not to Vitas, and I believe that is what she wants after more time to consider it than anyone has ever had. In any event, I cannot accomplish the vision without her. She has the technology and means to make it happen. But she needs someone to lead Vitans to it. We are bound together by the vision she created and that I may be able to fulfill."

"I hope you're right."

"Time will tell."

FIVE

NAPO

Shon slept that night in the woods outside Annec and ran over to GenLib in the morning.

When he entered the cave, the door opened and Kai said, "I must say, well done, Shon."

Shon said, "Say that again in a few hundred years or so. I intend to travel to the families over the next year."

"To face the challenges they might offer to your rule?"

"I doubt there will be many challenges. Mamercus did me a great favor by challenging me as he did. Their legates will report what happened in the Council chamber and most will not want to face such a sudden end as he did. I need to complete the conquest which requires that they accept the future I have laid out. I need to explain their role in it and how each family will benefit in the end."

"What do you require from me?"

"Start planning. We need to select a large region on a continent where those who agree to grow their population can send their progeny. There we need to build cities and factories to manufacture the ships. We need to design those ships, unless you have already done that. We need to decide which families to reveal to the citizens to excite them into joining the journey. We need to develop a plan for dealing with the revolts that will occur when people tire of the time it takes to get all this in place. Most importantly, we need to decide how to manage the process. We cannot do it ourselves. Familiarity will breed contempt and conspiracies. We must rule as you have, from the shadows. So we need to develop a new set of commandments, a new order based on the old, that will have a religious effect on the population to inspire them to persevere, not in fear of our retribution for failing to achieve the goals we have set down, but rather in their belief that the goals are their destiny sent down by God as their purpose in life. And we need to find those who can guide their brethren along the way. Plan, plan, and plan some more. That effort will pay dividends in avoided rebellions and lassitude."

Kai said, "I concur, and planning is my forte."

Shon looked into Kai's eyes. "Kai, a divided rule will fail. One of us must rule. Will that be a problem between us as we proceed?"

"I admire your Magan bravado, Shon. Vitas now requires direct leadership. I am not that leader. I have told you that I believe you are the only one of us who can lead Vitas to its destiny. If I thought otherwise, I would not have empowered you to achieve what you have already accomplished. So I submit to your rule. Serve Vitas and I will serve you. You may rule the Galaxy someday without any fear that I have any interest in that. But you must understand that I will continue to rule Vitas in the shadows as I have for the past eight centimillia and, when you have accomplished the objective, the conquest of the Galaxy, I expect you to leave Vitas to me. Will that be problem between us?"

Shon said, "I can live with that arrangement, Kai."

Kai said, "Then how may I serve you today?"

"I need one of the shuttles from Canopus to get around. Sailing the seas was an interesting adventure but it's too time consuming."

"Might I suggest an alternative that will be less likely to be noticed and just as effective?"

"That being?"

"The Walls go everywhere you need to go. The trams inside them can be adjusted to go much faster. Their current limitations were set to accommodate occasional Hom use which required low velocity to maintain their requirement for safety.

"When you enter any Wall take the red tram you will find near where you entered and it will take you to anywhere there are Walls on Vitas. To travel to a special place I want you to visit soon press a red button located immediately below the control console. The button, connected to a sensor to detect the Magan mind will only work for a Magan and is programmed to go to this location from anywhere. No one besides me has been there in more than six centimillia. When you arrive, you will know why you went."

"Do all the red trams go there?"

There is only one red tram, Shon. It was mine. Now it's yours. It automatically moves through the Walls to the closest entry to where you are and will only open for you. Very similar to the way our lightship shuttles stayed close to us when we were off-ship. I will adjust its propulsion parameters and I will also need to outfit it with a windscreen to protect you from the increased velocity."

"So I will just walk out of the Walls where I need to?"

"Just so. Or close enough for you to run to your destination."

"How long will it take?"

"Four hours."

"Why don't you have your tram already going fast?"

"The truth is I can't stand going fast any more than the Hom can."

Shon smiled. "Very well, make it fast. I would like to take it to Montaña now."

"Rest and come down to the control room when you awaken. I will instruct you on using the tram and prepare a map of the Walls and their exit points for you to download into your memory well."

•

Shon walked into the control room four hours later.

Kai connected his memory well to GenLib and downloaded the maps as well as her work on the starships and factories she had designed for their manufacture.

Shon drew on the well's data and scanned the information. He said, "You have done a great deal of planning, Kai."

"I was surprised to realize that I had not thought about the living facilities that would be required for the workers until you mentioned that. I guess I tended to focus on the process of creating the ships. I will begin working on that at once."

"I'm not surprised you would focus on the complex part first. You are Chinese."

She laughed, "I'll take that as a compliment."

"As it was intended."

Kai's expression changed. "Shon, I am excited as I haven't been since I was accepted into the black-hole lightship program. But that didn't work out so well for me for a very long time. I'm worried about embracing this plan with the enthusiasm I feel at this moment."

He stepped over to her and took her in his arms. "Kai, listen to me. We are embarking on something no one has ever dreamed of doing. That dream is yours."

He stepped back and looked at her. "Both of us have demons inside us. I fear I my Magan impulses. I realized that when I spoke of who should rule. You think you are Kai again but I sense that you are Magan and will always be as I will likely also always be. Even as I speak, I cannot tell where in myself what I say comes from. We are cursed with this reality about ourselves and may never know the truth.

"We have a common vision that serves our Magan mentalities. Perhaps it also serves our other souls. But we are really four people and that may lead to differences and conflict when times get difficult. We need to establish trust among our four selves. That will take time. Until all of ourselves know our trust among us is well founded, we should behave with caution. A single misstep could destroy our vision and Vitas with it."

"Spoken like the Magan you are now, Shon. You have succeeded in reducing my enthusiasm but not my belief that you are more than Magan. I still see Shon. I hope you will come to believe that I am also Kai and not the Magan who would destroy you when she saw no further need for you. I hope you understand from our earlier conversation that I love Vitas. I see a greater destiny but, in the end, I care about this planet more than anything else."

Shon said, "Spoken like Kai, or a very adept Magan Kai."

She said, "I think it's time to stop twisting our minds and for you to see your tram."

She led him down a long corridor that opened into a tunnel. The tram looked like a translucent deep red bullet.

Shon said, "It's quite beautiful. How fast can it go?"

"Up to a thousand klicks per hour on the long runs."

"Do I need to control the velocity?"

"The computers will insure you don't go too fast. But, if it goes too fast for your comfort you only need to pull back on the control lever you will find between your feet. To accelerate within the bounds of safety, just push it forward."

Shon placed his katana and his disrupter into the second seat and sat down in the first seat.

•

Shon entered the destination point, the place he had first met the Great One in the Wall near Huascarán. The monitor just below the forward window showed a travel distance of 21,341 klicks and a travel time of twenty-three hours and fourteen minutes. He pushed the lever between his legs fully forward and the tram accelerated rapidly down the rail. He felt himself sucked back into his chair during the acceleration and then he felt little physical sense of movement when he closed his eyes.

But when he looked out of the windows he realized that he was moving at an extraordinary velocity along what appeared to be a very narrow tube shooting forward at a small point in the distance.

After an hour he drowsed off, awakening occasionally as he shot through the Wall westerly across northern Asiana. Somewhere along the route he noticed a slow deceleration and a near stop as the tram shifted between walls and accelerated again. He looked at the monitor and saw that he was now headed south toward Montaña. He spent part of the remaining trip contemplating his plans for the next few days, ate some food he found that Kai had stowed in the storage compartment under his feet, and drowsed off again for the remaining portion of the trip.

•

He awoke as he felt the tram decelerating and got out when it stopped, taking his weapons with him. The weather here made hiding his weapons under his clothes impractical so he slipped his katana inside his waist band and put his disruptor into the backpack he found Kai had also placed in the tram's storage compartment, anticipating his need.

He found himself inside a lowly-lit metallic tunnel lined with pipes and conduits with a narrow roadway, paved in what looked like a smooth slate without any seams, beside the tram's tracks, almost exactly the same in appearance as the tunnel from which he had embarked on the tram from GenLib. A few meters down the Wall from whence he'd come he saw some light entering from outside the Wall. He judged he had arrived at the point where Kai had appeared.

He walked toward the outside light and looked around until he found a switch on the Wall and flipped it. The Wall opened to blinding light. He stepped out into a familiar warm, moist atmosphere. Despite Kai's assertion that he could get wherever he wanted to go, he realized that where he wanted to go wasn't a short jog away. But he was in Montaña again and knew the area. He had two choices. He could go to the northeast and eventually arrive at the village where he was likely to find some of Maria's friends or he could go to Pinchincha, four hours traveling east and then bearing southeast, where he would likely find Rolando.

•

Shon set out for Pinchincha early the next morning and arrived midday at the White Tower.

He approached the tower where he saw some workers and approached them, asking to see Rolando.

The workers recognized him as the man who had spent some time in residence a while back and went to find Rolando.

While he waited, he thought back on his time here. *So much has happened since, but this quiet place brings back the memories of preparation and my time with Luciana and Maria. My time with Maria in the village feels like a lifetime has passed since that day she found me on the rock in the pond by the waterfall.* He walked toward the building where they had practiced in preparation for banishment. He heard a familiar voice.

Rolando called out, "Shon, I cannot believe it. You are here."

Shon turned, strode toward his friend, and embraced him, saying, "It's been a while, my friend."

"So it has. Luciana told us about the battle. It's invigorated all of the Resurrection. Where is Maria? I thought she was with you."

"I could not bring her with me. She is in a safe place. Where is Luciana?"

Rolando's face stiffened. "Shon, I regret to inform you that she returned after your battle but then she disappeared. We searched everywhere but we have no idea where she went. Come to the tower and break bread with us. Ginés is here. All he talks about is his desire to serve you in your quest for our freedom."

Shon said, "Let's break bread tonight. I would like a few moments before that alone if you will not be offended."

Rolando, a bit surprised, said, "Of course, come when you are ready." He walked back to the White Tower while Shon proceeded to the practice building.

•

Shon walked into the building and sat down. For the first time since he'd left Pinchincha he was separated from the great undertaking and all that lay ahead of him. He took the backpack containing the disruptor from his back and set it down beside him. The room was quiet, the light low. He sat down on the bench he had sat on with Luciana and Maria while they learned to throw the bogacho. Magan as he was now he still felt the feelings he had felt then. He accepted that feeling as if it belonged to him.

A man entered. Shon said, "Ginés, it is good to see you again."

Ginés said, "I have practiced with the sword every day since the battle."

Shon stood up and drew his katana. "Let's see what you've learned."

Ginés drew his sword and stepped toward Shon to engage him. He approached low with his sword held just above his waist.

Shon stood tall, his katana held in his right hand to the side, leaving his body open to attack.

Ginés closed and made a low swing directed at Shon's waist opposite his sword.

Shon moved his katana swiftly to block the attack and then swung it back towards Ginés head. Ginés brought his sword up to deflect Shon's swing. Shon's katana made contact and broke Ginés sword.

Ginés stood for a moment defenseless. Then, smiling broadly, said, "You have a good sword."

Shon began to laugh.

Ginés said, "It is funny?"

Shon laughed some more, and said, "You have some idea of what I have done with this sword, but the last thing I ever expected to hear was 'you have a good sword.'"

Ginés said, "I am not worthy to serve you."

Shon, smiling, said, "Your counter to my attack was perfect. It would be a great honor to have you in my service."

He suddenly tossed the katana to Ginés and said, "Take this sword and become my protector. When we go to visit those I defeated with this sword, I will need to use it to do what only I can do with it. Otherwise, it is yours."

Ginés could scarcely contain himself. He said, "I will serve you with my life."

Shon, no longer smiling, said, "Beware, my friend. I have enemies who will challenge your skills even with this weapon in your hand."

Ginés said, "If I fail you, with my dying hand I will throw it to you." He flung the sword back to Shon.

Shon caught it and flung it back to Ginés. Shon said, "You are a worthy wielder. I hope you will never have to return this great sword to me again except for those occasions when I must have it in my hand."

Ginés said, "How shall I address you?"

Shon was struck by Ginés' accidental insight. Even Kai had not raised this point. He needed a title to rule Vitas.

Shon said, "Let us walk to the White Tower as I ponder your question."

He thought: *The Deinoc will call me Khan if I retake the Khanate; the Hom will call me Consul or possibly Augustus; the Council and the Society will likely call me Princeps. Kai titled herself Gaia; the Hom titled her Librarian; those families that she dealt with in Amassona titled her the Great One. But a litany of titles is not the answer for me; I need a single title to lead Vitas to a common cause. So what should the Vitans, the families and the communities, as a whole call me? I need a title not ever used by anyone else so it stands for the leader of the new order.* He smiled. *I have already been titled with the same title by the Society, by the Great One, by the Hom, and by the Deinoc.*

Shon turned to Ginés as they arrived at the White Tower and said, "When you feel the need to address me formally, call me, Traveler."

"Yes, Traveler."

They went into the White Tower and joined Rolando for dinner. Shon explained his plan to increase the citizen communities without disclosing his longer plan for them.

Rolando said, "The Society will accede to your plan for us?"

Shon said, "In time. I traveled to their capital in Europa and explained my vision for the future. They require some time, but I believe they will agree."

Rolando said, "You are a dreamer, my friend. They will never agree to change the way things are."

"Trust me, Rolando. As I defeated those who sought to kill me in Amaz, I will persuade the Society to agree."

"Tell me about those you faced in Amaz," said Rolando.

"In time. Now I need to rest and find Luciana."

They had a meal together and talked about the times before Shon's banishment. Then Shon left them and went to sleep in the room Rolando had kept for him as it was before he left.

•

Shon arose early the next morning and went to see Ginés.

Ginés awakened with a start and, recognizing Shon standing over him beside his bed, said, "Traveler, what is it?"

"I must leave for a time. Wait for me to return. Tell Rolando I have gone to find Luciana and that I will return soon. When I do, we will move forward. I will need the katana."

"Yes, Traveler." Ginés took the Saya with the katana from under his bed and handed it over.

Shon left and ran into the jungle.

•

Madra went to Luciana's home which the Therizi had constructed for her at the edge of the central community in Napo beside the shore of a small lake fed by a mountain stream. She found her sitting by the lake. Carpia was perched on a branch nearby.

Madra made a harrumph to announce her presence without alarming Luciana.

Luciana turned and rose to greet her visitor. She said, "There is news?"

"I regret to say the news is not completely current. Our family has been considering what Madriana learned at the Council meeting two days ago before I was permitted to discuss those events with you."

Carpia flew from her perch to Luciana's shoulder. "Madra, pass the formalities, what happened?"

Madra said, *"Something that has never happened before."*

Carpia squawked, *"What?"*

Madra told them of the extraordinary battle that took place in the Council chamber and how Shon took power over the Society with a challenge that any inclined to oppose him should do so within one year. She told Luciana how Shon had saved her father.

Luciana said, *"Shon killed Mamercus?"*

Madra said, *"Yes, but it was Mamercus that tried to kill him first and your father with him."*

Luciana held her tongue, pondering what she had been told. She said, *"Will the Society rise against him or support him?"*

Madra said, *"Those are not precisely the choices. The choices are rising against him or to submit to his absolute rule."*

Luciana said, *"There will be no vote of the Council to elect him?"*

Madra said, *"They already voted to elect him. But then he gave them a year to submit."*

Carpia said, *"Madra, what will your family do?"*

Madra said, *"We were not warlike before he came and, besides his insistence on being our absolute ruler and his possession of dangerous weapons about which we are naturally quite concerned, we see nothing about his proposal to cause us to rise against him. We also believe he can easily kill any challengers with his great weapon and the smaller one he used to kill his Deinoc foes."*

Luciana said, *"Where is he now?"*

Madra said, *"No one knows."*

Luciana thanked Madra for her visit and, when she had departed, she turned to Carpia. "I do not believe that Mamercus would do anything that might jeopardize my father's life no matter the cause unless my father ordered him to do so. I can easily understand that my father would not accept an outsider into the Council to rule them. In your view, what really happened?"

Carpia said, "Shon was prepared for betrayal. And he had an ally, the Great One. Where else would he get such a weapon and who else could make the Hom weapons impotent? Most likely it was your father's plot to begin with, so he must have been willing to die to kill Shon."

Lucian said, "For both of them to risk death meant they truly feared that Shon's plan for Vitas would be the end of them and the Hom."

Carpia said, "But why did Shon let Octavius live? He is a much greater threat to him than Mamercus. From Madra's tale, Shon actually saved Octavius."

"He must have done it for me, I think. But, to have spent the time saving my father in the midst of the attack described, means that he must have felt little real danger from the Hom."

Carpia said, "Which means he didn't fear their disrupter."

Luciana said, "Which means you are correct. Your Great One gave them a bogus weapon and told Shon."

Carpia said, "You seem disturbed."

Luciana said, "She betrayed the Hom."

Carpia said, "They were trying to kill Shon, Luciana, who I think has been working with her since he met her at the Wall in Montaña. The plan for Vitas must come from her. He said nothing of going to the stars before his encounter with her. She must have been waiting for him to appear. And, when he did, she seized the moment and instilled him with her plan, most likely very well planned given all the time she has had to conceive it. If they hadn't initiated the attack, Mamercus would be alive. You should be thankful she saved Shon and your father."

Luciana put her hand out.

Carpia flew from her shoulder onto her hand facing Luciana.

Luciana said, "I know I should be grateful for that, but shouldn't the Society be concerned that their leader for so many millennia would risk dying?"

Carpia said, "It sounds like they have no idea that he risked dying because it looked like he was faced with Shon's fate until Shon saved both of them."

Luciana said, "I understand that's what likely happened. What I don't understand is why my father is so fearful of Shon that he would risk death for himself and Mamercus to kill him."

Carpia said, "I suggest we wait. Shon will come to you eventually and you then you can ask him yourself about his plans for the Hom."

•

After attempting to contact the Great One at the Wall on Montaña's southern border, Juku had spent the next two weeks traveling north across Montaña toward Napo. As he neared the border between Montaña and Napo, he received a communication from his family about Shon's appearance in Annec. He climbed up to the top of a huge tree and sat on a large branch were it joined the trunk. It was his custom to think on top of large trees while sitting back against their trunks. He resumed his contemplation of why the Great One had left Shon to face the Deinoc without any assistance from her and why now she had undoubtedly assisted him in prevailing over Mamercus. It became clear to him that the Great One had a plan for Shon but that the plan required him to complete some portion of it on his own. Juku wondered, *why?*

•

Shon decided it was time to visit Amaz again. He returned to the Wall where he'd left his tram and rode it to the Wall which was closest to Sir Orda. He left the Wall and ran to the Deinoc capital, avoiding the Deinoc he observed along the way. He entered the Great Hall surreptitiously and waited for Batu to enter. He waited for nearly a day.

When Batu entered, Shon stepped out of the shadows and said, "Greetings, Batu."

Batu jumped two meters into the air and turned as he landed to face him.

"*Aargh, Khan!*" He calmed himself. "*Forgive me for addressing you as Khan as I know you are not. I heard about what happened in Annec. Have you returned to challenge for the Khanate?*"

"*For the moment, no. I will return soon for that purpose.*"

"*Why not now?*"

"*To do so now would put the Deinoc in opposition to those in the Society that may still seek to defeat me. I do not need your help in dealing with them.*"

Batu said, "*Then why have you come?*"

"*I have come to see you and to determine whether you are still with me.*"

"How shall I address you until you become Khan again?"

"Call me, 'Traveler'."

"Traveler, I am still with you though your methods are inscrutable to me. Why risk the attack you suffered in Annec when the Deinoc were pledged to you? We could have helped you."

"If one family joins me against the others, they will forever be tainted in the eyes of the others. It is important for the Society to remain intact to achieve the objective I first spoke of before our Deinoc family and which I have spoken of before the Council. When I come again to assume the Khanate it will be as the leader of the Society, not the Deinoc. The Deinoc have an important role, but not one that will be needed until we go out to the stars. The Deinoc must be patient and their time will come. Then they will receive what I have promised."

"We have lived in Amaz for a longer time than I hope you will require of us to wait."

"The time for waiting will be much shorter, but much more difficult to endure as you have a purpose now. You must maintain order here while I lead Vitas toward the new Order. Can you do it?"

"Those of the Deinoc who seek the Khanate focus on that and not much else. As I do not seek that role, I am viewed as their counselor and can work in the background to keep order here. If that changes, how will I find you?"

"Call out in your mind to the sky and I will hear you and come."

"As you order, Khan, er, Traveler."

Shon left the hall and slipped back into the jungle where he returned to his tram in the Wall.

He set the coordinates to go to the Wall closest to Napo.

•

Juku ceased contemplating and climbed down from his tree and set off for the Napo capital to visit Luciana and Carpia.

•

Shon arrived at the Wall adjoining Napo and ran into the jungle bound for the capital, Napo.

He found the city the next morning and moved around its perimeter observing until he located Luciana's house. He found a small clearing and called out to Carpia in her family's mindcast, hoping Luciana wouldn't hear it.

Shortly Carpia flew up and alighted on a branch nearby.

Carpia said, "I trust you have a good reason for worrying Luciana beyond measure, Shon."

Shon said simply. "It was necessary to put my plan into action."

Carpia squawked, "Your plan for Vitas, Shon? Or the Great One's plan for you?"

"They are the same, Carpia."

Carpia squawked, "Not a very good plan, in my opinion, if it so adversely affects those who care about you. And what of Maria?"

"She is as well as she can be for the time being."

"Hardly the most encouraging thing I've heard today."

Shon sighed. "Carpia, the Great One saved Maria and she will return her to me someday. In the meantime, she is safer where she is than here. Which brings me to Luciana. Is she well?"

"As well as she can be knowing her father and you were nearly killed by Mamercus and Octavius."

Shon peered at Carpia. "Why do you include Octavius in that remark?"

"You don't think Luciana knows that Mamercus would never have endangered Octavius without being told by him to do so?"

"I see. Let's hope no one else sees it that way. Octavius has sworn his loyalty, for the time being at least, and I have no desire to kill him unless forced to it by his own action against me." Shon paused and said, *"Come out of the jungle, Juku."*

Juku lumbered out looking a bit sheepish to Shon's eye though he couldn't be certain, as Juku had that look about him generally.

Shon said, *"Greetings, Juku. I guess you can hear Carpia's mindcast. A great deal has passed since our paths last crossed."*

Juku said, *"Indeed, that is so."*

Shon said, *"I need to see Luciana."*

"And tell me what?" Luciana stepped out of the jungle on the opposite side of the clearing from where Juku had emerged.

Shon smiled. "You are stealthy."

"I learned from the masters, all assembled here I see. Did you all plan to discuss my fate without me?"

There was another rustle in the jungle and then Madra stepped into the clearing, saying, "*And without me who taught you Deinoc?*"

Shon said, "*Greetings, Madra Ameyali. Well, here we are together again as we were before we went over.*"

Carpia said, "*Except for Maria and Ginés.*"

Shon said, "*Carpia is correct. But Ginés is well and Maria will be. Still we are not all as we were before as I am now different than I was before.*"

Juku said, "*The Great One changed you?*"

Shon said in a quiet voice, "*No, she gave me a vision for a Vitan future that could come only by my undergoing a change that could occur only if I faced the Deinoc alone with the lives of those I most cared about in gravest peril.*"

Luciana said, "*Shon, I have no idea what you are trying to tell us.*"

Shon said, "*The Great One and I come from the same past when Vitas was Earth. She came back long before me. You who helped me so much have a right to know about us.*" He proceeded to tell them about his turning Magan and his intention to pursue the Great One's vision for the future. When he finished, he said, "*So there you have it.*"

No one said a word.

Shon said, "*Is it that bad?*"

Luciana said plainly, without mindcast, "How could it be worse? I thought I knew you, but you are a stranger to me now." She turned and walked into the jungle.

Madra followed her.

Carpia alit and flew off behind them.

Juku turned away and lumbered after the others. Just before he disappeared, he turned back for a moment and said, "*It is difficult to imagine and embrace the future the Great One and you have in mind for us.*"

•

Shon stood there for a moment and when he was sure they were gone, he allowed himself a small tight smile. He needed to get them out of his life for the time being. They presented a danger to him and he presented a grave danger to them. Enemies would find it much easier to deal with him when he had them to protect. But doing what needed to be done had been easier to accomplish than he had imagined it would be.

As he returned to the Wall, he saw that the challenge ahead would be even more difficult than he had imagined. The citizens and families would assume the worst in him if his closest friends could so easily do so.

When he arrived at the Wall, he entered into it and boarded the Red Tram. He decided not to return to Pinchincha immediately as he had intended. He looked at the red button below the console and thought, *Now is as good a time as any to see whatever it is that Kai wants me to see. I'm also curious to learn why there is a special button for only one destination on Vitas and no maps or directions to where it is.* He pressed the button and leaned back into his seat.

As the Red Tram sped, he thought about Maria, in stasis on Canopus, *I wonder how she will feel about me when she awakens one day and sees what I did while she slept.* The memory of a lovely day on a rock below a waterfall entered his mind as he fell asleep.

SIX

WÜTÁISHAN

When Shon awakened, he raised the tram's windshield and stepped out into a small room, the smallest he had seen since he began using the Red Tram. He faced a red door in the wall opposite the tram behind him. The red door had a name inscribed on it, Wütáishan. This room did not appear to have an exit in the Wall like his stops before except for Annec where the room was much larger but was not situated in the Wall.

He deduced he was not in the Wall, unless this door was another form of passage through the Wall. He took two steps toward it, now a hand's reach away, and it opened. He entered what appeared to be a small elevator cab with a panel across the cab from him. The panel illuminated and a schematic appeared with three buttons set vertically on the panel. The bottom button was etched with a numeric "zero," The middle button with the word, "Base," and the top button with the word, "Peak."

"Peak" sounded more interesting than "Base," so he pressed the Peak button. The door closed behind him and he felt force from the floor indicating that the cab was accelerating and moving upward. Judging from the pressure on his feet from the acceleration and its swift change to normal gravity and then the deceleration to a stop, Shon calculated that he had risen about two thousand meters.

The door opened. He stepped out into a chilly breeze and walked down a narrow metal-clad path walled by the same metal as the Wall and open to the sky until he came to an opening with clear sky beyond that looked out over the area below him. He noticed that this path seemed to circle around a rocky mound rising on the uphill side of the land beside the path on one side about a hundred meters higher and, when he looked down on the other side, he saw that he was standing on a platform set into the side of a mountain. Was this what was inscribed on the door, Wütáishan? Perhaps it was another mountain like Huascarán

He looked out toward the horizon to the south under the glare of a mid-morning sun and gasped. His Magan mind instantly spun up and overtook his Shon/Magan persona.

Spread out to the horizon was the largest and tallest city he had ever seen on Earth before he left for the stars, if indeed a city was what it was. Hundreds, perhaps thousands, of narrow towers rose over a thousand meters towards the sky, much like spires. They were similar in their lower floors to those in Montaña, but narrowed to points unlike Montaña's towers' expansive top floors. Interspersed among them were thousands of lower structures of vastly varying dimensions. Some were squat and massive like huge warehouses, or even factories. Others were architecturally elegant and some even looked like ancient gothic churches, though all appeared to be covered with the same metallic material as the Walls were made of.

This would normally have been enough to excite his Magan self, but what had immediately caught his Magan brain's rapt attention was the motion of some sorts of vehicles on wide roads and a vast rail system running between the buildings. And it was a lot of motion: machines, vehicles, and robots were swarming everywhere and there was no sign of any Hom or any living being at all.

He walked along the metal-clad path around the mountain's peak to look at the expanse to the north of the mountain and slowed his pace as he approached a Wall that blocked transit to the other side, except that a door in it opened for him a few steps before he reached the Wall. He walked in and saw another door across the Wall. So he exited the Wall through that door. He was dumfounded to see what appeared to be the same city he had just been looking at on the other side. He drew on his memory well to be sure he wasn't mistaken and images of both cities appeared in his mind and began to match like points until it was clear these cities were identical.

The thought that came into his mind made him smile and

frown at same time. *When Kai remarked that she had not thought about the living facilities that would be required for the workers, she was toying with me. Her self-deprecating remark that she tended to focus on the process of creating the ships is laughable as I see the truth before me now. My condescending remark about her being Chinese having anything to do with it must have warmed her heart as she replied, "I will begin working on that at once."*

I am so far behind her. She had never needed any living facilities for her workers because her workers aren't alive; they are the Mechanica that don't eat, sleep, or require living facilities of any kind at all. Her workers must have been working for hundreds of thousands of years making this place. I wonder just how vast this place really is. Is the mountain itself filled with more surprising capabilities like Huascarán and Genlib? What else has she already done? And why did she build twin cities next to each other, yet each out of the sight of the other?

I must stop thinking of Kai and start thinking of Magan Kai and, in that vein, try to deduce why she needs me at all. Obviously she had been proceeding with some plan before I accidentally appeared and gave her another approach to her goal. What was her plan before, the one that didn't involve me? Is that still her plan? This revelation hardly seems amenable to the trust she promised we would have between us.

Shon called out to her through his mind to tell her he had seen what she wanted him to see and to learn why she had decided to reveal all of this to him this way. He got no response after trying for some twenty minutes or so. He took the lift down to Base and found his way into the southern city. As he walked out onto a street, the Mechanica nearby immediately became inert until he had passed them by at some distance unclear to him after which they began to do whatever they were doing before.

He heard a voice, Kai's, in his head about 35 minutes after he had reached out to her.

She said, "I cannot engage in discourse at the moment, Shon. We are too distant. But I assume you are calling because you pressed the red button so I will tell you about where you are. You are in or on Wǔtáishan, a great mountain in Asiana. That is good. I am sure you have now realized that we will be able to proceed with our plan very quickly because we are already past creating the infrastructure we need. Oh, and, yes, that includes the ships we will need to transport the first expeditions. They are by me now, on the other side of the Sun in orbit at the same distance from Vitas, hence the nearly thirty-five minute transmission delay.

"This is actually a good time to tell you what you want to know about my intentions and what I was going to do before you appeared. I do want us to trust each other; we will not succeed fully otherwise. I was coy because I believed you really needed to see what one person can accomplish unaided by anyone else and, to do that, you needed to see humankind's most magnificent engineering achievement all made possible by one human, even if not the standard version, and all done in secrecy.

"To move to the stars, we must essentially mislead or brutally force our Vitan races, human and nonhuman, to get into ships with low probabilities of survival so that those who survive can conquer the uncountable number of planets that are out there for the taking, albeit a hard taking.

"Before you appeared, though I always hoped you would, I developed a plan to use the Predation Agreement and all of the citizens and most of the Families' desires for more progeny and population to force them to contribute population to my space program which I call "Sky."

"I put it off for millennia, because even I, Magan as I am, was repelled by what would be required to make it happen.

"Then you appeared, and I have come to believe you will be able to gather the population we need to do what must be done without destroying the culture of Vitas. I will explain that when I come back.

"You probably have surmised from this conversation that I never really had a problem going fast in the Red Tram. In fact, I slowed it down for you. But the tram was often too slow for where I needed to be, so I have a lightship shuttle for travel on Vitas and a lightship for travel off Vitas which I only use to visit the consolidated-black-hole lightships stockpiled out here on the other side of the Sun."

Shon thought, *She really is God. There is no way, had I arrived first back on Earth and then become fully Magan, that I could or would have created Vitas, Enlightened an entire society of extinct species, created the Mechanica, controlled the whole Earth and the Moon beyond, created some sort of gigantic metroplex with a vast army of Mechanica that I also produced, and beyond it all, also constructed unified force lightships to use the Vitan population to take over the galaxy. Undoubtedly, she has also built in protections against anything I might attempt to stop her. And I don't want to stop her. Why not go out and populate the galaxy and even beyond?* He focused back on listening to what she was saying.

"Gird yourself up and start acting like God and the leader you are and bring the population we need to make this happen without ruining Vitas.

"I am with someone I am about to bring out of stasis to tell her she will one day return to Vitas. I will not tell her what we are going to do and I hope she will support what we did when her time comes to see you again. If you can accomplish what we need the way I think you can, she may support you. If you cannot or if we simply are acting beyond what a good person like her can countenance, then her return to you one day will be no gift. Magan life is not about happiness. It is about duty.

•

Her first conscious sensations were dreamy, violent vague images, sudden severe pain, then no pain at all. Dreamy became more a state of awakening and she felt cold. But also frightened by whatever the dreaminess that was fading had instilled in her awaking mind as she opened her eyes and faced a whitish wall so near her face that she felt a claustrophobic panic as she tried to fathom where she was and to escape into open space at the same time.

She closed her eyes and tried to calm herself. As her brain became more alert, an image flashed in her mind, a reptilian tail swinging towards her. Her eyes sprang open wide, bulging with terror. Then as quickly as it had appeared, the tail vanished.

The space around her was dimly lit and she looked around. She saw that she was trapped in a glassine container. She called out, "Shon," but there was no answer. From the corner of her left eye she saw a young woman walking towards her.

The woman reached out and moved her arm downward beside the container and the container opened.

She turned her head to the woman and said, "Where am I?"

The woman replied, "You are on the godship, Canopus, where you were taken after the battle with the Deinoc."

"Did we win?"

"Yes."

"Shon?"

"He became God."

Something about the way the woman said that word made her capitalize it in her mind. She paused for a moment, "And you are?"

"The God before Shon."

She peered closely at the face of the woman searching for the meaning in what she was saying. The face she looked into was not at all like the faces of someone she'd ever seen, none of those faces looked quite so beautiful, so inscrutable. She said, "I don't understand anything about what you've just said to me. What is a godship? Canopus? What do you mean when you say you were God or that Shon is? Is Shon dead? Is that why you are calling him God? Please tell me he lives."

"He lives. One day you will understand it all and then it will not matter to you."

She watched the beautiful, inscrutable young woman move her arm downward beside the container and saw her press a little button.

The container closed and she drowsed off, back into the deep sleep of stasis, her last thought was that Shon was alive.

•

Shon listened until he heard Maria ask whether he was dead and then he began screaming with the full power of both of his minds. But he was seventeen minutes away from being heard by anyone where Maria and Kai were and he was already seventeen minutes behind what had already happened there, literally an eternity since Maria was already asleep when he began to scream.

Shon's mind felt sadness, fear, anxiety and despair.

Magan Shon's mind hardened and took another step in replacing Shon Ó Conaill, commander of the lightship Canopus who loved a Vitan women name Maria Monterro, a citizen of Montaña, and a Hom woman, Luciana.

Magan Shon loved these women, too, even though he knew they were unlikely to love him back like they loved Shon when they sensed how different he was. Because he knew them through Shon, who was not really like him, he had learned that somehow he loved those whom Shon loved.

But Magan Shon was very angry with Kai who denied Maria a life with Shon because Magan Shon was well aware that would be a life with himself, maybe only himself. Whether better only him or including Shon, he wasn't sure. Either way was better than what appeared to be Kai's plan, denying both of them Maria for a long time.

●

The Great One pondered her original thought about Shon when Canopus was discovered approaching Vitas and she had wondered if she would even notice or much care. She decided she cared. But she wasn't so sure about Magan Shon, whom she needed to conquer the galaxy.

EPILOGUE

All are but parts of one stupendous whole, Whose body Nature is, and God the soul.

Alexander Pope, *An Essay on Man*

The Lord God Shon descended from the Sky to Wǔtái and created Wǔhǔ to be the home of the People before they journeyed to the Sky.

The First Tablet of Manju

In the year sixty-nine thirty-three of the seventh decamillium in the ninth centimillium pursuant to the First and Second Directives written in the First tablet of Manjǔ, two cities arose in eastern Asiana: Resurrection in Gurjar on the eastern shore of the Great Ocean and Wǔhǔ on the Great Plain below Wǔtáishan, the mountain of five peaks, the abode of Shon, Lord God of the People.

The First Directive afforded every sentient being on Vitas the opportunity to increase their numbers by providing a newborn to the Society for each increase in the population of their community or family beyond that previously proscribed under the Order until the population of each community or family doubled.

The infants provided to the Society were taken by their parents to Doors in the Walls which divided Vitas into the Communities and the Society Properties. The infants were left at the Doors. After the parents departed, the Doors opened and the minions of the Lord God, the Mechanica, took the infants inside and transported them to the Wall bounding Wǔhǔ, where they were deposited through the Wall Door into the Temple of Manju before the turn of the day. Each child received a Horn of Hearing and thus became one of the People. Each morning the

Temple Door opened onto Wŭhŭ and the infants were delivered into their future lives as the People of the Sky.

The Second Directive afforded any citizen in the two hundred communities on Vitas the right to take the Oath of Exodus to forever leave their community to reside in Resurrection. The Oath prohibited them from ever returning to their communities or thereafter communicating with the citizens of their former communities.

The History of Vitas as recorded in a file stored in the GenLib Repository with access strictly restricted to the Librarian

www.ingramcontent.com/pod-product-compliance
Lightning Source LLC
Chambersburg PA
CBHW030750030726
47497CB00001B/218